MATERIAL THINGS

MATERIAL THINGS

BASED ON TRUE EVENTS
SET IN THE 60ˢ & 70ˢ

THE UNTOLD STORY OF A YOUNG ENTREPRENEUR
WHO MADE A KILLING IN THE JEANS BUSINESS

LARRY SPENCER

Copyright © 2019 by Larry Spencer

All rights reserved. This book or parts thereof may not be reproduced in any form, stored in any retrieval system, or transmitted in any form by any means—spoken, written, photocopy, printed, electronic, mechanical, recording or other wise through any means not yet known or yet to use—without prior written permission of the publisher, except provided by the United States of America copyright law.

This book is a work of both fiction and also based on fact, real events and real people. However all the names, characters, some places and incidents are products of the writer's imagination and have been changed. Any resemblance to persons, living or dead, actual events, locales, or organizations is entirely coincidental. No legal or moral allegation is made as to the actual or potential activities of any organization, institution or government nor to any individual, living or dead.

Library of Congress Control Number: 2018914176

ISBN: 978-0-578-21232-6

Book Cover and Interior Design: Ghislain Viau
Cover Art: Bodgan Maksimovic
Author photo Laurie Spencer @ Lolo Spencer Photography

For Laurie, Kate and Riley
For countless reasons

In every American there is an air of incorrigible innocence, which seems to conceal a diabolical cunning.
—A. E. Housman

CHAPTER 1

NOVEMBER 10, 2016

7:30 a.m. Valencia, California. A neighbor calls 911 and reports what might have been the sound of a gunshot ringing out from the house next door. Police arrive at the home of Logan Alexander, sixty-nine, and discover a body sprawled in a pool of blood on the floor of the garage. In the victim's grip is a .357 Magnum revolver.

It's one horrific sight. First responders ID the body as the homeowner, wearing nothing but his boxer briefs and a sweat-stained Grateful Dead T-shirt. A fitting item of clothing in keeping with this unfortunate tragedy. He is noticeably thin and scrawny, almost anorexic, as if he hasn't eaten in months. It's reported that the victim is DOA with a self-inflicted gunshot wound to the head. It appears to be an apparent suicide, but they're not ruling out foul play. The only witnesses to this horrible scene were his lawn mower and 2012 Toyota Camry, its engine still idling as if to say, *I saw it go down.*

Authorities surmise the VIC must've tried carbon monoxide fumes but when that didn't work, he took the quicker way out—a bullet. The cops rule out robbery, as there is no sign of a break-in.

The medical examiner, a woman thorough at her job with years of experience, has seen too many of these cases. You never get used to the horror or the gratuitous deed. She confirms the head wound was the cause of death. At close range it entered and exited the skull through the brain. Time of death was approximately 6:30 a.m., an hour ago, maybe less.

They transported the still-warm body to the Los Angeles County Sheriff's Morgue for further evaluation. The VIC's wife, Joyce Alexander, who had been out of town, was notified to come in and ID her husband. There was no evidence of any suicide note left behind to provide a lucid reason for this gruesome incident. None was really needed. His wife had anticipated this day would come—but a lot sooner than it did.

Two days after, on the other side of the pond, Matthew Street sits alone in his kitchen in Scotland. Matthew is now a vibrant and striking sixty-nine years of age. With his long, chaotic, silver-gray hair and dark-tinted welder-like tinted glasses with leather side panels (to keep out any rays harmful to the retina), he looks more like an aging rock star than a retired interior designer.

He presently makes his home in Edinburgh. But that wasn't always the case. He spent the majority of his life growing up in Southern California, which he holds responsible for giving him far-reaching knowledge of what would be his greatest triumph, as well as his supreme downfall in the garment industry.

He had just finished feeding his cats when the phone rang. It's his friend Chris Styles, who he's known since seventh grade. Chris, a one-time TV comedy writer, had just written *Fade Out* on his first screenplay, "In Search of Ina Byers." He had left television behind for the much-maligned bureaucratic reason—ageism. Discrimination against anyone whose pubic hair turns prematurely gray. The entertainment community figures your imagination is the first thing to go. Then you can't get it up, which they see as a sign of writer's block, until finally your thesaurus becomes so outdated its primary function is that of a doorstop. This is the requiem for a seasoned writer with years of knowledge still crammed in his mind, aching to be used again.

It's 1:15 a.m. in California, so you can bet this call was not a frivolous inquiry about the weather. It had to be serious, and Matthew was guessing this was one of those rare holy crap moments that jolt you out of your comfort zone. Someone had died. Someone he knew. Either in an awful twisted-like-an-accordion car wreck or a body was found in a shallow grave somewhere in the Mojave Desert. With his ear pressed to the receiver, Matthew waited with trepidation for the news—he was right on target, speculating death. Chris, his voice at a low pitch, tells him that their estranged friend and former business partner, Logan Alexander, shot himself in the head this last weekend.

"Accident?" Matthew asks.

"Intentional. In his garage. In front of his car and the lawn mower," he says. Chris always had to throw in a treacle breaker to lessen the morbid description.

"Guess his life got too much for him," Matthew says flatly with no emotion whatsoever. Maybe a self-satisfied smirk at best.

"It's a real shame," Chris says.

"Is it?" Matthew responds.

"Look, there's a memorial service if you're interested." With that comes a pause. "Yeah, I realize it's a long way to travel to preserve the memory of a guy who fucked you over but—" Chris never finishes his sentence.

"You going?" Matthew asks.

"Yes. No. Maybe. I'm on the fence. The guy was our friend up until the early seventies. Just because he was an unsympathetic lowlife doesn't mean I have to be one."

They both agreed that Logan Alexander never got the hang of what it was like being one of the good guys. The real crime here, Matthew thought, is that he never got to enjoy his kids the way a father should. He cheated them out of memories. Matthew felt bad for his wife Joyce, who knew he struggled with alcoholism but stuck with him through all the hell and anguish. And then there was the mother of his children, Emily. Both these ladies knew he was a handful, but also saw something unique in him that never surfaced. Our friendship had broken up into small pieces of resentment and bitterness.

"If you decide to go, I'd love to see you, man. It's been a while since we shared a hug and a glass of burgundy," Chris says.

"I'll let you know, but don't count on me," Matthew says.

"Don't rule it out," Chris said before hanging up.

Matthew got other calls and emails, and most people were saying Logan could never overcome the hard-line depression, the feelings of emptiness and the colorless life he was struggling to turn around. Matthew took a deep breath, not because he was feeling a sense of personal loss, but because this once nailed shut CHAPTER of his life was just pried open like a can of foul-smelling sardines, and he hated the idea of going backwards to a time and place that disrupted his now peaceful existence.

MATERIAL THINGS

Matthew crosses to the stove and puts the kettle on to make a cup of tea. Tea is a big deal here in Scotland. Actually, anywhere in the UK. It's an addiction. Soothing. Kind of like a heroin fix with milk and two lumps of sugar. As fast as he turned on the kettle, he turned it off even faster. He needed fresh air. This unexpected news, although not surprising, demanded attention and rumination, not a cup of Earl Grey.

§

The Firth of Forth is a large firth on the east coast of Scotland and the estuary of the Forth River; location of Edinburgh. This is where Matthew came to savor his solitude, and remember his lovely wife, Melinda, who kept him strong and mentally indestructible before he lost her.

He thinks to himself: why would I fly for twelve hours and pay my respects to a person who disrespected me? As he cradled this thought, he's reminded of the words of wisdom Melinda, whose memory was alive in his heart, whispered to him before she took her last breath. She made him promise to make amends with his adversaries, and heal the one growing ache that has gnawed at him for the past forty years. She was, of course, talking about coming to grips with Logan Alexander, the same guy who didn't have the courage to grow old, so he decided to take the coward's way out with a bullet to the head. Her words inspired Matthew and gave him a new perspective. He resolved that showing up at the funeral would help erase the contempt that's been lingering since the early seventies. Matthew picks up a stone, kisses it, then sails it into the Firth of Forth, and watches it skip over the water before it slowly sinks and disappears in just about the same spot he had spread Melinda's ashes a year ago. This moment of sweet acknowledgment was his way of giving her a heads-up that he was about to fulfill her wish, as well as telling her she's never far away from his thoughts.

Chris and Matthew agreed to make an appearance together. As a team. As protection against the mourners and grief-stricken friends who might be out to challenge their audacity of showing their faces.

CHAPTER 2

It began exactly how you would expect a funeral would start—a person dies, then a solitary black hearse slowly makes its way up a steep incline to a burial plot. We can visualize and almost hear the muffled sounds of mourners weeping in their cars and grabbing tissues from the travel box that sits idle on the dashboard and hasn't been used since the last death in the family five years ago, when Uncle Ed slipped off a ladder and broke his neck while trimming a tree branch. Death: it happens and it's not always pretty. And in this case, death was beyond comprehension. Horrific and regrettable.

Matthew and Chris trail the small procession of ten cars and a vintage Ford pickup truck that looks totally out of place. They are not crying. They do not have tissues. They did not have an Uncle Ed. What they do have is a feeling of trepidation about even being there in the first place. Not really sure how these people are going to react about seeing them again after forty years of invisibility. Maybe they won't react with words but just stare or shrug or spit in their direction like they were the friggin' enemy. They would not see this as an act of redemption but as a jab in the ribs.

At the burial site are, of course, the usual family, friends, and drinking buddies Logan had amassed at local bars during his last few conscious days. Logan Alexander by definition was your typical example of an alcoholic who refused to dignify himself with any level of sobriety. According to his Logan's buddies, liquor gave him courage, strength, and suppressed the ugliness in his life. The Ford pickup truck, with its radio blaring The Doobie Brothers' "This Is It," belonged to a member of Logan's former speedboat racing crew—a marine mechanic who once worked on his high performance engines. A frivolous recreation that proved to be a costly investment that brought him nothing but conflict between him and his father, who saw this activity as just another road to nowhere that siphoned off his bank account.

As predicted, the mourners are noticeably surprised to see Matthew and Chris in attendance. They decide to keep a safe distance, standing in the back almost covertly. Most, if not all, knew of the bad blood between Logan and Matthew Street. The Jon's Drawer clothing store feud that dates back to 1974 was a highly sensitive topic and usually never brought up in mixed company. If at all, period. It begins to rain. Why is that a shocker? It's not. It's a funeral, and funerals usually take place under murky, cloudy, depressive skies. Why should this one be any different? So there everyone stands, maybe twenty-three of them, getting soaked while some rent-a-preacher recites Psalm 23: "The Lord is my shepherd . . ." Both Matthew and Chris make eye contact with Emily, the mother of Logan's grown child. She has managed to remain attractive and fit, wearing her hair shoulder length and very blonde. And Joyce, his widow, who seems to be in a trance, staring blankly down at the ground. Maybe in prayer. Her eyes register more relief than pain. In spite of the situation, the women find the strength to force a smile in our direction. Matthew nods. Chris smiles back. It's awkward as hell, and Matthew wanted to get the fuck away from this whole dismal feeling as fast as possible. But he is not surprised by his feelings. He knew what he'd be in store for—deadly stares, self-satisfied smirks, and clenched fists.

§

The guys head for their car before the Mexican cemetery worker, who first crosses himself, lowers Logan into the ground. And before they have to witness the tears when they throw dirt on his casket. Tears they cannot and will not shed themselves. The lumps in their throats are not produced by the grief they felt for an old friend, but is rather a reminder of a time and place that will always be significant and pivotal in their own lives, when they were just pups trying to make a name for themselves.

Attending the funeral was probably enough to satisfy Matthew reaching closure. Yet he and Chris felt a need to go to the post-funeral gathering and sample the catered deli before taking off back to their own reality, away from the unpleasant bouquet of death. It was being held at Logan's home in Valencia. Valencia is a bedroom community stuck in the middle of the Santa Clarita Valley. Logan's house was a modest California ranch-style, three bedrooms with a two-car garage on a small lot and a brown front lawn that was dying of thirst. For most of his youth Logan had lived in the lap of luxury. But when he stopped bringing in a paycheck, he had to rely on his wife Joyce to survive. Some say this alone was the cause of him losing his self-respect and excessive drinking. He was no longer the breadwinner, and this was an insult to his manhood. It was like cutting off his balls. What little balls he had left to cut off, that is.

Again, Matthew and Chris are on the perimeter of the crowd, out of the way of the people who look at them with indifference. Lots of stares. A few courteous nods in their direction but for the most part not many engaged them. The family dog was the only one who showed any interest, approaching them with a tennis ball in its mouth. Looking to be petted and told everything was going to be okay now that his master will no longer be taking him for walks or tossing that saliva-soaked tennis ball for him to fetch. Matthew grabbed the ball and, as a symbolic gesture, tossed it across the yard. Displaying a glimmer of sadness, the dog just loped for the ball, knowing this game he so loved was not the same.

The guys were leaning on a three-foot pony wall, drinking beers and wondering why people spend so much money on food and drink at these gatherings. For what purpose? Is it the party atmosphere that is supposed to bring joy to this morbid occasion? Matthew never saw the benefit of catering a funeral. Dead people couldn't care less if you're having a good time at their expense—if anything they're pissed that their loved ones are spending money frivolously on macaroni salad and fried chicken. A ridiculous rant, for sure. So Matthew got off the subject of food when Chris opens up about a nail-biting situation that took place in the late sixties. Three in the morning. Logan was drunk. His parents out of town. He calls Matthew and says he hated his life and was going to end it by sucking on the barrel of a shotgun. This was an obvious cry for help, so he and Matthew raced out to the house in Chatsworth and took the shotgun away from him. Fortunately, it wasn't even loaded. But that wasn't the point. The point being, if it were loaded, could they have made it in time to prevent this suicide from happening? They would never know. Logan recovered from whatever was bugging him, and the guys never talked about it again to anyone. Not even to themselves.

"Should we mention it now?" Matthew asks Chris.

Would it help them to understand Logan's recent state of despair—that went back over forty years ago? They paused a moment before making that decision—no. All they needed to know was that he blew his brains out last week. They didn't need the added drama while they mingled and quietly spoke of the deceased as if he were looking over their shoulder, listening.

Finally, someone approaches them. He looks drunk, teetering like he's wearing high-heeled pumps. He introduces himself without a handshake because his hands are busy. One is holding a drink; the other is tugging on his pants that keep slipping down below his waist. He is a shit-faced mess.

"Hey, I'm Alan Randall," he says, his speech slurred. "A friend of Logan's and the last person to see him alive." We aren't that open to starting a conversation and just nod and smile without saying a word. But that doesn't stop him from filling in some details. He rambles on at lightning speed. "Logan and me had several drinks the night before he did himself in, at a local tavern in town. Mulligan's. Truly great ambience. It was happy hour, so I picked up the tab. I always picked up the tab. The man had no money. Ever. Got an allowance from his wife, which he usually spent at the local liquor store on beer and cigarettes. I already told the police all this in detail. I think. But I forgot to add that Logan told me he was going to end it all later. I thought he was just overreacting—that it was just the Maker's Mark talking, and I didn't take him seriously. I was wrong not to come forward and say something. I was wrong. I should've tried to stop him, but I didn't because like I said, I didn't take him seriously. I should have. It's my fault he's dead. It's my fault all these people are here grieving and crying and speculating about his death. I'm not even sure if speculating is the correct word to use in this time of misery."

Matthew decides to speak up. "Sorry, for your loss."

"By the way, I bought a pair of jeans from you guys in '73. They ripped. I want my money back." There's a long, awkward pause right before he tells them he's fucking with them. They nod and smile again just to be courteous. He stumbles off and heads directly for a trash can, where he pukes. That was enough to drive them away from the crowd. They take a walk to avoid the chance of another "special drinking friend" experiencing a sharp pang of guilt approaching them with additional scintillating recollections.

"You remember that guy from '73?" Chris asks.

"You're kidding me, right?" Matthew says.

"Yeah, I'm kidding."

"Well, to satisfy your curiosity, I don't remember. You?"

"He looks very familiar. Think he was a 29 long, wore his hair shoulder length, love beads around his neck, leather wrist band, rose colored aviator glasses, and finished every sentence with the word groovy."

"You realize you just described 85 percent of the guys who roamed the earth during that era?"

"Like I said, he looked familiar," Chris says.

Matthew takes a deep breath, then says, "You ready to leave? I've had my fill of this inhumation."

"I'm ready when you are," Chris says.

"Know what really pisses me off? Not one person has made any attempt to thank me for coming five thousand miles to watch them bury a man they know I had issues with."

"You didn't have to come."

"Yes, I did. I promised Melinda. She expected me to show up and make amends. Ruling out shaking his cold, dead hand, I'm not sure what I'm supposed to do."

Chris gets his bearings and suddenly realizes they're now standing near the entrance of the garage.

"Let's check out the crime scene."

"What? Why?"

"Because I think it'll help close the door on this mental blockage of yours."

"Standing inside a stuffy garage will not provide psychological relief."

Chris grabs him by the arm and pulls him inside. The garage has the distinct odor of death. They have no idea what death smelled like but if it had a smell, this smell would be it. It's dimly lit. Chris finds a switch and fluorescent overhead lights illuminate the area like a nuclear flash. The walls were covered with photos of Logan's racing boats and the vintage cars his father once had in his pricey collection. There was also a picture of Logan receiving some kind of an award at a Concours d'Elegance classic auto show. This was an existence that seemed foreign to them. The damn lights started to buzz so they turned off the lighting and stood in the dark until Chris had the presence of mind to switch on the high beams on the car. Much better.

Matthew sat on a wooden crate marked MARINE ENGINE OIL, while Chris leaned against the fender of the Camry. Some of the crime scene body chalk line was still visible, as were dark bloodstains embedded in the cement. It was a little creepy, but it got them to thinking out loud.

"Could we have prevented this?" Chris asks.

"Us? There's no way. He deserted us and left us for the buzzards to pick off our carcasses. He was a cruel, uncaring sonofabitch."

"That's not what I asked," Chris says.

The answer was still this: there was no way they could have stopped Logan Alexander from committing suicide. He was doomed from the day he was born into wealth and given everything but what he really needed—affection, compassion, and parental guidance instead of the family checkbook.

Suddenly from behind they are interrupted by a woman's soft voice.

"I'd love to hear more."

The guys, a bit startled, turn to see an attractive woman dressed in dark clothing and wearing tinted sunglasses to possibly hide her tears. She is somewhere in her late forties, holding a bottle of wine and three glasses. Both Chris and Matthew agree she is the spitting image of Emily Harwood, her mother. Not a tough call, since she is Logan's grown daughter. She introduces herself as Kate Harwood. She had taken her mother's last name at an early age, after Logan stepped away from his responsibility as a full-time parent. Emily's second husband nurtured her through her teens and into adulthood. Matthew apologizes for bad-mouthing her dead father. It wasn't meant to be heard by anyone but them, because they knew a hostile, unattractive side of him that no one else did.

"He had his rare virtuous days too," Chris says, trying to back-pedal from the offensive name-calling.

"I'd really like to know everything about him," Kate says. "It was not an accident that I followed you guys in here. I'm looking for some insight into what he was really like. I've been left in the dark."

"Ask your mother, stepmother, aunts, uncles—or his drinking buddy, Alan something or other," Matthew says. "This is not something I personally want to get into. Or should get into." He then turns to Chris. "Enough bereavement. I have a plane to catch in twenty-four hours."

He starts for the door. Kate continues her dramatic plea.

"Thing is, I did ask and all I got was the sugarcoated version," she says. "I know through the years they've left out a lot of unspeakable, wicked stuff to spare my feelings."

"It's probably better you were spared than hear the truth," Matthew says.

"He's dead. He's not going to care what you say about his character," Kate says.

Matthew stops at the door, turns back and looks at Chris, who says, "I have no problem giving her answers. She deserves some sort of understanding of the guy whose DNA she carries. How it might affect her. Or if it already has affected her. Or how it may affect her children."

"She may not want kids after we reveal the harsh realities," Matthew says.

"Up to her," Chris says.

Matthew takes a breath.

"Okay, so if we agree to plunge into this head first, you gotta take into account it's not all going to be a feel-good narrative," Matthew says. "There were moments, I have to admit, when Logan was a considerate, generous man. But those moments were far and few between, and most of the time he was—excuse the expression—a drunken prick. If you're prepared to be shocked and blown away, and take possession of your own feelings, we'll gladly do this. Otherwise, live with what little you've got."

"I'm prepared to experience a host of different feelings," Kate says.

"Where'd you like us to start?" Matthew asks. "With the good, the bad, or the ugly?"

"The beginning would be great. Work your way to the middle and the end." Kate looks down. "Well, looks like we're standing over that bloodstained area already."

Although Matthew was still reluctant, he saw this as a way to bring closure to his own demons regarding Logan Alexander. He agreed to be honest and leave nothing to chance. Kate poured each of them a glass of wine. Matthew makes a toast like they were going into battle.

"To both uplifting and upsetting memories of times past. Hold onto your emotions, here we go."

They each take a healthy swallow.

CHAPTER 3

It was January 1969. They were in their twenties. Rebels. Nonconformists. They all smoked in those days, thinking this made them look cool and gave them an air of sophistication. Some of them thought they were ready to become husbands and tackle car payments and household budgets.

Logan Alexander was the best man at Matthew's wedding to Andrea Harberson. Chris was his groomsman. The thing to focus on was that Andrea was his girlfriend all through high school. Since she had no desire to go to college or pursue a career, getting married was her life's ambition. Matthew thought they were too young. So did Chris. So did a lot of people. In any case, except for the fact that they caught Logan stuffing one of the bridesmaids behind the rectory, it all went according to plan. The *I do's* were said. *Till death do us part* was promised. Matthew should've listened to his friends and family—even the florist rolled her eyes and gave him a dubious look. Logan, especially, was a nonbeliever. Time and time again you'd hear him spouting off, making an overcompensated case about how great it was to be single and not tied down. These are always the same guys drowning their sorrows in alcohol every night and doing their best to convince everyone (but mostly themselves) what a great life they have.

After three years, three months, and eight days, all hell broke lose and Matthew was accused of adultery. Andrea claimed he was having affairs but had no proof. It was all circumstantial. A feeling, she said. Insisting she could tell just by the look in his eyes that he had been screwing a redheaded slut. She knew she was a slut with red hair. How? No one knew exactly how. Maybe she was clairvoyant. But if she were a mind reader, she would have sensed this was coming way before she took the marriage vows. He was also seen by her sister, an unreliable source, kissing another woman in the supermarket. A total fabrication. Nevertheless, Matthew Street had to live with these allegations for a long time. He was interrogated every time he came home from work fifteen minutes late.

§

Matthew's men's hairstyling business was going full throttle after only a year. Called it VIP Men's Hairstyling. Okay, sure, this name was in conflict with the counterculture that was happening during this era, but it gave the place a splash of class. The shop's ambience was very eclectic, functioning under a vintage tin ceiling with an undercurrent of old mixed with new furnishings.

It was on a Tuesday morning in May, when Andrea comes into the shop armed with a pair of red lace underwear. She holds them up, waving them in front of Matthew's face as evidence of his adultery, ranting about how she found them in his sock drawer. He wasn't sure if she was accusing him of wearing women's panties or that it belonged to someone he slept with. Of course he pleaded not guilty to both allegations. She called him a lying cocksucker, threw the panties in his face, hollering how she wanted his cheating, lying, despicable self out of the house by midnight. She may have used the words *lying cocksucker* at least a dozen times during the course of this rant. With mouths agape, everyone in the room falls dead silent, waiting for him to retaliate with his own set of disgusting names. Like bitch, whore, cunt. Or worse, if there is a worse description of the indignation he should be flinging at her. Instead he grabs his stomach to try and relieve the sharp pain that's pulsating from his peptic ulcer. His client shifts in his chair nervously anticipating a delayed reaction, like gouging a trench in his scalp with the electric clippers.

Christopher Styles is in the shop, hanging out. He is sitting in an empty salon chair and has a front row seat of the whole live drama. He slides out of the chair, picks up the panties off the floor, and examines them delicately, like they are marked as Exhibit A in a criminal trial. Then, with all the fervor of Atticus Finch or Clarence Darrow, he makes his case:

"We can rule out that these belong to the accused, Matthew Street. For one, they're too small. And I don't see him wearing this shade of red. So, if you ask me, she's shifting blame because these were left behind by the girl she's been banging. The girl she was having a savage affair with while the defendant was working his ass off bringing home a paycheck to keep her and her lover in wine, cheese, and sexy red lace lingerie."

Having finished his summation, he sits back down. There's a pause while everyone stares at Chris, baffled by his spicy speculation. Keep in mind that Chris is a bizarre guy with a really sardonic sense of humor. Almost to the point where it pisses off most people. But he's talented in so many ways. He was attending Chouinard Art Institute, studying to be an animator. You'd always see him wearing the same outfit. It was kind of his artistic public image. Tight jeans, long sleeve chambray shirt, khaki safari jacket, leather opened-toed sandals, a Marlboro cigarette dangling from his lips, while always clutching an open can of Pepsi.

Matthew says, "Look, I appreciate your support, my friend, but the idea of Andrea and another girl is beyond ridiculous."

"Let me prove her infidelity," Chris insists. "I'll follow her, take pictures of them having illicit sex. Which would be my pleasure. Anything for you—just name it."

"If you really want to help, I could use a place to stay for a few days," Matthew says.

"Done. Just so happens my sofa is available." Chris holds up the panties. "And you already have a change of underwear."

CHAPTER 4

Laurel Canyon and Wonderland Drive. A community filled with the fragrances of weed and patchouli oil. Chris lived with Craig Fergus, an aspiring film director, in a two-story stucco house that they leased. It had no charm, no character, bad carpeting, and ugly furniture. What it did provide, however, was a spot in the center of what was happening during the height of the hippie/counterculture movement. Peace, love, and flower power was demonstrated throughout the canyons at a time when marijuana, LSD, and hashish ran rampant and was widely used in social circles.

Chris was dating this Jewish girl, Susan something or other. Matthew had forgotten her last name. Actually, he had probably never met her. Not important.

On Matthew's second night there, when he came home from work, exhausted, he caught them fucking on the couch. His couch. Both totally naked. They didn't seem to care that he was standing over them, watching like a pervert. Chris looks up and introduces them in a breathless voice: "Susan, this is my friend Matthew Street. Matthew, Susan Greene."

"Nice meeting you, Susan Greene," Matthew said, attempting to be polite and not tactless. Susan was in a state of euphoria and was completely oblivious that Matthew was even there. Her goal was to reach a climax and nothing was going to get in the way. Her large tits jiggled like filled pastry, as Chris pumped harder and harder, trying to achieve a state of utter bliss.

"Five minutes. I need five more minutes," he says to Matthew, hoping she'd be motivated and influenced by a time limit.

Matthew went to the cupboard to get a swig of Maalox. His ulcer was acting up and this foul-tasting stuff seemed to help. He stood and watched them fuck while guzzling half the chalky-flavored bottle. In his mind, he was rooting for Susan to quickly spew her vaginal juices.

After fifteen minutes, Matthew figures the promise of spewing any juices was not going to happen. He left the room and went out for some fresh air and a smoke. At night it was quiet except for the sound of cats and mockingbirds. It had a smell of eucalyptus, and in the spring, which was the rainy season, a lot of wildflowers would spring up. Laurel Canyon had a distinctive smell to it. Some say the Laurel Canyon music scene began when Frank Zappa moved to the corner of Lookout Mountain and Laurel Canyon Boulevard in the late sixties. Who knows, it could all just be an anecdotal account just to romanticize the area.

§

It finally hit Matthew as he went back inside—he'd be sleeping on a stained sofa that reeked of sex, sweat, and semen. He found a sheet and covered the couch after Chris had taken Susan home. Laurel

Canyon is an area that's hardly fraught with crime. It's a laid-back, peace-loving community. Until tonight, that is. He's taking a needed respite on the couch when he hears a gunshot that cracked the air like thunder. He sprang up like a nervous cat whose tail had just been stepped on and instantly dove behind the sexual sofa for safety. He could've sworn the shot came from right outside the window. Seconds pass, and he hears the jangle of keys and someone trying to open the door. He crawls to the kitchen like a combat soldier, intending to grab a large knife for protection. These guys have nothing that resembles a large, sharp knife. A spatula is his only weapon of choice. Not good enough to defend himself against a handgun. Was he nervous? Damn straight. He notices a baseball bat leaning against a far wall. He goes for it. Then focuses in on the door handle. It begins to turn. Just like in a classic noir film right before some goon enters, blasting away with a submachine gun, mowing down everything in its path. He stands in the middle of the room, closer to the door than he probably should have, and let loose with a warning.

"If you dare come in, you'll be met by a Louisville slugger to your fucking head, motherfucker!" he yells, his voice cracking with nerves.

He can only hope that this goon takes him seriously. The door swings open, and just as he was about to take a healthy swat at this guy's skull, he sees it's Chris's roommate, Craig Fergus. He is startled and also pissed by his hostile greeting.

"Holy crap! What is with you, man? Are you insane? I live here, remember? And take your greasy mitts off the bat, it's signed by Jackie Robinson. Worth a bundle."

Matthew apologizes for his incoherent bat-shit behavior. Told him he thought he heard a gunshot right outside the door. He panicked. Been under a lot of stress lately. Craig claims that it was nothing but a car backfiring. Matthew was not convinced he was right. Of course, he knew what was going on with his marriage and didn't seem to be sympathetic. Told him to take a Valium and chill out. Matthew didn't need a tranquilizer, nor did he need his medical advice. What he needed was his life back on track again. Craig excused himself. Said he had to get ready for a date with some starlet. As he climbed the stairs he stopped halfway, turned, and announced that Selig Levy killed himself by jumping off the Golden Gate Bridge yesterday morning in the dense fog. Matthew had no idea who the fuck Selig Levy was, or why he thought this was a noteworthy piece of information that would interest him. Maybe he was a celebrity or just some guy he knew from the old days. Or a junkie. Or a rabbi. He had to stop trying to guess who this stranger was. It would drive him nuts, like a tune you can't get out of your head. The name Selig Levy would continually replay like a broken record over and over until he made a connection.

As Craig disappears upstairs, Matthew sets his precious Jackie Robinson bat up against the wall, gently. Thinking if it's that valuable, why have it lying around collecting dust, or for anyone like himself to use as a weapon. Deduction—he thinks Craig is full of shit. Taking a closer look, he sees no real signature anywhere on the bat. Only an illegible chicken scratch. A little personal enlightenment on Craig Fergus—self-centered, arrogant, not a team player. Eats off of your plate as well as his own. Like me, he married his high school sweetheart. Better to keep her name out of it because this wasn't a warm and fuzzy story. Knocked her up, moved to San Francisco, gave the baby up for adoption, got divorced. Not nearly a storybook ending. Craig had lots of personal issues for as long as Matthew can remember. Spends more money on therapy than most people pay rent.

MATERIAL THINGS

In the years ahead, Craig will marry three more times and have a total of four children by two different women and an insurmountable amount of child support payments. This will add extra days to his shrink visits. His biggest fear is his own mortality. Death frightens him so much it's Matthew's belief that this guy is going to have a fucking heart attack trying to stay healthy.

§

Matthew couldn't get out of there fast enough. He decides to take a long drive to clear the cobwebs. He goes to his car that's parked at the curb. He was driving a silver '63 Corvette convertible. As he slides in, he feels something stick under his shoe. A rock, a nail, a stale piece of gum? Not sure, so with interest, he leans down and grabs it and holds it up. It's dark and his vision is hampered. In the glove box is a Zippo lighter. He snaps it open. Flick the flint roller and it lights up like a torch. What he sees in his hand blows him away. It's a fucking bullet shell. A car backfired, bullshit. Someone was out here plinking lead, just as he suspected. This only convinced him even more that he needed to resolve his problems fast and get the fuck out of Laurel Canyon and away from Wonderland Drive. A smart premonition on his part, because let's for a brief moment move ahead to 1981—eleven years from now. The Wonderland Murders, involving porn star John Holmes, would occur, shocking the nation. By then, Matthew would hope to be very far away from that infamous couch. Lights out. As he closed the Zippo, it clicked with cold metal authority.

CHAPTER 5

Matthew heads straight for Malibu Beach. The beach had always had a calming effect on him. From the canyon it was twenty-three miles, a good forty-three minute drive via the 405 Freeway. He got off at Sunset Boulevard, then hauled ass to where Sunset ends and runs into PCH (Pacific Coast Highway) and the ocean. First he stops at Malibu Wine and Liquor and buys a six-pack of Heineken and a Twinkie for dinner. By the time he made it to the beach, it was now eleven p.m., cold and misty from the sea breeze spewing off the surf. He pulled into a parking lot that overlooked the sand and surf. He didn't park too close to the edge because the saltwater spray would totally destroy the Corvette's paint and maybe even corrode the frame. He just sat in the car, drinking beer and listening to the waves crash onto the beachhead. The moon glistened off the water and created this amazing iridescence. In the distance, he could see the lights of a ship. Maybe a cargo vessel making its way overseas to the Far East.

He decides to stretch his legs and walk along the beach. He rolled up his pant legs to his calves. The wet sand oozing between his toes was like a foot massage, without the nimble hands of a masseuse. The salt air cleared his sinuses. After about a half mile, in the distance he thinks he sees a figure coming towards him. It was hard to make out since the moon was his only light source.

As the figure drew closer, or he became closer to it, he realizes it was a girl walking her dog. Or to be more accurate, a dog with a girl in tow. Judging by her silhouette, she was tall and thin, with long hair that stopped just below her shoulders. The dog, he couldn't say what breed it was or how long its hair was. But it spotted him, detached itself from her grip, and ran towards him at full speed with its leash dragging behind like an extended tail. The girl screamed out a command— "Olive, stop!" The dog ignored her and just kept coming at full speed. God, how he hoped it was friendly. He was in no mood to go to the ER and get a rabies shot. An idiotic statement. When is anybody in the mood to get a rabies shot?

As it turns out, the dog was a Doberman, and way too friendly, as it stuck its nose in his crotch. She spoke softy. The girl, not the dog.

"She likes you," the girl said as she approached. "She only sticks her nose in people's business that she likes. Her name is Olive."

"Yeah, I heard when you tried to control her. She hard of hearing?"

"Stubborn. She has a mind of her own."

"Yeah, that seems to be the temperament of most women these days—having a mind of their own. Nothing personal. It's just that I'm going through this warped brain phase. Have a nice walk."

She suddenly finds this whole encounter disconcerting. "Okay, well, nice talking to you," the girl says. Then she grabs Olive's leash and starts to leave.

Matthew instantly apologizes for his rudeness, explaining how he and his wife are about to be no more, and it's made him very uptight. The girl changes her position and turns back, pointing out how she and her boyfriend are about to split the sheets themselves. What was at first an awkward encounter turns out to be a commonality of interests—being in an unbearable relationship with the wrong partner.

"Can we start over? I'd like to start over," Matthew asked calmly. She thinks about it for a beat, then starts to ramble on about her life.

"I'm a waitress at Moonshadow's Restaurant in Malibu. Work nights. Long hours. Decent tips. It's our only chance to stretch our legs."

Matthew looks at her dog's legs, then hers. All six were trim and shapely. She was wearing cutoff jeans and a crop top that showed her small breasts and accentuated her nipples. After further inspection, she looked familiar. His next line was your standard hackneyed phrase but he didn't know any other way to ask.

"Do I know you?"

"A cliché, but I forgive you. Maybe you know me from the restaurant. It's a popular meeting place for the in-crowd."

"No, never been to Moonshadow's, and I'm definitely not part of the in-crowd." He keeps staring, trying to put a name to the face. She notices him furrowing his brow.

"You alright? You suddenly seem into be in deep, painful concentration."

It finally hits him. "Wait. Yes, I do know you. You're Lydia … no, Lila … no, Linda something or other. Right?"

"Very good memory, young man. Linda Tarlow."

"You came into my shop once for a trim."

"A trim? For me or Olive?"

"You. I'm a hairdresser. Mostly men. Women stress me out. Fuck, there I go again, being an insolent dick."

"No worries. I know what you meant. Cutting women's hair can be a daunting task. They're chatty and malicious, and rumormongers."

He just nods to play it safe. He then knelt down and began to pet Olive, just to show the animal-friendly side of his sardonic personality.

"Actually, I do remember you," Linda says. "You had the name of a street for a last name, like Elm or Maple, right?

"Street is my last name."

"Right. Street. Very clever."

"Matthew Street."

Her face suddenly lights up, remembering the moment. "It's all coming back to me," she says. "The name sounded more like a private detective from a Dashiell Hammett novel than a hairdresser."

He smiles knowingly. You gotta love the fact she knew about Dashiell Hammett. This is not the first time Matthew has been associated with this genre.

"I think my parents intentionally gave me this name so that I'd get harassed and have to fight my way out of confrontational situations with people who wore trench coats and had a Maltese Falcon hidden in their attic."

She laughed. Matthew liked her. She had a great laugh to go with her great legs. It was like he just struck gold. He thinks he made an impression on this babe. He loved her look. She looked healthy, but not athletic-healthy. Like the kind of woman who'd once had an eating disorder and learned the dangers, but there was no way she was about to get fat.

"It's uncanny that I ran into someone I know on the beach this time of night," Matthew remarks. "I take it you live around here?"

"I do. With the boyfriend. Like I said, we're in the last stages of calling it quits."

"Staying afloat in a relationship these days can be brutal," Matthew said, not very convincingly.

"It's okay. We weren't much of a couple. He's a musician. In a band. Always on the road. That should give you an idea of how promiscuous he is." She adds with contempt: "But he always tells me when he's unfaithful. He's generous in that way."

Matthew thought: why stay with this dude?

"Before you ask, the reason I stay with him is because, well, I guess I'm afraid of what's not out there for me. I've been meaning to leave. But I'm a huge procrastinator. A bad hang-up. Anyway, how about you? You must have an interesting reason why you're roaming the beach at night with your pants rolled up. Are we grunion hunting?"

"What? Grunion? No. A woman apoplectic with rage threw me out of my own house. Staying on a couch in Laurel Canyon. Needed a break from reality. The salt air seemed to fulfill that need."

There was this long, unpredictable pause. Their eyes met, and hers seemed to actually twinkle like a movie special effect. Matthew felt close to her. Like he was supposed to take this chance meeting a step further. Then, without permission, he leaned in and kissed her. It was amazing. Her lips were warm and salty from the sea breeze. They broke the kiss.

"We must be on the same wavelength—I was hoping you'd do that," she said, then kissed him back. He thought she was a natural beauty. This whole thing was freaking him out. It was one of those rare infatuation-at-first-sight moments that really don't exist. But did exist because he's living it. Twenty minutes later, they were making out in his car. She kissed more intensely than most people fucked. You could just tell that this was going to lead to heavier stuff. Sex was inevitable. But he wasn't sure he could pull it off. Or if the timing was right.

His confidence level had dipped to an all-time low. He hated to admit it, but there was this guilt factor he was still dealing with. As if he was cheating on his wife, Andrea. Which is an absurd thought, considering she's already convinced he's been unfaithful, on an ongoing basis, with whores, sleazy chicks, and loose women off the street looking for a daytime quickie. He was already a marked man before he stuck his hand down Linda's pants. When he got her off, her face registered complete euphoria. Guess he still had what it takes to perform with his digits at least. They shared the last beer, replacing the conventional after sex cigarette. They both had the presence of mind to not go all the way. They zipped up their pants, decided to exchange numbers, and wait a decent amount of time before moving forward. Which was a total of three minutes. Sex with her was something you'd never forget and want to repeat as soon as possible. So they did it again a half hour later. After they finally caught their breath, she went east, Matthew went west. By the time he got back to his car the sun was in its starting gate on the rim of the horizon. It was fucking magical, according to him.

CHAPTER 6

VIP Men's Hairstyling. 9:45 Tuesday morning. Matthew was fifteen minutes late for his first appointment. If his wife were waiting, she'd accuse him of performing unspeakable acts on another woman, and wouldn't let him out of the house until she tested his underwear for traces of semen and lipstick stains. Yes, he swears, it got that bad.

Didn't matter that he was late. Logan Alexander was his first appointment and he had already been drinking, which meant he couldn't care less about the time. Logan himself was not on any schedule. He didn't have a job, nor did he have to work. His family had big money and he got an allowance larger than most CEOs.

Matthew pours himself a cup of coffee, and a large strong one for Logan, then settled in, shampooing him. As he massaged his scalp, a rush came over him. He could still taste the sea salt on his lips from Linda. He decides to run by everything that had happened to him in the past week. That he was booted from his house, now living in the canyon with Chris Styles and Craig Fergus, and that his marriage was about to explode in divorce court. It's odd, because Logan didn't seem to be that shocked by it. His reaction was almost apathetic.

"Chicks, man, they're unpredictable," he says with no facial expression. "One day they can be reliable, the next thing they're accusing you of fucking their housekeeper. I know. I've been there."

That totally threw Matthew, but sometimes when Logan drinks he has trouble putting sentences together that make sense. What he really meant to say is that he had a crush on this girl's housekeeper but never got to first base with the girl or the housekeeper. So he stopped seeing the girl because he couldn't face being shot down by the help. This was his clever way of dumping the girl who never put out for him, so he blamed it on the housekeeper, who could have been just invented for this particular tale. Very convoluted. But not far-fetched for Logan Alexander, who fed his ego by putting himself on this invisible pedestal and idealizing his imaginary accomplishments.

Matthew starts to open up and tell him about his night on the beach with Linda Tarlow and her dog Olive. It got as far as them making out in his car—with Linda, not the dog—when David Ackerman, his second appointment of the morning, arrives a good forty minutes early. David was a strait-laced business guy who still wore a part in his hair. He made his living in his father's shirt business (California Knight Fashions) and had a showroom in the apparel mart downtown. There was a reason he was ahead of schedule. Today he brought in a dozen men's knit shirts carefully wrapped in plastic, that he wanted Matthew to display and sell in his shop. They were a very unusual style and weave. Like kite string that was hand-knitted together by a bunch of old ladies living in a retirement village in

Miami. Logan, never one to ignore a chance to argue against anything he dislikes or feels is unlawful, speaks up.

"None of my business, but I'd be careful. Stolen goods, maybe? The cops come in and arrest you for larceny. You go to jail, and you're cutting hair for convicts in Sing Sing on the Hudson River."

Of course, David Ackerman takes umbrage and defends that notion. Guarantees this is a legit business proposition.

First and foremost, there was no way Matthew is putting these shirts in the shop. He's running a hair salon, not a fucking Macy's. Plus, he didn't know crap about the clothing business, except that shirts came in small, medium, large, and extra large. This was the extent of it, so it's not surprising that he flatly passes on David's offer.

"Look, Matthew, there is nothing you need to know," David says. "You put a sign up, shirts for sale—I'll supply the sign—you take the money. Simple. Unimpeded by any fancy deals. This is not a scam. I know you. You get weird about things you don't understand. It's a legal business venture."

"Me, I'd still be cautious as hell," Logan says.

David gets upset. "But I'm not asking you to agree or disagree."

"No, but you are asking me to buy one of those weird fucking shirts," Logan replies. "And my intuition tells me to stay clear of them. They look fragile, not to mention pretty fucking ugly."

Matthew jumps in. He becomes a little irrational, explaining that his life up to this point was a virtual shit hole. He's on the verge of a divorce, maybe losing half his shop to a person who thinks he wears women's underwear, and this dude strolls in and wants him to push menswear. Why?

"Why me, David?" he asks.

"Because you have the foot traffic. Because you cater to guys who want to look better and want to display a good sense of style."

He needed an impartial opinion from someone besides Logan, who is still buzzed. He defers to Dean, one of the other stylists. Dean is older than them. Not by much. Thirty something. Smart, witty, a little crazy. But good crazy. A throwback to the beat generation. You'll never see him wearing anything but dark clothing (mostly black turtlenecks). A far-out dude with a groovy attitude. On the wall over his station are photos of his idols: Jack Kerouac, William Burroughs, and Allen Ginsberg. Matthew holds up one of the string shirts for judgment.

"Dean, need an honest evaluation."

Dean squints his eyes to adjust his vision, as if the shirts will look more appealing through a narrower aperture "Not my bag. Too à la mode for my taste. But the needlework seems boss."

"Think they'll sell? Matthew asks.

"Depends on how much bread," says Dean. "If they're pricey, you'll be using them to mop up spills."

Matthew turns to David, who suddenly rattles on like a carnival pitchman. "Eight ninety-five. Out the door. No tax. My dad's label, California Knight Fashions. My cost is free. I supply the goods from our downtown warehouse. They're closeouts. Reduced prices to get rid of superfluous stock. You get half. We both make money. What have you got to lose?"

There's a pause, then Matthew reluctantly agrees to a test run. Logan rolls his eyes dramatically.

"For no more than a month," Matthew stipulates.

"I'm telling you, man, you will be shocked at the appeal," David said right before he left two-dozen shirts.

"If you ask me, they're going to appeal to fucking hungry moths," Matthew fires back.

As expected Logan left without buying a shirt. He hated them. Thought they were cheap-looking. This was Matthew's biggest fear, that most people will regard them as crap and want their money back when they shrink in the wash and form back into their original balls of string. So what? It's costing him nothing except shelf space and maybe some raunchy remarks about keeping his day job.

Fifteen minutes later Matthew is cutting David Ackerman's hair—shorter than usual, because David wanted space between cuts. In truth, this was probably a money-saving thing with him.

After a few beats, Chris comes in just to shoot the breeze. He does that a lot when he's bored and needs to recharge his batteries and reenter the earth's atmosphere. Today he looked noticeably different. He had a very attractive girl in tow that he just picked up hitchhiking on Ventura Boulevard. Exotic looking. Born in Israel. Living in Studio City with her parents. Chris introduces her to Matthew. He shakes her hand. It was soft and warm. Her name was Anne Fraser. Maybe nineteen. Beautiful. Dark hair, incredible green eyes, olive complexion. Amazing overall features. Matthew couldn't take his eyes off of her. His stare was obvious to the point of being rude. She noticed.

"Something wrong?" she asks.

He needs to take a breath before answering. "No. Everything is perfect. Everything is in its proper place. Eyes, lips, cheeks—all perfect."

She smiles and walks around the shop taking in the ambience, while Chris attempts to talk to Matthew, but his attention is totally distracted by this girl. He admits to himself that she had him mesmerized, and any thoughts of Linda seem to vanish in the Malibu mist. This in some ways bothered him, because he had never experienced this kind of initial attraction with anyone, ever. Not even his wife. It was a good feeling, as well as a scary one.

All eyes follow her every movement as the sun backlit her just enough to expose her breasts through her gauzy blouse. He was suddenly consumed with jealousy, convinced that her exposure was not a command performance just for him. She turned to him. Their eyes made contact. She crosses the room and brushes up against him as she moves in the direction of the string shirts. There is a pause as she surveys them. She then crosses back to Matthew with a shirt (his size) in hand, and leans in close to his ear, her lips pressing against his lobe.

"I would fuck you in this shirt," she says just loud enough for him and David Ackerman to hear. David looks knowingly at him, his glazed-over eyes saying *I told you so*. Matthew so much wanted to put on the shirt right then and there and test her impulse. But of course he didn't, because he was fucking imagining all this. He was transported into another world. When he snapped out of this reverie, he was still cutting David's hair and Chris was introducing Anne to Dean at the other end of the shop. This whole situation had him baffled. But he's guessing all the female issues he'd been dealing with lately— his wife driving him out, Linda slathering him with affection, watching Chris get it on with Susan Greene—stimulated his sexual appetite. All of these situations ripped at his self-image, which was responsible for reality-testing and a sense of his personal identity. Bottom line, he needed a woman who would support him in his endeavors and show him that she likes him for who he is, and not who she wants him to be.

Twenty minutes later, Chris and Anne leave. Before she goes, she whispers a breathy goodbye in his ear: "Really nice meeting you, Matthew Street."

Matthew is pretty sure this was the defining moment he was hooked on this spectacular chick from Israel.

§

At the end of the day, Matthew is driving through Laurel Canyon headed back to Wonderland Drive, all the while thinking how he desperately needed to get his own place. The ongoing battle with his wife was getting more and more out of control. Her raging hormones and phone calls were a constant annoyance. He wouldn't put it past her if she had him followed and photographed. His neck was getting stiff from always looking over his shoulder for a slime bag lawyer to serve him divorce papers. Or a PI with a hidden camera taking a snapshot of him pissing in some restaurant men's room. Why was he waiting for her to make the first move? Fear? Of what? Conceding defeat? Being single again? Hoping for a miracle that would save this fucked-up marriage? Or all of the above? And then he switched gears and thought how a therapist would have a field day dissecting his defective marriage. He's also beginning to sense he's taking on the traits of a hypochondriac. A neurotic, as it were. The nagging question: does he seek professional help and take the prescribed medication, or just live with it and see where it takes him?

For now, he makes a conscious decision—get a lawyer and ignore the possibility of a brain tumor that's driving him to think irrational thoughts.

He makes it back and is greeted by Craig Fergus sitting at the kitchen table in his bathrobe, drinking soup and looking like death. He's home with a cold. Balled-up Kleenex is strewn everywhere like mini marshmallows. He looks pale and feverish. Why is he not in bed? Why is he spreading his germs throughout the house? Before Matthew inquires about his health, he asks if Chris had come by with this girl Anne. He says yes, but because he was sick they didn't stay long.

"So he didn't take her upstairs and fuck her?" he asks.

"I wasn't paying attention. I was too busy coughing and sneezing," he says. "But I wasn't that out of it that I didn't notice she was a bitchen looking chick with some serious green eyes. Why the sudden interest? You hung up on her?"

"Me? No. Not my type."

He quickly changes the subject, figuring he can get some practical feedback on a lawyer and shrink from Craig. After all, he's been divorced a few times, so he must have some insight. He gave me nothing. He was a worthless source of information.

"Trust me, you don't want to go with the guy who handled my divorces," he opines. "Useless prick. Took me to the fucking cleaners, then had the audacity to start dating my second wife as soon as the ink was dry on the fucking papers." Craig coughs up some yellowy phlegm. "Stay clear of me, I'm a fucking walking bacterial transmitter."

"So you can't recommend anyone?"

"Why bother, man? You're going to lose your ass anyway. You can't fight these chicks. Wait till you hear from her lawyer, and pay whatever they demand. Save on attorney fees. If you have half a brain, hide everything you can in an untraceable account in the Cayman Islands, or a coffee can you bury in the backyard, before they drain your accounts dry. My ex even took the fucking loose change she found between the sofa cushions." He sneezes and coughs up more phlegm.

Matthew couldn't take anything he said seriously. It's either the fever talking or he's just plain out of his gourd. And if that's the case, Craig's therapist is not doing a good job of saving him from the harsh realities of life, and is not someone Matthew would go to for his own obsessive issue. He figured he could wait another day or two before he's taken to the fucking cleaners. He did, however, seek out an empty coffee can, but had no backyard to bury it in.

§

It's now 10:30 p.m. Craig Fergus had finally gone to bed. Matthew is downstairs on the couch reading Jack Kerouac's *On the Road*. It's considered a defining work of the postwar Beat and Counterculture generations. But his mind wanders aimlessly, not paying attention to the words Kerouac has so brilliantly written, because his head is in the clouds and he seems to be more focused on hearing that next gunshot ring out in the canyon. Paranoia creeps in. He closes the book with force. The sound alone makes him flinch. He grabs and hugs the baseball bat, then lights a cigarette to help calm his nerves. He then hears the sound of footsteps outside the door and assumes it's Chris coming home from dropping off Anne Fraser. He's not going to make the same stupid mistake he made before, almost taking Craig Fergus's head off. He puts the bat down and waits for the door to swing open, almost like a wife ready to greet her husband.

Nothing comes. Nothing swings open. The shuffling outside the door continues.

He comes to his own conclusion: Chris is searching for his keys. He speaks through the door. "Relax, I got this!" he shouts. He opens the door and is instantly shoved back into the room with such force it propels him over the couch, sending his body into the kitchen table. Chairs go flying. It hurt like hell.

"What the fuck!" is his initial reaction, before two men in ski masks are standing over him with guns pointed at his head. The shorter of the two speaks in a calm, authoritative manner.

"This is a home invasion robbery. Do as we say and no one will get hurt. Nod if you understand."

He nods more than enough times. His is mouth is dry and he can't form words like *take what you want—please don't kill me.*

The shorter one speaks again. Maybe the taller one has no tongue, Matthew is thinking.

"A sliver of honesty. We're addicts. We want money, drugs, and jewelry. Whatever you can come up with will be appreciated. Now get them, we have a long night ahead of us."

Amazing how well-mannered and forthright they were. He tries to explain his awkward position—that he's temporarily sleeping on the couch they threw him over. He doesn't live here and he has no idea where these guys keep their money, stash, jewelry, or valuables, he says. Only thing he knows for certain is that baseball bat is a collector's item probably worth decent change.

"You need to talk to the dude upstairs nursing a bad cold—he's the tenant," Matthew says with a shaky voice.

"Get him down here," the taller guy demands, which rules out he's a mute or anti-social. Matthew gets to his feet and starts to head up the stairs, but he's told to stay where he is and get the sick guy down here without leaving the room. Matthew screams for Craig to come downstairs. Stresses that it's an emergency. No response. He's probably asleep and groggy from the antihistamines. After maybe three attempts Craig finally shows. At first he thinks this is some kind of prank and gets indignant, ordering them to fucking leave his house or he'll call the cops. He changes his attitude when one of the intruders fires a shot in the air and the cottage cheese ceiling rains down on them.

Craig Fergus quickly becomes accommodating, providing these guys with the exact location of his drug supply, including amphetamines and sundry other items stashed inside an empty gallon carton of ripple fudge ice cream in the freezer. Jackpot—there's a potpourri of hash, Thai sticks, cocaine, uppers, downers, and poppers. All this, plus jewelry and cash is then handed over to their captors without incident. Matthew happily surrenders his gold wedding band. For him, this act of compliance was a sign his marriage was doomed not to survive.

The thieves were thorough—tied them up with their own rope and left with the loot and the baseball bat. In a warm, sudden rush, Matthew felt good. God knows why. Maybe because they didn't gag them, knock them unconscious, or cut off a functioning appendage. After twenty minutes, they managed to free themselves. Decided not to call the police because, well, think about it—you're reporting a robbery by gunpoint by two masked men you can't ID. They'd ask them to make a list of everything that was stolen. Wedding ring, a baseball bat, and oh yeah, a whole shitload of illegal drugs Craig had stashed in his fridge. Not something you want to admit to the cops.

Craig found a way to blame Matthew for the whole incident because he made the mistake of opening the door to complete strangers. A ridiculous accusation, but Matthew wasn't about to argue the point with a guy running a fever, and who was also a card-carrying asshole.

His voice trembling with outrage, Craig urges Matthew to leave and find another couch to crash on.

"It'll be my pleasure," Matthew says as he gathers what little stuff he had. He heads for the door but turns back to slip in the last word: "Be sure and explain to Chris why you threw me out into the streets because I let in two crazed gunmen who were going to shoot the door off its hinges, then come upstairs and blow you away if I didn't. So, while you're thanking God you're alive, be sure and throw in a Hail Mary, full of grace, for me, asshole."

Craig's response is a classic example of being a true putz—he tells Matthew he owes him for a carton of milk that relieved his ulcer, plus the cost of the baseball bat. He wanted to tell Craig to go fuck himself but decided to act more aggressively and childishly, so he just slammed the front door hard enough where it caused the room to shudder and the bay window to shatter.

Matthew had no alternative plan, so he improvised and decided to drive to Malibu and see if he could somehow make contact with Linda Tarlow. A slim chance, but trying made it exciting.

Thirty minutes later the Highway Patrol pulls him over for speeding. Matthew reacts nervously because he has an open bottle of beer sitting between his legs. He covers it up with his shirttail as the cop slides up to him, keeping one hand on his gun.

"You in a hurry, young man?" he asks.

Matthew chose to ignore the question and went with friendly and naive. "Hey, evening, officer. What's the problem? What'd I do?"

"C'mon, you know what the problem is. I clocked you doing 80 in a 65 zone."

"Whoa, I swear I had no idea. Maybe my speedometer needs to be recalibrated. I'll get it looked at first thing tomorrow. Thanks for letting me know, sir."

Matthew puts the car in gear to roll on, but the cop stops him, reaching in and putting the gearshift back in the neutral position.

"Hold on, sport, we're not done yet." When a cop calls you "sport," you know this is not going to end well. He then asks for the standard license and registration and heads back to his cruiser, telling him to stay put. This gave Matthew time to dispose of the beer in a more practical way. Since his top was down, he chose to hurl it into the underbrush that was growing along the freeway. As bad luck would have it, the bottle hit a rock and shattered—just loud enough that the cop got wise to what was happening. Next thing Matthew knows, he's walking a straight line, and, with his eyes closed, touching the tip of his nose with his index fingers. A humiliating test of coordination as cars whizzed by, much faster than he was going, and seeing him put to shame.

Fortunately, the cop just gives him a speeding ticket and lets the open container violation slide. Matthew was grateful. Last thing he needed was a criminal record to go along with his pending legal separation.

The cop starts to leave when Matthew blurts out: "I need the name of lawyer."

"What? You're disputing the ticket? If you go to court on this, you're gonna lose kid, trust me."

"No. Hell, no! I'm guilty on the speeding charge. I expect to be in a heated divorce battle and I figured since you're in law enforcement, you could recommend a good lawyer."

There is a very uncomfortable pause. He could tell the cop was contemplating giving him a name or just driving off to cite the next victim.

"Thanks anyway. I'll just give her whatever she wants," Matthew said, playing the martyr. "Next time you see me, I'll be traveling by bus."

He puts the car in gear and is about to drive off, when the cop says, "Ed Baker, he's in the book. He's ruthless. Tell him Joey Siddens recommended him."

The cop gets in his cruiser and burns rubber. Somehow, breaking the speed limit worked in Matthew's favor tonight.

§

Matthew finally made it to the beach at 1:30 a.m. It's cold and windy. Even the seagulls' teeth were chattering. He gets out of the car and searches the area. Linda was nowhere in sight. Did he really think she'd be waiting for him? No. But it doesn't hurt to pin one's hope on a dream when you had no real plan. He then heads back to the car, intending to give up the search for Linda Tarlow, when he notices a phone booth near the pier. Calling her seemed like a good plan of action. A vagrant was sleeping inside like it was his own private suite at the Biltmore. Matthew tried getting him to move out of the way, but with no luck. He was immoveable, like a bag of cement, or maybe he was just dead. Hard to tell, and Matthew wasn't about to take the time to find out, so he straddled his body, which was covered in old newspapers and a tattered beach towel from the Santa Barbara Hilton. This guy gets around, Matthew thought.

The phone rang for what seemed like forever before he heard Linda's weak voice on the other end. She sounded desperate. She asked if he could come and get her and Olive. She gave explicit directions and said they'd be waiting outside.

Just as Matthew was exiting the phone booth, the homeless dude woke up, springing to his feet with catlike precision. Scared the living crap out of him. He introduced himself as Federico Fellini, the noted Italian movie director, and then asked for spare change. Said he had fallen on hard times. The movie business is not a dependable source of income any more, he claims. Absurd does not begin to cover this man's delusional state of mind.

All Matthew had was a ten-dollar bill—he'd used his only two nickels on the phone call.

"Gimme the ten-spot and I won't run my sword through your fucking heart," the bum says as he reveals a tree branch with a penknife Scotch-taped to the end. He goes berserk and tries to stab Matthew, in the fashion of Don Diego de la Vega (Zorro). He nearly stabs him in the gut, but bravery prevails and Matthew is able to elude his thrusts, grabbing the makeshift sword and breaking it in half over his knee, then tossing the blade over the sea wall into the ocean. Matthew's victorious *touché* echoed into the night.

Feeling defeated, the bum dramatically falls to his knees, like a stage actor appearing in a low-budget version of *Hamlet*, reciting verse into the night air: "Neither a borrower nor a lender be: For loan oft loses both itself and friend, and borrowing dulls the edge of husbandry."

There's a twist to this midnight madness—Matthew felt sorry for the poor guy and tossed the ten spot at his feet for his pathetic performance. He luckily got away from this whack-job without a scratch but also felt good for showing a bit of charity.

CHAPTER 7

The Surfrider Inn, Malibu. Linda, Olive, and Matthew pull into the first motel off PCH whose neon sign flashed VACANCY on and off, but in Linda's mind this was more than just a place that offered color TV: it was freedom and refuge. Her eyes were red and puffy from crying. They sat in the parking lot while she explained how her boyfriend almost took her head off because he caught her in the hall closet with the phone, trying to call Matthew and make a quick escape. He explains how home invasion robbers held him up at gunpoint, then got a speeding ticket, and finally was threatened by a homeless man with a knife.

"My God, are you all right?" Linda asks.

"Mentally, fine. Physically, my back and rib cage are in pain from being thrown across the room like a Frisbee into a breakfast nook and chairs."

"Thanks for rescuing me, Matthew Street," she says.

"My pleasure. Now, what's your story?"

Linda tells him that the boyfriend had his band mates over for a drug-fest and decided that was a good time to show how macho he was. He took a swing at her to heighten the drama that fortunately missed its mark. Thank God, one of his pals had the presence of mind to block his fist before the second swing was about to meet her jaw. She locked herself in the bathroom while he delivered insincere apologies through the door, claiming dropping acid was the cause of his unruly behavior. He promised to write a love song about this experience with her name in the title. It's just like a rocker to produce a record about his exploits, and how he treats women badly, and make money doing it. Not having any of his bullshit, she climbed out the window and waited with Olive for Matthew to show up.

He fell quiet, searching for the right words to make her feel better about herself. Nothing extraordinary came to mind. He decided the right thing to do was make her feel secure and safe. He held her close and tight in a warm shower until she stopped shaking. Her body pressed against his felt very safe for him too. This was something he and his wife had never experienced because she was too damn uptight about him seeing her every flaw in the daylight.

The water cascaded over them like they were in some kind of tropical waterfall, kissing each other so deeply they almost drowned from swallowing so much water. She ground herself against his outer thigh and whispered in his ear: "I want you to go down on me."

Sure, they had sex in the car a few nights ago, but this was different. This time it had meaning, significance. Somehow this seemed like a more intimate moment. The turning point in a relationship, if that's where it's headed. In his mind, this was breaking barriers—going from strangers just walking in the sand to a serious relationship in the making. This was not a quickie, cramped in the front seat of a sports car. He felt he needed to perform on a higher emotional level, not just fuck for fuck's sake. He wanted nothing more than to satisfy Linda, and here he was a nervous wreck, putting all the pressure on his pecker. While her Doberman looks on, evaluating his performance. His every move.

She knelt down—Linda, not the Doberman—and gave him a righteous blowjob that eliminated any sort of anxiety. They stumbled, still soaking wet, from the shower to the bed and made love. Or was it just radical sex and love had nothing to do with it? They took three cigarette breaks and slept for maybe two hours tops, until the sun started to blast its way through the ugly chintz curtains.

In the mist of the morning, when they go out to his car, there is some dude leaning against it. Olive growls like she recognized the guy. He looked like he could be your typical rock musician. Long hair, headband, tattoos, lots of chains hanging from his neck, smoking a Lucky Strike. Matthew assumes it's the boyfriend, and that he's in store for some jawing and pushing and shoving, and maybe even a little smacking and kicking and hair pulling. He automatically becomes defensive, brandishing clenched fists.

"Listen, dude, she's had it with your behavior. It's over. Recognize you're the bad guy here, man, and if we have to call the cops, we will." Matthew says all this with as much authority as he could muster without appearing like a pussy.

The guy is stunned. He says nothing. Linda nudges Matthew and, in a stage whisper, tells him that's not her boyfriend. She hasn't the vaguest idea who this dude is. Matthew turns back to the guy, now a lot less defensive and angry.

"So, yeah, okay, my error," Matthew says. "How can I help you, man?"

The long-haired guy launches into a story that they do not necessarily swallow—that he saw Matthew's Vette from the road, loved it, and waited for the owner to show up so he could make him an offer to buy it. There was a pause that gave them time to digest his claim. They don't want to appear like fools, so they just go along with his story.

"Appreciate the interest," Matthew says, "but it's not for sale."

Matthew, Linda, and Olive are getting in the car when the guy stops them.

"Look, my name is Phil Lesh," he says. "I'm a member of the band The Grateful Dead. If you change your mind, I'll be in San Francisco for the next two weeks at the Fillmore West. I'll pay up to four grand, cash. Which, by the way," he adds with confidence, "is the original MSRP."

Matthew and Linda doubt he's who he says he is, but it's an interesting anecdote they can retell for a few years until it gets stale.

§

Matthew dropped off Linda at a girlfriend's place in Santa Monica. She tells him that she wanted them to repeat last night's bedroom action real soon. Honestly, this was moving way too fast for him. He said he wanted the same thing but couldn't promise her that right now. She understood. Said if the wife thing managed to work itself out, she thought he was the best thing that could have happened to her and Olive, if only for a couple of unforgettable nights. Although he was pretty sure the marriage was not going to last another sunrise, he didn't commit to anything right now. Experience had taught him not to romanticize a sure thing.

MATERIAL THINGS

§

The following afternoon Logan Alexander approached Matthew with what promised to be a life-changing proposition.

"We should establish our independence and get a place together," he declares. "Roommates. Brothers in arms."

The timing couldn't have been more perfect, but Logan's drinking—and the fact most people didn't like his holier-than thou-attitude—were both issues. So, besides the obvious character flaws, price was a primary concern. The guy had expensive fucking taste, and Matthew couldn't afford to have expensive fucking taste. He was on a tight budget; Logan was on a bottomless expense account.

"Depends on the cost," Matthew says. "I need to go economy class or I can't hack it."

"Minor detail," Logan says. "The apartment is a two-bedroom furnished in Studio City. Three hundred-fifty a month. My end is two-fifty; your share is one hundred. Economical enough?"

In addition, this offer came with a bonus. Logan would only use it on the weekends to bring home chicks and party. The other five days the place was all Matthew's. Reason—a simple truth. Logan's parents demanded he live at home five days a week. It's the only way they can keep tabs on their wayward son. Plus, if he wanted to continue to get his lavish allowance, he had to follow the house rules.

It was a no-brainer. Logan had a place to shack up with his babes and store his wine and beer. Matthew had peace of mind. It got him out of Laurel Canyon and the away from the stoners, burglars, freaks, and the random gunshots fired off in the dead of night. They were scheduled to move in two days later. Not soon enough for Matthew, but he guessed two more days would not break his spirit.

The next day, Matthew is finishing up a cut when this very strait-laced guy comes in, wearing slacks, a paisley tie, and his shirtsleeves rolled up to his elbows. He figured he heard about the string shirts and was an interested buyer. The shirts, by the way, were flying off the shelves, making this a rare "who knew?" moment.

"Matthew Street?" he barks. Matthew just nods. He's not making any hasty acknowledgments until he finds out what this is all about. The strait-laced guy then hands him a manila envelope. "You've been served," he says energetically, as if it's a line from a Broadway play.

Matthew plays it cute. "Served? By whom? Who the fuck is serving me? A waiter? Who?"

"It's from the law offices of R.H. Brogliatti," the guy says, then turns and exits.

Matthew's premonitions were right. The motherfucker was a process server. Andrea had finally grown the balls to make her move. He felt sick inside, yet at the same time relieved. It was finally nearing an end. He didn't even have to call Ed Baker, the cop's lawyer friend, or stash all his loose change in that rusty Yuban coffee can.

He holds up the envelope to the light for a closer inspection. What was he looking for? A shredded marriage license? Photos of him kissing Linda on the beach? Linda and him checking into the Surfrider Inn? What does she think she has on him?

He felt the need to announce this sacred document to the room. "It's official. I've been served. Andrea has made it clear that she has given up, thrown in the towel. Can't handle the degradation of marital bliss."

No reaction, just all movement stops dead as he opens the envelope that's been hermetically sealed by some legal secretary's tongue—which, before this, he's sure was licking her boss's ass.

MATERIAL THINGS

He's baffled when he discovers they weren't divorce papers at all, but annulment documents. Reason? At that particular moment, he had none. He was stumped. But a few weeks later he'll find out that she was cheating on him with her boss, at her recent job at some Beverly Hills talent agency. She feared he'd find out and take her double-dipping adulterous ass to court. Matthew came out the winner in this battle of discontent. While this would have been a time to celebrate and rejoice for some people, he had no plan to yip it up and commemorate his liberation. The smart thing to do was to sign on the dotted line right next to where it said *nice going, pal*.

There was a smattering of applause. His receptionist, Tina, comes over and gives him a hug. She has tears in her eyes.

"And you're crying because …?" Matthew inquires.

"I'm happy for you. You're free," Tina says. "You can walk the earth now knowing you only answer to yourself."

As festive as it seemed, it was actually a real downer. It was a traumatic moment. Remember, this was his high school sweetheart, who he wanted to spend the rest of his life with. The first and only person he'd ever said "I love you" to. The woman he'd maybe have kids with. There was a feeling of failure that surged through him. He felt as if he had to return all the wedding gifts because he didn't live up to the vow "till death do you part." After three years, three months, and eight days, life with Andrea Harberson came to a gray and oppressive end.

Someone in the shop says "Mazeltov!" He turns. It's Anne Fraser, standing near the front door. Matthew blinks several times to make sure he isn't hallucinating again. She was gone in a whisper—a figment of his obsessive imagination. There was nothing in the doorway except space and air and what he thought was the fragrance of her perfume.

This was heavy. He just stood there in disbelief. Someone asks if he's feeling okay. Says he looks pale. He's reluctant to ask the obvious question, but he does so for the sake of his sanity: "Was Anne Fraser just here?"

He gets incredulous stares and a series of headshakes. He decides to take a much-needed break and get some fresh air. There was no way he could hold a pair of shears after what just happened. He walks three blocks to get a coffee. He didn't want a coffee, really, only a time-filler. A horn honks loud and steady. Crossing the street, he almost gets hit by a car. He's in another zone. He wants to be concerned about the Anne Fraser mirage, but he's not. He actually enjoyed seeing the sudden apparition. For a few minutes, she made him forget how depressed he was over the annulment.

§

Since the new apartment was not move-in ready until tomorrow, Matthew splurged on a hotel room at the Sportsmen's Lodge. He was told when he checked in that it opened in the 1880s, when the West Coast was still the realm of ranchers and fishermen. Was this historical information going to make his stay more pleasant? No. All he needed was a bed, a couple aspirin for his banging headache, and a wake-up call for seven a.m.

An hour later, Matthew is sitting up in bed smoking a joint. He just got out of the shower with only a towel wrapped around his waist. After another robust drag from the spliff, there's a knock at the door. He's puzzled. No one but his receptionist, who booked the room, knew he was there. He didn't order room service, so scratch that. Who was it?

He didn't open the door. Instead, he calls out from the bed: "Yeah?"

A familiar voice answers back. "It's me. Anne Fraser."

He had to pause. If it's really her, why is she here? Too many questions ran through his head. The first: was this just another hallucination? If not, what does she want? How did she know he was here, in this room? Does she think he's Chris? Is she in trouble and needs help? He still doesn't answer the door. His head spins.

"What'd'ya need, Anne? I'm about to go to bed."

"You, I need you! Can you open the door, please?"

"I can, sure, but to be perfectly honest, I'm feeling it's the wrong thing to do."

"I just want to talk. Nothing else."

"Talk. Sure. Let's talk about how you found me."

"It's hard to explain everything through two inches of wood. Let me in. Please?"

The last time he just opened a door, he was met by two masked men and a loaded gun. Reluctant, Matthew sets the joint on the edge of the end table and crosses the room, opening the door. A huge mistake. There she stood, wearing nothing but a trench coat. Naked underneath. He knows this because as soon as she steps inside, she spreads open the coat and reveals her nakedness. After he scrutinizes her amazing body, instincts tell him to call security, take the fire escape down to the street and run, but he becomes motionless. She moves closer. So close he can smell the distinctive flavor of her hair rinse.

He backs off, nervous. She tells him not to be nervous. All she wants to do is have sex with him. "If that's okay with you?" she asks.

No, it wasn't okay with him. She's Chris's chick. He discovered her. Matthew doesn't do other guys' women. It's morally wrong, he tells her. The fact he was hard as a rock was making this whole issue very difficult. Before he can retreat, she drops her coat to the floor, pulls off his towel, and then pushes him onto the bed. She is now on top of him and has made her mission quite explicit—seduction, copulation, fierce fucking.

"I thought you wanted to talk," he manages to get out.

"After we have incredible sex, we can talk about whatever you want," she promises.

Matthew tries to fight the urge, but has no willpower. He can't push her off. It's almost like he's paralyzed. Chris will never understand the circumstances. Their friendship will suffer. But Anne's sexuality is too powerful to resist. Only a few minutes goes by, but it feels like an hour of unbridled sex—and just when he's about to explode, he bolts awake in bed, gasping for air. It was nothing but a bizarre dream. Probably brought on by the effects of the weed and his underlying desires for Anne that surfaced earlier today in the shop.

It all seemed so real. He glances around the room, getting his bearings, when he notices the trench coat lying on the floor at the foot of the bed. Bizarre and defying common sense? Yes. Like a sequence from *The Twilight Zone*. He shakes his head and rubs his eyes disbelievingly. Maybe it's just another hallucination. He looks again at the floor. The coat has not disappeared.

A wave of anxiety rushes over him. Perspiration forms on his upper lip. He draws in a sharp breath and once again bolts upright in bed, startled, waking from what appears to be yet another mirage. Only now it's more of a nightmare. He goes to the bathroom and splashes water on his face to make sure he's truly wide-awake. As he does, the phone rings. It startles him. He looks in the mirror. His eyes are closed shut. Another few rings and his eyes pop wide open. Boom. He's been transported back under the covers in bed, still asleep. In a foggy haze, he slowly reaches over and answers the phone with a faint "yes?"

A woman's dulcet voice informs him: "Mr. Street, it's your 7:00 a.m. wake-up call as requested."

He says nothing. Just hangs up. He looks for the trench coat. This time it's gone. A sigh of relief. The trench coat seemed to be the pivotal object in the dream.

He quickly throws on his clothes and starts to leave. At the door he stops and looks back at the unmade, slept-in bed. For a moment he's torn between fantasy and reality—does he dare go back for dream-related seconds with Anne Fraser, or return to cutting hair in his dull real world? Of course he leaves, feeling he's made the right decision.

But as he drops off his room key at the front desk, the clerk tells him that a young lady inquired about him last night, but house rules prevent staff from giving out room numbers. The clerk, a little man with a Hercule Poirot moustache, then describes Anne Fraser down to her trench coat and beautiful green eyes. Surreal is an understatement. He turns ashen, then gets the fuck away from there before he bolts awake in the lobby, tripping over ranchers from the 1880s mingling after a cattle drive.

CHAPTER 8

The sun had slipped behind gray clouds. It was like someone had turned down a dimmer switch in North Hollywood.

Matthew finally settled into his new digs with Logan Alexander. A few nights later, Matthew, Chris, Logan, and Jon Lewis, his sister Patti's latest boyfriend, were having dinner at the Hamburger Hamlet on Sunset. The four of them sat outside on the patio abutting the sidewalk and watched the stream of characters parade by in an array of unusual looks, shapes, and sizes. All digging the strip scene, smoking joints out in the open. Braless chicks in thigh-high dresses, all headed for the Whisky a Go-Go to see Buffalo Springfield live on stage. In their wake were guys with hairdos down to their asses, Mohawks, ponytails, and slits for eyes because they were so loaded on their drug of choice, which was usually weed, acid, coke, or OxyContin. A few preferred an opiate—heroin, H, horse, skag, smack, China white. Whatever the designation, it was highly addictive and not a popular diversion with Matthew.

Jon, however, found it both interesting and staggering how much these kids must be spending on drugs—thousands to feed their habit.

"The drug dealers are cleaning up, making a fucking fortune," he observed. "If it wasn't illegal, this is the business I'd be in. Sleep late, no overhead, meet interesting people, live large."

But it was illegal and dangerous, so for the moment Jon wisely scraped that idea.

Matthew switches gears and quickly changes the subject to something less addictive and unlawful—clothing. Pants, shirts, sweaters, leather jackets, to be precise.

What had been an experiment became a source of wealth in those odd men's string shirts. Needless to say, we were fucking blown away by it. Jon, who ironically was also Matthew's accountant, mentions that the shirt sales were doing almost as well as the VIP haircut receipts.

While the waitress brought their food, Matthew proposed a radical idea to the guys. It included them, it included their ideas, and moreover, it included their money.

"I want to expand?" he said.

"What do you mean? Like gain a few pounds?" asks Chris. "Order two burgers," he suggests with a wry smirk.

They all ignored his inane suggestion, then Matthew explains this crazy vision he had the other night. Not the Anne Fraser reverie, which to be honest, was still locked away deep in the recesses of his subconscious, but the notion of opening a small clothing boutique in the back room.

He elaborates enthusiastically: "In today's market, the only place we have accessible to us that carries trendy trousers is a store called Mr. Slacks on Hollywood Boulevard. They cornered the market on casual dress pants. We should bring a new look to the party."

Jon wasn't paying attention. He was too busy ogling a chick in a see-through blouse that was walking by. Classy behavior for a guy who was about to marry Matthew's sister in a few days. Matthew lets it slide. The guy was only human, right? Truth is, they were all looking at this babe. They were all mesmerized by these kids who were making a statement. Peace, love, and flower power separated them from the norm and Matthew wanted to be part of this societal change.

Jon finally chimes in: "The back room of what?"

Matthew expounds, describing the back of his shop, where the pool table sits by itself, waiting for someone to give it some attention. It's wasted space. Perfect spot for a clothing store.

There is a pause while they take a drink of water just to make sure they can swallow this notion. Jon was jazzed on the idea and wants to hear more. Logan says he knows nothing about the apparel business except how to zip up his own pants. More importantly, there's no way his father would back him on this kind of blind venture, if only for a few thousand dollars.

"I'm out. But if it happens, I'll buy a belt," he says, attempting to stay in the conversation.

Chris is wary and wants to know "why me?"

"Why not you?" Matthew retorts. "You have a creative mind. You're a trustworthy friend, and you dress fashionably. Besides, I need your cash to pull this off."

By now, Chris had graduated from art school and had been working at a major animation studio for about six months. Felt trapped in the conveyer belt daily grind, so he walked away from it and started the Acme Cue Card Company, working on a multitude of TV shows. It brought in a sizeable paycheck and, more critically, he didn't have to answer to the Mickey Mouse corporate bosses he had been working for.

MATERIAL THINGS

Chris said he wanted to think about it. Without a clear plan, he was reluctant to invest in something he didn't know crap about. Matthew sort of agreed but didn't say anything for fear he'd scare him out of joining up. The lack of knowledge should have scared him too, but it didn't. What he did know was that they had good taste, an eye for style, and the determination to succeed. Not to mention the foot traffic from VIP. The word would get out and help boost business. That seemed like enough motivation for him to make this idea work.

They needed a sensible and practical idea. A design. Matthew already had some thoughts in mind but needed a few days to put those ideas to paper. And then, as if fate was listening to the conversation, this person sitting directly behind them clears his throat, then gently taps Matthew on the shoulder. He swings around to find an expressionless man with a square haircut, heavy on the Brylcreem, staring back at him. He spoke with a mouthful of food, excusing himself for eavesdropping.

"I couldn't help but overhear your conversation," he says. "I like what I heard. It's genius."

They eyed him cautiously. You have a right to feel uneasy about any person who thinks removing a pool table to make room for a clothing store is genius. Even though this dude had neither the demeanor nor the temperament of a dangerous lunatic, Logan grabs his fork for protection. The Brylcreem guy notices.

"Trust me, I'm no threat to you guys," he says.

He then nonchalantly hands them his business card. Nothing fancy. The kind of card you can get five hundred of for ten dollars. His name was Hal Exler. The card claimed he was a sales rep for a pants company called Male Pants. The four of them exchange confused but interested looks. Exler explains his company's specialty is selling and marketing bell-bottom pants to retailers. He wanted their business when they were ready to move forward with their plan.

"I want you guys to start the trend and be the foremost carriers of Male Pants bell-bottoms in the Valley," he says. "Start the revolution!"

Sounded like an incredible opportunity. Logan voices an opinion that bell-bottoms will never catch on as a trendsetting pant. Matthew and Chris wish they had recorded that statement.

"You'll never catch me wearing them," Logan says.

Nevertheless, to show his sincerity, Hal Exler paid their check. This was their first contact with the apparel community. It felt like a sign giving them the go-ahead to trash the pool table and turn the back room into a dramatic clothing store in the Valley.

"Start the revolution!" Exler exclaimed as he took his leave. By now they had figured out that was his catchphrase.

§

Matthew goes back to the apartment. It's a weekday, so Logan isn't around and he had the place to myself. He took a quick shower to cleanse his mind. Sat at the kitchen table and smoked a joint to modify it. It worked like a magic potion, and within an hour he came up with an incredible rendering. You gotta love the power of cannabis. He walked to the window and looked up into the starry night. For a brief moment, he thought how did he ever get to this place. Get to this moment. Didn't matter. He was here, and what mattered was he had to learn to accept his fate. He fell asleep on the couch, of all places, almost hoping in some perverted way that Anne Fraser would join him in his marijuana-induced state of mind and fuck his brains out. Even wanting this as just a fantasy was probably not a sane objective.

CHAPTER 9

It was agreed upon that Jon Lewis, Chris Styles, and Matthew Street would partner up with equal shares. They needed a retail license—but first, a name. They were all gathered at Jon and his sister Patti's apartment located somewhere in the Valley, near one of the freeways where the din of traffic rattled the walls like mini aftershocks.

In the mix were six of them, including one of Patti's friends, Betsy. Attractive. On the cusp of being your quintessential flower child. And since it was the weekend, Logan joined them. He was not your creative type, so his input would probably be limited to constantly raiding the fridge for a beer.

The room had a laid-back atmosphere. Mose Alison was playing in the background, underneath the conversation. Jon happened to be a modern jazz fan—music that was characterized by improvisation, syncopation, and a forceful rhythm. It was actually a refreshing break from The Stones, The Doors and the head-banging sounds of uneven-tempered rock 'n' roll .

Everyone was drinking, smoking, and scarfing the pasta and pizza that was offered, until Matthew corralled everyone around the dining room table to present his idea. Before VIP moved in, the store was a Mexican import store. So it had a theme to bounce off of. Arches, dark wood, beams, wrought iron. All that was missing was a piñata and a bowl of guacamole. Everyone seemed to be pretty much on board using the hardedge Spanish/Mexican motif.

Next on the agenda was coming up with a suitable name that would withstand the test of time. Suggestions are thrown out in the open—some not half bad, like The Fashion Factory, The Continental Clothing Company, The Street Scene—but they all seemed too esoteric. The frustration mounts. Everyone drank more and smoked more weed. By midnight they were all crashed in a chair or on the sofa. Yawns were being communicated instead of words. Time to call it a night. Maybe something will spark someone in the next few days. But it wasn't going to happen tonight.

What no one planned on was Logan getting stinking drunk, and trying to get Betsy to come home with him. He managed to corner her and get in her face. She backed off and quickly explained that she's not into dicks, but prefers the female anatomy, vaginas and other suitable parts. In a word, she's a lesbian. Logan sees this as a challenge more than an obstacle. He thinks he can woo her by being charming and delightful, and mentioning he drives an Aston Martin, and that his father is the western hemisphere distributor of Sony products.

Betsy takes it down another road. "Wow, very impressive," she says. "Seems like I should be sleeping with your father, not you."

Matthew jumps in apologizes for Logan's big mouth.

"No big deal," Betsy says. "I've lost count of every horny bastard that's propositioned me, thinking they have enough testosterone to sidetrack my affection for women. Get me to play for the other team. Comes with the territory."

She then crosses to Patti for protection from any more abusive remarks from Logan Alexander, and also to ask a favor—can she borrow her gray cashmere sweater. She's taking her girlfriend out for a birthday dinner on Friday and wants to look especially hot.

Logan could not resist an inappropriate comment. "You don't need a sweater to make yourself look hot, babe," he says. All eyes turn to him, with a look of disdain.

"What? The word babe is gender prejudice?" Someone needed to cool down Logan, who is still slugging down beers like they're going out of style. Too late. He goes, "You go out with me and I'll buy you all the cashmere sweaters you want, babe."

Chris tries to lighten the mood. "How 'bout if I go out with you? Cashmere or cotton?"

Patti breaks up the tension by saying she's getting the sweater. Betsy stops her. Says she'll get it just to get away from that misogynistic prick—just point her in the right direction.

"It's upstairs in the dresser, next to the coat rack, in Jon's drawer," Patti says.

As Betsy begins to climb the stairs she turns back to the room and pauses for a moment. None of them knew it at the time, but the next statement would change the course of history and make this evening's get-together a smash hit.

"I dig the name Jon's Drawer—for the shop," Betsy says. "It's a natural."

We all exchanged knowing looks. Except for Logan, who was still bent on getting into Betsy's pants. Betsy was right on target. It felt like a saleable brand. Matthew could see it on a marquee. On merchandise bags. On business cards. In newspaper ads. He could hear in his mind people talking about going shopping at Jon's Drawer. They gave credit to both Patti and Betsy. This was to be the designated name—Jon's Drawer. Brilliant.

The mood suddenly becomes celebratory. Everyone was hugging and kissing one another like they had just won the Academy Award for best ensemble group in a living room. In all the excitement, Logan grabs Betsy and tries to kiss her. This did not set well with her. She shoves him away and very loudly tells him to fuck off.

Logan was not someone who liked rejection. He became verbally abusive and said he could change her tune about digging girls if she gave him half a chance. It was obvious that this was not going to end well, when Logan again tried forcing himself on her and she gracefully kneed him in the nuts. He lets out a yelp and falls to his knees in pain. Betsy leans down to his level and says, "Well, I'm guessing you won't be trying to hustle and abuse any women until the swelling goes down."

Everyone apologizes to Betsy for Logan's uncivilized conduct. Matthew feels the need to explain that, during the week, Logan lives with his parents and is treated like a caged animal, aching to escape and look for prey. And when he's finally let out on the weekends, away from the authoritarian control of his parents, he takes advantage of his freedom. Drinks himself to oblivion and makes every effort to mate. Fortunately, Logan is too drunk to comprehend the self-deprecating image Matthew has just revealed.

Matthew and Chris lead Logan, who is gingerly cradling his throbbing balls, to the car. It's been one helleva night for Logan Alexander. But despite his rudeness and drunken behavior, his weekend was nothing less than spectacular, and worth all the negative criticism and insults he got. He thanks Matthew for being such a good friend and allowing him to be himself among their social group—unlike his family, which was always judging and trying to control him.

CHAPTER 10

The following morning, Matthew, Chris, and Logan are having coffee at Tiny Naylor's restaurant in Studio City, on the corner of Laurel Canyon and Ventura boulevards. A prime haunt for those who want to meet and greet and shoot the shit for hours while siphoning gallons of caffeine into their system. Once in a while, they'd order an egg and hash browns so it didn't appear as if they were hijacking the table for a twenty-five cent cup of coffee. Jon couldn't make it; he was busy with last-minute wedding plans. What plans? You drive to Vegas, pull up to a tasteless wedding chapel and get married by a former dealer who after getting caught cheating at blackjack, became an ordained minister through the mail. Plus, as a wedding gift, you get a complimentary breakfast and a ten-dollar chip redeemable at The Sands Hotel. This did not require extensive planning.

Logan, drinking his third cup of coffee and sucking on his forth cigarette, is nursing a serious hangover. He recalls nothing from the night before.

"Did I get laid last night?" he asks.

"No, none of us got laid," Chris says.

"It was a dry night," Matthew says.

Logan says, "Then why do my balls feel like someone took a sledgehammer to them?"

"You ran into a knee," Chris says.

"Can you be more specific?"

Chris says, "You tried to fuck a lesbian. She took exception."

Enough about his pain. Matthew had an idea about the Jon's Drawer logo and was eager to run it by Chris.

"It's so not conventional," Matthew said with excitement. "And you're gonna paint it on the storefront window."

Wait a second. Hold on. Chris got nervous because he was an animator, not a sign painter. Hire a sign company. No, Matthew wanted them to be involved in every aspect of the birth of Jon's Drawer. Plant the seed. Watch it grow. *Start the revolution.* They would be the mother, the father, and the midwife.

Chris nods and starts to take a sip of coffee. Matthew reaches over and grabs his hand. No coffee. Pay attention. Chris does. Matthew explains in detail how he wants a Tiffany glass-style logo combined with Coca-Cola-style italic lettering. There's a pause as Matthew waits for Chris to leap out of his seat and proclaim him a genius. To be honest, Chris did not experience the same sensation of heightened emotion as Matthew did. He holds his tongue—doesn't want to sound critical of his friend's idea. Mattthew shoots Chris a stare, then slides a fresh napkin in front of him.

"What, wipe the smirk off my face?" Chris asks.

"Draw. Create. Do your artistic thing, man. A rough sketch is all I ask."

Did Matthew expect Chris to sketch this logo on this flimsy napkin? Yes. He's looking for instant gratification. Chris is looking for something to draw with. A pen, a pencil, a fucking sausage link. He snags a pencil that's resting on a waitress's ear. Matthew hovers over him like a test monitor, just waiting for him to cheat or make a mistake. Chris erases a line and Matthew flinches. The pressure was enormous. He felt like all eyes in the restaurant were focused on the damn napkin. Waiting for brilliance. A Picasso rendering of a Coca-Cola font.

Then came some relief from Logan. "You know what I feel like doing?" he said, standing up. "Puking." He rushes to the head. Matthew had a premonition that this was going to be a regular weekend ritual with Logan Alexander. But it was worth the price of paying low rent, and the alone time Matthew got five days a week.

Then, without warning or reason, Matthew is suddenly intoxicated with excitement. "We definitely need some sort of grand opening with spotlights and balloons, wine and finger food," he thinks out loud.

Chris stops drawing to slow him down to a crawl. "Maybe we're getting ahead of ourselves," he cautions. "We gotta build a store first before we think about grand openings and finger food."

Matthew takes a deep breath, then nods in agreement. He's projecting the future with great expectations. He shares an idiosyncratic thought.

"You know, sometimes I imagine myself looking back on right now and I think, where will I be sitting or standing or lying when I look back on this moment? Will right now, when I look back, be something spectacular as it feels now, or just a yawn?"

This was a question for a sixty-five dollar an hour shrink to dissect, so Chris just gave him a polite nod and left his weird reflection linger in the air.

§

Logan came out of the bathroom cleansed and refreshed. The three of them escape the stark reality of the coffee shop, leaving behind the indecipherable napkin composition, and head for the Rose Bowl swap meet in Pasadena. This was the ideal venue to find bargain antiques to maybe use in the store. The circumference around the Rose Bowl is jam-packed with vendors and serious buyers and looky-loos. A variety of objects are being offered, from antique furniture to hard to find auto parts and eight-track tapes. Most of these vendors get there at two in the morning to set up and get a prime spot. People came from all over the state to buy or sell or just browse. It was like a big outdoor fair without the livestock, cotton candy, or some huckster trying to guess your weight.

It wasn't unusual to run into someone you knew, and today was no exception. Matthew was negotiating a price on a maple armoire he thought would be perfect to display sweaters, when both Logan and Chris spot a familiar face in the crowd. A girl, who is all over some older dude and is showing enormous, hands-on affection.

It was Matthew's ex, Andrea. Logan and Chris exchange concerned looks. Knowing this would not be a welcome sighting for Matthew, they attempt to block his gaze as she and the boyfriend walk by them. But their human barrier is futile and Matthew, in his peripheral vision, catches his ex-wife in a serious lip lock with this man. He reacts. His upper lip curls in disdain. She does not see him, yet. As he starts to approach and confront her, the guys intervene, trying to distract him. He ignores them. He has things to say.

Matthew is now face to face with the boyfriend, who is short and sports a five o'clock shadow. There is a moment of fear when Andrea realizes who he is, and whatever is about to be said will probably not go down as a friendly exchange. Matthew is surprisingly personable. He introduces himself as Matthew Street, Andrea's ex-husband. The boyfriend senses trouble, and instantly clenches his fist. Chris and Logan inch up right behind Matthew in case a skirmish breaks out.

Chris says, "We have your back, buddy."

Matthew goes on to say how he just wanted to get a closer look at the man who was fucking his wife while they were still married and trying to reconcile. She'd accused him of being a cheating cocksucker, when all along it was her who was being deceitful behind his back.

Andrea is now tugging on the boyfriend's arm. She of course feels uncomfortable and desperately wants to flee.

"I know this is awkward and embarrassing," Matthew says, "but I couldn't pass up the opportunity to finally lock horns with a piece of work like yourself, sir."

The boyfriend starts to say something but Matthew cuts him off.

"Stop. Wait. It's not your turn to retaliate just yet. I'm not done getting all that angst out of my system. One more thing you might find useful. She does not like anal sex. Makes her sick to her stomach and you'll have to swear to God Almighty never to put your thing in that orifice again. Yes, she'll call your cock a thing."

Now Andrea decides to speak up and defend herself, claiming what Matthew just said is pure fiction. All bullshit.

"He's clearly pathological," she posits, "projecting disdain only to bully you into taking a swing at him so he can sue you for assault. Not worth clenching your fist over this loser."

The confrontation devolves into a fierce verbal duel. Words like bitch, spineless adulterer, and frigid are tossed back and forth. A sob breaks from Andrea. Tears leak out. Matthew may have gone too far. He feels empathetic, but he doesn't want to feel empathetic. He wants to be revengeful. He looks at the boyfriend, trying to tell him with his eyes and body language to defend her. Pounce on him. Call him out.

"Do something chivalrous, for fuck sake!" he finally blurts out.

The boyfriend finally does speak in a controlled manner, saying he refuses to battle Matthew with threats or nasty language to make any kind of settling point.

"She is now with me, not you, which gives me great pleasure, and gives you angst and a feeling of emptiness," he says with a broad fucking satisfied smile.

With that he leads Andrea away. Matthew takes a deep breath and, frustrated, throws his arms in the air.

"That was a really unsatisfactory face-off," he says to the guys. "Why'd you let me come here today? You should've sensed trouble."

Logan makes what he believes is a feel-good suggestion. "Time to hoist a few, lads. Let's get sloppy drunk and disorderly and curse all the ex-wives and girlfriends until we feel vindicated by their harsh, savage treatment of us."

CHAPTER 11

A few weeks slide by, and on this particular day it decides to rain. Foul weather has a tendency to slow things up, cramp business, and make people irritable. Such was the case of four of Matthew's customers who cancelled on him. This alone gave him the motivation to maybe throw in the VIP towel and consider the apparel business as a full-time gig. But he's rushing what could end up an economic failure. So far he's only sold those string shirts—which, by the way, were still a hot item, much in demand. Who knew the popularity of crocheted twine?

When he arrives at work he's greeted by Anne Fraser, who's anxiously waiting to see him. She looked great even rain-soaked and was wearing, of all things, a trench coat. *The* trench coat. This caused Matthew to shudder inside. But he kept his cool and his nerves hidden. Let's keep in mind that the only time the two of them had any real contact was when Chris had picked her up hitchhiking a few weeks ago. Other than that, their only link was in his fantasy, his hallucinations. He lights a cigarette to cover his tension that was now seeping through. She opens up about why she was there. She came to ask for a favor. A favor? What sort of favor could Matthew possibly give her? Maybe to keep her out of his dreams and lewd thoughts.

She explains how she's planning to pursue a modeling career and would like to use his shop as a backdrop for some still shots. After hours, of course. Matthew almost felt disappointed that it had nothing to do with him personally. She waited for his answer that didn't come right away because he was deliberating if there'd be any fallout between him and Chris. Did he need to get permission from Chris? He hated to use the word permission but it seemed appropriate. Fortunately, she wasn't offended by it. She made it clear that she and Chris were just friends. He wasn't her type. Sure, he was nice. But she preferred a more eclectic personality. A little rough around the edges. But nothing so rough that it hurts. Then Matthew thought, was he a little rough around the edges? Was he Anne Fraser's type? For no other reason than to boost his ego, he hoped so.

"Just give me a heads-up on the day and time you plan to shoot," he says. She is ecstatic and thanks him with a kiss on the cheek. Her being so close brought back the memory of the same scent of her hair rinse that wafted in his hotel dream. Matthew watches as she disappears through the door. He knows this whole fantasy thing is crazy and surreal. To justify his delusions he philosophizes how most guys fantasize about being with movie stars and beautiful, untouchable cover girls. This is no different than Chris imagining he's fucking Raquel Welch while pumping Susan Greene. For the moment this satisfies Matthew's absurd state of mind before it really gets out of control.

§

Suddenly from the back room, there is a loud crack. Almost like a car had just crashed through the wall. It made Matthew and everyone else jump nervously. He quickly goes to assess the situation.

"Everything cool? Anybody hurt?" Matthew asks generally.

Jake McGrath, their contractor, is a friend of Jon's from Palm Springs. He pokes his head out and gives him a succinct explanation. He's chewing on a slice of pepperoni pizza, so his words are a little muddled.

"We're bringing down a wall to make room for the pant boxes you designed. It's not exactly an easy task. We have to work around a load-bearing wall."

It won't be long before we're selling pants, shirts, sweaters, and a variety of accessories to the people of the Valley. Exciting. Also a bit unnerving. Matthew's on edge and takes it out on Jake.

"I have no clue what a fucking load-bearing wall is," he grouses. "Just don't take out the plumbing—I'm planning to take a leak in the near future."

Shrugging, Jake goes back to the bearing wall. He usually works on bigger commercial projects, but things were slow and he badly needed the work. He came up here with his wife, Sage. A dishwater blonde beauty. Jake and Sage did not go anywhere without each other. Sage, however, was a long-established, habitual kleptomaniac. This recurrent urge to steal, without regard for need or profit, was a serious habit that she had a tough time breaking. Shoplifting was her specialty, but she also targeted oblivious women who would set their purses down in restrooms and restaurants and grocery shopping carts. An easy mark, an easy lift, she would call it. This was a skill she had been honing since she was eleven. She admits it's a sickness and has been seeing a shrink to try and suppress her obsession, and try to understand why she does it. Her therapist believes she sees each theft, no matter how big or small, as an individual challenge. She feels a sense of accomplishment when she gets away with it. Like she's beaten the odds of getting caught. Stealing was also a mood changer. Once she took a woolen scarf just to make herself feel better about the cold winter. Never wore it; just the fact she had it made her feel warm and toasty inside.

Jake was fully aware of her felonious lifestyle, but tends to look the other way and ignore that it's a serious issue.

He admits, however, to himself and no one else, that when they were down and out and needed money for rent, food, gas, and miscellaneous drug expenses, her lifting someone's wallet was a bonus. On a positive note, she hasn't stolen anything in almost a month. For her, this was considered progress.

During a lull in construction, Sage and Matthew get to know each other better. Actually, it's him getting a deeper understanding into her life. She starts by opening up about one of her most irreverent lifts.

"I've only been caught stealing once. A woman's Gucci purse from the bathroom at Melvyn's Restaurant. A very high-end eatery that caters to the Hollywood elite like Sinatra and the rat pack." Matthew feels like she's giving him a guided tour. "The woman was in the stall peeing. Her purse was on the edge, just inside the stall door. Just as I snatch the bag another woman enters and catches me, yelling 'thief!' Her shrill voice bounced off the tile walls and seemed to echo throughout the entire restaurant. Waiters burst in with no regard that it's the ladies room. I was caught red-handed with the evidence stuffed under my arm in plain sight."

She was only given a year's probation because she convinced the court she needed money to buy medication for her ailing bedridden grandmother. She also admitted to Matthew that she had no sick grandmother, but the lie worked in her favor.

"Do you feel remorseful for any of your thefts?" Matthew asks.

"Not really. But I'm learning through therapy to overcome the urge and rid myself of the stigma of being a kleptomaniac."

"Hope you make it," Matthew says. "Just do me a favor and don't steal or lift or rip off any of my customers, or you and Jake are history. Clear?"

"Crystal," she says.

Not convinced, Matthew keeps close tabs on her. He can't afford for her problem to become his problem.

CHAPTER 12

Jon, Chris, and Matthew were meeting up in West Hollywood at Barry Marcus's office, to sign a legal contract between them. Barry was someone Chris and Matthew went to school with. He was not your typical pin-striped suit lawyer, but more of a jeans and blue blazer kind of guy, with a joint resting comfortably inside his jacket pocket for those rare, paranoid clients who have a tendency to freak out in court. An advocate of pushing to make marijuana legal, he primarily handled drug cases but was doing them a favor because he loved the idea of the store. He thought of these guys as Renaissance men having a dream and not just sitting on it, but following through with it.

Barry's office was haphazardly decorated. The furniture didn't match, and there were framed photos of unrecognizable people on the dark wood walls. His diploma from USC Gould School of Law hung at the center of a far wall that was otherwise covered with an assortment of artwork, from line drawings to an autographed poster of The Grateful Dead performing at the Fillmore East in New York on February 11, 1969.

All this was topped off with the aroma of red sandalwood incense so strong they could feel the fucking burn deep inside their lungs.

They talked and decided each would take on a third of the responsibility, a third of the profits, and a third of the headache. Equal partners in Lewis, Street & Styles. Sounded more like a vaudeville act than a corporation. The guys sit across from Barry's vintage solid oak desk, an heirloom dating back to the early 1900s that had once been a dining room table and the setting for untold family gatherings. Matthew preferred to stand and lean against the wall. He felt it gave him a little power being higher than them, having once read in a magazine that height implied authority.

"So, you guys want something to drink or smoke or maybe some stale cashews that have been here since 1959?" Barry holds up an open can of nuts that are mixed with hard unwrapped candy and paper clips. They pass on all offers. Although the paper clips were tempting.

"Then you don't mind if I have a glass of wine? I work better when my mind is convoluted," he says, trying to fuck with their heads.

"Go for it, man," Matthew said.

"Just be sure to dot the i's and cross the t's, and underline all the sexy parts," Jon quips.

Matthew had to admit doing this was both exciting and a little frightening. In comparison, when he opened VIP, it was a lot different. The only thing he had at stake was a pair of shears and a blow dryer. Not an inventory of clothing that could clothe an entire

Third World country. Clothing that they still had no idea how to buy, sell, and display.

Barry explained the contents of each page they were signing. So far no one had any objections or real concerns. These guys were only twenty-four years old and wet behind the ears. For his part, Matthew felt a sense of maturity. That alone scared him. Then his own immortality came into play, when they got to the page that stipulated who gets what if one of them dies. Or two of them died, or all of them died together in a plane crash or came down with some sort of horrible incurable disease. They all thought this was something you put in a will, not a partnership agreement. Barry thought it'd be a good idea to add a codicil, just to cover all bases since they were young and foolish and prone to high-risk situations. High risk? What was Barry thinking—that they'd walk a tightrope over the fucking Grand Canyon just to sell a pair of bell-bottoms? No fucking way. But not a bad idea for a publicity stunt, Matthew thought to himself.

Halfway through the meeting, a girl enters with lunch from the Old World Restaurant on Sunset Boulevard, a block from Barry's office. Her hands shook as she set the tray down on his desk. Story goes, she was once one of Barry's clients who was arrested for possession of narcotics when pulled over for erratic driving, nearly mowing down a group of people waiting at a bus stop.

Hooked on Quaaludes, Barry helped her get straight, got her a job as a waitress, and she's been eternally grateful ever since. How grateful it's not determined. Her name was Nicole. Short-cropped hair. Cute figure. Great tits that seemed to want to free themselves from her off-the-shoulder gauze blouse. Rumor has it that Barry once took her to dinner at Antonio's Mexican Restaurant, a Mexican place on Melrose, and was so fucked up on ludes, she passed out as her chicken enchilada dinner was being served under her nose.

Despite the mishap, if at all true, Matthew kind of dug her boho style that was in sharp contrast to Linda Tarlow and Anne Fraser. Okay, before anyone accuses him of being fickle, bouncing from one girl to another, try to understand where he's coming from. He's young, adventurous, and loves the idea of a challenge. After he was kicked to the curb and called an adulterous prick, he decided to play the field, and not get hung up on one woman. For Matthew, that was just asking for trouble.

Justifying his own actions, he invites Nicole to their opening, then introduces her to the guys. "Nicole, meet the guys, Jon and Chris. Jon is the one trying to look down your blouse. Chris is the one nervously sucking on a paper clip."

"Hi," she says timidly without looking up.

Matthew puts on his best sincere demeanor. "You should definitely come. It should be a total blast. We're planning to serve wine and finger food and stuff."

This piqued her interest. She finally looks up at Matthew, and says, "I love wine, and finger food and stuff is my favorite."

The guys laugh appreciatively at her sense of humor.

She grabs an ink pen off Barry's desk, then writes her phone number on the palm of Matthew's hand. It's a little damp from nerves. "Relax," she says. "I promise this won't hurt a bit."

Matthew thinks to himself: hurt him? Is she talking about scratching her number on my skin—or about any emotional consequence that might come out of this connection?

"Call me," she says. "And if you must play with yourself, be smart and use the other hand."

This exchange was far from being just cute. It was arousing. But it had gone far enough. Barry interjects.

"Okay, enough adorable socializing, I need more signatures from you dudes. Nicole, goodbye—thanks for the lunch."

Nicole leaves with a big tip while Barry shoves a stack of more documents in front of them.

"Should we be reading this crap, or can we assume you're not fucking us?" Jon asks.

"Just sign the fucking papers," Barry commands. "The last thing I need is a damn pants store."

They didn't read a thing. They just signed wherever it said sign and date. For all they knew, they were signing away their firstborn and every ounce of their sperm to a lawyer who, by this time, was on his third glass of Merlot. But that wasn't an issue. They were officially becoming partners in what they believed was going to be one helluva venture.

Losing most of their appetites, they each ate a French fry and left the club sandwiches to mingle with the stale cashews and paper clips for the next client.

Done. Ecstatic. "Barry, send us a bill—we'll send you back a pair of bell-bottoms as payment," Jon quips.

As they're about to split, the door bursts open and what appears to be a lunatic fucked up on some high-octane drugs bolts in and waves a gun in their face, demanding they hand over all there money, jewelry, and what's left of the lunch. His eyes were like slits; sweat beaded on his forehead and he had horrendous body odor. The hand holding the gun shook so bad you'd have thought he suffered from Parkinson's. He was obviously coming down from a heavy dose of something like heroin and in bad need of a fix.

Barry knows the guy—Jimmy Ray Bigelow. He represented him in a possession case a few months ago. A heavy meth addict with a penchant for violence.

Barry tries to calm him down. "Jimmy Ray, it's me, Barry Marcus. What's going on here, brother?"

Jimmy Ray shows his teeth and becomes irate.

"What's going on? You know what's going on, man. You can see what's going on. You have to be an idiot to not realize what's going on, man!" he says, his voice quivering. "I have a gun, man. I'll use it if I have to and I'm desperate and need fast money to score some dope."

There's a pause before he shares more of his personal character flaws.

"Plus, there's my fucking excessive cocaine habit, that has wreaked havoc over the years, and which will require partial reconstruction of my fucking nose—changing my outward and possible inward appearance. This all costs serious coin. That's everything what's going on."

Okay, so the fact Barry knew this guy did not make them feel any better. Matthew's heart was almost pounding out of his chest. On the table they had set down a watch, a ring, and about thirty dollars in cash between them. Not enough for a manicure, let alone a nose job, that's for sure. He wanted our car keys and planned to sell it to a Mexican car dealership in Tijuana.

Barry hardly carried any cash. Used a credit card most of the time. So his contribution was zip. He tried to tame the guy's rage by offering an Oxy and a Xanax he had stashed in his desk drawer from a previous meeting. Jimmy Ray wasn't having it.

"A waste of a high. I need at least five Oxy's to get cool and make a difference," he insists.

Now he decides he needs a wardrobe change and wants Matthew's pants, Chris's shoes, and Jon's shirt. Why he couldn't get all three items from one person was baffling, but never questioned.

As they slip off their clothes, Matthew's palms went from damp to clammy. Nicole's phone number was just about smeared away. He looks over at Chris, as he begins to remove his shoes. He knows his MO. Chris gets anxious and frustrated. He has no patience for ignorant, illogical people. He enjoys challenging idiots. He's about to open his mouth when Matthew jumps in.

"Don't do anything stupid, man, it ain't worth it."

Too late. Chris suddenly gets brave and threatens to call the cops, who he promises will riddle Jimmy Ray with bullets and end his pathetic life like the lowlife fucker he is. There is a long nerve-racking pause. The guys look at Chris like he's lost his mind and just sentenced them to death, which was just mentioned on page twenty-four of the codicil.

Jon speaks up. "What's preventing this crazy-ass motherfucker from shooting all four of us and skipping out of here with our loot, my car, and a new pair of pants?"

"He won't," Chris says with sudden confidence.

"He won't what, skip?" Matthew says.

"He's not going to shoot us," Chris says.

"How can you be so sure?" Barry says. "You psychic? Women's intuition? What?"

"Yeah, you a mind reader?" Jimmy Ray says in the kind of shaky voice a junkie has when they're strung out and can't form sentences longer than five words.

"I know a real gun when I see one," says Chris. "And that is a gun that's dripping water onto the floor."

Jimmy Ray Bigelow drops the water pistol, then falls to his knees, surrendering with his arms in the air. He apologizes profusely for being such a nuisance, but his drug habit controls him. He has no willpower to quit his $300 a day habit. He begs them not to call the cops. He can't handle another stretch in the slammer, he says.

"A dangerous venue for me. I'm not well liked in jail. My personality rubs people the wrong way." Go figure.

Chris is not that understanding. As he picks up the phone receiver, he yells at Jimmy Ray: "You should've thought about jail before trying to rob us! You're going down big time, for attempted robbery and scaring the crap out of us!"

Before he starts to dial, Barry grabs the receiver. He wants to handle this in his own unique way: call in a favor and get Jimmy Ray enrolled in a rehab program.

They leave while they still have a modicum of their self-respect—and their clothes.

CHAPTER 13

The following day, Matthew woke out of sound sleep at 5:30 a.m., when Chris called, hyperventilating with tragic news. He bolted to his feet when Chris revealed that Barry Marcus was dead. He made him repeat it, because the statement was surreal to the point of being an out-of-body experience.

It was announced on the news and in the papers that the authorities had found Barry's bloody body slumped over his vintage oak desk. Jimmy Ray went off the deep end and stabbed Barry eleven times with a letter opener, then swiped his credit cards and the signed Grateful Dead print. Senseless was the word of the day.

LA TIMES HEADLINES - JUNE 23, 1969

A police plotter photo of Jimmy Ray was on the front page. Under it was the article that read: *Police are looking for a prime suspect, Jimmy Ray Bigelow, in the murder investigation of attorney Barry Marcus. Bigelow was last seen running away from the murder scene early Tuesday afternoon, with blood covering his hands and face. Jimmy Ray Bigelow, a native of Allentown, Georgia, is presumably on the run and may be headed for Mexico, according to law enforcement. This assessment was corroborated by the testimony of three of Mr. Marcus's clients held at gunpoint by the suspect prior to the attack. According to these witnesses, Bigelow burst into Marcus's office desperate for money, drugs, and food. Bigelow, a manic-depressive, known junkie, and feckless mama's boy who has been institutionalized several times for drug abuse, is considered highly dangerous. Extreme caution is advised. Do not approach. Call your local police.*

The guys closed the shop for the day to honor Barry's memory. They stretched a black sash across the front door. His murder was so upsetting it made their flesh crawl. He was a great friend, who looked out for the underdog. You can't help but think that if they had stuck around until that asshole walked out the door, Barry would still be among the living. Branding themselves as major fuck-ups wasn't a strong enough description to cover their guilt.

§

Saturday, June 25. It was a gloomy day. Only because they're burying a friend, not because the weather forecast sucked. There were easily over two hundred people gathered outside the chapel at Forest Lawn, plus a good seventy-five inside. You gotta figure everyone there was a card-carrying pothead, stoned and feeling a sense of tranquility, yet at the same time grief-stricken. This was an era that brought them all together in a harmonious balance of peace and love.

Seeing as Barry's an old friend, the guys were asked to say a few words. Jon passed. Matthew was too distraught and ad-libbing in front of an audience made him nervous. Chris was another story. In some strange way he felt flat-out responsible for what went down—forcing Jimmy's hand and setting him off into a violent rage. Chris wanted to get up and accept full responsibility, but the guys couldn't allow that to happen. It would only make matters confusing in the eyes of the mourners, who already had enough grief to ruminate on.

Some of his closest lawyer friends and peers said a few words. The guys never knew this about Barry Marcus, but he was a big proponent of the civil rights movement—a decades-long movement with the goal of securing legal rights for African Americans that other Americans already held. This did not come as a surprise. Barry was a person of integrity and honor—a real *mensch*. Being that his favorite rock group was The Doobie Brothers, they played "Jesus Is Just Alright" over the PA system during the ceremony.

A good hour and a half later everyone is at a private wake, being held outdoors at a friend's home in Brentwood. An expanse of clear sky. Not a cloud obscured the deep serenity. A very mellow gathering of friends, relatives, and contemporaries. More speeches were given. Tributes were made from elevated chairs and glasses of wine were lifted in toasts. An extra large tip jar sat prominently on the open bar. It was filled with cash and checks to be donated to Barry's favorite charity: The California Initiative to Make Marijuana Legal.

Because Logan knew Barry from high school, he decided to tag along and show his respect. Besides, he never passed up a gathering that had an open bar, no matter how dark the occasion. His drinking was becoming more and more serious, to such a degree that the guys had to watch his behavior. The last thing they needed was Logan embarrassing them during a celebration of life.

The four of them infiltrated small groups, which were reminiscing and sharing stories about Barry Marcus. They retold their last minutes with Barry and how he ordered a club sandwich lunch while they signed partnership documents. This turned out to be a rare PR opportunity for them to campaign for the upcoming opening of Jon's Drawer. Barry, they're sure, wouldn't have minded their ambitious motivation. He would have wanted them to move forward and fulfill their dream. He was that kind of unselfish dude.

Nicole, the waitress from The Old World, had tears in her eyes when she approached Matthew. She was wearing a miniskirt cut just above her knee. Maybe a touch inappropriate for a funeral, but who cared, she looked outrageous. She gave him a serious hug. They had not spoken since their last meeting in Barry's office. Her phone number unfortunately rubbed off on his palm during the face-off with Jimmy Ray Bigelow, so contacting her was impossible. It occurred to him that going out with this girl wasn't really a priority, but more of an attraction. A fascination.

"You never called," she says. He told her how he lost her number in a moment when he was in danger of maybe being shot between the eyes and killed by a lunatic. She was sensitive enough to understand his dilemma.

"Here's my number again." She hands him a Wrigley's Spearmint gum wrapper. "Stick it in a safe place—where it's not penetrable by dampness or rain or sweat or lunatics. Call when you're ready to be with me." She walks off, frustrated.

He wasn't sure if he was ready or not, so he tucks the wrapper in his wallet next to Hal Exler's business card. (As a reminder, Hal was the rep from Male Pants who had a premonition they would make it big. From his lips to God's ear.)

And then, not more than twenty minutes into the gathering, Matthew spots a familiar face in the crowd. He notices Anne Fraser getting a drink at the open bar. His stomach churned, and he had to blink twice to make sure she was real. She saw him looking back at her, smiled, and headed for him. His heart jackhammered. He took a couple deep breaths before she glided up to him.

"It is you," he says, totally blown away.

She smiles and says, "Yes, it is. My father once hired Barry to get me out of a legal jam when I was fifteen. Arrested for possession of marijuana. One joint. Ridiculous charge. Spent an hour in lockup. Not a grand experience, even for just an hour.

I know you must be churning inside, since you guys were the last ones to see him alive." She then kisses him gently on the lips, trying to soften the emotional pain.

He was really glad to see her. Unlike Nicole, Anne was a calming presence. She had to split, but before she left they discussed her upcoming photo shoot at his shop. They set a date for two weeks from now. He walked her out. In his peripheral vision he could see Nicole, craning her head, watching them. She looked worried. She sensed she had competition.

Matthew volunteered to drive Anne home but she had a driver and car waiting for her. It was then that Matthew discovered that Anne Fraser came from serious money. Her grandfather was the inventor and CEO of Fraserware, a top-of-the-line cookware company that had been around since the 1900s. Matthew's feelings for Anne would not change just because she comes from an affluent family. She kissed him goodbye. He watched the car turn the corner and disappear down the street. He checked his watch. He wanted to know the exact time he became totally infatuated with Anne Fraser.

§

In another area of the backyard, Chris and Logan are closely watching some young dude comfort an older woman who is weeping. He has his arms wrapped around her almost like a son comforting his mother—albeit a little too gropingly. As they eavesdrop on their conversation, it's apparent, by his intonation, he considers himself deep and abstract.

"You know what I think about when I'm this close to another body?" he is saying.

The woman, with her chin buried in his shoulder, shakes her head.

"I think one day, this body that I'm holding in my arms will stop breathing one day . . . stop living—just stop. Look at me. Isn't it a pretty devastating thought, that as alive as we are right now, we'll just stop?"

The woman pushes herself away and just stares at him, almost frightened.

"Who the fuck are you again?" she asks.

"I'm Barry's second cousin, Eli Markowitz, from Westchester County, New York. You?"

"Mindy. Barry's therapist."

"One day, Mindy, you'll happen upon my name in the *New York Times* obits, and you'll remember this very moment when we were on the brink of intimacy."

"You're a real fucking piece of work, you know that, Eli?"

As she walks away, Chris and Logan hang back, ready to pounce on this sick fuck, who lies in wait for yet another fragile female needing consolation. It's their belief this guy is a professional funeral crasher, impersonating family and taking advantage of vulnerable grievers.

§

At the other end of the lawn, another episode was taking place. A local reporter for the *Citizen News* somehow slipped in under the radar and caught up with the four of them standing at the edge of the swimming pool area, trying to comprehend this senseless act of aggression. Since this was designated a high priority murder investigation, it was deemed a human-interest story.

The reporter, overweight, had on a well-worn corduroy jacket that was too small for him and in badly need of a shave. Him, not the jacket. He was drinking a beer in one hand while holding a small notebook in the other. He was pushy, unctuous, and displayed what seemed to be a tasteless personality. He grinned a lot, displaying a wide gap between his two front teeth. This space caused an unwanted spray when he spoke, so the guys kept their distance, avoiding his putrid spittle and the bombardment of chewed mixed nuts he was spewing. His news beat was to cover and track down all the events regarding Hollywood murders and the underworld drug scene. He wanted any dirt he could dig up on Barry. They told him in the nicest possible way to go fuck himself.

Logan, being Logan, saw an opportunity to be rude and belligerent. He grabbed his notebook, tore it in half, and then tossed it in the pool. A little drastic, but it sent a message that he wasn't fucking welcome and was popping his scandalous questions at the wrong people.

"I'm just doing my job. Nothing personal," he says in his own defense.

Matthew comes back with: "And we're just protecting our friend's reputation from this kind of disastrously mishandled situation by you and your right-wing fucking newspaper printing lies just to sell papers."

This interaction of intense hostility continued until the reporter took umbrage and took a swing at Matthew. Jesus Christ, this fat fuck was dangerous. Luckily the blow didn't find its mark. Matthew tried to control his temper but something came over him, and he retaliated by shoving him into the deep end of the pool.

"I can't swim!" the reporter screamed as he went under like a rock. In a moment of civility, Matthew thought about jumping in and saving this poor schlub, but ruled against it when he remembered he was wearing his favorite pair of pants.

Someone finally fished him out, plunking him down poolside like a beached whale. He was gasping for air and spitting up water but no one rushed to his aid to perform CPR.

As he was shown the door, Matthew gets in the last word.

"Write anything scathing and we'll come to your office and break your typewriter fingers."

Not sure what he accomplished by that threat, but it felt right. It felt virtuous. Truth to tell, Matthew never knew he had the balls to engage the enemy. He didn't really like it. He was a committed pacifist.

§

By now Jon had separated himself from all the commotion and was checking out the bartender across the lawn. She resembled a tough chick version of Stevie Nicks, wearing a black tank top, low-rise jeans, and lots of rings on just about every finger. Jon was blown away by her boho appearance. As he crossed the lawn heading towards her, he casually—and almost with the sleight of hand of a seasoned magician—slipped off his wedding band and slid it into his inside pocket, where a rabbit might appear at any moment.

"What can I get you?" she said, in a raspy voice, probably caused from smoking too many cigarettes.

"A beer, plus your name and a time when I can pick you up to go on a buying trip with me to New York," Jon says in one breath.

MATERIAL THINGS

"Amazing. You're coming onto me with a trip to New York. Is this a game show? Am I on camera?"

"No and no. This is a legitimate offer. So what's your answer? Yes? No? Maybe? Leave me alone before I call a cop? What?"

"How do I know you're not like a, you know, serial killer—like that crazed Zodiac dude?"

"Good question. I realize it's a ballsy request on my part. A total stranger strolls up and asks an attractive bartender for a beer and a date to NYC. Cautious and skeptical. Good qualities to have. What was I thinking? Appreciate the beer and the conversation."

Jon turns to leave when Chris sidles up.

"I'll have what he's having, please," Chris says.

"One Coors coming up," she says.

As she pops open the bottle and pours, Jon asks Chris to validate that he's not the notorious Zodiac Killer. That he's just a regular guy who is about to open a jeans store in the Valley and is going to New York to buy inventory—not to murder anybody in a dark alley.

"And why am I giving her this long, exhaustive résumé of yours?" Chris asks.

She jumps in. "Because he's invited me to go to New York with him, and I want to know he's safe to travel with before I accept."

Chris leans in conspiratorially. "Here's the deal. A friendly warning," he says, exercising his slick wit. "Stay clear of this dude. He's not the Zodiac Killer by any stretch. He's worse. He's married."

Jon rolls his eyes, caught. Chris apologizes to Jon for outing him, but he had no choice but to be honest. Jon differs. He could've kept that information to himself. Chris moves off. Jon turns back to the girl. Guilt in his eyes. He admits he wasn't completely honest.

"Yes, the real truth is, I'm married, but not happily. It's only a matter of time before we split the sheets. Before she kicks me to the curb."

"For cheating?"

"No, for falling out of love. It happens for reasons too many to count. You can't survive on constant arguments, altercations, and a lack of trust. So please don't judge me for trying to pick up an attractive girl, who blew my mind when I saw her mixing drinks from across the lawn. Guess I was starving for some attention again. I'm Jon Lewis, by the way. Maybe when I'm free and less attached, you'll consider having coffee with me."

She stares at him mutely. It won't be the last time he'll strike out.

"Have a nice life … uh, shoot me a name so I can complete the sentence," he adds desperately.

"Sharon Gage, she says.

"Have a nice life, Sharon Gage." Feeling defeated, he turns to leave. "Okay, coffee. But in Manhattan."

Boom—he's in.

CHAPTER 14

While Jon was off buying and fucking his way through the New York apparel district, the rest of the crew kept working their butts off trying to finish the boutique. They gave themselves a deadline of three weeks, but because of unforeseen circumstances, like the contractor getting the flu and working with a fever, it slowed them down to a crawl. Sage would sometimes show up with chicken soup and sandwiches. She'd always be out of breath, like she had been running—or, more likely, being chased. Matthew never questioned how she paid for any of it. Assuming his ham and cheese sandwich was stolen, he ate fast, so as not to leave a trace of evidence.

§

It rained hard and steady that night. Thunderstorms with intermittent lightning flashes raged in the distance like a celestial fireworks display. The power eventually surged and finally went out just as Matthew was about to microwave some Stouffer's frozen lasagna.

It was a weekday so he was alone. Logan, of course, was at his real home with mommy and daddy, being a good, sober son, and telling them what they want to hear: of his plan to look for a job, which never comes to fruition but makes them feel he's conscientious, and aware he can't sponge off them forever—but hoping forever never comes.

Matthew sat in the dark with a flashlight whose battery was almost dead, causing the light to flicker like it was sending out a Morse code signal. A lone scented candle also offered a little light. He was not prepared for a natural disaster. He was not prepared for an unnatural disaster. His mind wanders aimlessly in the dark. Shadows become eerie, larger than life figures. The phones were out too. Dead. He had no communication with the outside world.

Twenty minutes pass, and he's eating a bag of potato chips for dinner—by now the candle had melted into an unrecognizable glob of wax. The flashlight ultimately faded out. He had no way of seeing, except when a lightning flash would illuminate the room. He felt trapped on an island that was about to sink into a city street.

Suddenly, there's a knock at the door. Or was it just thunder? The knock came again. Of course he became suspicious. In the dark, he grabs this ugly ceramic statuette that came with the place for protection from his unannounced caller. It's midnight, so that rules out a Jehovah's Witness trying to sell him on some bullshit religious doctrine. And then it occurs to him that he's actually asleep on the couch and dreaming that Anne Fraser, wearing her long-established trench coat, is at the door, coming to fuck again. If that's the case, he quickly opens the door to get this sexual fantasy started.

He was wrong. It was a woman about forty-something wearing a print dress that fell just below her knees. Never saw her before till now. Why was she in his dream? He wanted her out. She introduced herself as a neighbor and said she was afraid of the dark, and asks if she can stay with him until the power goes back on. Matthew is reluctant. For some reason his mind was transferring Anne Fraser into this older woman, because his subconscious knew it was wrong to have these illicit thoughts about a girl who made him feel better than any woman he'd ever been with.

"Sure, why not?" he says, despite his suspicion that she's just an apparition. "Come on in."

As she crosses the threshold he intentionally touches her arm just to be certain she's real flesh and bone. She is. Then he notices she's gripping a vibrator in her hand. Now he's certain this has to be a dream. He must be foreshadowing his preoccupation with having sex with Anne Fraser. Crazy? Yes. Insane.

He goes along with whatever this is and asks her what's with the vibrator. She says it's the only thing that calms her down in a tense situation. Does he buy this explanation? Maybe. Yes. No. Fuck no. Why can't she vibrate alone in her own dark apartment? If in fact she's really a neighbor and not a figment of his imagination, or worse, she plans to rob him and the vibrator somehow morphs into a Colt .45 revolver.

Before they go any further with her so-called plea for safety, he needs a name, apartment number, and an explanation. Out of all the apartments to chose from—he asks out of curiosity and sheer paranoia—why his? Keep in mind, it's dark and difficult to make out the features on her face—until lightning strikes again and illuminates the area. She was attractive. Her name is Angela, lives in apartment 12, and chose this apartment based on the names on the mailboxes. She says she was attracted by the name Matthew Street.

"It seemed like you'd be an interesting person to sit in the dark with," she says.

He offers her something to drink. She requests a citrus wine spritzer. Not capable of making that in the dark, he tells her. Besides, he had no wine, no lemon, no lime, and no seltzer. She settles for a Budweiser and what's left of the potato chips.

They sit in the dark, quiet and still, for a good fifteen minutes chugging their beers, until she decides to start a conversation.

"Charles Manson is a pretty interesting guy, don't you think?"

He can't help but gasp. "Interesting? The man is a sick fuck and a maniac."

"But that's what makes him thought-provoking."

This is not something he wants to discuss during a blackout. Now he's certain she's real, because he would never in a million years conjure up a dream where Manson is the central character. He had to stop her obsessive interest before he was forced to take matters into his own hands and use her vibrator as a gag.

"Okay, listen, you need to change the subject, or you're gonna have to pick another name on the mailbox. You're kind of freaking me out."

"Sorry, I was only trying to make idle conversation rather than sit in dreary silence."

That dreary silence is suddenly broken when a jolt of lightning and loud, rumbling thunder shakes the room. This is followed by the sound of her vibrator humming at a constant pitch. This seemed to shut her up. Lightning strikes once again, illuminating the room like daylight. Matthew can see that she has pulled her dress above her waist; her legs are spread wide as she services herself. As she leans her head backwards against the sofa arm, there's a look of mingled fear and pleasure etched upon her face.

Matthew must admit this is a slight turn-on, as well as embarrassing. He's thinking this has to be some sort of sexual fantasy and has nothing to do with her being afraid of the dark. Yet her fascination with Charles Manson, an emblem of insanity, violence, and the macabre, didn't seem to rattle her nerves as much as the weather.

"If you'd like to service yourself, I have no objections," she says to him as she continues her erotic escapade. He has to admit, it was difficult to pass up, so they took it a step further and fucked until they passed out from exhaustion.

It's now four in the morning when the power shoots back on again. The phone rings, and Matthew bolts from the couch and picks it up after the third ring. Angela was still passed out. It's Jake. He sounded excited. Not good excited. Catastrophic excited. He reports how the rain settled in one area, weakened the roof, and caused a cave-in.

It now resembles a cheap water feature. "Come quick and bring a large sponge!" he says.

Matthew wakes Angela and sends her back to apartment 12. He closely watches her cross the pool area and climb the stairs to her place, just to make sure she is who she says she is. She forgot to take her vibrator. You could surmise a prime excuse for her to come back during the next storm.

§

Traffic lights are blinking wildly because of the power outage. Matthew ignores them and makes it to the shop in record time. Rather than battle the weather, Jake and Sage slept in the store all night.

10:00 a.m. The rain had stopped. Sun peeked through the remaining scattered clouds. A few trees uprooted. One fell hard onto a car and totaled its hood. Some streets were still flooded, so Matthew drove slowly and cautiously. Emergency crews out repairing electrical lines. But for the most part we're back to a Los Angeles state of mind. The leak wasn't as bad as expected. Easily fixable. Just water that needed to be pumped out to avoid mildewing. Jake was already on top of it.

Armed with a cup of coffee supplied by Sage, Matthew is just finishing up a cut with his free hand when Nicole pays him an unexpected visit. She obviously got tired of waiting for him to make the first move and wants to take him to breakfast. She starts to literally drag him towards the door, like he was a dog she was about to take for its morning walk. He resisted. For one thing, he's not a breakfast kind of person. But primarily, her aggressive nature bugged the shit out of him. Too controlling for his taste. He had enough of that in his marriage, and he told her how pushing him was not the way to get closer, if that's her ambition. That she needed to give him space.

"My wife was clingy and distrusted me," Matthew says. "I can't do clingy again."

Nicole understands. She apologizes, thinking his feelings stem from being hung up on the Israeli chick.

"So, what's the deal with you and the Israeli chick?" she asks.

The deal? What's the deal? There is no deal. And if there were a deal, it wasn't her business. This is what he meant by clingy and being domineering. Nicole was fishing for anything that would make her feel better about where she and he stood. Matthew played it safe. He felt she deserved an answer to her prying question.

"Anne is a friend." Strong emphasis on the word friend. He mentions how she wanted to use the store as a backdrop for a photo shoot. "She's hoping to get into modeling. Why do you ask?"

"Nothing. Just saw you talking to her at the funeral. She's very attractive. I hear her family has bucks. You sleeping with her?"

Again, pushy and in-your-face aggressive. This was a hard question to answer, if in fact he was going to answer, which he wasn't, because—well, because it was all psychological. Subjective. Yes, he was sleeping with her, but in a dream state. And as he saw it, dreams are a manifestation of things to come. Of things people wish for. So as nicely as he could without being a complete dick, he satisfied her curiosity with a convoluted answer.

"If I were sleeping with her, I probably wouldn't say. It would be unfair to her and to me."

Nicole gives him her best empty stare and a low-pitched hmm, then turns and walks away, feeling rejected and snubbed. Life is full of disappointments.

Her inquisition made Matthew tense for the rest of the day. Also, he was teetering on the ledge of falling on his face. Worried about failing and forced to cut hair for the rest of his life would cause anybody great mental anguish. And while we're on the subject of insanity, the Anne Fraser fixation is on the cusp of being a major psychological issue that probably needs to be treated, but for some reason he's procrastinating because he likes its effect on himself. Sick? Maybe, maybe not. Other than going into the clothing business, it gave him purpose.

§

A week later. He slept with Nicole for no other reason than he needed physical pleasure. He needed some sort of release. His last close encounter was with Angela, his neighbor, during the blackout. Please keep in mind, so that he's not characterized as a user or an opportunist, Nicole came to him. Willing. No one pressured her into having sex. She was there for the taking, and he might have taken advantage of her favors.

Okay, fine, now let's talk about how Linda Tarlow fits into all this. For the moment, their relationship, if that's what you want to call it, is on hold. Treading water. Nicole knew nothing about Linda. If she had, this romp in the hay probably never would've taken place. Or maybe it would, because Nicole would try and distract his attention towards other women and push harder to make herself appear like a more significant player.

In the morning, Matthew drives Nicole home. On the way, she decides to open up about her childhood. Her parents always hoped she'd become a model or a lawyer, she tells him. Quite an imbalance.

"I wasn't interested in either. I wanted to be a drug addict or an alcoholic like Janice Joplin," she says with serious purpose. "I was good at it too."

Did he take her aspiration for truth or hyperbole? He actually found her goal to be real. Nicole was a rebel. A nonconformist. A person he could tell defied the Establishment and parental guidance. Janice Joplin, it's certain, was her hero, and he hated knowing this about Nicole. It was not a smart objective, admiring and emulating a self-destructive celebrity. It was actually ignorant and empty-headed. Matthew was honest with himself and didn't want to associate with someone like her. Yet there he was, about to drop her off and tell her how he had an incredible night fucking. It wasn't a total lie, it was just him being hypocritical and wanting to surround himself with people who had proper aspirations and goals.

When he dropped her off, he kissed her goodbye, like they were a couple, and she was telling him to have a nice day at work. Truthfully, it felt uncomfortable. Brought him back to his strained marriage. The only thing missing was her calling him "darling" and demanding he be home for dinner exactly at 6:30, or else no dinner or sex for a week. Yes, Matthew's tardiness ceased all incoming vaginal activity for a full seven days. Sometimes longer. Which is probably why he takes advantage of getting it when it's thrown in his face.

CHAPTER 15

Matthew made it to the store and was met by an unpleasant exhibit of cartons. There waiting for him, sitting in the middle of the room, stacked almost to the ceiling, blocking any path to the exits, were thirty boxes of clothing out of New York, Chicago, and San Francisco. The size a washer/dryer combo would come in. The boxes formed a labyrinthine route to the center of the room. At first he thought it was a mirage. Or a fuck-up made by a delirious delivery boy on crack.

But it was no error, it was Jon working on overtime. The result of his buying spree in New York. Matthew's ulcer went berserk. Jon had gone to extremes, maybe trying to impress that bartender, Sharon, he took with him. Nevertheless, the summit stood tall, waiting to be triumphed. Matthew lets out a disgruntled scream that rattles the walls. Jon enters from the back room with his arms stretched in the air, surrendering.

"Guilty. I may have gone too far," he says. "It'll take some time for me to get acclimated to the apparel climate. I bought what I liked, not what I thought was going to be best sellers. Hopefully, I didn't fuck up so bad that we're in the red before we get out of the starting gate. We'll make it work. We need inventory—we got it."

The bigger issue—where do they store this massive fuck-up? They had no storage space. Their only alternative was to send them on the red-eye back to New York, until they were ready to open their doors. Jon suggests they close down VIP men's hairstyling until they can come up with a solid plan of attack. Not going to happen. Matthew needs an income.

They seem to be overwhelmed, until Dean speaks up with the perfect fix. Get rid of the seventy-five-year-old Chinese tailor next store and use the space as a storeroom. Brilliant? Maybe. Problem is, it would goose up the rent. Then there was the minor issue of how to talk the old tailor into moving. Then there was the bigger issue of not speaking Chinese. This was not going to be an easy feat. Dean had another suggestion—arson, an accidental fire.

"I know a guy who'll do it for three hundred bucks. He's a pro, with references and pictures."

Jesus fuck, an arsonist with references? The idea of setting this poor Chinese man's sewing machine ablaze just to house a few boxes of pants and shirts was a bit unethical. Not to mention, the smoke fumes would seep through the walls like a black fog and their entire inventory would reek like an ashtray. Arson, although thorough, was a really sick idea. Making a deal seemed to be the smarter choice.

Matthew resolved to talk to the guy himself. Alone, with what he thought would be a hell of a proposal. A proposal he had not yet formulated in his head that was now pulsating in rhythm with his heart.

The next morning, after Matthew teaches himself how to say hello in basic Chinese—*ni hao* (pronounced nee how)—he goes face to face with the old guy, who is wearing dark glasses. Keep in mind Matthew's never been in this man's shop before, so the stench of cigarette tobacco and his yellow-stained teeth and fingers are nothing short of disgusting. He has planned what he wants to say, and has even brought a bottle of sake as a peace offering. He realizes sake is Japanese. Maybe Jack Daniels would've been the smarter bribe.

The old guy greets him with a bow and instantly begins measuring his inseam. Matthew backs off, doing his best to explain he isn't there for a fitting. He seems to understand, so Matthew gives him a sincere "ni hao." He seems confused by the greeting, then offers Matthew a cigarette. It occurs to Matthew this guy is not Chinese. Maybe Japanese or Korean or Vietnamese. He passes on the smoke. He lights up one for himself, even though there are at least three burning in an ashtray that is spilling over with butts on his sewing machine table. Then it crosses Matthew's mind, as the old guy feels for the ashtray and taps his cigarette against the edge of it, that he is blind. Or at least partially blind. Either way, he is a tailor with a vision handicap, which explains the dark glasses. This in itself is a remarkable accomplishment. To confirm his suspicions, a red tipped cane is leaning against a far wall. Matthew finally introduces himself as the guy who owns the shop next door. In return he gets yet another bow.

"I just wanted to say that I'm sorry I haven't been a better neighbor," Matthew says, forcing a fake smile.

The tailor mutters something in broken English that is hard to decipher. It sounds like he is offering his daughter's hand in marriage and trying to sell Matthew on the fact she has perfect teeth and is a virgin. Matthew nods, then gracefully turns his offer down and gives him the bottle of sake. Before accepting it, he feels the features of Matthew's face. Guess he likes what he touches, because he smiles. He opens the sake, sniffs its aroma to diagnose the contents. He smiles again with appreciation, showing his yellow teeth that had a few missing. He pours himself a drink into a paper coffee cup. The old tailor also reeks of garlic, probably caused by his highly pungent diet.

Enough socializing. Matthew finally makes his proposal. That he needed his place for storage, and, if possible, it would be helpful if he could see fit to relocate his tailor shop somewhere else. He would be willing to spring for his first rental fee on the new place and also help pay for the move.

There is a long pause. Matthew isn't sure if he understands or is about to tell him in some Mandarin dialect or broken English to go fuck himself. Instead he takes another drink of the sake and lights another cigarette with the butt of the cigarette he is smoking.

Before Matthew has the chance to repeat himself, this young Asian girl, probably the available virgin daughter the old man was trying to pawn off on him, comes in from the back room. Nice looking, sexy. Her alabaster cheeks flush with warmth. She is shoveling rice from a bowl into her mouth with chopsticks without dropping a grain onto the floor. An amazing feat. She has a terrific mouth. Great lips that appeared soft to the touch. She speaks English with perfect diction.

"I apologize for my father's marriage proposal. He's been trying to sell me off to every white guy who walks through the door, the attractive selling point being that I'm a virgin. Which I'm not, but it makes him feel better. So, you interested? I'm free in an hour."

"Sorry, I tried marriage and it didn't seem to agree with me. Ended in a battle of who gets the silverware. Name's Matthew Street. I own the shop next door." He offers his hand.

"I know who you are. I'm Helen Funai."

They shake. Her grip is firm but her hands are soft. He begins to explain the reason for his visit and recaps the conversation he was having with her father. She interrupts him halfway through his commentary.

"I heard your proposition."

Here it comes, he thinks. The verbal attack. How dare he take advantage of a blind old man, who scratched and scrimped his way from Osaka to make his fortune, and he, this privileged white guy, has the nerve to try and shatter that dream.

Before she has a chance to paraphrase any of that, he gives up and apologizes for wasting their time and hopes they understood his dilemma of needing more storage space with the upcoming launch of their clothing store. Before he reaches for the doorknob, the old guy bows, coughs, then lights another cigarette. Just as he's about to walk out, the daughter blocks his path and offers a suitable provision.

"You pay the first month's rent and the cleaning deposit, and find us an acceptable store in Woodland Hills—with a window, where he can watch the sun rise in the east."

Matthew leans in and speaks softly. "Not to be disrespectful, but how can he watch the sunrise if he's blind?"

"Partially blind. He has vision in his left eye."

A pause. Was this a lot to ask for? Should he come back with a counter offer, eliminating the sunrise? Is he going to be taken in by her adorable smile?

"Okay, I can do that," Matthew says without hesitation.

They shake again to seal the deal. He turns to her father. He looks frail. His hands are rough from too many sewing needles puncturing his small fingers like self-inflicted acupuncture pricks. This time

Matthew bows out of respect. It occurs to him this dude and his excessive chain smoking was not going to last through too many more sunrises. Matthew intended to find a real nice rental space for him to tailor what could possibly be his own burial suit. By now the old man had downed half the bottle of Sake. He was looped for the day. This had to have an effect on his vision. However you looked at this, this dude had a talent and was kind of a phenom.

Matthew went back to the shop having no idea what this whole endeavor was going to cost them. But it couldn't be avoided. They were desperate for space. He told his receptionist to check the classified ads, then sent her out to Woodland Hills to hunt down a commercial office space for Mr. Funai. She had no clue who this Funai guy was. He didn't bother to explain. He gave her gas money and instructions.

"Nothing extravagant. A window that faces east. Just big enough to hold a sewing machine and a large ashtray."

Until they could find the tailor a suitable space, they had no alternative but to stack and arrange the boxes in a way that made things tight and claustrophobic—causing some pissed-off clients to find another hairstylist. Fine. They held the door open for all those disloyal pricks.

That night. The Doobie Brothers were blasting through the wall speakers. The place reeked of sweat and weed. They were hauling ass, sawing, hammering, plastering, removing splinters from their hands and repairing an occasional broken finger. Jake repaired the leak in the roof and was putting the finishing touches on the pant cubbyholes that would house the styles by size. Even though they had a definite plan they were ad-libbing as they went. It was a system that no one had ever tackled in the jeans business. Their heads spun with inexperience. They were more than just wet behind the ears.

They were virgins. And they moaned and purred with every thrust of their hammers and pumping action of the saw blades, waiting to come to a climax and get this store open for business.

Every now and then an unexpected challenge would arise. In this case, it was a water heater. Unattractive, located directly in the middle of the room. A plumbing nightmare, it would have been a major task to move it. Solution—they needed to camouflage its ugliness. Matthew thought: what would Michelangelo do under these circumstances? Easy—he would not have opened a jeans store in the Rome of 1509.

Then he had the brilliant idea of painting it as though a vintage American flag was wrapped around it, then cover it with shellac to give it that antique feel. It resembled a forty-gallon contemporary art sculpture by Red Grooms, an American multimedia artist best known for his colorful pop-art constructions depicting frenetic scenes of modern urban life. Matthew was a big fan of Grooms and later sent him a photo of the water heater and a pair of bell-bottom jeans, just to show his appreciation of his artistic depictions. He never heard back, so he wasn't sure if he even got the pants. He would like to think he included the bell-bottom jeans in his next artistic piece of Americana. But he knew better than to hope.

Air. Matthew needed some air. The shellac fumes mixed with the drift of marijuana smoke was making him nauseous. He checks in with Chris, who's in the midst of painting the Jon's Drawer logo on the front window. It's slow going because he's not a sign painter. He was right; they should've hired a sign painter, not a cartoonist. Besides, it looked lopsided and oblique.

Chris has taken a break and is in mid-conversation with Helen, the Japanese tailor's daughter. That statement alone sounded like the title of a kids' fairy tale. Chris is doing his best to have her notice him in a different light. Not as an American artist painting a distorted sign, but as an American GI interested in maintaining close relations with foreign neighbors. In a few choice words, he's trying to hustle her, applying friendly tactics used during World War II, but instead of offering a chocolate bar and nylons as an inducement, he's bribing her with dinner at the beach and a crop top. It was hard to tell if he was making headway, because they were interrupted by the untimely arrival of a police cruiser pulling up out front.

Two uniformed officers slither out. One of them opens the back passenger door, allowing their detained female to exit. It's Sage. She looks worried and disheveled. The cop refers to his spiral note pad before speaking.

"I'm looking for a Jake McGrath," he says. "Either of you him?"

They all answer with a solid shake of the head. Sage clears up the confusion.

"He's in the back working," she says. "He's their contractor."

Chris volunteers to get him. Everyone had a pretty good idea what the problem was even before the cops told them. Turns out she was caught trying to steal a bottle of champagne, some Carr's English crackers, and a triangle wedge of brie at Ringside Liquor on the corner of Moorpark and Whitsett.

Sage defends her unscrupulous deed. "I wasn't thinking straight. It was there. I had no money. I saw the opportunity. I took it, not thinking of the consequences. It's a sickness. I have a sickness. I'm trying very hard to fight back the urge, but I'm still not there yet."

Matthew intervenes, trying to save Sage from a night in the lockup.

"Any chance you can let her off with a warning?" he pleads with the cop. "She's seeing a shrink, and they've been working on her problem, incessantly. Still haven't quite got to the bottom of her disease, but they're making great headway. If it helps, I can vouch she'll be on her best behavior from now on." Sage has trouble being strong and can't hold back the tears.

"I swear I'll be good!" she vows, raising her right hand in the air.

There's a pause as the cop ponders a verdict.

She thinks the worst. A cascade of horrors: arrest, shame, poverty, death in the electric chair. However, leniency fortunately prevails tonight. The cop tells Sage how lucky she is to have friends who care about her psychological well-being. And if he or anyone else ever catches her stealing again, she's going to end up in jail for a very long period of time. Sage, realizing she's skated by with a slap on the wrist, thanks him, profusely.

After the cops drive off, she promises to make it up to Matthew. "Make it up to me by not doing it again," he says.

Sage confides in him, confessing as to why she tried to lift the goods from the liquor store. She and Logan Alexander had planned to rendezvous, and these comestibles were her contribution for what promised to be an evening of spirited sexual activity. Why she admitted this to Matthew, God knows. Maybe she wanted him to intercept this before it was out in the open and got back to Jake and ruined her marriage. Matthew, Chris, and even Helen kept this sordid information all to themselves.

Jake finally materializes from inside the store. He is noticeably pissed and threatens to leave Sage if she ever pulls this stunt again. This was a threat he's made several times, but this time you got the feeling he meant it. There was a pause, during which Sage was keenly aware of Jake's threat being genuine this time. She wanted badly to please him, to say something like: "This is a turning point, everything is different now. I've changed, I've been redeemed." But she knew she couldn't make this pledge, because this sickness was hard to cure. If in fact there was a cure. The ugly truth was, shoplifting could lead to bigger crimes like bank robbery or a jewelry heist. And a heist of any magnitude could land her in the big house. Matthew did not envy Jake McGrath's future trying to keep Sage in check.

In the meantime, Helen the tailor's daughter makes her move on Chris and accepts the dinner date. Chris is thrilled until she lays down some heavy ground rules. She won't fuck him, no matter how much he spends on her or how charming he is. She doesn't fuck on the first date. Second base is highly unlikely but not out of the question. And for Chrissake, do not under any circumstance take her for Japanese food. The man was rejected at the curb. A sad commentary. With that kind of stiff proviso, he's undecided, struggling within himself if even having this date is worth it. Probably not. Maybe change it to a breakfast, which would eliminate any idea of combining sex after waffles.

He looks over at Matthew for guidance, hoping he'd give him direction. A shrug was the best he could do.

So as not to keep anyone in suspense, Chris got damn lucky that night and in fact scored big with Helen Funai. Why? Who knows? Perhaps his stars were in alignment and some sort of divine intervention played a role in it. He and Helen went strong for a long while before she dumped him for someone of her own brand—an Asian businessman with serious coin.

CHAPTER 16

August 1969. Saturday. Opening night. The store is completed and ready to accept the open minds and wallets of the public. Everything in its proper place. Racks are filled. Shirts and leather jackets hung with intricacy. Dressing rooms are built to specifications. They laid used wooden planked flooring to give it that rustic feel. Their biggest advantage was that they featured top name brands that were getting public attention. Male Pants, Kaminsky, A. Smile, Sisley, Michael Milea shirts, Viceroy pants. It's weird, because they had a buzzing suspicion that they were onto something big.

By 9:00 p.m. the place was rockin' like an urban juke joint to use a very old hip term. In the mix are familiar faces, strangers, invited guests, and crashers who came all the way from the other side of the hill. Plus a lot of stragglers off the street, pulled in by the distinctive scent of marijuana wafting up and down the boulevard.

In the background you could hear the music of Creedence Clearwater Revival blasting through the shop's music system. For the most part everyone was blown away by the store, and even more so by the fashions.

Matthew was standing in a corner, alone, leaning against a wall and soaking it all in, when this very cute petite chick approaches and hands him a glass of wine.

"You look like you could use someone to talk too," she says.

"Sure. What do you want to talk about?" Matthew replies.

"A job."

"What kind of job? Blow job, hand job, nose job?"

There's an awkward pause. Then Matthew apologizes for being so rude, explaining that he's a bit loaded, and this is why he's letting this wall help keep him in an upright position. She laughs before she introduces herself as Dede Copeland, a college student who picks up odd jobs as a seamstress. She tries to sell him on the idea that he's going to need someone to hem pants and make alterations.

"I'm a necessity," she declares. "I'll charge you by the pant, plus 2 percent."

Matthew liked her confident approach and her instincts. He gave her the job, not even knowing if she could even thread a needle or was just looking for idle conversation.

Of course, their favorite girlfriends came to see them off and wish them luck. It made for some nervous moments, but for the most part everyone was cool. No one fell on each other in a gladiatorial frenzy of yowling, scratching, and yanking wisps of hair. No punches were thrown. No drinks thrown in anyone's face. The word "bitch" was not being tossed around frivolously.

Jon invited some guy he met on his buying trip to New York. Ronny Cooper. He was working as a waiter in the Tribeca Kitchen. Seemed like a nice enough dude. He noticed that Nicole was sort of all over him. Figured he must've had a huge sparkling personality, if you catch the implication.

Matthew was still leaning against the wall when this Ronny approached him, lighting a Swisher Sweets Blunt before asking in a very matter-of-fact, businesslike way if he was interested in buying some primo coke. To Matthew's sensibility, primo meant expensive. Didn't matter, cocaine was not his drug of choice. It wreaked havoc on his sinuses and was even worse on his psyche. Too foggy for his taste, he tells him. Not sure what that meant, but he's certain he got the drift that he wasn't interested.

Ronny was pushy and handed Matthew a couple sample lines carefully wrapped in tin foil. It was very apparent this guy was either a serious dealer or was striving to be a serious distributor. Fine, the store can't expect to cater to only nuns and choirboys if they're in the business of selling clothing to the masses. There's going to be a lot of offbeat, unconventional whack jobs who cross over the threshold with the crazy idea that Jon's Drawer has the answers to the life they're looking for—standout originality.

Ronny Cooper walked away in the haze and rejoined Jon and a few others out back, where a snorting party was forming.

At the time, neither Chris nor Matthew, and possibly not even Jon, had known this was going to be a regular habit—cocaine gatherings with Ronny Cooper, sampling and purchasing his primo blow.

The end of the night arrived quickly and people started to clear out. Eleven o'clock was the designated hour to close the doors and call it a night. It was a city noise ordinance. A few lingered. One of them was Matthew, who fell asleep in a shampoo chair with the back of his head resting awkwardly in a really uncomfortable rinse bowl.

CHAPTER 17

Following morning. The sun blinded Matthew and the light from the front window showed dust specks floating in the air. He woke up still asleep in the shampoo chair. No one bothered to wake him and steer me home.

His back hurt, his neck was stiff, his head throbbing like someone was beating a hammer against the wall of his skull. He was a mess and he needed to pee, badly. The place reeked of wine, stale beer, cigarettes, weed, musk oil, a hint of Shoyeido Nijo Japanese rain-scented incense, and fresh brewed coffee.

Before he got out of the chair, he turns his head just enough to see Anne Fraser walking towards him with a hot cup of coffee. Another dream? Another hopeful sign? Perhaps. Still not straight from last night's drug-fest, he rubs his eyes awake. It was no hallucination. It was her. She was dressed in a new pair of bell-bottoms and T-shirt. She looked outrageous. She approaches, hands him the coffee. Kisses him on the lips. Just soft enough to make it count.

"Good morning," she says.

"Have you been here all night?" he asks, voicing his assumption. She nods. "Yes. I watched you sleep."

"Really? All night?"

"The weird thing is, you called out my name a few times."

This explained his morning erection. It was difficult for him to comprehend. He needs fresh air. He excuses himself and crosses to the front door. It was still unlocked. He opens it and sucks the morning mist into his lungs. When he turns back, Anne is gone, and he is just waking up again in the shampoo chair.

Again, this vision was all in his imagination. By now, you would think these images would scare the piss out of him, but they didn't. He really loved the idea of her showing up in his life in such a freakish, mystifying way. Eventually this will make more sense. Or drive him to the loony bin. "Maybe I need to lay off the drugs for a while," he says out loud.

When he finally heads for the bathroom, he notices the pant cubicles are in total disarray. Shirts tilted off their hangers. Miscellaneous clothing piled inside the dressing rooms. Cigarette butts stomped out on the floor. Glasses of unfinished wine sitting atop his Red Grooms water heater, and one pair of panties casually hanging from a wall sconce. It looked more like the morning after an orgy than a stellar opening.

He checked the receipts from last night. He could barely make out the numbers that were scribbled on invoices like Sanskrit. Failing to get a read on a total, he wondered where the sales money was. He thought maybe Jon blew it up his nose. Okay, sure, that was an unfair evaluation. But not all that far-fetched.

He opens the door to the toilet and there, sitting on the john, slumped over with drool running down his chin, like a hideous bronze replica of Rodin's *The Thinker*, was Logan, his elusive roommate. He shook the hell out of him.

"Hey, man, time to get the fuck up."

Nothing. Not even a change of position. Matthew pees in the sink before he nudges him again, only harder, almost propelling him off the toilet seat. This seemed to get his attention. He stirs awake, coughs, and without missing a beat swivels around, lifts the toilet seat, and pukes as if he's performed this pirouette before. The retching sound seems to bounce off the walls like bad opera. Matthew knew this to be a time-honored ritual for Logan Alexander.

Matthew hands him several paper towels to wipe his face, and the residual barf he got on his pants, shoes, and the wall. He looks like an infant sitting in his highchair, who went berserk with the strained carrots. You can bet he had no clue where he was, who he was, why he was, wherever he was.

"How're you doin', man?"

"Not sure. Am I at home or in jail again for a DUI?" he murmurs. He has to be reminded of last night's event, which seems to register through his blank, bloodshot eyes with a blink and a nod.

"I could use a drink," he barks. He grabs a half glass of wine parked on the floor. Unbeknownst to him, it had a cigarette butt floating gently on the surface. He drinks, then spits it out before swallowing this mixture of wine and tobacco.

Matthew manages to get him in presentable enough shape to be seen in public. A half hour later, they're going for coffee at Tiny Naylor's. Matthew drove Logan's Aston Martin. How he talked his father into letting him drive that car, God only knows. This was a prized possession in his collection of fifty vintage automobiles. Worth a fortune. One ding on this baby and Logan would not see daylight for months, if not years. Which meant no place for Matthew to live, so he handled this car with extreme gentleness, as if they were driving with a case of nitroglycerin in the trunk.

As they go, Logan begins to sober up, recalling the night before. "I spent a cool hundred on some slick duds last night," he says, trying to be groovy but he just doesn't make the grade as a far-out cat. More bourgeois than anything else.

"I appreciate that," Matthew says. He looks around. "Where are they?"

"Not sure. Maybe I didn't buy anything but was about to, then I got sidetracked. I was pretty fucked up."

He then starts to open up and reveal how he partied with Sage. Spectacular girl. They shared a bottle of Jack D in the parking lot, then had this wild make out session in his backseat.

Logan looks around, and sure enough there's a pair of underwear sitting there in plain sight like a souvenir of his achievement. He turns back and smiles triumphantly. "Amazing lady in so many ways," he says.

There is a shudder from Matthew. Obviously Sage did not fulfill her promise to stay clear of Logan Alexander. This could mean serious trouble. He asks Logan to cool this infatuation with Sage, for obvious reasons—if her husband finds out, all hell will break loose, and he'll come after him with a fucking crowbar. Not to mention, this love fest could jeopardize Matthew's working relationship with Jake, and he needed for him to remain his contractor for future gigs. Logan promised he would cool it. He said this still half bagged, while he puked one more time on the side of the Aston Martin. So his reassurance was questionable at best.

They forgo getting coffee and make an unscheduled stop at a hand car wash. Admittedly, this was a selfish gesture. Matthew didn't want to risk the chance of losing the apartment and sleeping on someone's couch again solely on account of Logan not returning the car in pristine condition. Matthew paid for the car wash because Logan's wallet was missing. He was pretty sure this was some of Sage's handiwork. A sudden, uncontrollable anxiety rushes through Matthew. He decided to wash his hands of Sage. If she gets arrested, she's on her own. No more Mr. Nice Guy coming to her rescue.

CHAPTER 18

With opening night behind them, they tallied up an impressive twenty-five hundred. Not too fucking shabby for selling jeans at seven dollars a pair and shirts priced between six and eight bucks.

Matthew didn't relish the phone call he had to make to David Ackerman. His string shirts had served their purpose, and it was time to cut the umbilical cord and move on. He thought David would figure that out for himself. He didn't. He became petulant and irritable. He virtually became unglued and picketed the store on the grounds of unfair business practice. After three hours walking the picket line by himself in the hot sun, with his makeshift sign that read *Boycott this store. Unfair labor practice*, David gave up the fight, after he was humiliated by a local news channel that accused him of trying to deny the small businessman from making a living. He became irate, brandishing his sign like a sword and trying to keep customers from crossing his picket line. He was eventually arrested for assault. The publicity helped, and a cultural blend of people wandered in just to see what all the hoopla was about. Ackerman was fined five-hundred dollars and ordered never to come within a hundred feet of the store, or he'd be arrested for trespassing on private property. That was the last CHAPTER—the string shirts died an ugly death and were replaced by the trendy Nik-Nik shirts.

§

The following week, Jake and Sage headed back to Palm Springs. Family crisis. Matthew and Chris were relieved, anticipating friction between Logan and Jake if it ever got out he had a private backseat moment with Sage. Before they split, Matthew was about to confront Sage about lifting Logan's wallet. He had no proof, but it was pretty much a given she had pulled this off. He approached.

"Sage, we need to talk," he said. She had that guilty faraway look in her eyes like she knew he was about to nail her for lifting the wallet. Before he had the chance to come down on her, she hands over the leather alligator wallet. She couldn't confess fast enough.

"It was there for the taking and I couldn't resist. The temptation was too much," she says. "I guess I still have that bad seed growing inside me, but then I thought about the consequences—never seeing Jake and another sunset again. Wasn't worth the grab."

This time Matthew didn't give her the praise that he's sure she thought she deserved. In fact, once she was out of sight, he checked the contents. Cash, credit cards, and an unused Trojan condom were still there. He guesses that, by psychotherapist standards, this was considered a breakthrough.

§

Business was moderately humming. Foot traffic was marginal but promising. It's amazing how the word got out so fast. Through their pants rep, Hal Exler, they learn about the weekly tradition of mart day—a regular occurrence the guys will come to hate. On any given Wednesday, retailers hit the California Apparel Mart on 9th Street, in downtown Los Angeles, to buy inventory. A collection of retailers and wholesalers from around the globe, the mart is lined up with endless showrooms. It's actually a grueling, head-banging activity, as these ruthless, take-no-prisoners reps try to sell the piss out of their garments. The only decent thing, but it wasn't Matthew's bag, was these crazy wholesalers offered inducements like wine, cocaine, maybe a bagel and cream cheese, or a powdered donut to induce a sugar intake that speeds up your heart rate. All this hoping to get retailers loose so they'd buy till their accountant runs amuck. God knows how cream cheese induced their buying power.

But Mart Day was something you had to endure to keep up with the fashion scene. The guys let a couple of weeks go by before they again ventured into this apparel nightmare.

§

Wednesday. 8:00 a.m. The traffic on the 101 Freeway is brutal. Bumper to bumper. A parking lot. Chris was sitting in the backseat. A nervous wreck. Biting his nails to the nub because they were moving at a snail's pace.

"How do people make this hellish trip every day and not want to kill themselves by the time they reach their destination?" Chris wonders aloud. "It's a fucking mystery."

"Roll your window down and ask the driver in the car next to you," Matthew suggests.

Chris takes up the challenge. He rolls his window down and screams at the car next to them—asking the driver why he tortures himself every morning.

Of course the guy can't hear him, and probably can't see the road for that matter. His car is filled with smoke like he's driving in his own personal fog. They witness him taking a hit from a hash pipe, which answers the question of how he handles every arduous stretch of asphalt so effortlessly. He's in his own fucking stratosphere, and by the time he gets to work he couldn't care less about the drive or selling life insurance to the people on planet earth.

Then, out of nowhere, Chris—who's always in another dimension himself—blurts out: "I think while we're downtown, we should get the Jon's Drawer logo tattooed on our asses. I know a place. Cheap, and the needles are clean."

There is an incredulous pause. Matthew then turns and gives Chris a dubious death stare.

"You're serious?" Matthew says.

A beat before Chris answers. There is a minutiae of doubt rendered on his face. "Yes. Serious," Chris says, utterly committed to the proposal.

"For what purpose?" Matthew asks.

"A show of solidarity. Cohesion. Unity."

"You get it first, and if we like it, we're in," Jon says.

"If we hate it, and think it's a really lame move, you'll be marked as the partner who went for individuality over common sense," Matthew argues. "And how do you know the needles are clean? Rumor?"

Chris replies, "It was mentioned in their Yellow Pages ad."

"Well," says Matthew, "that testimonial is good enough for me."

Chris decides to muse on the idea that now seems like a risky challenge. Their first appointment was at nine o'clock with Stan Tendler, the founder of Kennington shirts of California. They enter the showroom. Nothing fancy. Plain white walls. Two racks on rollers with an assortment of about fifty shirts hanging idly. Just the three of them and the rep with his female assistant. They always hire an attractive young lady to exhibit the shirt in a more fashionable way, waving it in front of their faces like a bullfighter's cape. They offer them your basic morning menu—either a bagel, a donut, or a generous serving of cocaine. While Matthew had the bagel, Chris went for a donut, Jon disappeared for a brief moment and snorted a line of coke off a compact mirror, provided by the female assistance. Jon was never one to turn down a free drug sample.

They're on the clock. They have one hour to go through the whole line and pick and choose between fifty styles. The rep takes them through the line—shirt by shirt, print by print, price by price. All of the styles were great, but they bought what they felt was going to appeal to their customers, breaking it down into sizes: three extra-small, four small, five mediums, four large, two extra large. They're not done; that was just one shirt—one style, one print, that comes in different colors. Jesus Christ, the pressure mounts. They had to determine, right there, how they thought that particular shirt would sell. How many medium-sized people might buy it or not buy it. It was like a fucking game show.

The rep attempts to help. Most of the time they buy what they like for their area. What Nebraska might like, Studio City might use for a dust cloth. This is just one label. They left ordering a total of four styles, in different colors and prints, seventy-two shirts in all. Their cost: somewhere in the neighborhood of five hundred dollars. Not bad for seventy-two shirts. Remember, it's 1970.

Their next appointment was at 10:10 with Hal Exler at Male Pants. Another floor, another cup of coffee. Another powered donut.

Same exhausting routine. Only pants. Lots of fucking pants in a wide range of materials. Low-rise, high-rise, medium-rise. Mart day is a pisser. A fucking nightmare. Jon didn't care because he was stoned and nowhere to be seen. They tracked him down back at Kennington shirts—where he ordered another dozen shirts for a quickie blow job from the female assistant. The apparel business is clearly not strained by a sense of ethics.

§

Six hours later, their minds are like scrambled eggs. It's all they can do to stand up. After a rigorous buying spree, they find themselves at a tattoo parlor on South Hill Street called The Ink Pad. Matthew can't make sense of why they agreed to undertake this ridiculous and unwise endeavor. He was nervous. Not because he anticipated the prickly pain but because this was something he was always against. Marking your body seemed almost barbaric. But it felt right in this case. It felt acceptable. Three guys showing that they are inseparable, in business and in friendship, etching the Jon's Drawer logo on their asses to commemorate a milestone in their lives.

Chris, as advertised, went first. His eyes glazed over. The tattoo artist, not Chris. A burly guy. Long hair past his shoulders, like John Lennon. His body covered with tattoos from his neck down. His head was the only space void of any indelible design. He reeked of beer, and there were four empties and a bottle of Seagram's sitting in the trash can near him. They concluded they were letting a drunk scribble on their skin. Jon feared the worst. "What if the alcohol muddles his train of thought," he mused, "and he somehow inscribes the word MOTHERFUCKER in a font size you normally see on a marquee sign?" Matthew clenches his fist for no other reason than to make sure he still has feeling in his hand.

MATERIAL THINGS

Chris wanted a cigarette and a Pepsi to calm his nerves. You would think he was about to have bypass surgery. The tattoo artist offered them a joint for courage.

"What about a shot of Novocaine?" Chris asks. His wiseass remark earned him an incredulous look from the tattoo guy.

They shared the joint like it was their last request before going in front of a firing squad. The sound of the buzzing needle puncturing the skin was a bit off-putting. It was minuscule but sounded like a fucking jackhammer. They made a collective decision, and voted against having the logo inscribed on their asses. No way were they going to pull their pants down for this dude. The calf area seemed to be the most suitable area. Small but formidable. In red ink for emphasis. The Coca-Cola letters that read Jon's Drawer.

Chris winced as the needle pierced his skin. Beads of sweat formed on his upper lip. Jon and Matthew were having second thoughts until this attractive Mexican girl walked in and wanted her boyfriend's name tattooed on her left breast. This calmed them down and quelled their fears. They watched as a second tattoo artist went to work on her, marveling at the intricacy of the name "Philippe" being lined out and replaced by "Alejandro" directly underneath it. This was the third name on her left breast. The right one had its own list of former lovers X'd out. She didn't flinch, so they couldn't show signs of being pussies from the Valley no matter how much it stung.

Afterwards, the Mexican babe says, "I'll be back in six months. That's when these hombres usually dry up."

When they finally walked out of there, they weren't really sure if they'd made a mistake or not. They chalked it up to a period of youthful experimentation. Chris covered his with a Band-Aid if he ever went to the beach. Matthew said he would only fuck in the dark.

Jon was already considering getting it removed the following week. But all in all, it was a grand fucking moment in the recent history of Jon's Drawer. Well, maybe not as grand as much as fucking stupid.

CHAPTER 19

Hanging up the hair dryer seemed like the right move. The boutique took off like they never expected. Sales skyrocketed. According to Jon's calculations, they were making more than VIP Men's Hairstyling.

Jon and Chris came to Matthew and ran by a suggestion. They were foaming-at-the-mouth excited. They suggested shutting down and sending VIP to an early grave and expanding Jon's Drawer to a much larger boutique with a wider selection of clothes. Also, taking a sledgehammer to the wall connecting them with the former tailor shop and making it predominantly a jeans room.

Matthew took a deep breath, which was followed by some slight regurgitation of vomit in his throat. You just don't make these kinds of life changes without giving it some serious thought. Mull it around. Ponder it. Turn it over in one's mind. The guys wouldn't let him think twice about it for fear the reality of this proposal would sink in and scare him unconscious. They were anxious. Their eyes said yes, go for it, drop your scissors and hang up your hair dryer—having all the hallmarks of a gunslinger in the Old West retiring and hanging up his six-shooters.

The gunslinger reference rattled around in Matthew's head and gave him a far-reaching idea on how to design the store. In the American West motif. He went for it and told his receptionist to cancel his appointments for the next couple weeks. He never picked up a pair of scissors again except for the ribbon-cutting ceremony. She took it the hardest. Tears in her eyes. She had been with Matthew since he first opened his doors. He gave her the option of staying and selling clothes or moving on. She chose to move on as did Dean, who had a gig waiting for him in San Francisco. He had talent. In the months to come, Dean would open his own shop in the Haight-Ashbury district called The Cutting Edge. Tina, his receptionist, chose to travel and backpack it through Europe.

§

That night, Matthew was at home in his usual pose—on the couch, smoking a joint, while listening to Crosby, Stills, Nash & Young's album, *Déjà Vu*. He stared up at the ceiling, trying to come up with a design for the new augmented Jon's Drawer. He'd been in this position for a good hour and a half, and all he had was the idea of installing a tin ceiling, when there was a knock on the door. It startled him. Interrupted his train of thought. He thought about ignoring it until he heard Linda Tarlow's voice on the other side.

"Hey, it's me, I know you're there. I can hear your brain working," she said.

He got up and opened the door. He just stood there staring at her for a good fifteen seconds before he asked her in. She had a bottle of wine in her hand. Red or white, he wasn't paying attention. His head was still in the clouds. The weed had taken over and cluttered his sense of reason, but not so much that he didn't notice that she looked great. Torn jeans and a faded black T-shirt, just short enough to reveal her belly button. He hadn't seen her for a solid three weeks. Maybe a month. This was a conscious evasive action. He had mixed feelings about Linda Tarlow. He was pretty sure he was over her. It all happened so fast with the two of them. He was in a hopeless state of mind. His wife was on the verge of calling it quits and he was in pain. He was certain he was looking for some solace, and there was Linda Tarlow walking on the beach towards him, almost like some sort of divine being coming to make him feel better about himself and lick his wounds.

"You haven't called me in a good month," she says.

"What's going on? Why are you here? How did you know I moved?" This line of questioning probably wasn't the most tactful approach. Sounded like he wasn't glad to see her. Truthfully, he wanted to be alone.

"I brought wine," she says, holding it up.

"I see. What's the occasion?"

"I'm pregnant," she blurts out.

Matthew beat a hasty retreat back to the couch, before he passed out. The color drained from his face. It was suddenly hard to swallow. This was impossible. He was careful. It couldn't have been him who knocked her up. He was careful. He realizes he's repeating himself just to make sure that any person pointing a blameworthy finger in his direction knows he was a responsible lover. And careful.

He managed to get out a moderate "Really?" He assumed she was here to celebrate. Break the news that he's the father. Maybe even her bags were in the car. Ready to move it. Without sounding tactless, he didn't need this. Things were really starting to click and the last thing he needed was a kid clutching for attention. Or an abortion to take care of, if that's what she wished. But why would anyone bring wine to celebrate an abortion? Trying to open the wine became a monumental task. The strength seemed to disappear from his entire body. She noticed his nervousness. She smiled as she placed her warm hand over his and took the bottle from him. She opened the wine and then poured them each a glass, raising hers in a toast.

"To my beautiful baby," she says. She only takes a small sip, because alcohol could cause birth defects, she explains.

This was more information that Matthew needed to know. She was definitely having this baby. He needed to breathe and inhale more oxygen. He takes a deep breath and chugs his glass of wine. She notices how edgy he is and tells him to relax. Easy for her to say—she's not the expectant father.

As she pours him a second glass, he thrusts his mind into rewind mode. She just toasted to *my* beautiful baby, not to *their* beautiful baby. Maybe it was just a slip of the tongue. He's not so quick to think he's off the hook. He starts to ask her if this is their kid, but she beats him to it and sets the record straight, saying he's not the daddy—it's her ex-boyfriend's. She actually came over to break it off with him, but wanted to do it face to face, and not be rude and distant about it.

Okay, why couldn't she have told him this at the door and avoided the drama? Did she want him to sweat, because she secretly wished he was the father, not the abusive boyfriend who tried to smack her around when they were together? Didn't matter. Of course, he was relieved. Not so much that it wasn't his baby, but because he wasn't ready to take on the enormous responsibility of being a dad and probably a husband again.

She wanted to run by a name. Get his opinion. Kirby, if it's a girl. A boy—also Kirby. She waited for his response. What could he say, he hated the name? Of course not. "Yeah, I love the name Kirby," he lied. "It's perfect for a girl or a boy." Then he thinks to himself, *Kirby for boy—a mistake. He'll be nothing but a bully magnet.*

She stayed another fifteen minutes, then got up and slowly crossed to the door, acting as if she had something to say. She did. She turns back with tears in her eyes.

"If I can be perfectly honest, I wish it was yours," she confesses. "I think you'd make a better father than him. But life has it ups and downs, and sometimes the *downs* outweigh the *ups*. Whatever the fuck that means. See you around, Matthew Street. Keep the wine."

And with that, she disappears into the night.

CHAPTER 20

The sun was just starting to set when Chris, Matthew, and Jon returned from an all-day location shoot at Knott's Berry Farm in Anaheim. They must've taken at least a hundred Polaroid shots of the dusty, weather-beaten ghost town and its facades. The outing brought back childhood memories of visits to the ghost town with his family. In his head, Matthew fancied that he was riding shotgun on the bumpy Wells Fargo stagecoach line, carrying a gold shipment to Tombstone. In his wildest imagination, he pictured bandits with red and white-checkered bandanas covering their grubby faces riding up alongside the stage in a cloud of dust with six guns blazing, seizing the strongbox and robbing all the passengers.

This chimera alone had inspired him to go with the American Western motif. They all agreed the look would fit perfectly on the boulevard. The idea would hopefully blow the minds of everyone who walked, ran, or drove by.

MATERIAL THINGS

They took separate cars. While Chris and Matthew headed back to LA, Jon took a quick side trip to Palm Springs to visit his mom and talk Jake McGrath and Sage into coming back to build the western trading post facade. If the city would allow horses and buckboards, they'd have them centrally parked out front with the Ford Mustangs and Broncos.

After a half hour on the road, Chris needed to take a leak, so they stopped at a Sinclair Gas Station that was going out of business. Everything about it looked vintage. Rusty. Even the attendant was timeless.

Out front was an old barber chair for sale. What that had to do with a gas station, no one knew, but they're thinking there's got to be a great story behind it. It was the kind of chair that had a leather strop hanging from the side for sharpening razors. It's a well-known fact that barbershops were centers of social interaction in small towns and big cities alike. Matthew was sure there were hundreds of patrons who sat on this throne of discourse and spun their yarns to the barber, who listened with rapt attention—while clipping away to the music of the lies he's heard over and over, always with a different ending. Hell, the barber could probably tell some whoppers himself. You could almost smell the witch hazel that permeated the air.

As Matthew examined the chair, he suddenly felt like he had been transported back to the late 1940s. This was a classic Pagano barber chair in mint condition. Black cushions. Shiny steel frame. Flip-style footrest and old-fashioned pedestal. He imagined that Baby Face Nelson or John Dillinger got a hair cut in a chair just like this. Matthew had to have it for the store.

While Chris went somewhere around back to pee—probably in an empty oilcan—Matthew went inside to ask about the chair, and nearly tripped over an old hound dog sleeping in the doorway. The critter would have been more at home in a rustic cabin deep in the Ozarks, but there he was, bloodshot, droopy eyes, wrinkled forehead, long, floppy ears and all.

"How much you want for it?" Matthew asked. It was like he was dealing with some old dude who looked like Gabby Hayes and smelled like the inside of an old cowboy boot. His skin was as leathery as the strop. He spit tobacco juice before answering.

"The dog ain't for sale, the chair is eighty-three fifty." Okay, where in the fuck did he come up with such an odd number? "Don't try and haggle me down," he added. "I look old but I still got plenty of spine left in me, Young Turk."

Matthew shot back with: "I'll give you seventy-five and you deliver it to me in Sherman Oaks." This time Matthew spit on the floor. He thought for a moment, then just nodded and spit again, just for emphasis and color.

According to this old guy, it was 1906 when his mother dragged him to Sal's Barbershop on Main Street in South Bend, Indiana, where he grew up. Forced him to sit still in that exact chair or she'd smack him silly. Nice parental behavior in those days. He understandably hated the experience. Wailed at every snip of the scissors. He bought the chair to remind him of how much he hated his mother for pressuring him to do it. She died when she was eighty-three and a half years old. Same number as his original asking price for the chair. True or not, the old coot's story captured Matthew's imagination and he forked over his asking price—eighty-three fifty.

Just like the water heater, he planned to use this old chair to display merchandise. So far he's got a design concept, a tin ceiling, and a barber chair. The boys were headed in the right direction.

CHAPTER 21

It's been nine months since they opened Jon's Drawer in the back room. They gave themselves a deadline of April 1 to finish and transform VIP into a killer boutique. They worked their asses off virtually day and night, and on weekends. Hammered, nailed, painted stained, snorted, drank, and smoked their way through construction and a few days impeded by foul weather.

Hanging over the storefronts were rustic signs made from used, weathered lumber that mimicked Knott's Berry Farm's western township facade. The lettering echoed Old West signage circa the 1860s. It was truly a work of vintage craftsmanship.

Jake was doing one helluva fucking job, but failed to steady himself while attaching a railing suggestive of a saloon straight out of Deadwood, South Dakota. He fell off the roof onto the sidewalk, spraining his wrist and cracking two ribs. Really unfortunate. An ambulance was quick to respond and patch him up. Jake begged for some pain meds. They never knew for sure if it was for relief, or that he just wanted to get high on five 80-milligram OxyContin tablets. But he managed to get through it. Ironically, the EMTs vowed to return to buy a pair of bell-bottoms, so the fall wasn't a total loss.

With only one good arm and the help of some prescription drugs, Jake managed to complete the entire job two days ahead of schedule. His last labor-intensive task was installing double-hung saloon doors on the dressing rooms. His idea. Brilliant. The partners were more than thrilled with the outcome of the whole job. It was everything they imagined it to be and more. The Old West had come to Sherman Oaks in 1969. The only thing missing was an authentic dingy saloon offering whiskey and sarsaparilla, evoking images of languid belles and parched cowboys.

CHAPTER 22

April 1, 1969. The Grand Opening had a Hollywood premiere flavor to it without the formal tuxedos and the pesky autograph hounds. Even the local news station came on the scene and gave them a hefty plug.

Jon loved to be in the spotlight. Shove a camera in his face and he became a whole new animated guy, talking like a carnival pitchman. Shove some coke up his nose and the conversation becomes random, and he would stretch the truth like a politician. Matthew caught up with him in a corner trying to explain the definition of the term "Keystone" to this very attractive chick. He listened as the definition rolled off Jon's tongue like a seasoned buyer from New York's famed garment district.

"Keystone is a retail term related to pricing inventory. It's a method of marking merchandise for resale at an amount that is double the wholesale price or cost of the product. Keystone essentially means that if the cost of the product were, say, fifty dollars, then the selling price would be set at one hundred. Dig what I'm saying?"

She rolls her eyes, giving him an incredulous look, then fires back with: "I fully understand what you just threw at me, but to be brutally honest, I don't give a shit about this whole Keystoning thing. I'm here to get wasted, have a good time, and buy a pair of jeans no matter what the cost."

Jon, feeling a sense of stupidity, staggers away into the crowd in search of a more affable audience.

The girl then turns to Matthew and introduces herself as Betty Farrell. She's a stripper at the Condor Club in San Francisco's North Beach district—went by the exotic name of Cinnamon Cynda. She could've been a fashion model. She was that attractive.

"Why'd you become a stripper?" Matthew asked her.

"I'm working my way through school. San Francisco Conservatory of Music. I play the cello."

Wow. He had no idea if she was putting him on or not. But her story was something to marvel at.

This was just one of many fascinating discussions the partners participated in on their opening night. Doctors, lawyers, schoolteachers, mothers, fathers, addicts, rock stars, musicians—a motley crew all flocked to see what all the commotion was about bell-bottom pants, flowered print shirts, and fringe leather vests.

Then things got real interesting and dangerous at the same time when Jimmy Ray Bigelow showed up. He's wanted for murder in two states and walks in like he's fucking Al Capone, gunning for Eliot Ness.

He lights a cigarette and takes a drag, inhaling through his nostrils and blowing a smoke ring that hovers over him like a cheap halo. He then squints his eyes doing a three-sixty look around, like he's casing the joint and intending to rob, pillage, and plunder . . . or looking to have a showdown with one or all of the guys who witnessed the scene at the office of Barry Marcus on that vicious day. Chris is the first to spot him. He pulls Jon and Matthew aside.

"Remember that dude who murdered, Barry Marcus?" Of course they remembered. "He just walked in."

"Where? You sure?" Jon says, noticeably panic-stricken.

Chris begins to speak in a hushed tone. "Leaning against the barber chair, drinking a cup of wine, smoking a cigarette and sniffing uncontrollably, like he's high on coke or got a bad cold."

Chris thinks they ought to call the cops. Now. Without hesitation. They were in major jeopardy. They agreed this crazy-ass fuck came to kill them. With them out of the way, he could maybe get a lesser sentence with an insanity plea. Jon volunteers to go call the cops. Maybe not a good idea, Matthew says. If this idiot has a real gun this time, things could get dangerously ugly, people could get hurt. Bad publicity for the store. Or good publicity—depends how you look at it. But if they were dead, any kind of public attention would do them no fucking good.

They needed a sure-fire plan of attack. Predictably, Chris comes up with a foolish one: take the guy down by throwing a pillowcase over his head, bind his hands with a telephone cord, then throw him in the trunk of a car until the fuzz arrives.

Both Matthew and Jon give Chris a dubious look. Matthew says, "Okay, cool. Where the fuck do we get the pillowcase?"

"If someone has a better idea, I'm willing to listen," Chris says.

Taking that as a bold dare, Jon suddenly gets a dash of courage. He moves towards Jimmy Ray at a slow pace so as not to freak him out. You can bet his heart was beating like crazy, because Matthew's was. His guess, Jon had no idea what he was going to say or do. And you can bet he wasn't about to explain the term "Keystone" to fucking Jimmy Ray Bigelow. But you never know.

Jon's now maybe five feet from Jimmy Ray, fists clenched at his sides, when he suddenly stops cold. Having second thoughts maybe? Exercising better judgment? Neither. Jon had noticed a guy he knew from Palm Desert. Freddie Garcia. Freddie had a justifiable reputation as a guy you didn't want to fuck with. He'd been a boxer and had recently cultivated an ultimate fighting obsession. Freddie liked violence—seemed to like getting hurt as much as he liked hurting people.

Jon gave him a friendly hug hello and then explained his dilemma. Freddie was more than willing to handle it.

"I can do this, amigo," he says, speaking with a slight Mexican accent. "You want this *pendejo* dead, or just fucked up enough where he can't ever breathe through the windpipe no mores?" (English interpretation: *pendejo* means asshole.)

Jon pondered Jimmy's fate. Death or windpipe? "Preferably not dead," Jon decides.

Freddie cracks his knuckles, then his neck, then his dick for all they know. He then swaggers over to Jimmy Ray with bravado. Forces a friendly smile, flashing a gold tooth. Says something in Spanish. (You can bet it wasn't *buenos dias, mi amor*.) Then he lands a ferocious sucker punch to the temple, decking the guy. It's a beautiful sight, but Jimmy Ray is still conscious. He grabs the .38 special that's tucked in his belt and points it at Freddie's head.

"You're a dead man, motherfucker!" he yells.

There are screams and gasps throughout the store. Jimmy Ray shoots but the gun misfires. Freddie responds lightning-fast. He kicks the gun out of Jimmy Ray's hand to the wooden floor, where it slides a few feet away. As Jimmy Ray reaches for it, Freddie leaps onto the floor, grabs the gun and, without missing a beat, fires three shots into Jimmy Ray's chest, killing him instantly in front of the mesmerized Jon's Drawer opening crowd.

There's complete silence while the crowd reacts, trying to comprehend if this is real or a dramatization of a classic noir assassination.

Matthew turns to Chris. "Guess we can blow off the pillowcase idea," he deadpans.

The cops, the coroner, and the EMTs show up within twenty minutes. It was a spectacle, lit up like a movie set. They stretch yellow caution tape around the entire perimeter of the shop. No one was allowed to go in or out until questions were answered. They toe-tag Jimmy Ray, then toss his corpse in a body bag and haul it downtown to the morgue.

In their report, the police clear Freddie of murder and call the attack an act of self-defense. This night will play in the partners' nightmares over and over for years to come.

The local news picked up on the story and gave them some decent publicity. Jon made sure they mentioned the store's name, address, and hours of operation.

The guys agreed to give Freddie Garcia a reward—two pairs of pants and a leather jacket. They stuck a hundred dollar bill inside the jacket pocket, with a note that said "Thanks, amigo."

Two weeks later, they appeared in court to identify Jimmy Ray Bigelow as the man who murdered Barry Marcus. All charges were dropped against Freddie Garcia, who was given a personal thank you by the FBI, the LAPD, the mayor Sam Yorty, and the Marcus family for his heroic act of taking a high-profile killer off the streets.

Unbeknownst to anyone, Jimmy Ray had a wife who planned to sue the city and Jon's Drawer for his death. She had no case. It was clearly open and shut. Besides, she was serving a thirty-year prison sentence for assault with a deadly weapon with intent to kill. Even so, the guys were a little nervous about her maybe wanting to retaliate and seek revenge against them and Freddie Garcia. It made for a couple of sleepless nights.

CHAPTER 23

The shop fell into a comfortable, and contented purr. The publicity of the ill-timed death of Jimmy Ray Bigelow made the grand opening a huge success and boosted business.

The boys couldn't have been more jacked, and they desperately needed to hire sales people to help out. Jon and Matthew couldn't hack it alone, and by now, Chris was writing full-time for television—early mornings to midnight gigs—so he was useless during the week.

While Jon did the hiring, Matthew handled the buying. Today, he was perched in the parking lot buying T-shirts out of this guy's banged-up VW bus with a British Union Jack painted on the rooftop. Tony Clarke, a Brit from London, must've had two to three hundred British Army tees he was peddling in all different colors. He had bought a complete warehouse filled with Henley-type underwear shirts. Matthew had to pay close attention as he hawked his wares in his thick Liverpudlian accent.

"These are never before seen or sold across the pond, mate. You'll never find these for sale in the penny dreadful," he said. "It's an original Henley. Named after the traditional uniform of rowers in the town of Henley-on-Thames. Hundred percent cotton. A bloody smart investment."

Even without the history lesson, Matthew had a good feeling about Tony and an even better feeling about the merchandise. This felt like a trend. He took three-dozen to start, banking on his gut instinct they'd appeal to the in-crowd.

He called them English Tees and displayed them on a table draped with the British Union Jack. Sure enough, they became an instant hit. A best seller. Once again the guys were blown away by the popularity of a simple cotton shirt.

Tony made it a habit of coming around every few weeks to restock the table. On every visit he'd show up with a different chick he had picked up hitchhiking across America and Canada, wanting to come to Los Angeles to stake their claim in the rapidly growing music and movie business. Most of them never got to see the inside of a studio and either ended up as a waitress, a streetwalker, or going back to the Midwest and working on the family farm. It's the mystique of Hollywood.

Before peddling shirts, Tony Clarke worked in the shipping department at Harrods, the legendary department store in the ritzy Knightsbridge district in West London. But he was fired when he was caught stealing and selling the merchandise on Carnaby Street in Soho. Did time in a category D prison.

Jon was on top of finding them some very attractive, competent employees. He handpicked four fresh bodies. All of them came with their own personal baggage, strengths, and weaknesses. Elaine Russo and Michele Newhouse arrived on their first day fittingly already dressed in Jon's Drawer clothing. They looked outstanding. Jon had somehow stolen experienced Michele from a less hip clothing store called Country Club Fashion in Encino. She was young and willing to be less high fashion and more organic. Laurie Forester and Sheila Crane, two other girls, had the sting to be ace salesgirls and were anxious to be a part of their growing family. All four girls showed extreme enthusiasm, knowing they were about to undertake a first in the Valley—introducing bell-bottom jeans and funky accessories.

§

A week later Chris comes into the store. He looks wiped out. Television is taking its toll on his body. Bloodshot eyes. Bags. Unshaven. Weight loss. A wreck.

But when he sees Michele, who is folding T-shirts, he suddenly snaps out of this cave dweller ugliness and becomes almost human again. He goes crazy with infatuation. Instantaneously hooked. A shudder racked his body. He's certain he's just fallen in love. He wondered if that was even possible. What had it been, three seconds? People could know each other for three years and never love each other. Why couldn't someone you just saw for the first time seem like someone you've known for years? It's not possible—he knows that—but he makes his move anyway. It was impulsive and deliberate.

"Hey, I'm Chris, one of the owners," he says, offering his hand. She shakes it firmly.

"Michele Newhouse, I'm one of the new guys," she says. "No offense, but you look sickly. You okay? Because if you're coming down with something, I'd really like my hand back. I'm sort of a germophobe."

He releases her hand. "Not to worry. I'm just tired and only look like I'm dying. I'm a TV writer. Work crazy hours. The price of being imaginative. You sacrifice that GQ look for wit." He then makes an awkward transition. "So, I've heard a lot about you."

"Really? I've worked here no more than two days and already I'm being talked about around the water cooler," she says just as a customer approaches, waving a pair of pants in her hand and asking if they came in brushed denim. Michele goes into her pleasant, helpful salesgirl mode.

"Sorry, no. But they should though, shouldn't they? A brushed denim would be so stylish. And you would look so great in brushed denim. Know what? I'll mention it to the boss and have him contact the manufacturer." A beat. "Wait, he's standing right next to me. Boss, we should check with the manufacturer to see if these come in brushed denim, don't you think?"

Chris, has no fucking idea who the manufacturer is or what brushed means. He's only focused on one thing—impressing Michele.

"Absolutely. I'm on it."

The customer goes off to browse. Chris is impressed by Michele's saleswomanship.

"Well, I have to say you are good at what you do. The way you handled that girl was amazing. You did a stupefying job. How about dinner Saturday night?"

Michele chuckles. "Wow, I like how you shoehorned in *stupefying*, while at the same time you managed to ask me out. Must be part of the creative genius."

"Are you putting me on?"

"No. Yes. Maybe a little. Sorry. Just being a smart-ass."

"You're fired."

"What? Really?"

"Yes. No. Just going for cute. So, about dinner?"

Although she was flattered, she flatly turned him down because, well, there was a boyfriend in the mix.

He responds with a disappointing, "Oh, well my loss," then turns and walks towards the back room. She hollers after him: "Brushed denim! Don't forget!"

Michele looks to Elaine, who had been watching this very strange moment materialize, then seem to vanish into thin air.

"That was weird, uncomfortable, and kind of pathetic," Michele says.

Elaine shrugs. "He's a TV writer. They have insecurity issues. Look, it's no secret he wants to sleep with you and will do whatever it takes to get in your pants. So be prepared for several more attempts on his part. He'll come back clean-shaven and refreshed. Ready to attack again."

Michele cocks her head. "Attack?"

"Attack is wrong. More like swoop down. Like a vulture lunging for its prey."

"Did he ever come on to you?"

"I'm not his type."

"What's his type?"

"You are. Dark hair, dark eyes. Beautiful complexion. Sexy. Erotic. Hot. Fuckable."

Michele almost blushes over Elaine's bold evaluation of her. Elaine can sense that she feels awkward. She apologizes for being honest and hopes she didn't make her feel uncomfortable. Michele just shrugs, feeling self-conscious that another girl sees her in that light. Michele fears her job might be at risk if she snubs Chris's advances. Elaine agrees and suggests the two of them should have dinner and discuss how to approach this dilemma—woman to woman and in detail.

Have a game plan. Michele likes this idea. It could be fun, as well as a chance to get to know Elaine better.

Through this understanding of what men want, Elaine and Michele established this instant attraction. You could see it in their eyes, a fondness that neither of them had ever experienced before. It caught them off guard. The idea of an infatuation was mind-boggling. Even so, they in fact planned to meet on the weekend. This date, so to speak, was more than just two girls having dinner—it was the beginning of a very close link they hadn't foreseen.

They choose a restaurant in Hollywood. Away from the Valley. Away from their regular hangouts. Neutral ground. The Musso & Frank Grill. A popular haunt frequented by Hollywood celebrities.

They were both noticeably nervous while perusing the menu. The fare was a tad pricey but that didn't seem to affect their mood or their pocket book. The waiter, dressed in black pants, red jacket, and black bow tie, is casual enough when he takes their order. Surprisingly they order the same dish—a Cobb salad with a side of fries. It's a commonality of interest they seemed to like. It makes them more at ease to realize they share similar tastes. The girls each order a glass of wine and are asked for their ID. Another unexpected coincidence—both were Scorpios, born in November. As they dine, Elaine catches Michele looking down her blouse during a lull in the conversation. She says nothing but is turned on by her gaze.

They finally get to the central point that generated this dinner. How should Michele proceed with Chris Styles? Or should she proceed at all? It's apparent he's not going to let up until Michele agrees to either go out with him or she breaks up with her boyfriend. Michele confesses there is no boyfriend. It was just a ploy to keep him at a distance until she decides how to deal with a guy who seems to have a take-no-prisoners attitude.

Elaine thinks generating a fake boyfriend was brilliant. She also likes how this conversation is almost conspiratorial. Michele poses the question: what would the consequences be if she refuses to sleep with him? Fired? Collect unemployment to make her rent?

"Maybe just a hand job would keep your job safe," Elaine suggests wryly.

Michele likes the idea of having an alternative plan. A hand job could be her saving grace. This opens up the subject of sex and the last time they had any. They discover it's been a while for both of them.

Michele admits if she doesn't get any soon she just may have to relent and go out with Chris. "My hand just doesn't cut it these days," she quips.

They share a giggly laugh and hide their faces in embarrassment as other diners look over at them. They get more into it, and Elaine confesses she's always wanted to sleep with a girl. "Just for the sake of youthful experimentation," she quickly clarifies.

There is an awkward pause as Michele takes this as an invitation. A come-on. She turns her attention to her Cobb salad, not knowing how to respond. Is she expected to say she's had the same fantasy? Sure she has, but probably every girl has. It's part of the female psyche. Admitting this now feels almost like she'd be proposing that Elaine and her jump into the sack and satisfy this girl on girl dream after dessert. Or maybe they *are* the dessert.

The whole idea of this notion excited Michele. She shifted nervously in her seat. Elaine is very attractive and sexy. Incredible figure. Full lips. Michele puts her fork down, reaches across the table, and puts her hand on top of Elaine's. She does not flinch. In a soft whisper, Michele makes an assumption that could backfire. She looks deep into Elaine's blue-brown eyes and says, "If we have sex, it has to be something we keep just between us. It can never leave our lips or our minds. It can never become shop gossip. We chalk it up to—like you said—youthful experimentation, and move on. In the store we will smile, because we'll have this moment locked away in our personal journal. And if we ever want to repeat it, which we will because it's going to be incredible, we shouldn't—with each other. Agreed?"

Elaine is caught off-guard; she smiles with great pleasure, then puts her free hand on top of Michele's. This was a very pivotal moment in their otherwise heterosexual friendship. Nothing else needed to be said. So ended the meal portion of their evening.

CHAPTER 24

The Aquarius Theatre, July 21, 1969. 8:00 p.m. In the mix are the usual Jon's Drawer suspects—plus Jon's drug-dealing friend Ronny Cooper. They're located smack in the middle of what appears to be a madhouse as Jim Morrison sings "Light My Fire" to a packed house. It's an insane visual, like Hieronymus Boschs' painting *The Garden of Earthly Delights*.

Logan was invited but passed on account of the loud, unrestrained, head-banging music and getting bounced around by sweaty, stoned people who are rude and tactless. This coming from a guy who gets shamefully drunk and pukes all over himself and whatever is in his path.

Despite the fact they can't even hear themselves think over the din of the ear-splitting music, they make fruitless attempts at conversation. Matthew's heart was racing. He noticed his friend Nicole, totally out of it, holding onto some guy who was keeping her from falling onto the floor. He was positive this was the work of a diet of extensive amounts of Quaaludes. He chooses not to make his presence known. Better to keep clear of her when she's nearly unconscious. Besides, she probably wouldn't have any idea who he was—or, by the looks of her condition, where she was.

Matthew leaves their small group and heads for the edge of the crowd to scan the room. Without appearing biased, he had to admit they were, without a doubt, the best-dressed people in the auditorium. Even better than Morrison and the other Doors. People are actually staring at them, because they were so together fashion-wise. Either that, or they looked like total freaks. When there was any kind of break in the action, fans would approach one of them for apparel information, like they were living/breathing mannequins.

"Where did you get those far-out threads?" was the call of the wild from some stoner, her enlarged pupils larger than the Doors drummer John Densmore's cymbals. Here's the brilliance of Michele Newhouse: she was smart enough to bring a stack of business cards.

People clamored around Michele, nearly crushing her to get a card, as if it was a backstage pass to hang out with the Lizard King. Hey, if half the people who took a card came into the store, it would pay off. And if half those people bought something, it'd be worth the lofty price they had to spring for six tickets.

Jazzed that Michele had the foresight to think of bringing business cards, Chris got carried away and kissed her to show his gratitude. This took her by surprise. She quickly withdrew and broke away from the kiss, wiping her mouth with the back of her hand. Whoa, that was weird and Chris knew it. He apologizes for his boldness.

"Look, I got carried away," he says. "It was wrong of me. I overreacted. I'm usually not this forward or stupid. Sorry."

Elaine rescues her, slipping her arm through Michele's for moral support. "Apology accepted," Elaine remarks, "but let's not forget, she has a boyfriend. She is committed to another guy."

Chris nods his head vigorously. "Yeah, thanks, I needed that reminder."

Michele and Elaine exchange knowing looks. There's a pause, an overpowering silence just between them.

Someone interrupts the girls' private reverie and passes them a hash pipe. They each take a long hit. You can hear the smoke creak in Michele's chest. This was her first time with hash. It took immediate effect because unbeknownst to them it was blended with cocaine. The girls didn't seem to be bothered by it and took another hit before passing it back. While Chris is witnessing this sharp intake of hashish, the girls give each other an exuberant high five, then a quick kiss on the lips. Chris reacts big.

"Excuse me, what the hell was that all about?" he says, almost choking on his own spit. Michele's reaction time is slow. Elaine seizes the moment and takes control.

"We're floating on whatever that was handed to us from perfect strangers, and have no control or recollection of what we're doing or saying," she says convincingly.

Michele agrees with her assessment. "Drugs have a way of altering your inner consciousness. By the way, I love working for you. You're the best boss. Just an honest observation."

He thanks her for the compliment, then tells both of them that they're doing a bitchen job, then moves off and joins Matthew, who is still standing on the perimeter of the crowd.

The girls smile and turn their attention back to the stage. Elaine slips her hand through Michele's fingers and says flirtatiously, "You never know, maybe later you may get lucky."

"God, I hope so," Michele murmurs hornily.

After the third encore, performing "The Celebration Of The Lizard," they lost Jon and Ronny in the crowd somewhere. They took off to hunt down and surely score with a couple of diehard groupies. By now Jon was hanging by a thread as far as his marriage to Matthew's sister, Patti, was concerned. He was dead meat, but he didn't seem to care. Matthew knows firsthand how tough it is to maintain a stable marriage. He doesn't take sides; neither does he blame either of them for what seems to be the end. If anything was to blame, it was the concept of *free love* in this extremely liberal generation.

After the concert, they are heading out when one of Morrison's roadies approaches them. Slender kid, long hair, tattoos up and down his arm, pasty. Probably has no idea what the sun looks like—only seen it in pictures or through the window of the tour bus as it rhythmically rolls through town after town to the next gig. Seems Morrison had heard all the commotion about their store and wanted to come in after hours sometime.

"Fuck yes," Matthew says as cool and calm as he can without seeming like an overanxious pimply teenybopper.

"What a great fuckin' stroke of luck," Chris enthuses. "The Doors in our pants! That could make a clever ad campaign slogan." Matthew doesn't hear him. His attention is focused on some groupie chick giving the drummer head behind the cyclorama.

While Michele hands Morrison's roadie a couple cards, and sets up the Lizard King's visit to the store, they continue their mission, looking for Jon and Ronny, who they heard had somehow wangled their way backstage. They caught up with them just as they were brokering a drug deal with the band and some of the backstage crew. They played it close to the vest, trying not to be blatant, out-in-the-open pushers. But as far as Chris and Matthew were concerned, it was obvious and fucking transparent. They turned their backs to the truth—decided to let it slide for now, thinking maybe they were overreacting and being mistrustful since Matthew and Chris were both under the influence of Acapulco Gold and hash. On the ride home, Jon plays it loose and vague.

"Before you cross-examine me, we just exchanged a few joints for an autographed album Morrison's going to send me," Jon claims.

Matthew didn't buy the excuse, but he also didn't question Jon's bald-faced lie. Despite that unsavory drug deal, the concert was a mind-blowing experience they'll all carry with them the rest of their lives.

Matthew fell asleep that night with an annoying ringing in his ears from standing too close to the amps, and "Break On Through (To the Other Side)"—repeating in his brain till he fell asleep while bobbing his head on the pillow.

§

Handing out business cards really paid off. They spent the next week moving lots of merchandise and building an amazing new clientele. The latest growth spurt for the entrepreneurs was a shoe store they opened next door called Acme Shoe Emporium. Chris and Matthew had gone into partnership with another friend, Gary Frankel, an overweight guy with a talent for eating an entire rump roast in one sitting. He wasn't the most attractive person on the dance floor, so girls weren't exactly throwing their room keys in his direction. Since his social life wasn't going great guns, he spent most of his leisure hours alone in the dark, hatching up ways to bilk people. He and Sage would've made a good villainous team. But he was a superstar when it came to business. He had a knack for starting out with a single idea and producing excellent results, always turning a profit.

Just like their lack of knowledge in the clothing business, this was another area they went into totally blind. They knew shoes went on your feet and came in different sizes and grains of leather. Beyond that rudimentary knowledge they knew bupkis. They again counted on their fashion instincts to order stock. San Remo boots and an assortment of platform shoes for both men and women became an upward trend almost overnight.

§

Two weeks drift by. It was a morning just an hour after sunrise, when Matthew discovers Jon in the parking lot sleeping in his car. He knocks hard on the window. Jon flinches awake.

"What's going on," Matthew asks through the glass. Jon keeps the window rolled up.

"I left. Patti and I finally slammed the door on the marriage. It was only a matter of time, and the time was last night after she threw a stack of glossies in my face."

"I need more than just glossies."

"Photos of me with some naked chick doing a line of coke on her stomach. She had me followed. Caught. I had no excuse."

"Sorry to hear that, Jon, but let's be honest, you've been fucking around on her for a long, long time. She must've had a whole album of salacious photos."

"It's too early for me to ponder the definition of *salacious*, but I'm guessing it's not good."

"Not worth trying to save the marriage?"

"You know how that goes, man. Chicks get it in their heads you're unfaithful, they want nothing to do with you. They're packing your suitcase and showing you the door."

Jon climbs out of the car. They both head into the store. You can never tell by his facial expressions if Jon Lewis is being sincere, but he apologizes to Matthew for his unconscionable conduct and promises to help Patti out financially if she needs more that she's getting out of the divorce. There is a pause during which neither of them knows what else to say. Jon ultimately breaks the awkward silence.

"Look, the last thing I want is for us to have issues," he says. "I hope we're cool, man."

"I'm not cool with my sister being heartbroken," Matthew replies, "but somehow we'll get past this. We have to. We have a business to run. A suggestion—don't get married again until you're sure your wife's stomach is the only one you want to snort coke off of. Just sayin'."

§

Friday night. The Old World Restaurant. Matthew is driving through Hollywood on his way to take Nicole Benson to dinner. For the record, they were no longer intimate but when he heard she cleaned up her act and got an auspicious and challenging position at a popular teen magazine, he took her out to celebrate. She deserved at least some recognition for her efforts from somebody. She had burned a lot of bridges during her highly drug-induced days.

At the table, Nicole was unduly fidgety. They hadn't been sitting for more than ten minutes when she began to play with her fork, stabbing the prongs in her hand over and over like her palm was a baked potato. Matthew thought she was about to puncture a vein and spill blood all over the white tablecloth.

"You planning on eating with that fork or stabbing yourself to death?"

She looked up at him. Her eyes were nearly all pupil. This was not a good sign. He may have spoken too soon about her cleaning her act up.

"Not sure," she says.

"So, there's a chance you might stab yourself until you bleed out on the table?"

She stares at him. Her eyes look far away empty.

"Wow, that is one trippy visual, don't you think?" she says aimlessly.

"Trippy and deadly," Matthew observes mordantly.

"You gotta learn to lighten up, Matthew Street," she says right before her eyes roll back in her head and she passes out head first into her dinner salad.

Nicole appeared more of a wreck than ever. Truth be known, Matthew was pissed. She had promised him, "no drugs tonight." For a moment, he actually thought about just leaving her but that would've been cruel and unjust. Instead, he got help from the busboys, who carried her out to the car. Her eyes appeared to be welded shut. Her mascara now blended in with the salad dressing. She had taken on the look of a circus clown. He couldn't help feeling a sense of pity for her. No argument, Nicole was a good person. She never wanted to hurt anybody. She was lost in a world and a lifestyle she only knew one way how to handle, through drugs. People were staring, whispering how sad and pathetic it was as this scene played out. Matthew was embarrassed—for her, not himself.

It was a good half hour before he pulled up to her curb in front of her apartment. She was still out of it. Of course carrying her limp body to the door was going to be a daunting task. No busboys in sight. She still had salad dressing on her face and a couple croutons in her hair. She reeked of Roquefort. The inside of his car smelled like a French cheese factory.

If you'd ever try slinging a person over your shoulder, you know it's difficult and cumbersome. Matthew nearly drops her while searching for her keys. He got her inside and gently lowered her onto the couch. He found a washcloth and cleaned up her face, removed the croutons from her hair, then threw a blanket over her. She would never remember how she got home or that she passed out head first into a bowl of lettuce. He left a note suggesting she try and cool the drugs for while, or the next time she may not be so lucky—and fall head first into a bowl of soup and drown.

CHAPTER 25

It's been three years. Jon's Drawer, along with Acme Shoe Emporium, was on an eventful roll. The team was bursting with pride after recording another sensational year of sales.

Today Matthew gets an unexpected visit from Linda Tarlow. He'd be lying if he said she didn't look superb. Pretty sure she just had her hair and makeup done. He's thinking, what's the occasion? Last time he saw her she was pregnant. This time she comes in like a runway model, with her three-year-old daughter, Kirby. So, she'd had a girl—a girl saddled with a weird, androgynous name. Linda gives him the same generous kiss hello as when she had last said goodbye. It bothers him because he feels she must want something. She does; this explains the makeover.

She pulls him aside out of earshot of her daughter. She opens up and tells him she's no longer with her nameless boyfriend, adding that he split two years ago and never took full responsibility for his kid, and that he's a fucking deadbeat piece-of-shit dad. Why did he have to hear this? Not his problem, and certainly none of his business, until the little girl speaks up like she had just been cued to express cuteness and innocence.

"Maybe you can be my daddy," she says, looking up at Matthew with her baby blues.

This plea coming from this adorable little girl would break anyone's heart. And it does. Heads turn. For a brief moment Matthew thinks he hears an *awww* being expressed around the world. This touches a nerve. He gives Linda an incredulous stare, waiting for her to jump in and explain the harsh reality to her daughter. Nothing. No comforting words. It was almost as if the kid was speaking on behalf of her mommy. As if this was rehearsed.

Matthew was actually offended. She stepped over the line. Matthew leans in close to Linda so that the kid doesn't hear that he can't and won't fill this void. She has a father who needs to step up and accept responsibility.

"You disappoint me, Linda," he says icily. "And by the way, spending a shitload of money on your hair made no difference in my decision not to be the kid's parent."

"Just so you know, I did not brief the kid. This was not a setup."

"Sure it was, and we both know it."

Having failed in her attempt to persuade Matthew to team up, she tries to give him one of her memorable goodbye kisses. He backs off.

"No more pseudo farewells," he says. He does, however, kneel down to Kirby's level and sets the record straight. She's only three, so who knows what wisdom he can administer that she'll actually grasp and understand. Matthew takes a deep breath, then levels with the tyke, like Ward Cleaver lecturing Wally and the Beaver about one of life's hard truths.

"Look, I'd loved to be your daddy, but you already have a daddy, and he wouldn't be happy if I took his place. Plus, who wants a daddy like me who doesn't know the first thing about parenting? A daddy who's never around because he's too busy with work and needs to deal with the pressures in his own life? Selfish, I know. But that's how it is. Know what I'm saying?" A long blank stare from the kid says it all. "No, of course not. That stuff I just said was way to convoluted for a three-year-old to understand, and I'm sure it went totally over your pretty little blonde head."

"Huh?" she says.

"Exactly my point. On the plus side, you have Olive, who is part of your family, right?"

With tears in her eyes, Kirby tells Matthew that Olive got killed when the dog was hit by a car. Upon hearing that devastating news, Matthew has no more to say. He looks up at Linda. "Sorry about Olive," he says with a crack in his voice.

The drama is almost too hard to bear. When he gives Kirby a hug goodbye, she tries one more time to persuade him to be her father. And one more time he has to pass, because he couldn't give her the attention she deserved. He couldn't teach her how to ride a bike or toss a ball. He might have laid it on too thick, but he was trying to make an effective point that would hit home more for Linda's benefit than the kid's.

This was the last Matthew Street ever saw of Linda Tarlow. But through the rumor mill he heard she moved to Las Vegas and became a cocktail waitress at one of the luxury hotels on the Strip.

§

As the store profited, Jon started spending more. Buying fancy cars—a Porsche, a Bentley. New furniture. Expensive jewelry, designer sunglasses, a Gucci wallet to house his cash. He got caught up in what Matthew called an overindulgence in material things. The need to buy, buy, buy.

Jon also made a new friend, who he met at the used car dealership—Bud Collins. Bud was also looking for a classic car, but the price was way too steep for his bank accountant. Bud was one of the few people in their circle of friends who wasn't a native of Palm Springs. His accent suggested Texas. He looked like an older version of Jack Bruce from the rock group Cream—but without the English accent and the talent to play guitar and sing. At first sight, he seemed like a genuine, unaffected guy. But Chris was wary. Chris was suspicious of everybody—including the fucking bagger at the Safeway Market—until they proved themselves trustworthy.

It wasn't long before Bud and Jon became real chummy. Close. Inseparable. They shared the same likes and dislikes. Smoked the same cigarette brand (Marlboro Reds), lusted after the same type of woman—any attractive blonde or brunette who would lay down for them—loved the jazz scene, hated the movie *Love Story*, and despised that *Saturday Night Fever* disco crap that took over the nation like a plague. And this was just after only two weeks of them palling around.

Okay, sure, admittedly Matthew wasn't suspicious of this Bud Collins at first. But Jon's obsession with him started making him nervous. His biggest doubt about Bud Collins was the fact he never wore any of their clothing. Bell-bottoms seemed to be beneath his sartorial preference. He dressed like he just stepped off a cattle drive—Tony Lama boots, snap button Western shirts, and Lee jeans. Carried his cash in a small wad in his front jean pocket and his pack of cigarettes inside his sock—this was a military-type custom,

Matthew observed. Makes you stop and wonder why Jon was even friendly with this dude. Maybe the sheer fact that he wasn't the norm was the attraction. Jon spent less and less time at the store and more and more time hanging with Bud Collins and Ronny Cooper. So far, it didn't seem to interfere with the day-to-day running of the business, so Matthew and Chris had no complaints. But it was a legitimate concern.

These guys were doing lots of drugs, and the last thing they wanted was a partner who couldn't function and was tripping over his tongue trying to explain the term Keystone to a customer who didn't give a shit about pricing a pair of pants.

Jon's fixation on being ostentatious rubbed off on Matthew. He found himself checking out a clean 1955 Rolls Royce on a consignment lot in Brentwood.

"Why a Rolls?" Chris wonders.

"Look, I'm having fun being extravagant," Matthew replies defensively. "It's a phase. It'll pass. And when it does, I'll trade it in for a bus pass."

Chris says wryly, "I get it. Some people get their kicks bowling."

The lot was selling the Rolls for an elderly lady whose husband had died inside the car. Sitting behind the wheel while in the garage, with his wrinkled, arthritic hands gripping the steering wheel. And he was dressed for the occasion in his best Brooks Brothers suit.

"How'd he die?" Matthew asks the dealer quizzically.

"Carbon monoxide emissions did the trick."

He didn't press for more. Didn't need to know why he had enough living with this old lady and used his precious car as a coffin.

"There's a Polaroid of the old guy in the glove box, as he took his last breath," the dealer says. "Took it himself."

"Not interested," Matthew says flatly. He didn't need the haunting apparition of this old man in the act of shuffling off his mortal coil.

The old bag wanted twenty-five hundred. They settled on seventeen-fifty. It had serious miles on it. The old guy must've driven from sunrise to sunset, just to avoid going home to this woman.

§

The shop, the clothing, and the era influenced people in all kinds of different ways. The impact was hard to make sense of in some cases. With the good came the destructive. The anti-Establishment versus the Establishment. Blue-collar, lunch pail-carrying workers as opposed to your white-collar, eat lunch at a bistro professional.

It is early morning when Sister Melinda Francis, from Saint Charles Borromeo School in North Hollywood, comes into browse. She's young, maybe twenty-nine, and wears a traditional habit. She wants a pair of bell-bottoms.

At first, Matthew thought someone was putting him on. This had to be a gag. She assured him it was no joke. He wanted her to swear to God but that would've been a little sacrilegious. She said she wanted to be a part of the 1970s cultural revolution. And in doing so, she planned to shed her habit for a pair of jeans. According to her, after the Second Vatican Council in 1960, many religious communities made the habit optional, limited its use, or stopped wearing it altogether. This reflected the signs of the times.

She went in the dressing room, took off her habit and tried on the jeans. It was like she was inside a confessional booth. Matthew was surprised that she even came out to check herself in the mirror. *Holy Mother of Jesus* was his private reaction. She had a terrific figure. She could thank God for that.

"Peace out," she remarked as she left the store, confident she was doing the Vatican proud.

Matthew was far from being a religious cat, but just to stay on the Catholic Church's good side, he gave her a big discount.

§

Sunday. They stay open until one o'clock. Trimmed hours for the working stiffs who need the weekend to do their errands. Shop. Escape the suffocated office environment.

It was four o'clock when Anne Fraser arrived for her photo shoot, wearing a short black dress, and leather boots. Professionally applied makeup augmented her already striking facial features. Her photographer, attractive in her own right, was female. She set up light stands with umbrella modifiers and reflectors. Very professional. Matthew slipped on Bob Dylan's *Blonde on Blonde* album to help set the mood. She started shooting randomly just to get into the right frame of mind. Click, click, click in rapid succession. Sexy was an understatement. Matthew watched with rapt attention, mesmerized by Anne's rapport with the camera. She knew what she wanted from herself, even though the photographer gave her direction. She tilts her head left, then right. Swings her hair from side to side. All the while, she's utilizing the shop's ambience in her favor.

Anne then perches herself on the barber chair, her legs spread apart, and swivels in a merry-go-round fashion. The first thing Matthew notices is not her random poses, but that she's not wearing underwear. Yet the photographer keeps shooting at various angles, zooming up her skirt. This seems odd to Matthew for a modeling portfolio. Anne goes with the flow. In fact, she pulls her dress up high above her thighs showing even more thigh. Was this for his benefit or were these shots intended to be used elsewhere? An adult magazine, maybe. He doesn't try to second-guess it. He collects himself, thinking maybe he's having another fantasy episode. If so, this is a sign that he needs to get professional help. This is getting way out of hand.

Then, without warning, she removes her top, flinging it across the room, all the while posing for the camera as it clicks away at her exposed torso. He'd be lying if he said this wasn't turning him on. She then crosses to Matthew and kisses him hard. He doesn't flinch as the photog moves in closer, snapping picture after picture, the lens almost touching their lips. Very artsy shot, he thinks. Not out loud because his mouth is busy.

She takes a breath, then asks, "Enjoying this?" He answers with an emphatic "yes." "It gets better," she promises, and removes her skirt. She is now totally naked except for her knee-high leather boots. He doesn't for a second budge because he's too involved with her physical attack on him from head to toe. This is a deviance every man should experience once in his life. If not twice.

Then she leans in and whispers in his ear: "I'm leaving for Israel on Monday, and I wanted us to have a memento of our time together."

The memento came in the form of some heavy-duty sex. They made love on the floor while her photographer, who must've been turned on herself, didn't miss a beat and kept capturing the moment, changing lenses as they did their thing. It was truly amazing. It felt like a dream, or that he was on an acid trip, it was so surreal.

They've been at it for over an hour and are pretty much drained of energy, but not tiring of each other. As they get dressed, Matthew suddenly smells the distinct odor of cigarette smoke wafting through the room. He looks over and notices the photographer, with a cigarette dangling from her lips. Even more perplexing, she too is naked, and is putting her clothes back on like she has just reached her own thrilling climax.

"I'll have the proofs ready for you in a week," she says, adding as she exits: "Oh, and nice meeting you." Thing is, they were never introduced.

It was doubtful Matthew would ever see Anne Fraser again. Her decision to visit Israel had been purposeful: in order to see her bedridden grandfather again before he died. But as soon as she crossed the border into Israel, she would be grabbed and forced to enlist in the Israeli Defense Forces.

§

Two weeks later an envelope is slipped under Matthew's door. It contained the photos. As Matthew examines them, he is reminded of one incredible sexual rendezvous. And then something catches his eye: a close-up shot of Anne's thigh bearing a tattoo of the Jon's Drawer logo. This was eerie and puzzling. How was this possible? Was it always there and he overlooked it? Or did the photographer somehow generate a sketch from his leg? Whatever the answer, the saga and mystery that surrounds Anne Fraser will baffle Matthew Street for years to come. He'd fallen hard for her, and lost all common sense in the swirl and storm of emotion before. Never this fast, however. He'd never been so overwhelmed by the driving force of a person. It spooked him, and he vowed to back off from any further romantic ties for a while.

§

But that pledge didn't last long. Two months later, he's on the road, having just picked up Tanya, the latest female in his life. As they drove down the boulevard, she gazed adoringly at him with her big, brown eyes as she snuggled her head into his shoulder and licked his face. She was a stunner. She should be: she was a four-year-old Afghan hound. Peering out the open car window with the wind flowing freely through her hair, like a model being shot in front of a large prop fan by a fashion photographer, she was quite an eyeful.

Matthew pulls up to the curb in front of Jon's Drawer, and his view suddenly changes from routine to extraordinary. Standing outside was the most amazing-looking blonde girl. Sitting obediently next to her was a gray Afghan. He had to meet her. The girl, not the dog. Okay, so with Linda and Nicole being ancient history, and Anne Fraser for the most part an untouchable in another country, it would be careless of him to pass up this opportunity. What an incredible twist of fate! She could be "the one." Although, to be perfectly honest, he wasn't looking for "the one." A companion? Maybe. A girlfriend? Not really. A steady sexual partner? Sounds like an extraordinary plan but not a priority.

With Tanya by his side, and his heart thumping, he tries to speak without mispronouncing the word "hi." He gets no response, only a nod. He tries another tactic: playing on their obvious similarities.

"Very cool dog. I'm well-known as a mega fan of that breed," he says.

Now came an even longer pause. Wow. He couldn't even get a smirk out of her. It was apparent she wasn't interested in his dog, him, or his dry humor. Or maybe the word "mega" threw her.

"Well, nice talking to you," he says with a tinge of sarcasm. As he turns and heads into the store, he hears a quiet murmur.

"I don't speak English," she says in a very unfamiliar accent. It wasn't French, German, Spanish, Russian, or anything he recognized. Not that he's a person skilled in foreign languages. He asks where she is from. She just shrugs as if she doesn't know where she came from. He gives up, throwing a *ciao* over his shoulder as he heads for the front door.

And then another unexpected twist—her friend comes out of the store. He had just made a purchase and must've overheard his attempt at trying to strike up a friendly conversation.

"She's not European, if that's what you're wondering," he says.

"Oh, okay," says Matthew. "Hey, I'm sorry, I didn't know she was your girlfriend."

The guy laughs. "We're not a couple," he says. "I'm gay, you see. My name's Jeffrey, by the way."

Matthew was already beginning to gather that from his mannerisms and flamboyant attire.

"I'm Matthew," he says. "I'm trying to get her to understand me."

Jeffrey then starts to talk to her—in sign language.

Matthew looks her straight in the face and declares, admittedly rather rudely, "Holy crap, you're deaf."

She clears her throat like she's about to speak but then signs to Jeffrey: "Tell him I'm a mega fan too." Jeffrey translates, then reveals she can read lips if you look directly at her. Which Matthew does. This time he clears his throat and speaks slowly and distinctly.

"Why did you tell me you didn't speak English?" Matthew asks.

She signs to Jeffrey. It takes a while because she has a lot to say.

Jeffrey translates: "She speaks English, just not well enough for most people to understand her, so rather than make it difficult she chooses to not say anything."

Matthew makes sure he's looking directly at her when he says, "I get it. No big deal."

She signs to Jeffrey again, her fingers flying at Mach speed. He again translates for Matthew's benefit.

"She says she knew you were interested in her, and it's frustrating for a deaf person who doesn't speak very fluently to shy away from hearing people. Makes it hard to form relationships."

Matthew turns back to her and says: "I'd like to take you for coffee or waffles or just walk our dogs together in the park and watch them pee on the same tree. Jeffrey is more than welcome to chaperone."

She looks at Matthew, her face as blank as a sheet of paper. He again turns to Jeffrey for help.

"You think maybe my choice of words was a little bit too acerbic?" Matthew says. "Talking about peeing on a tree may have crossed over the line."

Jeffrey raises his hands in the air as if to say leave him out of this, you're on your own. She then speaks in her own voice. Not close to being normal. Sort of nasally. But it didn't matter; she made the effort to actually speak, even though she felt uncomfortable. This was a big step, and Matthew knew it.

"Okay. Coffee. But no Jeffrey. Let him find his own tree to pee on."

He was rocked by her sense of humor. Everything about her intrigued him. He played it cautious—didn't want to push it. He almost didn't get her name—Heather Wilcox. His newest friend. She lived at home with her parents and her precious dog. He never got the dog's name. But he did get that it was a hearing guide dog—trained to alert Heather to household sounds that are necessary for safety and independence. These dogs are trained to make physical contact and lead their person to the source of the sound. An alarm. The harsh blare of a whistling teakettle. Someone screaming *help*.

Matthew found this amazing. Crap, his dog only responded when she heard a can of dog food being opened, the jangle of car keys, or the word *walk* found its way into a conversation.

CHAPTER 26

Drugs and denim, Matthew observes trenchantly, are an unlikely combination.

Jon is handling the cash register, making a sale to a young couple no more than nineteen or twenty. They look like they just returned from a Summer of Love festival in Griffith Park. Both were glassy-eyed, clearly high. They were huddled up against each other, looking haggard and sexy the way young people can look for a little while, until they just look haggard. The girl's hands were shaking. Maybe jacked on meth or coming down from a bad trip. Hard to tell. Matthew was not an expert on adverse drug symptoms.

After Jon wraps up the sale of over two hundred in cash, he pulls them into the back room while Matthew watches the front. He hasn't a clue what was about to go down. Jon whispers so as to not draw attention.

"Listen, you guys seem like cool people who could use a little, you know, boost. I'm just the guy who can help you settle the nerves, if you catch my drift."

"Yeah, we're a little strung out," the kid says while his girl continues to shake. "We've been on liquid oral analgesic, toothache medicine, for two days, and it's not cutting it."

"Tough. I feel for you. It's strictly a cash deal."

The girl nervously tugs on her boyfriend's shirtsleeve. She looks desperate. Jon kneels down next to the water heater. From underneath a Persian rug he removes a couple loose bricks in the floor and takes out two cellophane baggies.

"You interested?" Jon says, dangling the drugs enticingly.

"Coke?" the kid asks.

Jon shakes his head. "I've got coke, weed, ludes. This is ground heroin."

"I've never had it," the girl says.

"I have. It's just what we need," the kid says. "How much?"

"Thirty dollars will get you 1.5 grams. If you're a steady user, it'll get you through two to three days," Jon says.

Without missing a beat, the kid pulls out a wad from his jacket pocket. Some of the bills spill onto the floor. He doesn't bother to pick it up, but the girlfriend does. They just spent two hundred on clothes. You have to figure either he sold his Fender Telecaster or robbed his grandmother's gravesite for the jewels she was buried with. This is a common practice with addicts, desperately robbing family graves for drug money.

"Here's sixty," he says, handing Jon three twenties.

Jon takes the cash, then grabs an English T-shirt off the pile, wraps the heroin around it, then stashes it into the Jon's Drawer shopping bag like it was part of the sale.

"The T-shirt is on me. Tell your friends to ask for Mark Twain, if they're interested in scoring really primo narcotic." He adds emphatically: "Just be very cool and cautious about it." Jon, obviously covering anything that could be traced back to him, always used a pseudonym in these transactions. He changed his name every few months just to be on the overly paranoid safe side.

At this point the guys were totally in the dark that Jon had been actively selling drugs and paraphernalia out of the store, his car, and at home for a good six months—maybe longer. It soon became very apparent that he was making a lot more money than Chris or Matthew pushing something, and it wasn't hip apparel. Prime example—Jon would take these regular trips to Vegas, sometimes with Bud, but mostly with Ronny. They'd splurge on hookers, bet on sporting events, and spread cash around like it was Monopoly money. And of course, they snorted cocaine off fancy glass coffee tables in deluxe hotel suites. These guys were virtually and literally living the high life.

§

Vegas. Sin City. Jon is at the Flamingo Hotel & Casino where he's losing his ass at the crap tables. The room is filled with cigarette smoke that wafts in the air like a dense fog rolling in off San Francisco Bay. As Jon places another large bet, a friendly cocktail waitress in a sexy outfit serves him a complimentary drink. He's oblivious she slid up to him as he's in another zone, absorbed with the little red cubes he holds between his fingers, mentally trying to direct them to show mercy and not come up seven. He desperately needs to roll an eight—his number. He has three thousand dollars riding on it. The players surrounding the table urge him to go for it. The noise is deafening. His luck has been putrid, so he asks the waitress to blow on the dice, hoping it will change his fate. She accommodates him with a gentle puff.

Jon tosses the dice across the table, letting them glide to the other end where they ricochet off the pyramid bumper rubber and stop dead in their tracks near the come line. The silence takes on kind of an intelligence as one die is still spinning, waiting to land on it's back. It's a four; the other die is also a four, too. He's rolled a hard eight—he's a fucking winner! The other players erupt in a deafening congratulatory roar. Jon looks to heaven, as though God had something to do with it. He then turns to the waitress, kisses her hard on the lips, then hands her a hundred dollar chip for her magical "blow job." She is stunned—not by the kiss or the generous tip, but by the fact she recognizes Jon Lewis from an old memory.

"This is fucking unreal," she says.

"Yes it is," he says. "You are my good luck charm. Do not move from my side as long as I'm in Las Vegas."

"Jon, it's me, Linda Tarlow."

Jon, clearly being a smack too high, does not recognize the name, nor does the face look familiar.

"Sorry, sweetheart, but I've drawn a blank," he says.

"I dated Matthew Street for a brief moment," she persists.

This did not jog his memory. And truthfully, this girl didn't look like someone Matthew would go for. Matthew had a type and she wasn't it. Her makeup was heavily applied to hide the deep lines usually associated with heavy drug users. But to be nice, he makes it seem they're old friends.

"Yeah, right Linda. You gotta excuse me, I've been at this table going on six hours straight trying to win back the five grand I dumped."

She smiles and says confidently, "So, let's win it back."

He thought, was this a ploy? Was she a shill to entice patrons to drop more money? Didn't matter—he was going for it.

Since there are no visible clocks in Vegas, it was hard to say if it was just two hours later or two days, but either way Linda was still by his side while Jon raked in another twenty-five hundred. Appreciative, he buys her breakfast and learns her life had spun out of control ever since she crossed the Nevada state line over a year ago. Desperate for attention and someone to help provide for her kid, she hooked up with a dealer from the MGM Grand. This was a mistake because he was a loser in more ways than one. A heavy gambler himself, he'd lose his paycheck, always trying to double it at the gaming tables. Unfortunately, her take-home pay didn't cover their expenses. They shared rent, food, childcare, and a hefty addiction of cocaine and amphetamines. Jon's first impressions were spot on, thinking she was a serious user.

A waitress comes over and tops off their coffee. Attractive. Thin. She has dark hair, sky blue eyes, a flower petal mouth—the sort of chick who most men would pay top dollar to fuck because she looked sweet and had that innocent, virginal look. Thing is, she's primarily a dancer hoping to catch her big break as a showgirl in a top Vegas review.

She knows Linda. They exchange a friendly hello and some insignificant chitchat about how she's been on her feet for six straight hours. Linda then introduces Jon. Jon nods politely. He looks wiped out, like an unmade bed, and is not in the mood to have a conversation about feet.

Linda casually reaches inside her purse for a small envelope the size of a pack of cigarettes and slides it surreptitiously over to the girl. She in turn slips her a ten-spot. After the dancer/waitress leaves, Linda explains to a curious Jon that it was six Fenphedra diet pills.

"I have a little side business. Diet pills, Quaaludes, uppers, downers, Tinas, Lucys, Aimies. It's small-time but it helps pay the bills."

"Who's your source?" Jon asks. "Don't need a name, just an idea of his or her skill set. Local, out of town? Italian, Jewish, Mexican, Polish, Russian?"

"None of the above. Some pimply-faced kid who delivers for a local drugstore in town. I pay him 10 percent of the gross."

Jon saw an opening and could not pass up a chance to be her main Vegas supplier. She listens with rapt attention as he runs down the full gamut of his menu, his cost, and the password—Mark Twain. She's stoked. They make a deal on a handshake and a kiss. It was a profitable connection for both of them. The crazy thing was, Jon could never remember Linda from the store or her ever dating Matthew. But he kept his memory skid to himself so as not to hurt her feelings or damage their new working relationship.

By the time Jon leaves Vegas, he has won back his original five grand, plus another three. His friend Ronny has made some important contacts, promising to ship a good amount of high-grade weed to some guy working out of a trailer park in North Las Vegas. Jon never mentions the Linda Tarlow sighting to Matthew for obvious reasons. No sense opening up a fresh can of worms that is likely to have a negative outcome on everyone and rock the drug boat.

§

Deep in the San Fernando Valley, an unfortunate power move was about to be played. Logan's father, James, was cutting off his lifeline. That generous allowance was on its way out. They wanted him to get a job and see how the blue-collar working class lives. Learn some responsibility. No more sponging off mater and pater. His dad did, however, give him a job at his stereo plant. An entry-level position in the shipping department working alongside—and coexisting with—the other grunts. He could live at home and pay minimal rent. This was a wake-up call for Logan Alexander, who was twenty-three at the time and not ready to spread his wings and fly far from the nest.

It also rattled Matthew's world and would change his monetary value system. His incredibly small monthly rent payment would come to an abrupt end, forcing him to find other accommodations. Hopefully not the back seat of his car or a park bench. To be honest, he was ready to go solo. There were too many weekends he would stagger home and find Logan and some bizarre chick, usually a barfly, spread-eagle on the kitchen table.

Figuring it's always good to have somebody else's unbiased opinion, Matthew asks Chris to tag along in his search for new digs. Most apartments they checked out were totally tasteless. No character. Paper thin walls, cottage cheese ceilings, ugly shag carpeting, faux wooden blinds from another era, and closets the size of fucking gym lockers. He needed something with personality, something to whip up his creative juices, and of course, something not outrageously priced.

It was right after they checked out the third or fourth apartment that Chris decides to open up and share the fact that Michele Newhouse finally agreed to go out with him. His persistence paid off, he says. Matthew, of course, was blown away. Chris, on the other hand, didn't seem that thrilled. What's the deal with that? The guy had been pining over her for months, for Chrissakes. She was the center of his fucking universe. Something was not copacetic.

"Talk to me, man—what's bothering you?" Matthew says.

Chris speaks in a hushed tone, as if he's spilling trade secrets and there's a tape recorder hidden under the dashboard.

"Why don't you see me throwing confetti? Here's the thing. I'm a person who loves the chase, and once I cross the finish line, so ends the thrill of victory. It's sort of anticlimactic. A sad commentary, I realize, but it's how I'm wired. I push and push and push, then when I win, I back down. Am I a bad person for feeling this way? Maybe. Maybe not. Probably. Yes. A shit-heel."

Matthew never knew this about Christopher Styles. The Chris he knows is not that shallow. He would never put a girl on a pedestal just to knock her off.

"You're bullshitting me, right?" Matthew says. "This is you being cute and cynical, right?"

Chris explains his fucked-up theory in detail. In the event he senses he's about to be dumped, this is his way of taking control, and saving his self-esteem—pouncing on their ego before they destroy his. This was more than a theory; it was a neurosis that needed to be closely looked at by a shrink, in a controlled environment like group therapy. This was his defense mechanism: mowing down people before they chop him to bits. From what Matthew could gather, Chris was always anticipating when the tide would turn on him and he would drown in a whirlpool of self-absorbed unhappiness when he's told to take a hike. Constantly has his guard up. Who lives this way?

Matthew, having heard enough, takes him home. The kicker is, Chris tells him he's seeing Michele that night but is thinking of canceling the date. Out of fear, he says. Did he feel this same way about the Jewish girl, Susan Greene? No, he says. Because in his mind, losing her would not be psychologically harmful to his ego. Matthew wasn't about to try and understand his fucked-up set of principles. It's his theory that getting the heave-ho by a nice Jewish girl was something he could handle emotionally—as opposed to getting dumped by a Gentile, which he saw as a fate worse than death. No way could Matthew even begin to try and understand this insane ideology.

§

The next day, Matthew gets lucky and finds a pad that suited his aesthetics—his artistic temperament. A cabin-like, one bedroom dwelling. The walls were covered in dark knotty pine. Slanted beam ceilings. Fireplace. Hidden behind and surrounded by large sycamore trees that gave the impression you were living in Lake Tahoe, but without the lake. Picturesque. Quaint. Dark. Private. It was his own little getaway from the concrete jungle and the bullshit of world affairs and foreign policy issues. Four of his other close friends all lived in this oasis off of Burbank Boulevard in this typically obscure neighborhood of North Hollywood. Very convenient. It was a fortress against any disturbance, and the sound of the nearby freeway hummed you to sleep like ocean waves.

On his fifth night, he and Heather were in bed, making out, with George Harrison's *All Things Must Pass* album on repeat. They'd lost count of how many times the arm had reached the end of the record, and the needle made that scratching sound, before it started again.

They'd been at the kissing, touching, dry humping, and oral stages of their relationship for a good month. They had not reached actual intercourse. Every time they'd get close, they'd stop. Actually, he would stop. He was the one who stepped on the brakes and decelerated.

It was getting frustrating for both of them. Heather was a virgin. He would be her first, and she was a little naive about what to do birth control-wise. He, of course, recommended a condom but she wasn't in favor of it.

"No," she says. "I want to make love the way it was meant to be—with a natural naked penis that's been circumcised."

Whoa. Matthew wasn't about to instruct her on the virtues of safe sex. This wasn't his call. Desperate times call for desperate measures.

MATERIAL THINGS

The very next night they go see her parents. Mainly his idea. The anxiety floods him, suffocating him from inside.

He pulls into her parents' driveway. The house is your typical California ranch style. Tree in the front yard that could have once accommodated a tire swing. Or not. She noticed his apprehension.

"You okay?" she asks gently.

He shrugs. "I'll be fine." In truth, he was a fucking wreck. His throat felt tight. He could hardly form spit.

"Just be sincere and to the point," she instructs him. "Try not to use the word vagina or pussy." She was attempting to make him more at ease with her droll humor. It didn't work.

They walked up to the front door. She held his hand tightly. It wasn't too late to turn back. Of course, that would mean they'd never have sex and the relationship would eventually lose its momentum and die a slow death, never getting past the dry humping stage.

The night before and on the way over Matthew had rehearsed what he planned to say. Straight and to the point. No speaking vaguely or euphemistically. Everything was good until they went inside and his brain suddenly stalled. He stammered and tripped over his own tongue, but finally got up the courage to speak. But what came out was off subject. He complimented them on their furniture and the interior color of the walls. He wasn't honest. They had no taste. The furniture was dreary. The drapes were as dull as dishwater. Why was he privately criticizing their obvious lack of color and design knowledge? Should he say something? Of course not. It would be rude and offensive. But maybe they would appreciate his creative input. His heart was now beating out of control. He was positive it was loud enough for them to hear through his shirt. Relax, he tells himself. He's only asking for permission to sleep with their daughter, not for her kidney.

Finally, he takes several deep breaths and gets to the point. He speaks slowly and deliberately, as if they were deaf too.

"Mr. and Mrs. Wilcox, I …" Suddenly feeling a residual spasm of uneasiness, he pauses. He grabs Heather's hand for support, and also to make the moment feel more romantic and less sordid.

"Heather and I share this really special relationship. We're at a stage where we plan to have, you know, sex. We both want to be mature, responsible people, so I believe it would be a smart idea, and in our best interest, if we—if *you*—give her some peace of mind. I'm talking birth control pills."

He waits for their reaction. He expects at least a look of shock, a gasp, an incredulous "what?!" But he gets relief instead. A sigh that seems to last for twenty minutes. They had anticipated this day and were going to mention it to Heather themselves. Mr. and Mrs. Wilcox give them their blessing to fuck. Matthew's words, not theirs. But that's why they were there, to give his penis the go-ahead. Mission accomplished.

Matthew had done his job. A deep comfort flows through him. He can't wait to get out of there and breathe again. But since they had just established their sexual relationship, Heather's parents feel the need to invite him to dinner to commemorate the occasion. Who does that? They do. Their little girl is growing up. But Matthew passes on the invitation, revealing he has made plans to take Heather to this new jazz restaurant in Studio City called The Baked Potato. Then it occurs to him, as he's telling her parents this, what a moronic slip-up. She can't hear. But they are quick to point out that she can still eat a potato and feel the vibrations of the music.

After they leave, Heather praises Matthew for not using sign language to illustrate two people fucking.

CHAPTER 27

The Baked Potato. The cigarette smoke, along with the red lighting, seemed to drift through the claustrophobic nightclub like a blanket of scarlet fog. Heather looked outrageous. Matthew was proud to have her on his arm. The Don Randi Trio was on the bill. They were seated close to the front. Matthew had no idea why they got such special treatment, until he realized the manager was a big fan of Jon's Drawer, decked out in a double-breasted brown bell-bottom suit and a paisley neckerchief.

He could tell that Heather was both excited and a little on edge. He was sure this environment was new to her. After the first set, Heather goes to the bathroom. He crosses to the tip jar on the piano and drops in a few bucks, along with a business card. He notices another card. A Jon's Drawer card. Jon is here. Matthew scans the room like a sniper but doesn't spot him. He lets it go for now when harsh cry from the back of the room pierces the din—"I don't speak fucking English!" It's Heather's distinctive nasally voice.

Matthew rushes to her rescue, nearly colliding with another guy. He's so absorbed in getting to Heather, he doesn't realize it's Jon's friend Ronny Cooper, the drug dealer. It's unclear if he recognizes Matthew, but at the time it doesn't matter.

When Matthew arrives in the back, he knows what to expect. Some drunk is trying to put the make on Heather. He thinks she's a stuck-up bitch because she didn't respond to his come-on and called her out on it.

It wasn't that Matthew didn't want to stick up for Heather and punch this guy. He just didn't want to have to explain that she's deaf. That would have been humiliating—make her feel small and insignificant. This was something else he had to learn to deal with—people misunderstanding her, and him having to step in and rectify the situation without incident or embarrassment. This relationship was proving to be difficult but if he was in it for the long haul, he needed to take the good with the complex.

He managed to pry this guy off her without a skirmish. Told him that she was a refugee from Budapest who just got off the boat last week and is still trying to adapt to American customs and values. That she hasn't learned to distinguish a gentleman from a prick. This guy was so drunk he had no idea Matthew had just insulted him. Heather smiled, appreciating that he came to her rescue.

That ended their night of live jazz music at The Baked Potato. Matthew drove Heather back to her parents' house, where she felt safe and protected by the menagerie of stuffed animals decorating her bedroom. Did he mention she was adopted? This is not a criticism but just some personal insight. Her birth mother had taken a daily dose of aspirin during the pregnancy, which caused the hearing defect.

They are both very quiet on most of the ride home.

"I had a good time tonight," she suddenly blurts out.

He's not really sure she meant that, but under the circumstances, you take what you can get from Heather Wilcox.

"We'll do it again soon," he says.

This prompted a gale of tension-breaking laughter, because they both knew going back was unlikely in the near future. But they decided to chalk it up to a memorable experience to write about in their diaries, if they had diaries—which they didn't.

Heather makes an absurd suggestion: "Maybe we should stop and buy diaries."

"No, we'll use our brains as our diaries," Matthew counters. "We'll make mental notes. That way your mother can never read your personal thoughts and question your raunchy sexual behavior."

She looks at him deadpan, then lowers her head and buries her nose in his crotch, not unlike Olive had done. But Heather's nose wasn't as cold and wet.

On the way home, two things were foremost in Matthew's mind: why was Jon's business card lying in the tip jar, and why was Ronny Cooper there? He's guessing these guys were not there for the sounds, but huddled in a smoky back room with the band, putting together a drug deal. He thought about going back to the restaurant and doing some covert investigating. What good would it do if he caught them in the act? None. So he went home and put this night behind him and filed it in his mental diary.

§

It's 1:30 when Matthew takes his dog out to pee on one of those sycamores. While he's watching Tanya do her business, his neighbor Gary Frankel comes out of his place. He couldn't sleep and he's gnawing on a turkey leg for a late night snack.

"How's it going with the deaf girl?" he asks. Keep in mind tact is something this dude does not possess. And Matthew wonders why he's always home alone cuddling up to a turkey leg.

"She has a name—Heather," Matthew says coolly.

"Okay. So, how's it going with the deaf girl— Heather?" Gary says, thinking that'll be a sufficient response to his fucking impertinence.

Anger pierces Matthew deep in his gut. He can only hope Gary chokes on that turkey leg, and the only person close by to perform the Heimlich maneuver is him, and he chooses to just watch him suffocate. Malicious? Yes. He's in no mood to save a life tonight.

§

The next morning there's a heavy drizzle. The streets are slick, which means every lousy driver who never should've been issued a license is on the road demonstrating their horrible skills. A person has to drive defensively in these conditions—to protect your vehicle from inattentive pricks that don't know which way to turn their wheels when they enter into a skid.

Such is the case when Matthew is suddenly read-ended while sitting at a stoplight. Pissed? Fuck yes. Practically foaming at the mouth, he leaps out of his car and angrily hurls his keys at this guy's windshield. A kid not more than nineteen or twenty slowly exits his car in fear. His hands shake as he raises them in the air.

"My fault. Sorry. I fucked up," he says, his voice cracking. "I spaced out for a quick second."

Matthew, seeing how contrite—or high—the kid is, calms down and tells the kid to do the same.

"It's just a dent. No big deal," Matthew says. "Thank God no one got hurt."

"Yes, thank God. Are you a religious fanatic?" the kid asks.

"Me? Not really. For me, thanking God is just a knee-jerk reaction more than a religious edict."

They exchange information and it just so happens this kid, obviously high on something illegal and lethal, has no insurance but is willing to pay cash for the damages. They were no more than two blocks from the store and Matthew suggests they meet up and settle there.

"Small fucking world," the kid says. "I'm headed there myself. Going to do some business with Mark Twain."

Matthew cocks his head. "Mark Twain, the author?"

"No, the Mark Twain dude who has some righteous blow. I'm a regular customer."

"Can you describe this Mark Twain dude with the righteous blow?"

And then he proceeds to describe Jon down to his cigarette brand and even the Aramis cologne he wears. Matthew shows no emotion. Keeps a straight face. But inside he's fucking seething.

Not to attract any suspicion, Matthew decides to settle the damages with the kid on the spot. It's not really a bad ding. The kid gives him $150 in small bills—more than enough. His girlfriend is in the back seat. She slept through the whole ordeal, or had just OD'd on whatever they were sharing. Matthew prefers to think she was just napping.

Matthew then persuades the kid not to mention their little mishap. He tells him the car isn't his but in fact belongs to Mark Twain.

"Look, kid," says Matthew, "Mark Twain will be very annoyed if he finds out you fucked up his precious wheels, and the chances of you scoring any dope will not be in your favor."

"I dig what you're sayin', man. If I say anything, the word 'hush' will be the only thing expelled from these lips."

"Very well put."

This kid was obviously no rocket scientist but in his defense, Matthew got the feeling it wasn't his fault. He's guessing his parents are probably junkies and he followed in their footsteps. He was doomed at birth. You can't help but feel empathy for him.

Matthew got back in his car and drove slowly for the next two blocks. He was in a state of shock about Jon, feeling sick inside. He opened the window to get some fresh air. His head was spinning. He wanted to lie down anywhere that felt safe and secure and not in this country. He was just having an anxiety attack. It would pass. He knew he had to contact Chris and give him a full report. But how could he tell him that their suspicions were right—that the partner they've trusted the most was dealing drugs out of their store? He wasn't looking forward to that discussion, because he knew Chris's reaction was going to be rage and indignation, followed by prodigious puking.

Rather than calling Chris from the store, he stopped at a pay phone. Chris was working in Hollywood, so they decided to meet at the Denny's Restaurant at Sunset and Gower. A nondescript family place that never attracted anybody of importance. Safe and not at risk of a narc overhearing their conversation about Jon Lewis.

An hour later, they sit in a red Naugahyde-upholstered booth in the back, away from the windows and as far away from the sad, down-on-their-luck homeless people who ate there after begging for change on Sunset Boulevard. Who knows why they were so cautious, but they were, probably out of fear. It was their first time dealing with drugs other than the pharmacist at the Thrifty Drug Store.

"This is fucking surreal," says Chris. "We've associated ourselves with a drug dealer. A known pusher!"

Their waitress, a young girl with an over-bleached ponytail has chosen this emotionally-charged moment to refill their coffee. She looks at them with suspicious eyes, as she walks away to another table to serve her tasteless watery beverage to an obvious homeless man reading *The Wall Street Journal*. Later, he would use that same paper as a blanket to shield himself from the cold.

It was now very apparent—and totally unacceptable—how Jon was able to afford his opulent lifestyle. They agree his extracurricular activity was not great for business. If word got out that Jon was dealing, the store, plus their reputations, would suffer. More than suffer—their lives would be in the proverbial crapper.

They had done nothing to deserve this kind of treatment. Their friend took advantage of what they worked so hard to create. He'd used their success to gain his own power and fed it with his greed. They agree that they had to confront him and get to the bottom of this before they're implicated and arrested for illegal drug trafficking.

"Should I talk to him, or you?" Chris asks. "If it's me, I need to write something down. Make it smart, to the point, no dancing around what we're accusing him of. And not to worry if we hurt his damn feelings."

While it was obvious Chris was ready to send him to the gallows, Matthew suggests they just play the whole thing without causing a shitstorm.

"We need to get him alone, away from Ronny and his friend Bud Collins," Matthew says. "Those guys are fucking bad news influences. The idea is to get Jon to admit his transgression and tell us why he fucked us."

Chris, after some deliberation, agrees.

They left the waitress a bigger tip than the usual 15 percent. It was a subtle incentive in case she overheard their conversation and had the urge to tell the authorities of their drug connections.

As they walk out into the sunlight, feeling a sense of anxiety, they're confronted by the homeless man who was seated not far from their booth. He claims he overheard their entire drug conversation and threatens to blackmail them. It'll cost them ten thousand dollars in unmarked bills to keep his mouth shut.

"Whoa, old dude, you've got it all wrong," says Chris, thinking fast on his feet. "We're actors rehearsing our lines for a cop show."

The homeless dude cackles. "Bullshit! Cough up the dough or I go to the cops."

Matthew jumps in, waving some cash. "How about three dollars instead?"

The guy snatches the money from Matthew's hand like he was grabbing the gold ring on a merry-go-round. "This will do for now," he says, adding ominously: "But just to make you guys squirm a little, I have the name Jon ingrained in my mind."

The last they saw of him, he was walking down the sidewalk asking unsuspecting strangers for spare change.

"Think we need to worry about him?" Chris muses.

Matthew shrugs. "Maybe he'll die of exposure or get deadly food poisoning at Denny's."

As they walk to their cars, Chris decides to open up about his date with Michele. In a word, it was a bust. It never happened. At the last possible minute she got a sore throat and didn't want to subject him to the possibility of getting a streptococcal infection. Very considerate and convenient of her, Chris says, thinking it was just an excuse to blow him off.

"Probably for the best," Chris sighs. "I would've eventually been crushed, hurt, cast aside—totally rejected. I took a Xanax, masturbated, then went to bed."

Matthew shuddered. "More information than I needed to know."

CHAPTER 28

Matthew is face to face with Jon, standing so close he can almost smell his breath. Jon doesn't blink, just listens as Matthew, stony-faced, speaks in a stern but controlled manner.

"We realize this is an awkward position we're putting you in, but honestly, we don't give a flying fuck. We need answers. We deserve some explanation, man. A solid reason why you fucked us over. How you figured taking advantage of our friendship was okay."

Jon takes a much-needed breath, swallows hard, then exhales. "This is not easy for me to admit," he says.

Chris interjects with his own intensity. "Give it your best shot. And try not to insult us by thinking we're naive enough to believe you were in some sort of financial trouble. Like you had a gambling debt hanging over your head."

Jon's housekeeper, Anna, was vacuuming in the other room. This made Jon nervous, and although her English wasn't that terrific he shuts the door just to be on the safe side. He takes another deep breath before confessing.

"In all honesty, this whole drug thing gave me the opportunity to make a lot of fast cash. And it kind of spun out of control. I became the go-to pusher, and it was hard for me to stop."

"I'm curious, who got you started in this?" Chris asks.

Jon wrung his hands nervously. "That I can't say, and it's best you don't know."

"Ronny, I'm guessing. Never trusted that prick from day one," Matthew says. "He's a social pariah, if you want my biased opinion."

Jon continues his self-examination, almost mechanically. "For the moment let's forget Ronny, and concentrate on the why. Greed mostly. Popularity. I was fashionable in several areas. Clothing, drugs, and chicks. Chicks that wanted drugs and clothes. I ate up being in the spotlight. But I guess the biggest reason is I'm a pathetic addict myself. I got hooked on coke and other sundries. For me it was a free ride."

There's an awkward pause. "I've been at it a long time, long before the store. Long before my marriage to Patti," Jon admits, his voice heavy with regret.

"While you were my accountant at VIP?" Matthew asks. Jon just nods. Matthew just shakes his head. Chris gets incensed.

"So, I'm curious, when does it stop?" he demands. "If we're going to continue to be partners, it has to end. No fucking way can I sleep at night knowing this is happening under my nose. Knowing that some druggie is coming into buy a pair of jeans, with a special closeout sale on a gram of coke slipped in the back pocket."

There's another interruption as Anna the maid exits the bedroom and automatically starts dusting in the living room, where they are. This, of course, throws them off-balance, as they're still having a private conversation. Jon takes charge and leads her into the bathroom to clean next. As they go, the unexpected occurs when a nervous Anna brings up a personal issue.

"Don't forget, Mister Jon, that I needed the marijuana for *mi madre* with the cancer," she says as she hands him a ten-dollar bill.

Jon is caught off guard. The guys exchange stunned looks. Amazing, he's selling to his own maid. He assures her he hasn't forgotten and she'll have it before she leaves today. He then crosses back to the guys. His eyes register guilt and shame.

"I know. Not cool selling to my housekeeper. But in this case I'm doing a good thing. Her mother has cancer. Weed seems to help the pain. So don't criticize me for helping a sickly old woman."

The question is how many other sickly old women is he selling to? Maybe the entire population of local Salvadorian housekeepers.

"So, the bigger question remains, are you giving up this drug thing or what?" Matthew asks.

There is one of those long pauses where you know the answer is not going to be what you want to hear.

"Not just yet," Jon says. "I have a commitment to make to a friend. One last mission before calling it quits. One last major deal." He gives them his word, that this'll be his last push before he goes into retirement.

Matthew tries to measure this moment against others. It's one of the worst. About as awful as Andrea begging him to stay after she said she didn't trust him and that he was a lying, cheating pig. Relations have to be built on trust. No trust, he walks away and never looks back. This was definitely a no-look-back moment.

The guys see this as a no-win situation and are forced to present Jon with an ultimatum: give Anna the weed for her so-called sick mother, then hang it up, or else you're history. Out of the clothing business. A more significant issue to contemplate: if the authorities ever got wind of him dealing in the store, they'd somehow be implicated as accomplices running some sort of drug cartel and end up broke, with a record and jail time.

Jon agrees to these terms. Matthew and Chris are skeptical.

On the way home, Chris turns to Matthew. "Coffee?"

"I'll pass on the coffee and settle for a good criminal defense lawyer, and pray that Anna the maid wipes all our fingerprints clean in Jon's house."

§

3:00 a.m, in the Pavilions market parking lot, Sherman Oaks. An innocent enough neighborhood. Dimly lit. The lot is empty. Only a few stranded shopping carts are left behind. A small, plain white rental van creeps slowly into the lot and parks in the corner at a nearby tree that's naked of foliage. The engine idles for a few minutes, then shuts off, sputtering. There's no movement in the van, nor can we make out the driver. The window cranks down a little, then cigarette smoke drifts out from inside like a smoke signal coming from a bluff on the prairie. Two seconds later a butt is tossed out.

After a good ten minutes and another cigarette butt, a green '65 Mustang drives into the parking lot. It's not in the best of shape. It pulls up next to the van, where it maintains a steady idle.

After a brief moment, the driver of the van gets out. He's wearing a hooded sweatshirt, obviously to hide his identity. He goes to the side van door and waits. Then, as if on cue, the driver of the Mustang emerges. He wears a Yankees baseball cap. It's dark, and his head is down so he can't be recognized. A familiar voice cracks the air.

"Hey, bro, right on time," the van driver says in a friendly manner.

"It's fucking cold as ice. Let's do this fast, so I can go back to the warmth of my cramped studio apartment."

When they step out of the darkness and the shadows we recognize their faces. Jon Lewis and Bud Collins. They shake. Suddenly a pair of coyotes scamper across the parking lot at full speed. Not an unusual sight for these varmints to come down out of the local hills looking for breakfast. They ignore each other's presence. For some reason, maybe nerves, Jon decides to engage in small talk.

"Your Mustang. A '65? Nice."

"Yeah, '65. Piece of shit," says Bud, adding anxiously, "Let's get down to business."

Jon slides open the van door. Inside, Bud sees four very large Hefty trash bags, like black olives in a giant serving dish.

"I usually don't deal on this high a level, but you're an exception," Jon says. His promise to Matthew and Chris to quit pushing obviously didn't mean crap. Jon adds: "I can't stress enough how we need to keep this on the down-low."

"Not a word. I'm cool, man," Bud says. "So whaddaya got for me, quantity and dollars and cents wise?"

Jon goes into his seller's pitch. "Four Hefty bags filled with high-grade Columbian weed. Thirty dollars an ounce. Quarter pound goes for ninety. The entire package, street value, north of a hundred and seventy-five thousand. I spoke with my people and they're willing to let it go for seventy-five as we discussed, since you said you might be a regular customer."

"All sounds very cool to me. I'm jazzed."

Bud then reaches into his inside leather jacket pocket for an envelope of cash. As he does, Jon can plainly see that he's carrying a concealed weapon that rests in a shoulder holster.

"A gun. Wow. Nice touch," Jon says nervously.

"You never know when you might need protection," Bud says matter-of-factly.

"Protection from what?"

"The bad guys. The punks who want to steal your shit. Or worse, kill you for a lousy dime bag."

"Smart. Can't be too careful about the lunatics roaming the streets."

This was the last sentence Jon says before Bud whips out his credentials, revealing his true identity as an undercover narcotics officer and placing Jon under arrest for drug trafficking in Los Angeles, San Francisco, Orange County, and Barstow.

Jon, of course, is horrified. He turns a whiter shade of pale. At first he might have thought it was a big joke, but he knows better when Bud handcuffs him, then reads him his Miranda rights. Bud reveals that they, meaning the Feds, have been investigating his activities for over a year. About the same time Jon and Bud became friendly at the used car lot.

"Fuck. You're good at what you do, Bud. If that's your real name. Had me fooled."

"Names are insignificant at this point, Jon," Bud says.

He then jumps on his car radio and notifies a standby team that he's got the target in custody. Within seconds, two other unmarked DEA cars whip into the parking lot, lights flashing like a float in the Hollywood Christmas Parade.

They confiscate the evidence and impound the van. The last thing Jon says before they shove him in the backseat of an unmarked car seems appropriate: "I'd better get myself a good fucking defense lawyer." Then, under a shallow breath: "And where's fucking Barry Marcus when you need him? Underground in Burbank."

§

It was now 5:59 a.m.

There was the promise of a hot day, and the sun was rising behind the San Gabriel Mountains. They had no idea what Jon had just endured, but the phone rang off the hook, and woke Matthew from a deep sleep. It's his alarm company informing him that there has been a break-in at the store. It's actually just a recording so there was no way of talking to a live person, who was probably home in bed asleep like a normal human being. A casual response? No way. He leaps out of bed and wakes his neighbor Ritchie Barton, who he knows owns a gun. In case he needed protection from the thieves. What he didn't know is that Ritchie's idea of protection is a derringer the size of a deck of cards. Only two lousy bullets to defend themselves. Their adrenaline skyrockets. They have no idea what to expect. They could be met by nasty dudes with automatic weapons for all they know, and all they have is a cap gun. Matthew was hoping this was a false alarm. It's happened before. A couple rats somehow find their way into the store, have a party and trigger the sensors.

They were only ten minutes away from the store. Traffic was light—zero, actually. Matthew ran red lights and was driving like a fucking insane person. Nearly flipped over making a sharp turn. Remember, they're in a Rolls Royce—not exactly the best maneuvering car on the road. Calling the cops was not necessary. They would automatically get the same recorded message, as would Chris and Jon. Matthew could only hope they all made it there before the cops. They would need a key to get inside, or else have to resort to throwing a grenade through the window like it was an amphibious landing on the Anzio beachhead.

Matthew and his friend pull up to the curb. No sign of the cops, no sign of Chris or Jon.

Despite the lack of backup, Matthew and Ritchie decide to investigate themselves. Ritchie is brandishing his derringer like Doc Holliday. They move to the front window, shielding the sides of their temples to see inside better. A scary sight greets them: three guys wearing hooded sweatshirts stealing merchandise; a telltale hole in the roof reveals how they got inside. Matthew bangs on the window to distract them. It works. The thieves grab two sacks brimming with the merchandise they've swiped, leap atop the barber chair, and quickly climb back through the hole in the roof. From there they make their escape to the back parking lot.

Ritchie again tries to take control of the situation, shouting "Police! You're surrounded!" like he's Sam Spade from the classic noir flick *The Maltese Falcon*. This clichéd outburst was humiliating in front of the bad guys.

By now these douche bags have made it back to their car—a beat-up oxidized Ford pickup with a camper shell over the flatbed. No license plates. They burn rubber; the screeching echoes in the morning air like two alley cats having feral sex. The pickup turns the corner and hauls ass down Ventura Boulevard towards Laurel Canyon.

What possesses them, they haven't the vaguest idea, but Matthew and Ritchie chase after them as if they could easily scare them into throwing shirts and pants and leather jackets out the window. If they dare catch up with them, what's their plan? They had none. Then it occurs to Matthew, their destination could be fucking Mexico. No way was he going to Mexico to retrieve a pair of seven-dollar bell-bottoms that were made in Taiwan.

Ritchie is now shaking the derringer out the window, as if that's going to do any good. Ritchie, keep in mind, is this antsy/twitchy guy who can't sit still without the aid of a tranquilizer, or if someone ties him to a chair.

They look around to see if there's any sign of a cop. Nothing. Matthew backs off just to keep a safe distance. It occurs to him these guys could be really fucking dangerous junkies who needed to sell the clothes for drugs.

"Why we slowing down?" Ritchie asks.

"Strategy. Trying to remain aloof." Aloof? What did he mean by aloof? Like they're being antisocial?

Then up ahead they notice the windows being rolled down on the truck and a hand appears, holding a gun. They fire a shot at the Rolls. Ritchie fires back. His gun sounds like a firecracker. These robbers are not afraid. In fact, they suddenly make a U-turn in the middle of the street.

"Shit!" Ritchie yells. "Those motherfuckers are coming back after us!"

Try not to panic, Matthew says to himself. But it's hard not to be a little concerned when the people you are chasing decide to chase you with a cannon. Violence, mayhem, and bloodshed is inevitable. The scent of fear lingers in the air like a cheap perfume.

Matthew swings the car around and steps on the gas. He figures the safest place to be is at the shop, hoping the cops are waiting for them by now. It's been twenty minutes. This is some really poor response time, if you ask him.

Ritchie looks behind him. "Shit! The crooks are gaining on us," he says.

Matthew frowns. "Again with the corny gangster movie clichés?"

Up ahead, Matthew sees the all-night diner, lit up like a beacon of safe harbor. He tells Ritchie: "I'm going for it, man, so hold on."

"Going for what?"

"The diner. When we stop, jump out and hide behind the nearest waitress." Ritchie shoots him a quizzical stare. Matthew adds: "Once we're inside we'll be taking on heavy shellfire, but we should be out of harm's way."

Ritchie's jaw drops. "Why are you suddenly talking like General Patton?"

Matthew can't be more than 200 yards from the restaurant. He's actually steering the car directly for the front door. Another fifty feet, Matthew slams on the brakes and skids sideways to a hairy stop. In his rearview he sees the bad guys give up the chase and detour down a side street and out of sight.

Matthew and Ritchie heave twin sighs of relief. Their hands tremble nervously. Matthew detects an acrid scent permeating the Rolls.

"What's that smell?" he says, sniffing the air.

"I peed my pants," Ritchie admits. "Couldn't help it. I wasn't scared, mind you. I just had to pee and couldn't hold it."

This was a questionable excuse, but Matthew lets it slide. Why make a big deal out of a little urine?

§

They finally limp back to the store and find Chris and the cops on the scene, assessing the damage: an easily fixable hole in the roof and, from what they could determine, roughly two thousand dollars in stolen property. Jon, by the way, never showed. Chris tried calling him but got his answering machine.

The cops take a statement from Matthew and Ritchie, but they have nothing really helpful to add to their report. The cops label it a typical break-in with no little to go on, but they vow to be on the lookout for the truck and the merchandise.

"You guys were pretty stupid for chasing after them," one cop chides them, "especially knowing they were armed."

"We didn't know they were armed until they started shooting at us," Ritchie says. He displays the derringer. "Luckily, I had this baby with me."

The cop snickers at the sight of the tiny gun. "I'm going to have to confiscate that," he says. Ritchie is fined; he's lucky he's not arrested for carrying a firearm without a permit.

They hung out at the store until the sun came up. The place was ransacked pretty good. Clothes strewn everywhere. Roof plaster on the floor that looked like big chunks of dandruff. The guys found nothing typical about this.

They never anticipated getting their stolen goods back. By now they had probably been sold to another store either in Northern California or at a swap meet in the Midwest. With no clues, no prints, no nothing, the cops never ID'd the thieves. They found the truck a week later, totaled, at the bottom of a ravine in Carlsbad. It was stolen from a church parking lot in Orange County.

Both Chris and Matthew had their suspicions that it was an inside job. Not by any of their employees, but pulled off by a friend that had been involved in a lot of shady, underhanded deals. Credit card fraud. Check fraud. Insurance fraud. Not exactly a stellar résumé. They never said anything to the police about it because they had no proof, only speculation. Speculation got them crap. And why make their lives more difficult if they were wrong? But from then on, they watched their backs, and kept a closer watch on their turkey leg-eating friend.

CHAPTER 30

Federal building. 11000 Wilshire Boulevard, Los Angeles. Jon's lawyer was a Ms. Jamison, who sat on his side of the metal table wearing a suit and looking as bitchen as a model on the cover of *Glamour* magazine. If things were different, he would've put the make on her. Jon was now wearing your standard jailhouse orange jumpsuit. A far cry from his usual trendy attire. In lieu of a designer label, the word inmate was crudely stenciled on the back.

Ms. Jamison and a federal DA talked back and forth. Jon really couldn't follow much of it, but figured they'd come up with some agreement that would send him to prison for either a long time, or a reduced sentence since he had no recent priors. He did have a juvenile record—which didn't help his situation—for driving drunk with a suspended license and trying to pawn a stolen Rolex lifted from a local Palm Desert jewelry store.

The law defines Drug Trafficking as the act of transporting a large quantity of illegal drugs or controlled substances with the intent to unlawfully sell, distribute, or deliver. This is typically defined as a felony. And since Jon Lewis was arrested trying to sell to a federal agent, it made his situation very iffy. Iffy was not legal jargon, but to put it in terms we all understand: he was screwed.

The DA and Ms. Jamison walked outside and discussed Jon's options. After about a minute tops, his lawyer came back in. Jon could tell by the grim look on her face that his fate wasn't going to be a slap on the wrist.

"Their offer is a reduced sentence from ten to five years if you reveal your source," she said. "Names, addresses, nationality, place of birth, food allergies—whatever you can supply them with."

Jon's face turned ashen. He felt sick inside. "Okay, so what's the best deal we can get?"

"That is the deal. I don't think you understand the gravity of your situation, Mr. Lewis." No, he understood it; he just couldn't grasp the intensity of it.

Unfortunately, she wasn't done. There was an added stipulation. The Feds planned to set up a sting operation at a house in Laurel Canyon owned by the agency. Comely Ms. Jamison tossed her long auburn hair over one shoulder and described how it was to go down.

"It's up to you to get your contacts to take the bait, and deliver the goods. The Feds will move in, catch these guys in the act and you'll have an easy time of it while incarcerated."

Jon sat there wiping the nervous sweat from his brow with his orange shirtsleeve. He pondered his situation. It was dire. He really had no choice. He could tell them no deal, which meant he'd spend ten years in federal prison being passed around and shared like a cheerleader. Five years he could possibly do without a problem. He went back to his cell to sleep on it, and run his options by his cellmate, who seemed to be very familiar with the particulars of serving time in federal prison.

§

It's been a week. While the shop was pretty much back to a normal rhythm, their lives were still fraught with nerves. Jake, the carpenter, was patching the roof. The new clothing alarm system was installed. Elaine, Michele, Sheila, Laurie, and the rest of the crew were keeping busy attaching those damn security tags to the inventory. Following the break-in, this was a mandatory proviso by the insurance company, which refunded their losses and paid for damages. But the guys had it on good authority that they hadn't ruled out this might have been an inside job just so they could file a hefty claim. So the insurance premium skyrocketed. They had no choice but to pay the new premium.

Everyone was stumped as to the whereabouts of Jon Lewis. Anxiety ran rampant throughout their group of friends. They were constantly trying to get in touch with him. Even called the hospitals, police, his old Palm Springs contacts. Nothing materialized.

Recalling his one last hurrah of a drug deal, Matthew did not rule out that Jon could be dead and buried in the desert for all they knew. Sheila, who recently had been having an affair with him, had not made contact, so she was especially worried.

It was almost closing time when Bud Collins waltzes in with a couple of other dudes who they've never laid eyes on before. These guys smelled like cops. What was about to go down had them all shaking their heads in disbelief. Bud showed them his Federal credentials while the other two agents produced a search warrant and began to look for drugs and anything else that could connect Jon or the store to an illegal drug ring. Everyone was shocked to find out Bud was an undercover agent that had been assigned to make a play for Jon and bring him down. Chris and Matthew had an inkling of this, but nothing like what Bud described in detail. A Laurel Canyon sting operation to capture and bring down Jon's main source had failed. And while Jon was supposed to be taken back to jail until his arraignment, he somehow slipped away from the Feds, and was thought to be on the run.

Bud shows them a couple of photos of known Mob guys. One in particular was a Vincent Longo, Jon's Mafia drug contact. Nice Italian-looking kid in his early thirties. Vince got his start on the streets of New York in the fifties peddling dime bags. Been arrested for a slew of crimes ranging from grand theft auto to illegal prostitution. Bud wanted to know if he looked familiar. They all took a closer look at his mug shot. Never saw him before. Elaine, however, thought he'd be cute if he got a nose job.

Bud issues them a warning: if anyone knows Jon's whereabouts, they need to speak up right away. "Now. Tonight. Hiding information constitutes aiding and abetting a fugitive. Any one of you could be in serious legal trouble and serve jail time."

Chris, being Chris, who never misses an opportunity to say something harsh and intrusive, speaks up.

"Hey, man, I think it's pretty fucked that you gain his confidence then whip out your tin badge and hang his ass out to dry. Just my personal opinion, which I'm sure means crap to you."

Bud holds his tongue.

Chris's frustration was understandable but made them all a bit uneasy. Sheila, however, has her own agenda, and finds this whole situation a bit torturous and rife with bullshit allegations. She clears her throat and lets Bud have it. "If I knew where he was, you'd have to beat it out of me. Which I'm sure you people are good at!"

For Matthew, her outburst was a little over the top, but it got the point across that she wasn't giving up Jon.

Bud goes on the defensive, sounding an awful lot like Joe Friday on *Dragnet*. "Look, I know how you feel. It's a lousy job I've got, but it's what I've gotta do to help keep drugs off the streets so young kids don't become addicts or OD before they get to celebrate prom night."

"If Jon was in fact dealing, he wasn't selling to kids. That's not his style," Sheila says.

"Well, you'd be wrong, miss," Bud says. "We have it on good authority that he was selling to whoever had the price of a dime bag." This clientele, he adds, includes everyone from his Hispanic maid to the in-crowd cruising the Sunset strip.

At this point the other two agents, placid as can be, return from their search and divulge their findings. They uncovered Jon's stash hiding place near the water heater. Found nothing except an empty baggie. Still, this did not render Jon above suspicion. "Inculpable" was the word of the day. Of course, everyone showed mild disbelief and shock. Sheila claims they weren't aware of this hidden area in the floor.

"No one mentioned it was in the floor," Bud says.

Sheila is quick to retort. "I read James Ellroy's book *L.A. Confidential*. It described ideal hiding places. The floor, the wall, behind an A/C vent. It was very illustrative if you planned to hide anything, which he wasn't—hiding anything, that is."

That night ended with the understanding of how life sometimes throws you a curve and hits you smack in the fucking head and jogs your brain. Not everyone is a saint. Some of us become, for whatever reason, drug dealers.

§

Despite their disdain for Jon's elusive tactics, Chris and Matthew never gave up the search for him. It was like they were gumshoes in a classic mystery thriller, trying to track him down. For a week or more they drove by his house routinely at least once a day, and checked in with Sheila to make sure she had had no contact. The reason being, he may be on the run, but this guy still got horny and she was his sexual relief these days.

§

It was on a Thursday when things changed dramatically. Chris and Matthew made their usual drive-by of Jon's house. They'd always get out of the car, knock on the door, and look through the windows—always with the knowledge they were being watched by two undercover Feds in a gray unmarked sedan parked two blocks away. It was like a Hollywood movie but not as clever. These guys were so obvious, with their binoculars in plain view, fast food wrappers disorderly stuffed on the dash, cigarette butts piled onto the street like miniature snow-capped mountains outside their open car windows. There was no way Jon would return home unless he was stupid drunk—or just stupid.

Only this time, Chris and Matthew stay in the car and keep the engine idling. There was the usual mountain of unread newspapers and junk mail on Jon's doorstep. But something puzzling caught their eye. Sticking out of his mailbox was a stalk of freshly cut white lilies.

"What the fuck is that? Maybe from an adoring fan knocked silly by love," Matthew says a little naively.

"Very romantic, but not the case," Chris says. "I know this to be fact—the lilies have Mafia implications written all over them."

"A bit Kafkaesque, don't you think?" Matthew says.

"I'm telling you, it signifies there's a hit out for the recipient of the lilies. Jon Lewis is marked for assassination."

On that acute determination, they get the hell out of there fast and leave the lilies to wilt and die in the coffin of the mailbox.

CHAPTER 31

Somewhere deep in the Valley, Sheila was just stepping out of the shower, toweling off, while Jon lays naked in bed smoking a cigarette and drinking what's left of a Schlitz beer. The clock on the nightstand reads one a.m. The television is on but without sound. It was acting more of a night-light than anything else. With the Feds and the Mafioso Vincent Longo actively searching for him, both Sheila and Jon have wisely stayed away from Jon's house, as well as her apartment in Studio City. Paranoid, they didn't want to share their present location with anyone, and you can be sure they've taken every precaution to remain invisible.

Still naked and dripping from the shower, Sheila grabs a baggie from her purse and starts to roll a fresh joint. She is noticeably tense so it's difficult to maneuver the perfect spliff. Shaky, she drops the piece of the Zig-Zag rolling paper lined with the weed onto the rug. The marijuana scatters in all directions while the paper flies under the bed out of sight. Frustrated, she sighs and curses, then begins the challenging process all over again. Jon notices she's unduly anxious and tells her to forget the spliff and come back to bed.

"I'm still wet," she says flatly.

"I like my women wet," he says playfully.

She laughs, then climbs back into bed and curls up close to him like a kitten. All that's missing is the vibratory purr. She takes a breath before asking the question that's been haunting her for the past hour.

Sheila asks, "So, any brilliant thoughts about the next move?"

Jon is brief and to the point, saying his primary goal is to first contact Matthew and Chris and sell his interest in the store. It takes money to hide. It takes money to flee the country and start fresh. The first move is to get capital. Next, they need to find themselves a crackerjack forger who can quickly make them a couple of phony passports. Then they head straight for Canada without looking back.

"All this needs to happen within the next twenty-four hours," he says. "Fast and smooth with no hiccups."

"You said a couple passports," Sheila questions.

"Exactly. You, of course, are coming with me. Fake names, fake social security numbers, maybe even a cut and dye job on our hair. Need to run the whole gamut of deception. We have two tough elements after us—the Feds and the Mafia. We can't leave anything to chance. No bread crumbs. No paper trail."

Alarmed, Sheila feels her stomach clench. Her lower lip quivers before she speaks.

"You cold?" Jon asks.

"Scared."

"Understandable. So am I."

"That federal agent guy coming into the shop and giving us the third degree was cutting it too close for me. I almost slipped up and gave you away. Gave us away."

"But you didn't. So everything is cool," he says.

"No. It's actually not cool," she says.

He sits up in bed and takes a sip of his beer. "Okay, lay it on me, what's really bugging you?"

"I mean, what we have is really terrific. Better than terrific. Special. But the possibility of the Mob catching up with us—with me—is not something I signed on for. Know what I'm trying to say here?"

"I do. Yes. You don't want to die in a blaze of gunfire at the hands of a crazed Italian Mob boss. Neither do I. That's why the right cover is essential."

"Jon, I dig you, but—"

"But," he interrupts, anticipating her next remark, "in the morning, when I wake up, you'll be gone, having split in the middle of the night. Running as far away from this madness until you you're out of breath, gasping for your safety."

Sheila feels his disappointment pulling in around her.

"Baby, you have enemies. I have my whole life ahead of me," she says, trying to justify her reasoning for calling it quits.

Jon gets it. She then kisses him on the forehead, almost like a father would do before sending his child off to summer camp. Jon pulls her closer to him and begins to kiss her on every inch of her face, starting with her eyebrows. He then murmurs: "Just one more goodbye romp so I can take with me a lasting memory of when things were safe and perfect."

Her smile says sure, let's make love one more glorious time, while at the same time she's relieved that he understands and this crazy ride will soon be over for her.

And, if he's not careful, for him as well.

§

While all this was taking place, Heather had scored her much-anticipated birth control pills, and her and Matthew's relationship had shifted into another gear. It was everything she dreamed it would be. However, she wanted to do something a little more innovative and offbeat, like getting a motel room. She liked the idea of being sneaky and indecent for no more than an hour. This excited her; this excited him as well.

Night falls when they drive to the Shady Rest Motor Lodge in Studio City. The neon sign flickered in the night air like a beacon of ill repute. Eight dollars a room. For an extra two dollars you get a view of the empty pool, filled with rusty beer cans and an old tire at the deep end. A real dump, but indecent like she wanted. Matthew signed the register using a phony name, Mr. & Mrs. Johnson. Not exactly clever but he wasn't looking for shrewd. As he signed the register, he noticed that someone checked in the night before under the name of Mark Twain. This rattled him to the point of almost puking all over the check-in desk.

"Is this Mark Twain person still here?" he asks the grubby looking manager that reeked of cheap wine—all the while trying not to show any desperation in his voice and mannerisms.

"Can't say," he says. "I mean, I can say, but I have this privacy rule, not unlike doctor-patient confidentiality."

Matthew reaches in his wallet and pulls out a crumpled five-dollar bill. The clerk snatches the fiver and shoves it in his pocket, then checks to see if the room key has been replaced or not. By now,

Heather is getting anxious. All she wants to do is get a room and fuck on a queen-sized mattress with an ugly bedspread. She looks at Matthew, frustrated. He looks back at her so she has no trouble reading his lips.

"I know, you're in a hurry," he mouths, "but this Mark Twain could be Jon using an alias." He then turns back to the manager, who should have an answer by now. "Well?"

"Just missed him. Checked out maybe fifteen, twenty minutes ago. Saw him drive off in a yellow cab, or maybe it was a school bus. My eyes have a way of playing tricks on me when the sun sets and darkness covers the earth."

"You couldn't have told me all this for free?" Matthew gripes.

"I could've, but I saw an opportunity to make a sweaty crumpled fin."

"Was he with anybody?"

"Can't say. I mean, I can say but— "

"Never mind." Having a normal conversation with this con artist would be expensive, costing Matthew per word.

This whole ordeal puts him on edge. He's pretty sure he just made a connection and finally caught up with Jon and Sheila. He was in no mood to make love to Heather, but he promised—he was doing this for her.

But before they jump into the sack, he realized they got the room next to the one Jon stayed in. An opportunity to look for clues, if he could just get inside. Heather was chomping at the bit, anxious to get it on. While she got ready, he bribed housekeeping with another fiver to gain entrance. He checked it out with the precision of a private investigator, but unfortunately found only a Zig-Zag rolling paper under the bed.

He went back to Heather and her growing need for unconventional sex. The bed squeaked and rattled the walls at every pump and thrust of her hips. Again, this dark noir moment could've been fictionalized in a Raymond Chandler novel. All that was missing was someone in the adjoining room banging and yelling: "Keep it down, Mac, some of us are here to sleep."

An hour and half later, they checked out. Heather, totally satisfied, was beaming with joy at having fulfilled the raunchy sexual experience she'd fantasized about.

When they got back to the car there was another Zig-Zag rolling paper wedged behind the windshield wiper. Matthew looked around suspiciously, making sure there were no binoculars staring back at them. The paper contained a barely legible message that read: Chris's pad 9 p.m. Wed. Bring a $20,000 cashier's check. M. Twain.

Weird. How did Jon know he'd be here? Luck? Coincidence? Their paths must've crossed. That will be his first question at the meeting. He destroyed the evidence, chewing and swallowing the note. This night of sex and mystery made Heather very nervous. She told Matthew never to bring her back to the Shady Rest Motel again. Even if she begged him.

The next morning, around 10:00 a.m., Chris and Matthew get to the shop and are met by Bud Collins. Bud had his game face on. The guys had a sneaking suspicion that something wasn't right in the world. Elaine said he'd been here since she opened at nine and must've chain-smoked a whole pack of Marlboros waiting for them.

Bud pulls them into the back room for privacy. He clears his throat, coughs a few times, then lights the last cigarette in his pack. He tells them that the thinking within the agency is that Jon panicked and split for parts unknown. Bud also makes it clear his team of agents had spotted them scrutinizing Jon's house—and that they were aware of the Mob's white lilies message left in the mailbox. He had come to see if they had made any contact with Jon, since they last talked. Of course, Matthew never mentions the note attached to his windshield wiper. That would be a stupid gaffe on his part, developing into a stakeout situation at Chris's place and Jon's certain capture.

The Feds were willing to offer Jon protection against the Mafia, which was closing in on him fast. Bud was blunt, pulling no punches.

"Jon will be a dead man, if he doesn't come in from the cold," he says, like someone who has read too many John le Carré novels. "Bottom line, you don't double-cross the Italians or you'll find yourself hanging out a ten-story window by your ankles."

Matthew asks, "So, he's definitely going to prison?"

"No getting around it," Bud says.

"It's his first offense," Chris argues. "Can't he just get, like, a slap on the wrist—maybe pay a hefty fine and do some community service picking up trash along the 405 Freeway?"

"It's not as if he was littering," Bud says, still all business. "This is a serious federal offense. He's connected with some heavy drug traffickers, man. The Longo family ain't lightweights."

Their pleas meant nothing. Jon was a dead man. Time to order flowers and dust off the black suits, according to Bud, who was trying to scare them into opening up. They didn't scare that easily. They didn't open up. They gave him nothing.

§

After Bud split, Chris and Matthew took a walk to clear their heads. They had no destination; they just walked along the boulevard. Hardly said a word. They became paranoid, constantly looking over their shoulder. In their minds, every person who passed by them was a threat. Ridiculous stereotypical images ran over and over in their minds. Every cliché you can think of unnerved them. The backfire of a car made them duck.

And then, their illusions became a chilling reality.

A black Plymouth Fury whips around the corner and stops in front of them, blocking their path. They attempt to walk around, but the car lurches forward, again obstructing their path. The passenger window lowers and a guy sticks his head out. He looks familiar. He should. Not more than a few days ago, Bud Collins showed them his mug shot. It's Longo in the flesh, and he's even better looking in person. He introduces himself. His demeanor is civil. Polite. Well-bred. He tells them that it's urgent that he speak with Jon Lewis. The driver looked more like a dentist than muscle.

Needless to say, they're nervous—but not intimidated, until he says, in a calm, cool manner: "I'm giving you guys twenty-four hours to come up with Lewis's exact location. If you don't, I'm having one of my crew take out my frustration on your boutique. An 'accidental' fire. Very devastating and costly. It would be a pity if you boys and your employees were in the store when the incendiary device goes off. Not to mention your customers. The carnage would be unimaginable." He hands Matthew a business card. "Call Cafe Alma and ask for me when you're ready to give up your friend. And don't get clever and notify the Feds. They can't help you. Only your partner Jon Lewis can help you get out of this mess. Have a nice day."

They drive off, leaving Matthew and Chris to digest this drive-by threat.

Sure, they're a little stunned, and it took a good couple minutes before they understood the gravity of the situation. But Matthew wasn't that threatened. "I'm not intimidated by their strong-arm threats. It's bullshit—old school mobster tactics. This is the seventies, not the thirties. Not the era of Bonnie and Clyde and Al Capone. They may burn our store down, but they still don't have Jon. What have they accomplished? What good does it do if they take us out?"

Chris says, "Well, for one, we're dead at a very early age. Our lives are over. Breathing ceases. That alone is enough for me to be scared shitless."

Bottom line, they had to meet with Jon and let him know that he's gotten them into some deep shit, and they expect him to save their asses, and the store, from his felonious lifestyle by turning himself in. Easier said than done, but worth a shot.

§

It was Wednesday afternoon, the day they planned to meet up with Jon. As if there wasn't already enough tension and anxiety to go around, Logan Alexander, Matthew's former roommate, comes weaving into the store, feeling no pain. Clearly drunk, he reeked of cheap bourbon that seemed to exude from his pours.

He begins to unload about how he hates his job, his overbearing authoritarian father, and his father's company. He has difficulty relating to the people he's working with. He finds them beneath him. Furthermore, the pay doesn't even cover his nightly bar tab.

Okay, so they were busy and when they're busy the last thing they need is this kind of distraction. It's up to Matthew to quell his outburst. He's making the customers nervous. But it escalates into a war of words. Chris suggests he get a higher paying job. The truth is, he doesn't want to work at all. His parents created a monetary monster. He's been spoon-fed since the day he was born. He's spoiled, and he knows it's too late for change.

Chris tries to compliment him—tells him he's a natural to work in the auto industry. He should consider a job at a dealership for high-end cars like Porsche, Ferrari, or Maserati. This seems to appeal to his sensibility. He thanks the guys with a hug, then starts for the door. Suddenly he's distracted by a cute girl trying on some new jeans who's just stepped out of the dressing room. She's checking herself out in a full-length mirror. That's when things get dicey. Logan decides that her ass looks great in the pants and tells her so.

"You have the perfect ass to fit in those pants. When God created the female anatomy, He broke the mold on your ass." The word *ass* sends an alarm throughout the store.

The girl, rightfully embarrassed and insulted by his rude comment, throws a fit. She grabs her purse from the dressing room, dumps the contents onto the floor, picks up a small canister of something that appears to be Mace and sprays it into Logan's face. He feels this hot, blinding sensation in his eyes, followed by gushing tears, a strangling sensation in his throat, choking, and severe nausea, causing him to double over in agony. As he moans in pain like a beleaguered buffalo, the girl slides out of the jeans, tossing them on the floor, and then runs out in her underwear, gripping her old pair of pants.

Of course, Logan's conduct was unconscionable and needed to be dealt with. Matthew turns to him and says calmly, "You can't behave like some uncivilized wild man, Logan, if you expect us to let you come in the store ever again."

"What are you saying?" asks Logan, still blinded by the mace .

Chris chimes in: "We're banning you from ever coming back unless you're accompanied by your father or agree to a Breathalyzer test."

"Fuck you guys," are the last words Logan says before feeling his way out the door.

CHAPTER 32

That night they actually rented a car so as not to draw attention with their own cars. What they hadn't counted on was that the anxious Feds were already waiting for them at the house, in their unmarked car, so they drove around the block, parked in front of a random house, then snuck in the back door like thieves in the night. They waited impatiently in the dark, drinking Wild Turkey to take the edge off. It didn't seem to do any good.

Matthew checks his watch. Jon is twenty minutes late, so they assume he's going to be a no-show.

"Maybe Longo's crew got to him and he's dead," Matthew says.

Chris says, "Maybe he fled the country and he's sitting pretty in fucking Tierra del Fuego by now."

"No, he badly wants money. He wouldn't give that up so easily."

Chris curls his thumb and index finger around his chin thoughtfully. "It would be in our favor if the Feds caught up with him," he muses. "That way, we no longer have to answer to Longo. The headache would be in his court. If they wanted him that badly, they'd have to take him down in federal prison."

Another fifteen minutes pass. Still no sign of Jon Lewis. Matthew goes inside to take a leak and almost pees on the floor because he's nervous about turning on a light. Chris lights a Marlboro, then cautiously parts the living room curtains just enough to peek out and scan the perimeter. Nothing. Everything is still. He then crosses to a sliding glass door that separates the house from the backyard.

He stares blankly out into the darkness, where he notices a shadowy figure scaling his brick wall. After jumping out of his skin, he calls out to Matthew: "Either Jon's here or we're being invaded by the fucking Italians!"

Matthew comes out of the bathroom just in time to see a mysterious figure slithering along the grass like a combat soldier. As the figure gets closer the guys panic for a second, until they recognize that it's Jon. They slide open the doors, letting him crawl inside on all fours like a wild animal. Time was precious. He talked fast and in a whisper.

"I had to make sure I wasn't being followed, so I took side streets and cut through people's backyards. Nearly tangled with a mongrel the size of a fucking mountain lion."

They huddle near the fridge, opening the door a crack for light. There's no small talk. Matthew gets right to the point.

"How did you know I'd be at the Shady Rest motel?"

"I didn't. It was purely coincidental. I saw you pull in as I was leaving. To be honest, I was kinda blown away to see you and Heather get a room. That's when I made my move and left the note. I was in no mood to discuss this in front of that dipshit night manager."

"Let's just cut to the chase and tell us your plan," Matthew replies. "How you expect to avoid getting bumped off by Longo—who, by the way, came to us and threatened to burn our business to the ground unless we gave you up."

"You really put us in a compromising position, Lewis," Chris cuts in. "Truth is, we'd be better off with you dead than alive."

Jon quickly switches gears. "That's why I need the twenty grand. To flee."

"No fleeing just yet," Matthew says. "We have no check. We need a good reason why we're handing over so much money."

Jon takes a needed breath before he explains his agenda. A buyout. He figures it's a fair price. The least they could do is to forgive him for being such an all-around fuck-up and making idiotic decisions.

"There's no excuse for stupidity," Matthew says.

Jon grabs a dishtowel and wipes his hands from the dirt he picked up when he crawled to safety. Predictably, he launches into a self-pitying soliloquy.

"Ever since I was a kid, my mother raised me the best she could. But it wasn't good enough. My father left us when I was five. Never came back. Never had a father figure to keep me out of trouble and grounded. Only an alcoholic mother, whose best advice to me was to steal or marry into money."

"You realize you're blaming your parents for fucking us over?" Matthew says.

"I guess I am. It's all I got. Hold someone else accountable for my actions."

He goes on to add how he planned to give a portion of the money to help his mother survive her own set of heartbreak and financial woes, and a slice to Patti, his ex.

Desperate, Jon comes up with a really lame story to try and sell Longo: he suggests Matthew tell him he skipped town and went to Moscow until things cooled off.

"Tell him I've got relatives in Russia who will hide me. Encourage them to contact the Russian mob and ask them for a favor—to hunt me down like the lowlife dog that I am."

Matthew is incredulous. "Are you fucking serious? If I give Longo that bullshit story he'll laugh in my face, then blow it off with a 9 millimeter."

There's a knock on the front door, followed by a loud, powerful voice: *"Jon Lewis, we know you're in there. Open up! It's the FBI. We have a warrant for your arrest."*

This meeting was over. Jon swiftly leaves the same way he came in, slithering through the sliding glass door back into the dark of night like a prowler. Matthew and Chris exchange nervous looks.

"I'll handle the Feds, you shag-ass the fuck out of here," Chris says.

After a beat, Matthew slithers through the sliding glass door, but is met by two federal officers, guns drawn, waving the search warrant in the air. Bud Collins shoulders his way past them.

"Where the hell is Jon Lewis?" the narc demands.

Of course they lie, denying Jon was ever there. "We were just sitting in the dark," Matthew offers, "getting ready for a surprise party—in case he did show."

Bud frowns. "A party? Just the two of you? Bullshit."

Chris shrugs. "Well, the birthday boy didn't have many friends."

Bud and the Feds finally leave empty-handed. Jon obviously got away and this pissed off Bud, because he knew he had the fugitive in his sights and let him slip through his fingers. Even though they had no real proof that the guys were aiding and abetting, they were reprimanded by the Feds and warned that next time they'd serve jail time. Matthew saw this as just another idle threat to scare them into divulging under what rock Jon was hiding. No way were they going to lock them up when they were the only lead they had to Jon.

CHAPTER 33

Against their better judgment, like idiots they agree to give Jon's mother the twenty grand and let the two of them—and Jon's ex-wife Patti—fight over the split. Matthew and Chris cling to a slender hope that Longo buys their ridiculous Russian story, or else they're in for a major fire sale.

The plan was to withdraw the money in the form of a cashier's check, then take a road trip to Palm Springs. But first, Matthew takes his car in for needed service. The mechanic, Lonnie, your typical grease monkey, who still sports a ducktail, gives him a lift back to the store. An hour later, Matthew gets a call from Lonnie telling him that someone had installed a tracking device under his car frame. No big mystery. Matthew knew it was the Feds, following his every move, hoping he'd come in contact with Jon. For now, he leaves it intact so as not to give away he's on to them. He also decides to keep this discovery to himself and not share it with Chris.

With Jon now out of the picture and legally dissolved from the partnership, they had to assume other in-house responsibilities. The bookkeeping, for one. Matthew knew nothing about ledgers, balance sheets, or financial statements. He sought help from Dede, his seamstress, who was good with numbers and smart as hell. The guys left her alone with the books, for as long as she needed. After about a week of retracing Jon's complex system, she comes to Matthew looking panic-stricken. Her complexion pale, her expression serious, her eyes red from straining for too many hours on the calculator.

She finds Matthew on the floor checking out a new shipment of pants from Sisley Jeans. The smell of new denim made his eyes tear and wreaked havoc on his sinuses. It was like breathing in ammonia. Dede approaches and sits down next to him. In her hand was a balance sheet. The fact that the paper was trembling was a dead giveaway something was not good. She stalled a few beats before laying it on him. Seems Jon had cleverly embezzled over twenty thousand dollars. Panic scissors through Matthew; he thought he heard someone scream and didn't realize it was him.

Dede went over the numbers a thousand times and it always came out the same—twenty thousand in the red. Matthew was sickened. She explained how he managed to cheat them: "He took an average of seven-hundred a week using a bank counter check to cover his tracks."

It was never entered. Never recorded. To use a more felonious term, he was cooking the books and robbed them with a number 2 pencil.

Wasting no time, Matthew makes a desperation call to Chris, who was working on some crazy-ass bogus TV talent show called *The Gong Show* that featured weird, freakish performers who were a heartbeat away from being committed.

Chris wasn't shocked to hear Jon had bilked them and skimmed off the top. In his words: "We were sucked into his lying, cheating, malicious fucking world of crime."

"I'm afraid there's more," Matthew says.

"Of course there's more. He's a user. He has no value system. Tell me—but first let me grab a Valium."

Matthew paused, before telling him that while Dede was cleaning and straightening up Jon's hellish mess, she discovered twenty thousand dollars worth of unpaid, delinquent bills that had slid down between the desk and the wall. This was clearly a slap in the face. Their only alternative was to slap back—even harder.

And they did.

CHAPTER 34

Road trip. Chris and Matthew drove to Palm Springs and paid a visit to Jon's mother, Agnes Lewis-Baldwin. They take Chris's car to avoid being tailed by the Feds' tracking device that remained on the Rolls. Matthew had not yet told Chris about it. He left the car parked at the store, allowing the Feds to think he wasn't going anywhere for the day.

The desert heat was unbearable. Summer weather. 109 in the shade. You need to constantly hug an air conditioner or you'd melt. Agnes was only in her late fifties but looked like she could die at any moment. Growing old gracefully was unfortunately not in the cards for this woman. She served them iced tea that tasted like yellowish chalk dissolved in cold tap water and stale cake that must've been in her fridge since Betty Crocker was a teenager. Her kitchen was old and outdated. Cupboard doors hanging off their hinges. Sink stained around the drain. Curtains yellowed from nicotine. Jon grew up in this environment during most of his formative years, while his mother worked the night shift as a waitress at Sambo's Restaurant and Pancake House on North Palm Canyon Drive.

Agnes lit a cigarette and gave vent to a hacking cough that startled the cat sitting on the windowsill. It was losing its hair and also looked as if it was not going to make another sunrise. She knew why they were there and was naturally excited to get a hefty check for twenty thousand dollars.

She planned to use her share to tidy up her dreary house, then Western Union Jon a few bucks once she got word where to send it. There was a long pause before the guys explained how her son embezzled over twenty thousand from them and that giving her yet another $20K was out of the question.

"So, I'm getting crap? My Johnnie boy is getting nothing?" she says, disappointed and choked up.

"Afraid so, Agnes," Matthew says.

"But how will I survive? How will my only boy survive in a foreign country without money? He will starve and die, and that will be on your conscience," she says with an overdramatic tenor.

She starts to hyperventilate, gasping for air. It was hard to tell if this was a genuine problem or she was seeking an Oscar nomination. Even so, Chris finds her a paper bag for her to breathe in. She refuses to use the bag because it has the residual odor of a rotten banana. They wait as she regains her normal breathing pattern without the aid of a sack.

Once fully recovered, Chris then jumps in and reveals more of her son's shameful behavior. For instance, how they found the stack of unpaid bills he left behind that coincidentally totaled yet another twenty thou. Once again she chews the scenery, swooning, losing her balance as if she's about to pass out, but she doesn't, supporting herself against the hutch that housed her prized shot glass collection. And again she finds a way to recover, sticking her wrists under a cold running faucet. She dries off with a dishcloth, then begins to switch the blame on Jon's father for his mischievous, inexcusable behavior as the reason for Jon's criminal misconduct.

"His father was a conniver," she expounds. "Plotted and schemed and paid the price with a five-year stretch in the state penitentiary for check fraud and selling arms to the Contras." Sure, this was head shaking news but not at all unexpected.

During the entire visit, Chris sat there in an unsteady kitchen chair, marred by cat scratches, and listened to Agnes's in-depth recitation of Jon Lewis's backstory. According to Agnes, Jon had fled an adolescence whose catalog of woes had included drug use, countless arrests for disturbing the peace, a fondness for keeping company with women of questionable virtue, and one suicide attempt when life got to be too much for Jon to hack.

Chris didn't believe a single solitary word this nut job threw at them. In his assessment she was as much a bullshitter as Jon and the father. Swindling was in their blood. A family legacy. They left with a feeling of indifference. Agnes Lewis-Baldwin was not their concern or their responsibility. She would somehow have to survive through her own polluted guilt. They left her to dwell on the reality of her corrupt son over stale cake and diluted iced tea that she later spiked with Jim Beam.

§

That night, Matthew sat at home alone, drinking a can of Country Club and staring at the phone, trying to screw up his nerve to call Longo. Matthew twiddled the mobster's business card in his other hand. It's been a week since Longo threatened them with arson. Although Matthew wasn't intimidated by this so-called gangster's threat of arson via incendiary device, there was still the issue of trying to convince him of the ridiculous story that Jon split the country to lay low in Russia.

Finally, Matthew grows big enough balls to make the call. The phone rings at least six times before he hears a voice on the other end.

"This is Longo."

The Mafioso himself answering takes Matthew by surprise. He gets straight to the point, speaking with respect.

"Mr. Longo, sir, this is Matthew Street. We met on the street the other day. You threatened me with a lit match to my store."

"That wasn't a threat so much as it was just a way of getting you to act in perfunctory manner. Know what I'm saying?"

"I do, but I think you may have misused the word *perfunctory*. But what do I know? I'm not a grammarian, I sell pants."

"So, whaddaya got for me? Good news, I hope."

"Nothing but good news, sir."

Matthew tells him the whole Moscow scenario—how Jon made it to Russia and that he's using the alias Nikolai Petrov. Yes, it sounded like a stage name but how would Longo know? Petrov is a common name in Russia—like Smith in the United States. He'll be looking under every rock and dish of beef Stroganoff in the damn city and come up with ten thousand Petrovs living in a three-mile radius of one another.

"How do I know this is not some bullshit fairy tale you just conjured up to throw me off the trail and make me look like an ass?"

"I'd be stupid to try and deceive you, Mr. Longo. Your reputation as a powerful figure precedes you. Any further information I get, you'll be the first to know. So, we done here?"

There was a long, silent pause.

"For now, Street, your building and your pants are safe. I'll keep you posted when we take care of business with your friend, so we can all sleep better at night knowing this unscrupulous piece of shit is in the trunk of some car at the bottom of the fucking Black Sea. Sleeping with the fishes."

It was weird how this man suddenly became this stereotypical gangster. Then, as if Matthew was a winning contestant on a game show, Longo announces: "Meanwhile, you've earned a complimentary dinner for yourself and that cute deaf girlfriend of yours at my restaurant, Café Alma." He hangs up.

Matthew felt the call went well, but of course anticipated that somewhere down the line, Longo would catch on to the fact that Matthew was lying.

§

None of this resolved their problem of owing big money to their suppliers. They needed a miracle of some sort. They had no plan, and Matthew actually thought of going to Longo for a loan. Really bad idea? Maybe not. He figures as long as he owed him money, he wouldn't torch their only source of income, wrap his dead body in a shower curtain, and stuff him in a steamer trunk. Now who's spewing gangster clichés?

He suddenly hears a sound outside his window— footsteps crunching on top of leaves and twigs. His first thought is, it's the Feds making sure he's not hiding Jon Lewis under his bed. He goes outside to scope out the area. He sees nothing that looks suspicious. He's thinking it's time to remove the tracking device from his car and put it on a truck that's headed for Canada. Clever? Not really. An old diversion.

MATERIAL THINGS

§

It was on the weekend when Matthew woke at the crack of dawn and headed directly for a local truck stop diner in Bakersfield called Rosalie's Cafe. His purpose was to find a suitable truck upon which to attach the tracking device that's been on his car for the past month. Bakersfield seemed to be the ideal location because most truckers heading north towards Washington and Canada take Interstate 5. Since Matthew had no knowledge of how to physically make the transfer, he brought along his mechanic, Lonnie, who was a reformed felon and had some skill in this particular area. There was a labor charge of a hundred dollars—steep, but well worth the price of deception.

Parked in a central spot, they lie in wait for just the right truck. It was amazing the amount of truck drivers that rolled in for breakfast before hitting the road. What a thankless job, Matthew thought. An endless, solitary existence, and their only socializing is done on a CB radio, or when they stop at a greasy spoon, flirting with the waitresses and shooting the bull with their fellow truckers.

A good hour later, an eighteen-wheeler with Toronto plates rolls in. The perfect vehicle. A hefty, beer-bellied guy sporting a full beard and a straw cowboy hat gets out of the cab and heads into the diner for his caffeine top-off. Once out of sight, Lonnie immediately goes to work under the truck. Unbeknownst to them the driver gets his coffee to go and is headed back sooner than expected. Matthew thinks fast and springs into action, asking the driver for directions.

"Excuse me, sir, but do you, uh, know how to get to, uh … Placerville," he says, pulling a name out of a hat.

The driver isn't that accommodating. "Look, kid," he responds sharply, "I know you might think that every truck driver who rolls in here knows the whereabouts of every street, highway, and roadside eatery in the western United States from memory, but most of us don't. We sometimes get lost, just like normal folks. I remember once I couldn't find my way looking for Wayne, Nebraska. A small, nondescript town with a population of five thousand. Not exactly a jumping metropolis. Have a pleasant afternoon."

After this rambling dissertation he clambers into in his cab and drives off, leaving Lonnie flat on his back, lying in an oil spot. Matthew shrugs a "well?" Lonnie gives him a thumb's up. Mission accomplished.

With the tracking device securely attached to the underbelly, Matthew decides to play their game and keep his car out of sight, to make it appear he might be chauffeuring Jon Lewis to Toronto.

CHAPTER 35

The Canadian border. Dusk. Tony Clarke's VW bus with the Union Jack on the roof idles in a long line of cars, trucks, and RVs waiting to cross the border into Vancouver, BC. He has a passenger who is hard to identify, because he wears a baseball cap and dark shades. Probably a hitchhiker. Tony is notorious for picking up riders during the long haul from Los Angeles to Vancouver. Makes the journey less of a bore. Not to mention, in the event he falls asleep at the wheel, it's handy to have someone to prevent the bus from swerving into an oncoming car. This particular passenger appears nervous and edgy. Tony tries to comfort him in his Liverpudlian vernacular.

"Try to relax, mate," he says. "If they get a sense things are all at sixes and sevens, we're fucked. And the last thing we need is to be hassled by the Old Bill. No way do we want this little delay to go pear-shaped."

Tony's passenger nods, confused. Sixes and sevens? Old Bill? Pear-shaped? What the fuck is he talking about?

Fifteen minutes later they reach the border crossing and the border patrol checkpoint. A uniformed Canadian officer instantly asks to see their passports and ID. Both Tony and his passenger comply without protest. The officer studies both passports thoroughly, looking for any discrepancy. These guys have that Bohemian, nonconformist, beatnik look, so they're automatically profiled as suspicious drug users who might be smuggling contraband across the border. He asks that the guy riding shotgun remove his cap and glasses, making sure the ID picture and the man match. After he complies, the guy stays in the shadows, not revealing his full face. But it's not hard to detect that it's Jon Lewis trying to remain incognito.

It's nervous time when they're asked to step out of van while they inspect the contents. Standard procedure, according to the border officer. But Tony thinks otherwise, as he opens up the back. Jon, now out in the open and more identifiable, prays he's not recognized. Fidgety and uneasy, he keeps his head down during the entire search. The officer notices his restless behavior.

"Your friend okay?" he asks Tony.

"Yeah, he just needs to take a slash."

"A what?"

"A piss."

Next, they're asked why they're headed into Canada. Tony, trying to keep it friendly, speaks up. "Strictly business, mate. We sell those British-made T-shirts you're checking out in the back to the local retailers. Big sellers. This is my third trip. His first. I'm training the bloke."

MATERIAL THINGS

Jon doesn't respond, nor does he look up. The border Mounties finally complete their look-see and are about to relinquish their passports, when the officer asks Jon to step closer into the light. He checks him out closely. Jon is about to piss his pants.

"You look familiar. Have I seen you before?"

Jon suddenly gets talkative. Nervous energy. "Me? Maybe you have. Used to be a male stripper at the Chippendales in Vegas. Lost my physique. Fired my scrawny butt. Maybe there, you think?"

The officer suddenly feels emasculated. "Not a chance in royal hell you'd ever catch me in a joint like that. You boys can go. Keep an eye out for wild life. Meaning hitchhikers."

They drive off. Tony says, "Nice save, mate. I mean Mr. Twain." A half laugh from Tony confirms his collusion.

Jon says, "First liquor store or exuberant hitchhiker we come to who's holding—stop. I need something to help settle my nerves."

"Glove box. There's an Oxy in a tin box posing as an aspirin."

CHAPTER 36

It was February 1970. The young entrepreneurs were still breathing above ground but the store was gasping big time. Filing a CHAPTER 13 has unfortunately become a reality. Both of them being insomniacs, Matthew met up with Chris at Tiny Naylor's coffee shop at two in the morning to discuss what they thought might be their best way to get out of debt. The shop's usually empty at this hour, so they felt secure from any unfriendly ears listening to their conversation.

Chris orders coffee and a slice of boysenberry pie. Matthew, coffee and a glass of water to wash down the two Tylenol he needs to curb his banging headache. Leaning in and talking at a whisper, Matthew recommends they seriously think about going to Longo for a loan. Not the whole twenty grand, but just enough to satisfy their creditors. Half, he says. Ten thousand.

After the stunned silence that followed, Chris poses the question: "What happens if we need to skip a payment? Say we have a really bad month. I'm talkin' a cigarette machine takes in more than we do, and we can't come up with the full amount due. I'll tell you what happens. He doesn't have us killed or break our legs. No. He penalizes us a grand, then tacks on another 5 percent interest charge. We will be in debt to this joker for the rest of our lives. Which he will eventually end with a bullet to the back of the head."

"You're overreacting."

"Good. You noticed."

"If we want to survive, it seems Longo is our only saving grace. Yes or no?" Matthew asks.

"Let's run it by him and see what the interest rate is on ten thousand and how long he expects us to repay the loan, before his friend who looks like a dentist shows up at our door with a bouquet of lilies."

Matthew loads in two more Tylenol. His banging headache was now a full-blown fucking migraine. His ulcer is acting up and his heart feels like it's going to jump out of his chest. He was a mess.

While they were still trying to figure out how to remedy their financial crisis without it becoming injurious to their health or imperiling their store, Logan Alexander makes their lives a bit more complicated—he decides to tie the knot and asks Chris and Matthew to be his groomsmen. Emily Harwood was beautiful and smart. She and Logan met at the Marina Yacht Club restaurant and bar. She was having lunch with a girlfriend whose parents were members. Logan's family was also members, which made his move very convenient. He was at the bar drinking his lunch. He saw Emily from across the room and went fucking nuts. Never in his life had he seen such a beautiful girl. And she was just that, a girl, in her early twenties. She was wearing a short red dress, black boots, and a tan that seemed to glow even indoors.

Their eyes met. She smiled. He nodded. Smiling was not a facial expression that Logan ever displayed. He was more of a serious guy who hardly ever showed his exuberance for fear he might look weak. He sent over a drink by way of introduction, with a handwritten note on the coaster that read: *If you're free, I'd like to marry you in a month or two. My family will foot the bill wherever you'd like to exchange the vows. United States, Europe, South America, at this very yacht club—your choice.* This made a lasting impression on Emily Harwood, who went for the marriage proposal hook, line, and sinker.

Logan's father, James, was thrilled by his son's clever choice of words, and even more so by his choice of lady. His son desperately needed stability, and James was certain Emily was the someone who could provide that for him.

James said he'd give Emily the fucking moon if she'd marry Logan—an innocent enough bribe. She was twenty-two, he was twenty-four. Probably way too young for either of them. It was rumored that she got a new Mercedes from James as a wedding gift, and the moon was stashed inside the glove box, masquerading as a certified six-figure check.

§

So here they are a month later, dressed in rental tuxedos, stiff white shirts and clip-on bow ties, feeling a sense of doubt that this marriage should even take place. Both Chris and Matthew were guessing the cost of this amalgamation alone would have covered their debt to the manufacturers, who were still breathing down their necks, hungry for payment. By now, the entire forum at the California Apparel Mart and their New York reps knew about the Jon's Drawer fiasco. So far, only a few of them had totally abandoned them and threatened to sue for delinquent accounts. They set up a meeting with Longo for a week from today at Café Alma. Just the thought of it caused major acid reflux.

Strictly a guesstimate, Matthew gauged the life expectancy of these nuptials to be, well … short. How short? Four and a half years, tops. This measurement wasn't based on Logan's past romp with Sage, but with the bridesmaid he was fucking in the hall closet just minutes after the I do's, then getting a blow job right before the roasted chicken breast and new potatoes were being served.

Chris, Heather, Michele, Elaine, and Matthew were seated together near the head table. It was awkward for Chris. He and Michele never reconnected after that broken date when Michele supposedly contracted that streptococcal infection. But he got through the wedding, thanks to a 25-milligram Xanax.

Elaine and Michele, however, demonstrated a curious closeness, feeding each other with compliments and flattering remarks, and giggling like schoolgirls. Of course, no one knew of their special night together. This was and always would be highly confidential. Everyone assumed their good-natured attitude was caused by slugging down too much champagne.

They had just been served dessert—a three-layered chocolate-vanilla cake with a strawberry center—when James Alexander, his abnormal gait the result of being thrown from a horse in a childhood accident, hobbles slowly towards Matthew. He had since limped his way into unprecedented wealth via distribution of a Japanese firm's high-tech tape recorder. No one was willing to take on this unknown company's business, but James saw a profitable opportunity and took up the challenge, pushing the Sony brand in the United States and all across the western hemisphere.

James finally makes the journey across the expansive room to their table, arriving out of breath. He's a short, stocky man with a moustache that badly needed a trim, or to be shaved off completely. Matthew handles the introductions. James, being an overbearing bastard, doesn't seem to care who they are. He just asks if everybody could please excuse them while he talked with Matthew about "a matter of importance." They leave, finding it rude and impolite. While Chris and Heather head for the bar, Elaine and Michele go to the ladies' room to powder whatever they needed to powder. Maybe to share a spliff or a blunt or a kiss. Who knows? Just speculating.

James sits down and instantly begins to eat Matthew's slice of wedding cake, like he fucking paid for it. White icing, characteristic of residual cocaine, sticks to his unruly moustache. Done with the cake, he lights a cigar, offers Matthew one. He passes. He hated the stench of cigars. They reminded him of tired old men sitting in a private boys club discussing politics and the pussy they usually pay top dollar for. What James touches on next makes Matthew powerfully uncomfortable.

"My son is a rare disappointment, Matty," he says. Matthew is no dummy. He calls him "Matty" as if he can now confide his innermost thoughts without the fear of him spreading rumors. Like they're best friends. Like he's a relative allowed to hear family secrets. "You're a smart, clever young man and I trust you. You have balls and aren't afraid to take chances." Matthew had no idea where this is going, but did appreciate the compliments. And then came an alleviation of the pain Matthew was feeling and the future he was dreading. A band-aid to stop the bleeding, so to speak.

"I want to give you—on Logan's behalf, of course— $32,000 for a third of Jon's Drawer. A third of the stock. A third of the headache.

MATERIAL THINGS

This should get you out of the cellar and also get my son, a person who fails at everything, a chance at making something of himself, through your endeavors."

Matthew had to take a deep breath and loosen the top button of his shirt, which was now cutting off his air supply. This offer was staggering. There was relief from having to deal with Longo, but there was also the dreaded nightmare of having to cope with Logan as a partner. He asked a pertinent question.

"I'm curious. How did you know about our, you know, financial troubles?"

"Matty, I'm a high-profile business man. I have people on my payroll who find out things, when I want things to be found out. I have corporate spies. Sometimes I learn about things that come up unexpectedly. Like Logan getting laid in the hall closet minutes after today's ceremony. Makes it all very intriguing, don't you think? All this undercover spy shit."

There's a pause as James waits impatiently for an answer. Some sign that would give his son, who he continues to label as a failure, a chance to redeem his mistakes. Seeing Matthew's poker face, he rattles on.

"Let's also be honest, the chances of this marriage making it past five years would be a fucking miracle," he says categorically. "And that's when he's going to need some stability in his otherwise pathetic life. I'm looking out for his future. After all, he is my son."

Truth to tell, the idea of taking on Logan Alexander as a partner could be a huge mistake. Longo hasn't agreed to the loan yet, so figuring him into the equation wasn't even relevant. Matthew looks across the room and sees Logan looking over at them, wearing a sheepish grin—he obviously knows what's going down. On the other side of the room Chris leans against the open bar looking directly at James and Matthew. He shrugs. One of those body gestures that says *what the fuck is going on?*

Matthew finally replies to James's proposal. "I'm blown away by your offer, James. But I can't give you an answer, because, well, I have a partner, Chris. You know Chris Styles, who's over on the other side of the room, I'm sure wondering what the fuck we're talking about. Feeling left out."

James agrees. He made a mistake keeping Chris on the fringe of this conversation. He's an important feature in this deal. James assumes that Chris, like Matthew, has a smart business mind, and will go for the deal. Then, almost betraying anger, James stubs out his cigar in the slice of strawberry cake.

"There's more cake if you want it," he says, as if he's using that turn of phrase to cough up more than the thirty-two grand if needed.

James suddenly makes eye contact with someone in the guest party waving him over.

"Let me know your decision." He starts to leave, then turns back. "An important detail, Matty. Logan will strictly be a silent partner. No creative input. He does not want to tamper with success. Those are my stipulations, not his. Maybe once in a while you could throw him a bone and ask his opinion on something of little importance. The color of a shirt. Recommend a shoe style. Let him sign the Christmas card you mail out to clients. Nothing that demands a great deal of attention."

With that, James slowly limps back into the wedding crowd. A few seconds later, Chris, with Heather in tow, taps Matthew on the shoulder. "There's a lot to consider, isn't there Matty?" he says. "He offers us a $32,000 buy-in or we pass and go to Longo and still only ask for ten." Seeing Matthew's incredulous stare, he adds: "Heather read your and James's lips from across the room and gave me a full account of the conversation. She's very talented and handy to have around." Proud of her skill, Heather smiles.

"And I take it your answer is fuck Alexander's offer?" Matthew says.

"You read my mind, Matty."

Chris was clearly opposed. And rightfully so. Their love for Logan was slowly dissipating into thin air. He would be a liability rather than an asset. But they were desperate and running out of ideas to stay afloat. They mull it over for a few minutes. Longo or Logan. Either choice wasn't a winning scenario. Failing was not an option they wanted to face. A decision had to be made. They figure they had a week to decide their fate. With Longo they know what to expect—pay or suffer the consequences. With Logan it's strictly a crapshoot—akin to having someone seize your intestines and twist.

Heather, knowing both sides of the coin, asks who Longo is. A loan shark Matthew explains. Heather is stumped by the sobriquet.

"A loan shark is private person you borrow money from," Matthew explains, "and if you don't pay him back within an allotted time, he sends out gorillas to break your legs."

She nods, and then gives her opinion slowly and methodically.

"For me, the smart move would be go with the man with the limp. Seems to me he'd have a difficult time catching you guys on the run."

Her intuition helped them make a decision.

CHAPTER 37

Matthew, Chris, and Logan had done everything together since seventh grade: gym class, crank calls; on warm days they'd hit Sorrento Beach in Santa Monica and stay till the sun went down or until they were fried. They'd even taken their first sip of wine together in the summer of '53. Logan was the best man at Matthew's wedding to Andrea. He's seen him at his highest and lowest points. There had always been a trust between the three of them.

Relieved they didn't have to go to Longo, they cancel the meeting. Longo thought it was a wise decision. Said if they were delinquent on payment he'd have to take drastic measures, which he would regret because he'd grown to like these boys.

Instead, they set up a meeting with Logan after he got back from his Hawaiian honeymoon. Of all the places to meet, they agreed on the carousel in Griffith Park. It represented their childhood when they were all naive and free of any responsibilities or moral obligations.

MATERIAL THINGS

No liquor breath or they'd walk was their hard and fast stipulation. Yes, they made a big deal of this. Their reputation and livelihood were at stake. Not to mention, keeping their sanity. Another drunken outburst about a girl's ass could mean a lawsuit, followed by a banner waving in the breeze that read going out of business due to sexual harassment.

It was April 17, 1970. In the news, the world breathed a collective sigh of relief when the ill-fated Apollo 13, after six days of nail-biting suspense and anxiety, returned to earth with its imperiled astronauts all safe. They sat on a park bench just far enough away so that the tuneful Wurlitzer band music of the merry-go-round didn't hamper and drown out the conversation. Populated with bright wooden horses and laughing children, Logan decides this was the perfect time to tell them he's about to become a father. "Holy crap!" would've been the fitting reaction, but they kept it sincere and took it for granted that Emily Harwood walked down the aisle pregnant. This was not a criticism but more of a quiet observation.

After a few accolades, followed by a series of forced hugs, they got down to the business at hand—trust, alcohol, and keeping a civil tongue in the presence of customers. Logan makes it an easy transition.

"I know you guys are worried—no, probably scared shitless about my behavior—but I can assure you I'll do all my drinking at home, and won't interfere with the day-to-day running of the shop. When we're in the black, just send me my monthly paycheck."

Chris interjects with: "What if you do walk in drunk and decide to tell some girl she has a nice ass, or because you're lit you try and seduce her in the back room? What are we allowed to do and not do? What recourse—legal or personal—do we have?"

They wait for a response. He wipes his nose. Tousles his hair. An obvious stall, trying to think of the correct answer. The proper punishment. He had nothing. His eyes are blank and empty. He shrugs. Matthew makes a few gritty suggestions.

"The worst possible consequence, we run to your father and tattle like snot-nosed little kids. He'll disown you, never give you another cent. Your marriage will fail, and your dad will probably force you to join AA."

Logan couldn't argue because he knew everything Matthew described was spot-on fucking right.

"And this is why, gents, I intend to be on my best behavior," he vows.

Matthew also knows, but keeps this to himself, that his father would somehow find a legal way to take back his investment, leaving them no choice but to file for bankruptcy—or resort to getting down on their knees, begging Longo for a loan while giving him a hand job to prove their loyalty.

The pressure to make the right decision was fucking torturous. But despite the doubt, Street, Styles and Alexander Incorporated was formed on that afternoon in 1970. You could bet Logan desperately wanted to slug down a couple vodkas to celebrate. His power to control his drinking was still questionable and remained their biggest fear, no matter what he promised.

While Chris went back to the studios, Matthew headed for the store to let the guys know the outcome of this meeting. Logan stuck around and watched the screaming, crying kids and pondered what parenthood held in store for him. What the guys didn't know, but should have suspected, was that he had a flask hidden in his sock. So by the time he left the park he was pretty much sauced and probably wanted no part of being a daddy.

§

Later, Matthew gathers up the crew after most of the customers left. He tells them their jobs and the store are still alive and breathing, and they should treat Logan Alexander as an owner, but without creative license. He stipulates Logan was not allowed to change a fucking light bulb without his say-so.

CHAPTER 38

The end of the year came around in a whisper. It was late December. Like a seasoned designer who might have done Macy's New York, Elaine was revamping the front window display in an eclectic array of leather, lace, denim, and sprigs of mistletoe. Christmas cheer was in the air in sunny Southern California.

Chris, looking both excited and eager, comes in to discuss a personal situation with Matthew. It involves Michele. He's got what he believes is a sure-fire plan to try and kick-start this hopeful relationship with a weekend trip, driving up the coast to San Francisco and Sausalito. Get her into an all-new environment, away from the store and any distractions, he says.

Matthew pulls him aside before he has a chance to put this plan into operation. He gives him a blunt reality check, saying his intentions are noble but the weekend road trip spelled death.

"You're grabbing for affection and hoping that because you're locked in a room together for three days," Matthew says, "it will make the intimacy stronger and bring the two of you closer. It usually backfires on the basis that your whole demeanor is lacking what she now needs in her life. God knows what that is, but it's not you. You're out in cold, suffering the slings and arrows of love. Why spend the time and money, only to get hurt and sent back into the world mentally scarred and alone? You can't force feelings on another person, Chris."

There's a long pause while Chris lights one of his Marlboros. After two drags, he squashes it out in a nearby ashtray, then says, "Maybe you can force feelings in a way that doesn't seem forced or unnatural, but is real—genuine."

Matthew knows trying to talk him out of this is a lost cause. Pointless.

"You're going to do whatever you want. And you're also going against your own philosophy—protect your ego, before they shoot you down in a ball of flames."

This was sage advice to consider. But sometimes logic gets in the way of feelings.

§

On another day, Matthew was straightening a rack of blouses when Nicole Benson slithers up behind him, puts her arms around his waist, and sticks her bony knee into his ass. He flinched and may have even let out a mild "what the fuck."

"Jumpy, are we?" she says. He turns to her. She looked tired and wasted. In another zone. Her hair a mess. Makeup not applied very well. Lips cracked from the sun. A zit on her forehead. He hadn't seen her since the Jon Lewis bust. He was hoping she would have gotten her act together drug-wise, but that didn't seem to be the case.

"Hey, what's going on? It's been awhile. You look great," he lied. "Where's your other half?" This was a reference to Ronny Cooper, whom he heard had taken off for parts unknown.

"Mexico, Canada, Australia. Who knows? I'm not his babysitter. It's a mystery."

"So, you here to buy or browse, or did you just come by to stick your knee in my ass?"

It takes her a good minute to process this question.

"I needed to get something off my chest," she finally says. "A sad, pathetic, embarrassing thing that happened to me, and you were the only person I thought would understand and maybe sympathize with me."

"You want to sit down?" Matthew starts leading her to a chair, when she decides to sit down on the floor where they were standing. He kneels down to her level. "Lay it on me."

"I was let go from my job. Fired, actually. Never saw it coming."

"Sorry to hear that."

"Yeah. I fucked up royally. I need help, Matthew. I'm a waste of space."

She begins to cry. Matthew puts a comforting arm around her. He knew there was more to it than just losing her job.

"What else?" he says. "Why'd you get fired? What happened? Something not cool, I can tell."

"One of the secretaries caught me shooting up heroin in the lunchroom. She told the boss. The rest you can guess. They called the cops. They booked me for possession. My brother bailed me out. I have a hearing in a couple weeks. Probably get jail time."

"Wow."

"Yeah, it's heavy."

"Look, these things have a way of working themselves out."

"No, they don't. Nothing gets worked out; it only gets worse. The last full stint in rehab after my last possession arrest worked, and I thought I'd left my past in the past. Rebuilt my life. I stayed clean for two years, then fell off the wagon."

Matthew takes it all in as she continues to open up.

"I figured after you left me the note after that death-defying salad dive, which I apologize for, you'd be the one person who'd understand my sick, fucking habitual drug habit. I can't tell my parents, they'd disown me. Ronny is the most unsympathetic person I've ever been with. I had to tell someone. Anyone who'd listen. I need someone to tell me that things will be okay."

She is now sobbing uncontrollably, and customers are walking around them with concerned looks. Matthew assures them everything is fine.

"Everything is not fine!" Nicole hollers. "I'm a loser!"

That outburst begins to make the customers nervous. And Matthew as well. He gets her on her feet and starts to lead her outside.

"Look, I'm so sorry about all this," he says. "But the truth is, things won't be okay until you stop. I like you too much to sit around and watch while you kill yourself."

In truth, the whole thing was freaking him out. Sure, this was an era when drugs played an important role in social surroundings. But that doesn't mean shooting up in the lunchroom is an acceptable practice. He made a promise to try and get her into a drug rehab program—if she was serious about trying to get straight. The tragic irony was that she wasn't sure if she wanted to stop. She only knew she didn't want it to affect her lifestyle. She left as she came in—in tears, in doubt, and feeling like she was carrying the world on her shoulders.

§

It was right after the New Year, when Chris approached Michele and asked her to go on that symbiotic San Francisco trip with him. His expectations were high. He ignored any signs of rejection. This was his own do or die decision. Michele's honesty came without warning.

"Look, Chris," she says, "I can tell you've put a lot of thought and energy into this—into us—but I don't think we're going to be anything but good friends. You're a nice guy and I'm flattered, but I'm going to have to turn you down."

Before Chris, totally flummoxed, can reply, she adds: "But you know who might be interested in this all-inclusive weekend? Dede, the seamstress. I think you guys would hit it off."

She walks away, feeling a sense of guilt knowing she probably destroyed his self-esteem. It wouldn't surprise her if he fired her.

Chris considers the Dede suggestion for a minute, then decides to go to Las Vegas instead—get himself a hooker or, even better, catch some out-of-towner eager to sleep with a writer from Hollywood. This, he felt, would satisfy his hunger for female companionship.

He took the forty-five minute PSA flight into McCarran International Airport, five miles south of downtown Las Vegas. The terminal is strewn with travelers gripping the handles of one-armed bandits (slot machines), hoping to not go home empty-handed. The plunk, plunk, plunk of the coins is music to the ears of the weekend gamblers.

In the mix is an older woman, maybe in her seventies, who has been sitting anxiously in front of a machine for hours trying to win that jackpot before jumping on the bus back to her trailer park. Down to six quarters—and her fingertips stained with the familiar blackness from the coins—she looks straight ahead, her face reflected in the machine's glass face, its whirring cherries and numbers reflected back in her bifocals. She loses, hits the machine with her fist, yells out a frustrated "fuck you," slides out of the chair and takes a much-needed pee break.

Meanwhile, Chris steps off the plane, enters the terminal, and decides to test his luck at the first slot machine available. He walks up to the same machine the old lady just abandoned. Drops in a quarter. Pulls the lever. The three wheels spin his fate. Boom! Lights flash, bells go off. Three cherries. He's a winner! A $200 payout. His eyes light up, shocked at his good fortune. A change girl approaches and counts out two hundred dollars in twenties.

"Amazing!" he says to her. "One quarter. One pull. I should turn around and go back to L.A."

"Just the opposite," the girl fires back. "You must have the magic touch. This is a definite sign of bigger things to come."

Just then the old woman returns and claims the two hundred bucks that particular machine just paid out belongs to her. Most of what Chris won she had fed into the machine. This was her slot that she'd been playing for the last two hours. She only left it for a minute to pee. She called first dibs.

"Ask the change lady the rules, young man!" she demands. Then she instructs Chris to pay up, sticking out her hand that still shows the coin blackness. Obviously the old bitch didn't wash her mitts after she took a piss.

"I don't think so, lady," Chris informs her. "You can't lay claim to a particular machine. First come, first serve. But nice try. I admire your enthusiasm."

Failing to convince him, she has an alternative solution. She leans in close so as not to be heard or seen by adjacent players. Her breath smells like stale whiskey and cigarettes. She then flashes her sagging tits. Not an enticing sight. She then offers to give him a righteous blow job in a back storage room for half the winnings.

Okay, this proposal was offensive and disgusting. He of course passes and heads for the nearest waiting cab. She takes umbrage and screams, calling him a faggot and a right-wing fascist pig. Heads turn. This encounter is over when security approaches, calming her down and telling her to go home and sleep it off. The security officer tells Chris they call her Bandit Betty. She's been coming here for decades, and her appetite has remained insatiable. In her younger days, she managed to entice many a winner into the back storage room for a quickie.

Night falls over Sin City. This is when the town comes to life. The smoked-filled Flamingo Casino is packed with high rollers, blue-collar workers, and optimistic day-trippers anxious to try their sure-fire system on the gaming tables. Chris is having a celebratory drink at the bar. In front of him is a chip tray containing three thousand dollars in winnings he accumulated playing no limit hold 'em poker. The bartender, a slick-looking woman in her mid thirties, suddenly slips another drink in front of him.

"What's this?" says Chris, baffled.

"Compliments of the young lady sitting at the other end of the bar," she says.

Chris glances over and makes eye contact with a woman, maybe twenty-five. Clearly a hooker, though a decent-looking one.

"Thanks, but I should be the one buying you a drink," he says.

"The night is young." She slides down a few bar stools towards him. She stares at his chip tray.

"Quite a stack."

It's clear what she is, and what she wants, but she manages to make that part of her appeal.

"Yeah, I hit a lucky streak," he says.

She leans into him. "If you ask me, the lucky part is that you had the good sense to walk away from the table and not try to double the amount, and lose it all like most suckers who come to Vegas. You're one of the rare smart ones."

"Truth is, I really didn't come here to gamble. I came because I was depressed, hoping the night life and the bright lights and the booze would cheer me up."

"Has it worked?"

"Not yet, but like you said, the night is young—and not getting any younger."

"You staying in the hotel?"

"Yes, I am. Yes."

"Take me to your room," she purrs.

He looks at her, knows he's being worked. But it feels good to have a woman who wants him, no matter what the cost.

"How much? And don't base your price on my large stack, because you just might talk yourself out of a decent night's profit. I'm not about to go over one twenty-five. Anything bigger and I sit here until another lady slides up and buys me a drink, willing to negotiate and not stiff me because I happen to look like I'm going all in." He nods towards his chip tray.

"Once again, you've come out a winner," she says, grabbing his arm and leading him across the casino floor to the elevators. They enter and are met inside by an older couple. Probably been coming to Vegas since the fifties. The woman is dripping in fake jewelry, and he's wearing his best sporty toupee. Chris is noticeably anxious as he balances the tray in both hands. The old man seizes an opportunity.

"You kids interested in scoring some primo shit? I'm a rep at Pfizer Pharmaceuticals."

An incredulous death stare from the hooker shuts this crazy old man down.

§

Chris had sex until his penis gasped for air and screamed in surrender—enough, no more. Names were never exchanged and at the end of their sack time, neither had realized they once crossed paths nearly a year ago. He was not aware he just banged Linda Tarlow, and she was oblivious she just fucked Matthew Street's partner. How was this even possible? Maybe it was the booze, the grass, and the hash that fogged their minds. The mind plays tricks on you. If you've ever forgotten to note where you parked your car and spent what felt like forever wandering around looking for it … well, you know how that goes.

Chris was desperately in need of the touch of a woman. And Linda, who saw this as nothing but a business venture that paid better than being a cocktail waitress, ignored the personal touch and focused on how this john was going to pay for food on the table and a roof over her head for her and her daughter.

Chris slides out of bed and starts to get dressed as she watches with a satisfied look on her face.

"You like dogs?" she asks.

"Depends on where this question is going. Is it referring to a sexual position or a legitimate inquiry about puppies?"

"I used to have a Doberman. Her name was Olive. Died."

"Look, not to be rude but I prefer not to get into personal shit. Keep this romp between us strictly business, which brings us to the portion of the evening they call pay up time."

She just nods, complying with his request to keep it impersonal. "Most guys feel a sense of guilt and want to talk about how they're happily married and this experience was nothing but some kind of a midlife crisis that is sure to pass."

Whatever anybody wanted to call it, this was exactly what Chris needed. Unbridled sex. Someone to fuck his brains out with and remind him that he still has what it takes to get it up and keep it up for an hour. He hands her two hundred-dollar white chips. Although they agreed on just a hundred, he felt an unusual closeness to this girl but didn't now why. She was certainly grateful for his generosity, but takes nothing for granted.

"Does this mean you want to ride again?"

"No, it means you caught me in a charitable mood," he says. "It means that in another time and place I could like you and would ask you out for dinner or a movie, like on a regular date."

"I thought you wanted to keep this impersonal."

"You're right. I'm contradicting myself. Forget the whole dinner and movie thing. I'm young and a tad naive and still think dating is what most chicks want before they'll put out. This is why I like your profession. No expectations of needing to be wined and dined and told how smart you are."

"I'm not sure, was there a compliment in there somewhere?"

"Maybe. No. Yes. I don't know. I'm stoned."

With that thought lingering, she gets out of bed and starts to get dressed. Her body is bruised in places. Undoubtedly wounds of the trade. The biggest question remains to be answered—unless they fucked in a cave, and wore blindfolds, how did this girl overlook the Jon's Drawer tattoo on his calf? And if she did notice, why not say something? Why the anonymity? Embarrassment to reveal her true identity? Who knows? Doesn't matter, because this part of his weekend is over and it's time to head back to reality, feeling a sense of triumph. Along with his winnings and the whole encounter with a working girl, it all helped to redeem his masculinity that was destroyed by a girl who never gave him a chance. A shop girl who folded pants and made him feel, well, like a runner-up. He wanted to fire her but why should she suffer because she didn't want to fuck him in San Francisco? Childish? Yes. Or maybe not.

CHAPTER 39

Following weekend. Matthew lays awake most of the night, listening to the rustling of the sycamore trees and the hooting of a lone owl lost in the wrong setting, trying to find its way to a more hospitable change of scenery. His insomnia was brought on by racking his brain trying to figure out a way to soften denim material so jeans didn't look new and feel so Tin Man stiff.

It's three in the morning when he decides he needs feedback and calls Chris. Surprisingly, he is also wide-awake. Probably still pondering the loss of Michele and kicking himself for not following the rules of his own theory. Not the case—he was entertaining thoughts about a new woman in his life. For now, Matthew skips the interrogation about how and where he met her and goes directly to his own midnight madness.

"I've been cogitating about softening and fading new Levi's jackets," he says, "so they look and feel like they've been worn on the prairie over a hundred and twenty years ago."

There was a long reflective pause, then came Chris's input.

"All I know is that club soda will remove wine stains from a carpet. Any help?"

"None whatsoever."

"Call Scott Howard," Chris suggests. "His family owns and operates an industrial laundromat. He'll have answers. Gotta jump off."

"Wait, whoa, slow down! Who is she? Your new chick."

"No one you know."

"Try me."

"Her name is Claudia. She's Italian. At the moment she has no last name, but I'm betting it's also Italian."

"This is woefully inadequate information."

"She has incredible eyes and an overbite. That's all you get. I'm hanging up. We'll talk faded denim tomorrow."

They both hear the distinctive sound of a dial tone.

Okay, so after Matthew jumps off the phone with Chris, his imagination goes haywire. He's thinking this cute Italian chick Claudia is a plant. That Longo somehow found a way to splice them together and her job is to find out where Jon Lewis is hiding out in Russia. It's not as absurd as it sounds. Longo, he's sure, is getting heat from his Mob boss to do anything he can to finish this *stronzo* (Italian for "piece of shit"), who ratted on them and tried to fuck them over. At the right time, Matthew plans to tell Chris his theory. He won't buy it. He'll tell him to fuck off and call him vile names. And all because he's not about to allow Matthew or anyone else steal away his chances of having a meaningful relationship with this Italian girl with the overbite.

The following afternoon, a highly jazzed Matthew contacts Scott Howard to go over the denim process. What process? He knew less than anyone. But they both agreed washing the jackets in bleach and throwing in rough river rocks should give them that vintage, beat-up, aged look. For how long a wash cycle was unknown. And, would the rocks damage the machines? Probably. It was going to be trial and error and possibly costly.

§

As they were loading Scott's trunk with Levi's jackets for the denim experiment, they were interrupted by the high-pitched scream of a siren. A motorcycle cop was in hot pursuit of a silver gull-wing Mercedes, out of control and heading directly towards them. Making a split second decision, they quickly dodge out of the way before the Mercedes jumps the curb, crashes through the front window, and comes to a complete stop with its hood inside the store. Glass, chrome, and bent metal strewn everywhere. The window display looks as if a cyclone hit it. Smoke and steam billowing from the radiator like a spewing volcano. The motorcycle cop can't believe his eyes. He's been chasing after this lunatic for a good five miles. Nearly crashed himself when he hydroplaned through a puddle of water.

It didn't take long for a crowd to gather. A couple bystanders rush to the aid of the driver. He's trapped inside and his head is bleeding profusely. The cop calls in the emergency and while they wait for help to show up, Matthew makes a shocking discovery—this Mercedes belonged to Logan and it must be him inside with his head wedged between the steering wheel and the dashboard.

Matthew goes into panic mode. Says that's his friend, Logan, trapped inside. They need to get him out before he bleeds to death. The cop attempts to calm him down but Matthew is hell-bent on trying to pry the door open himself. No such luck. He's pulled off the car by his friend Scott.

Unhinged, Matthew starts to pace. He thinks to himself that Logan was probably driving drunk. Matthew knew this day would come when he'd almost kill himself. It was only a matter of time. If the courts have anything to say about this, Logan Alexander will be taking public transportation for a very long time.

Finally the goddamn ambulance and fire department arrive. As they pry him out, Matthew hollers: "He can't die, he's gonna be a father in a few weeks!"

They finally pry the guy out of the car, put him on a stretcher, and begin to treat his wounds. And then a shocker—this guy wasn't Logan Alexander after all. Who the fuck was he? A dead ringer. A look-a-like. An imposter. Still unconscious, the EMTs are able to revive him with smelling salts. And that's when the questions start flying left and right from the cops, the fire department, and even Matthew, who launches into a profane rant.

"Who the fuck are you man and what have you done with Logan Alexander? Is this a ransom thing? Is this about his family money? Say something, fucker!"

No one has ever seen Matthew Street this distressed. Especially about a guy he's not that fond of.

The cops finally get solid enough answers. The car was stolen from the parking lot of a local bar—a bar Logan frequented in Woodland Hills. The driver confesses to grand theft auto and claims he was paid five hundred to steal it, then drive to Tijuana. He had no name, no description of the person he dealt with. Nothing. Only a voice over the phone and a destination—a chop shop off the main drag in Tijuana called Nauchos. The cops know this MO—it's the handiwork of an auto theft ring called the Highwaymen, who work out of the San Fernando area. This was an on going problem that had been running the police ragged. The thief needed twenty-four stitches and was booked for GTA, speeding, running ten red lights, and reckless evading of a peace officer. A year max.

The good news is, Logan Alexander was cleared of any wrongdoing. But because of his excessive drinking, and his ongoing visits to the local bar, his father bans him from driving the expensive cars. From now on, a used 1965 Mustang would be his designated form of transportation.

§

Despite the unfortunate accident, the denim experiment went ahead as scheduled. Scott had displayed the final results for Matthew to evaluate. He was overcome with emotion. It turned out better than he imagined. Worn. Soft. Horse-and-buggy, rugged-looking denim. Whatever that meant; he just liked the reference to a dusty, bygone era. They accomplished what they set out to do, giving jeans that vintage look.

While the general public roared with approval, they couldn't produce the faded jeans fast enough. It became a fashion trend almost overnight.

It wasn't long before Hal Exler, the rep from Male Pants, comes in and buys three pairs. Different shades. Matthew wasn't surprised. He was waiting for this day to come. The copycats had reared their ugly heads. These guys intended to put the pants under a microscope and genetically clone them if they could. Eventually, most of the jean manufacturers got a whiff of their success and duplicated the look with there own processes. It was inevitable. For decades, the controversy lingered that Jon's Drawer actually gave birth to the faded jeans/denim look.

"Shit, let people challenge us being the first," Matthew mused philosophically. "We know what we did, and that we were fundamentally the mothers of invention."

It was a brilliant victory.

CHAPTER 40

It's been a week since Elaine and Michele had taken time off and hit the sun-drenched beaches of Puerto Vallarta. When Elaine returns (alone, by the way), she gives Matthew and Chris a handwritten resignation from Michele. She's had her fill of the apparel business. In the letter Michele thanks them for her employment and trust, and helping her find where she belongs in the real world. At the moment she belongs in Puerto Vallarta with the guy she plans to live with: Juan Medina Vargas, the assistant manager at an exclusive beachfront resort.

The boys took the news with a heavy heart. Michele would be missed. Elaine was also down about losing a friend who had helped her appreciate another form of sexuality within the zeitgeist of the hippie culture. But life goes on, and they weathered the sadness over time.

Months later, they spread their wings and expanded the corner on Ventura Boulevard to include their own little community of specialty shops. Their friends, who had witnessed Jon's Drawer's success, wanted to join in and reap their own rewards. Consequently came the birth of Jon Winkle's Bookstore, Homers Five and Ten, and a very classy, trendy women's boutique called Periwinkle. They flooded and overwhelmed the corner as a charming district for shoppers looking for unique gifts, clothing, and books. They had another grand opening and the local papers spotlighted them as a must-see attraction.

§

As these events were taking place in Sherman Oaks, meanwhile, somewhere deep in the heart of Tarzana, Logan Alexander and Emily Harwood also extended their family, with Emily giving birth to a girl—Katherine Isabelle. Soon after, they moved to the upper middle class section of Encino to raise their children in the lap of Democratic luxury. The house and the neighborhood were compliments of Logan's father. The only downside: it was located near a bar and grill.

§

With success also came disappointment. Matthew was sitting outside on a bench in front of the store reading a copy of the June 1973 issue of *Rolling Stone*. Rod Stewart, wearing a leopard skin suit, was on the cover.

Chris arrives and slumps down next to Matthew. He could feel the warmth radiating from his body. He sighs heavily, then looks at Matthew with serious eyes and wastes no time getting to the point.

"I'm done," he says flatly.

Matthew sees his own confused reflection in Chris's aviator sunglasses.

"Done with what?" he demands. "Done eating meat? Done dating women? Done with life itself? What do you mean by 'done'?"

Chris swallows hard, then explains how he wants to be bought out of Jon's Drawer. He wants out of the clothing business altogether. They can determine a fair dollar figure later, he says.

"I've had it with Mart Wednesday," he says. "And with pushy sales reps. Unfolding and refolding shirts and pants. Shrinkage. And earthy girls doused in patchouli oil with more hair under their arms than I've got on my chest and legs combined."

Chris goes on to say he was hired as the story editor on a new sitcom and intends to pursue a full-time career in television.

"That's great," says Matthew. "But can't you do both?"

"No, I don't want to do both," Chris says, almost betraying his anger.

This came as a huge disappointment. Chris's contributions and talent would be missed. But Matthew understood completely when he added that one of his biggest reasons for bailing out was that he no longer wanted to be in business with Logan Alexander.

"The man is a sizzling stick of dynamite waiting to explode," Chris opines. "He makes me nervous, and it scares me to death to think I could lose everything I've invested because of his erratic fucking behavior."

Matthew couldn't argue with him. "Yeah, you're right. We got lucky when that stranger hotwired Logan's car and drove through the window—it could have been Logan driving drunk. He dies and also kills a customer. The insurance alone would fucking bankrupt our asses. Not to mention the bad publicity. The papers would've crucified us."

"You're preaching to the choir," says Chris, adding, "Look, I'm not a quitter. I adjust. I see things through to the very end. I apologize if I'm leaving you hanging but I'd be a lousy partner, always knowing in the back of my mind that Logan held my fate in a bottle of Chivas Regal."

This conversation ended with Chris warning Matthew to watch his own back. "Stay alert," he admonished. "Don't drop your guard for a moment or you're fucked."

One warning deserves another. Matthew felt this was the perfect time to warn Chris that Claudia, his latest girlfriend, could be an informant for the Mob. Chris was staggered, nearly choking on his own spit.

"Are you on crack? That's fucking insane."

"Is it? Longo would do anything to get to Jon Lewis. Even if it meant infiltrating their friendship."

"Maybe, maybe not."

"Humor me," Matthew insists. "Where'd you meet her?"

"You're grasping at straws, Matt."

"Tell me where!"

"Okay, okay. Market. Aisle 9. We both reached for the same bottle of Italian dressing."

Matthew shrugs, indicating he believes it was an obvious setup. Chris is not convinced.

"I need more than salad dressing," he says.

"Give me a last name and let me check her out through my contacts downtown," Matthew suggests. "I'll call in a favor."

"What contacts downtown? You have contacts downtown? Since when do you have contacts downtown?"

This was not an easy thing for Chris to admit, that he might have been played by an attractive chick. He turns and walks away, noticeably confused and wary that Matthew might be right. Over his shoulder he says: "Mancuso. Claudia Mancuso. Let me know your findings, before she kills me in my sleep with an ice pick."

MATERIAL THINGS

Lawyer's office. Logan, Chris, and Matthew sign an official legal document dissolving Chris from Street, Styles and Alexander Corp. They settled on a fair five-figure amount. Nothing extravagant, because Chris knew Logan would get his father's five savage attorneys to fight it, and he just wanted to walk away clean with a few bucks and no hassle from a powerful Beverly Hills law firm.

§

Matthew's favor regarding Claudia Mancuso comes in. His source was a DA whose hair he had once cut. The results were glowing. She seems to be clear of any ties to Longo or the Mafia. No record to speak of. Never been arrested. A clean slate. Not even a parking ticket. But Matthew doesn't rule out that Longo used his influence and bought off the cops, making sure her record or any other discrepancy was untraceable. This seemed like a lot of trouble to go through just to hunt down and scoop up a small-time drug dealer like Jon Lewis. But maybe just the fact he betrayed the Mob was enough to piss off a lot of people. The tragedy of it all was, Jon never knew his source was Mafia connected until he mentioned Longo to the Feds. If it were Matthew, he would've suspected and assumed he was dealing with heavyweights. Jon either turned a blind eye or was just plain stupid.

Matthew goes to Chris and assures him that Claudia Mancuso was not a threat. But unbeknownst to Chris, Matthew kept a close watch on her for the next few weeks. Just to be on the safe side, he had his mechanic, Lonnie, follow her and report back to him. Lonnie had become a valuable asset.

CHAPTER 41

Matthew considers going to the ocean in August of '73. He hit Marina Del Rey early in the morning to look at a space that was available for lease. With the success of Jon's Drawer in the Valley, he had this urge to go to a beach city. He intended to introduce their look to the Coppertone-drenched folks normally seen wearing board shorts and flip-flops.

The place was located in a small shopping plaza right off Glencoe Avenue in the Villa Marina Center. You could smell the saltwater and hear the crashing waves from the parking lot, if you listened closely. Matthew noticed a security guard cruising the area in a blue car emblazoned with Marina Security insignia. This was a welcome sight—a deterrent for thieves who want to break in through your roof.

He was early and had to wait for the rental agent, Leslie Chase, to show. Anxious to get in, he was looking through the window like a peeping Tom, the for lease sign partially blocking his view. He kind of hoped the security guard would drive up and question him. But the guy wasn't even looking in his direction, but rather at a woman jogging along the perimeter of the plaza. She was fit and trim. Her breasts were not clamped down like normal runners, so they bounced with her every stride. She appeared to be running in slow motion, which made ogling her even more pleasurable for Matthew and the guard. Matthew looked guiltily away when the comely jogger caught him staring.

The interior was fucking fabulous. Matthew knew what to expect by the description in the *Times* classified ad. The art deco architectural and decorative style harked back to an era when people felt safe and secure. When kids could play outside till after dark. When a ladies silk dress went for $8.00, and man's suit cost a whopping $22.50. A throwback to the good old days when fashion-conscious people roamed the earth in tweed and rayon crepe in the Roaring Twenties. If he ever got to go back in time, this era would've been his choice. The most remarkable thing about this place was that it was move-in ready.

Twenty minutes later, he meets up with the leasing agent. Beachy. Attractive. Blonde. Tan. The familiar fragrance of her sunscreen replaced any sort of expensive designer perfume or unpleasant musk oil.

The agent gave him the once-over, from his long hair to his San Remo leather boots and back again, stopping at his blue eyes. He introduced himself and got straight to the point.

"I'm Matthew Street. Not to appear pushy and anxious, but when will the space be available?"

He could tell she was stumped by the abruptness of the question, so he rephrased it.

"When can I move in? I'm ready to sign at least a two-year lease."

"You know, I'm not sure." She laughed a nervous laugh. She was cute, but obviously a lousy broker. He gave her the benefit of the doubt, and figured she just got her license last Tuesday.

She opens up, brushing her hair out of her eyes on every syllable.

"I was so jazzed about meeting you. I've heard so much about Jon's Drawer."

She needed to start over again. She inhaled, getting just enough air so that she could speak in one breath and not stop mid-sentence, he was guessing.

"Okay, I should be completely honest. I'm not the rental agent you think I am."

"You're not Leslie Chase?" As she shakes her head no, her blonde hair bounces in slo-mo, like a model in a Breck hair commercial. "So who are you then?"

"A diehard fan. I'm looking for a job. I'd love to work for you. I'm into clothes. Into fashion. Into your look. I'd give anything to be the first person to introduce bell-bottoms and groovy accessories to the Marina crowd. Get them out of Bermuda shorts and tank tops."

She dropped her leather purse. They both knelt down to pick it up. She was wearing a low-cut T-shirt with no bra. Matthew got a glimpse of her tits. It was his assumption that dropping her purse was no accident, but part of her résumé.

How she knew he'd be here, baffled him. Maybe she was psychic and could also guess he found her attractive. The jogger ran by them again. The security guard also drove by, following close behind her. Could be this dude really isn't a guard but a stalker in disguise. Should he call a real cop, he ponders?

While he was watching the jogger run out of his peripheral vision, the fake rental agent wrote her real name and number on a slip of Zig-Zag rolling paper. He's sure this was to show him that she's hip and trendy. But he's guessing she never smoked a joint in her life. She looked more like a Nat Sherman filter tip cigarette kind of girl. To a lot of people, their store represented the nexus of all things hip and groovy. She desperately wanted to be part of this culture. He was flattered.

"Can I get you a cup of coffee or a glass of wine while you wait?" she asks.

"Curious," he says. "Where do you get a glass of wine at 8:30 in the morning?"

"In my car. I came prepared to celebrate in case I got the job."

Matthew ignores her optimism and just smiles politely, then starts pacing—he's anxious to get inside and scrutinize the premises. The girl doesn't leave. She just watches him walk back and forth. This makes him very uncomfortable.

"Well, it was nice meeting you"—he glances at the rolling paper like it was a crib sheet and choked on the odious name—"Andrea." This was not a name he wanted bandied around in any of his stores. She would not get a callback unless she agreed to legally change her name.

The jogger runs by a third time. Matthew thought this was just too weird and suspicious. Joggers typically run for miles in a straight path; she was running in circles. She stops directly in front of him, catching her breath. She gives him a friendly enough smile. He notices a bulge under her sweatpants. Up close, her face is masculine, with a hint of five o'clock shadow. Matthew deduces "she" was actually a "he" with fake tits—and, he's pretty sure, a gun strapped to his/her ankle. *And here I was, checking her out*, Matthew thinks, feeling his testicles contract in horror.

"Keep your nose clean, pal," she says in a deep, masculine voice. Then she gives him a friendly "arrivederci." Next, the security guard swings by and picks her up.

Matthew hits his mental panic button. It's those FBI pricks, still watching him like a hawk—an undercover operation orchestrated by the Feds. Or was it? The he-she said "goodbye" in Italian. Scratch the Feds and point the finger at Longo. The Russian thing had not panned out, so he sends a thug dressed as a busty chick to snoop and gather intelligence.

Whatever the case, Matthew ends up signing a two-year lease and agreed to take over the space at the first of next month. This gave them enough time to load in merchandise and add their personal touches where needed. He had this idea to put up a neon sign that resembled the marquee of the Pantages Theatre. Very twenties. Very art deco. Very vivid concept, he thought. He kept it to himself, for fear it would result in a verbal slugfest between Logan and him. Logan has a pessimist's aversion to everything new—a faith that it will somehow ruin him, not enrich him.

Everyone was excited about the new location, but no one was jumping at the chance to work there, because of the commuting distance. Even so, it needed a manager. Someone he could count on. Someone he could trust. Putting an ad in the local paper for an experienced manager was something to consider. Logan steps up and volunteers. He had a yacht docked at the Marina and thought it'd be the perfect setup for him. He could sleep on the boat. Ten minutes away. Couldn't be more ideal.

"What about life at home?" Matthew asks.

"Emily has it covered," he says. "She would want this for me. A job with greater responsibility. Not like some low-ranking shipping clerk in my dad's company."

Matthew didn't get it. He's a new parent. You'd think being a dad would be his top priority. Getting to know his kid. Guess not. Something was up. He's guessing his original end date was closing in on this marriage.

Unless Logan was willing to go on the wagon, the idea of him managing the shop was out of the question. This became an issue. He fought Matthew hard on it, assuring him he could do the job, and that he'd only drink after closing time.

And then he became somber. He sits down and bows his head in a pathetic fashion. The drama of this moment was almost laughable. He finally raises his head and looks into Matthew's eyes. A tear rolls down his cheek. Matthew thinks: Where did he get that tear? Did he bring it with him? And then Logan speaks in a hushed tone.

"C'mon Matty, we've been friends since our balls dropped. We're supposed to trust each other at some point. Let me prove to you, and myself, that I can be responsible. I'd like to feel useful and not be just the money guy. I know what you and my dad agreed to, but let's both show him he's dead wrong." Matthew knew that Logan Alexander wasn't strong enough to pull this off, but his impassioned plea got to him. Maybe this was a good move. It might bring them closer to again being the friends they once were as kids. Or it could backfire and really distance them and blow up in their faces. With considerable resistance, he finally gave in and agreed to it.

"You won't regret it, buddy," he says.

Buddy? He never calls Matthew buddy. It's an obsequious, boot-licking gesture. Nothing else. That alone made his decision questionable.

Logan goes outside into the blinding sunlight, where an attractive young blonde girl—a *new* blonde girl—is obediently sitting behind the wheel of his Mustang convertible. He slides in on the passenger side, and kisses her. She is checking herself out in the rearview, then turns to Logan for approval.

"Am I pretty?"

"Yes. Gorgeous. Now drive."

"Am I better in bed than your wife?"

"This is not up for discussion, Sherry."

"It's Meredith."

"Are you sure?"

"It's on my driver's license, so yeah, I'm pretty sure."

This exchange only validated Matthew's prediction—the marriage was on the brink of disaster. They drive off.

Off in the distance, a fishing trawler, headed out to sea, was bobbing up and down over the whitecaps. Matthew wished he were aboard, with his line over the side, hoping to reel in a less complicated life for himself.

§

9:00 p.m. Matthew is at home, hanging loose with Chris, eating cold pizza, slugging down beers and discussing the decision to give Logan managerial responsibility.

"It's a huge error in judgment, and we both know it," Chris says.

"He guilted me into it," Matthew explains. "Pretty sure he and Emily are about to call it quits, and I felt bad for him. It'll take his mind off the horror of divorce."

Chris crosses to the fridge to get another beer. "The only thing that'll take his mind off anything," he observes, "is a pint of Chivas Regal and a random fuck. You wanna another beer?"

"Sure. What's the worse that could happen?"

"He insults a girl who has a very large, angry boyfriend who beats him to a pulp, sends him to the ER, and they have to remove his spleen."

"Jesus. You, my friend, have conformed to a very perverted sense of values."

"It's the show I'm working on. Calls for edgy, macabre humor and has decayed my outlook on life."

Matthew suggests Chris gets himself a full-time companion—a dog or a cat or a fish. Someone to talk to and fill the void on those empty days and nights.

Chris considers the idea. "Sure, a companion. You like the name Olive for a dog?"

There's a pause from Matthew, as the name Olive jogs his memory, taking him back to a cold, misty night, long ago, on Malibu Beach. A warm feeling washes over him.

"Olive. Yes. Adorable. How'd you come up with that name?"

Chris says, "When I was in Vegas, the hooker—the one I told you about with the daughter—once had a dog named Olive."

Matthew reflects this picture in his mind. Sure, he knew that Linda Tarlow had relocated to Vegas, but working as a hooker seemed too desperate, and he hated to think she'd be that reckless and destitute. Then again, how many chicks in Vegas do you think once had a dog named Olive? He let it slide, only because if it was her, he didn't want it to be a thing between him and Chris. The likelihood of it being her was actually pretty strong. So he allowed himself to take it to another level.

"I forgot, did she have a name? The hooker."

"Never got a name. Only got what I paid for—unbridled sex."

The phone suddenly rings off the hook. They both flinch. Matthew lets it ring. Chris gives him a look.

"I'm not going to answer it because I just know it's not great news. I feel it in my bones."

"Want me to get it?" Chris says, after the fifth ring. "It could be important, like Logan calling from the ER needing a body part."

"Or Longo, finally fed up with us bullshitting him and giving him the runaround."

This was the first time Matthew wished they had nabbed Jon Lewis. Everything, especially the constant pushing and poking for answers, was getting to be too much for him.

Chris reaches for the receiver, but Matthew beats him to it. Big mistake—he should've let it ring and yanked the phone cord from the wall. It's Heather's mom. Don't ask him her name because he couldn't tell you. He sensed something was seriously wrong by the alarmed tone in her voice. He sat down to prepare himself for the worst. But he didn't expect the news she was about to lay on him.

"Matthew," she says, "this afternoon I took Heather to the doctor"—(crap, cancer!)—"and it seems"—(brain tumor!)—"well, she's two and a half weeks pregnant." He freaks.

"How is this possible?" he screams.

"Spleen?" Chris asks. Matthew covers the receiver with his hand and whispers to Chris—"Heather's mom. Says she's pregnant."

"Don't admit to anything," Chris says.

"We had taken every precaution," Matthew assures him.

He stands and begins to pace while her mother explains that she had been taking her pills as prescribed. Never missed a dose. He covered the receiver with his hand, then said out loud: *"Then what the fuck happened?"* He then drew a breath and said more calmly: "So how did this happen? I'd be interested to know how this happened. Faulty pills? Wrong dosage? She was taking a placebo all along?"

"Tipped uterus," Mrs. Wilcox says, like it's a diagnosis he should understand. His brain is getting tossed around like a tetherball. Does he need to refer to a medical dictionary before throwing an object against the wall? He covers the receiver again and turns to Chris.

"Tipped uterus. What the hell does that mean?"

"It means her uterus was tilted—on the bias," Chris says, not knowing crap about the condition.

Matthew swings back into the phone conversation.

"And another thing," Mrs. Wilcox says firmly, "Heather blames you for this and never wants to see you again."

"We're those her exact words?" Matthew asks. "That she's breaking up with me because some of my sperm accidentally got through her tipped uterus?"

"Matthew, I know this comes as a shock," she says, "but you can imagine how Heather feels."

"Can I at least speak to her?" He pauses as Chris mouths the words "she's deaf," pointing to his ear.

"If it's any consolation," Mrs. Wilcox says, "she will not take this baby to term. Your responsibility ends here." She hangs up without even a goodbye.

Matthew sits there, stunned. He tries to evaluate what just went down. Nothing makes sense because the part of his brain that chronicles logic shuts down.

"Heather blames me for her getting pregnant and never wants to see me again," Matthew tells Chris. "Somehow this was my entire fault. Like my dick caused her uterus to bend and tip and invite my sperm in for a party."

Chris observes: "It's a common female problem that no man, or even God himself, has control over."

That was a pretty bold statement—bringing God into the tipped uterus discussion. Be that as it may, in this bewildering moment, Matthew's life seemed to be spinning out of control. Andrea, Linda, Nicole, Anne Fraser, now Heather. Is it him or them? Someone has to ask that question. You can't ignore failure. Maybe Matthew needs to take a good look at himself and readjust the rearview mirror, so he can see what's coming at him, and sidestep being taken down before it punches him in the gut. Or maybe he just chose fucked-up women and doesn't realize they're fucked-up until it's too late. Choices are a manifestation of who you are.

Chris attempts to give Matthew support. But sometimes it's hard to take what Chris says as anything more than bullshit sarcasm just to get a laugh. In this case, he offers a bit of dime store philosophy that has a ring of truth to it.

"There is no reversing everything that just went down, my friend, so you just have to accept the consequences and try to move on as best you can. Here's my personal recommendation, coming from the heart. Sell that damn car of yours. Ever since you got it, it has brought you nothing but bad luck and aggravation. It's a black cat. A broken mirror. Bad mojo. Get rid of it. It's a curse that provoked Heather's tipped uterus."

Although Matthew wasn't convinced Chris's far-fetched interpretation was correct, he did consider the old man taking his life in the front seat could've siphoned all the good karma from the car. At sunrise he drove to the auto consignment lot in Brentwood and put the Rolls up for sale. It flew off the lot in two days, and he purchased a green Mercedes coupe that had no history of death or feminine wiles linked to it.

CHAPTER 42

Matthew's green Mercedes is parked on La Cienega Boulevard in Hollywood. He leans against the front fender, waiting to meet yet another leasing agent regarding a storefront rental. He's early, so he had time to grab a cup of coffee and a glazed donut. Always dressed to impress, Matthew is wearing a new Michael Milea print shirt and bell-bottoms. The guy always tried to look groovy.

As he watches cars whiz by, this boring time-killer is suddenly interrupted by a pedestrian who runs across the busy street, risking getting mowed down by an oncoming car with its horn blaring and brakes screeching. Close fucking call. Matthew almost witnessed a man being hit and probably (with his luck) landing on the hood of his green Mercedes—proving that even this car has bad mojo. Instead, this pedestrian who challenged death was fine but his momentum carried him across the street, where he stopped directly in front of Matthew's face.

He takes a moment to get his breath and blurts out, with an almost religious fervor: "I want to look and dress exactly like you. The shirt, the pants, the shoes."

Matthew backs off. This guy was wearing dark glasses, so it was difficult to tell if he was high or just another psycho who broke out from the local psychiatric ward. Matthew lets him lead the conversation, all the while making sure he doesn't pull out a knife, cut his throat, and steal his shirt just to undergo this staggering metamorphosis. A finger of doubt poked him lightly. He was prepared to toss the hot coffee into this guy's face, turn around, and hop in his car.

Matthew surveys this guy up and down and notices his nails are manicured, so he eliminated the psycho ward notion. Although who's to say asylums don't house manicurists these days? He wore an aloha shirt brimming with hibiscus and his pants were baggy and too short. Sensing Matthew's apprehension, he introduces himself and explains his mission for being in L.A.

He claimed to be Tom Sparks, an advertising artist on a business trip from Hawaii. He looked like a tourist who had taken a wrong turn, more than an artist type. Of course, it occurred to Matthew he might be a member of Cosa Nostra posing as a badly dressed out-of-towner. Another imposter, like the he/she Italian jogger.

Matthew flips out and rattles off a Russian Post Office box number—Varshavskoye shosse 37, Moscow, Russia.

"Tell Longo that's all I know," he spews in the ersatz artist's face. "And if you want fashion advice, buy fucking *GQ* or *Cosmopolitan*."

§

Trepidatious about extending this encounter, Matthew decides to cancel the meeting with the leasing agent and head back to the Valley. Driving over Laurel Canyon, he passes the Canyon Country

Store, which brought back shaky memories staying with Chris and Craig Fergus, and watching Chris fuck Susan Greene on his couch while he wallowed in self-pity about losing his wife. In the bumper-to-bumper traffic, he wasn't aware that this Tom dude was tailing him until he got to the store and saw him pull up behind his Mercedes.

Matthew rushes inside the store with Tom hot on his heels. Tom stands just outside the storefront, obviously unsure about venturing inside. A sense of panic scissors through Matthew as he breathlessly explains to his attentive audience that he's being stalked by a lunatic.

Elaine shows some balls. She crosses to the door and threatens to call the cops in her loudest, most intimidating voice. Tom gazes at her quizzically.

Matthew is slightly embarrassed, feeling he's acting like a pussy and should show some courage. Stand up to this character—give him a message to relay to Longo. Just to be on the safe side, he stands inside the door as he says his piece.

"Look, buddy, we've been through a lot and have had just about enough of the tough talk and the aggressive nature of Vince Longo. So, go back and tell him that whatever he wants to do, just get it over with and don't send his flunkies around to do his dirty work. Understand? This is not a difficult request."

The guy reaches into his back pocket. Matthew backs off, thinking he's reaching for a gun. Relief comes when he pulls out a wallet and shows him photos of his wife, cat, and house in Oahu. When he speaks, his voice has lost its religious fervor. He sounds like a guy apologizing for some misdeed he hasn't actually committed.

"This is my wife, Gina. The cat's name is Tim. I'm just a normal guy. I swear I have no connection with the Mafia. I'm not even

Italian. I am who I say I am, and I'm sorry if I'd caused you guys any undue stress."

With that he walks away, clearly baffled by this whole crazy experience that began over a pair of pants and a shirt.

§

Later, in the backroom, Matthew sits and ponders his fate. How had it come to this? He needed answers. He would be the first to admit that his persecution complex has spiraled out of control, and he's convinced that being highly suspicious of every person who has a picture of a cat in their wallet could cause him long-term psychological problems. He wrestled with the notion of either seeking help, or eventually being committed. Sure, this latter scenario was overkill, but he decided to see a shrink as a precaution.

He grabs the Yellow Pages and starts thumbing through like he's looking for a plumber. He looks under the M's for mental illness. There's a list of conditions to choose from: clinical depression, anxiety disorder, bipolar disorder, dementia, attention deficit disorder, schizophrenia, and finally obsessive-compulsive disorder. *Boom*, a winner! That's his category. He picks a doctor randomly, landing on a Dr. Jeffrey Kass, who had a Ph.D., a license, and an office with a couch. He made an appointment for just one session. He just needed to know if any of this behavior was justified or not. No delving into how his mother may have breast-fed him well into his teens.

§

Beverly Hills. Tuesday, four p.m. Matthew lies on a soft leather couch. He preferred to sit in a chair but it seems Dr. Kass preferred the idea of the couch because it relieved them the burden of eye contact.

"You don't like eye contact?" Matthew inquires. This seemed really fucking odd.

"It's distracting, and I find it tiring," says the shrink. "This way, we can both look wherever we like. Up at the ceiling. The door. The window. Your hand."

"Do you ever sleep while I'm talking?" Matthew asks.

"I may close my eyes but I assure you I am fully awake and homed in on your every word."

The doctor nervously sucks on the tip of his horn-rimmed glasses. Matthew reads this as an indication that he's the one who had a serious breast-fed nipple problem. Before they got into it, the doctor says that one session is not going to relieve the burden. It's a process that takes many hours to explore. For Matthew *hours to explore* was code for costly.

"Your paranoia could go as far back as your childhood," Kass explains. "Even while still in the womb. This is not a disorder that is cured overnight. It grows inside a person and can migrate for years."

On the word "migrate," Matthew bolts upright and turns his attention to the doctor. He has his eyes closed, his head facing up at the ceiling.

"Migrate? We're talking a slight psychosis here, doc, not about wildebeest relocating across the Serengeti;"

With his eyes still shut, Kass replies: "Often times I'll use a euphemism for a problem that settles in the subconscious and is unable to identify itself."

"Doc, I have no idea that psychobabble you just laid on me means, but what I do know is that this session is over. Thanks for the use of the couch. This piece of furniture seems to haunt me wherever I go."

He leaves, and as heads for his car, he makes his own diagnosis—you can't blame the womb for every malfunction in one's life. He also determines that his mental health is solid. His fear of going down in flames because of the Jon Lewis affair, and any Mafia vengeance, is not unnatural, and whatever happens—so be it. Armed with this liberating *que sera, sera* attitude, Matthew mentally pays himself sixty-five dollars for shrinking his own head.

§

When Matthew returned to the shop, there was a bottle of wine and a Hawaiian fruit basket waiting for him from Tom Sparks. The card attached read: *A small token from us folks at the Mob offices.* Matthew had a choice to make. He could either accept Tom's biting sarcasm or, fearing it contained a bomb masquerading as a pineapple, toss the basket out the window. On the advice of his employees, who were concerned about his whacked-out behavior, he made the rational decision to take Tom Sparks and his wife to dinner. This, they advised him, would help relieve his suspicions—but under no circumstances, should he mention his mother's womb.

The Smoke House Restaurant in Toluca Lake was not Matthew's kind of eatery but Tom's wife Gina was a great admirer of nostalgia, red leatherette booths, and waiters as old as the original menu.

They were seated in an advantageous spot commanding a perfect panorama of the comings and goings of the restaurant and its staff. They ordered drinks, then Matthew dove into a complex explanation of his paranoid behavior, opening up about how hectic and strained his life had become ever since the Jon Lewis drug fiasco, with the Feds and the Mafia haunting his every step and throwing off his game.

"I'm sure my store, my apartment, and even the flower arrangement on this table are all bugged," Matthew moans. "I usually go outside or turn up the volume on the radio to make sure my conversations are garbled."

"Oh, dear, it sounds like an awful way to have to live," Gina comments, smiling sympathetically.

"It has been pretty unnerving."

Tom tries to come up with some choice advice: "If it were me, I'd go talk to a shrink to help relieve the mental strain. These dudes can work wonders analyzing the biggest problem and making it go away in a snap," Tom professes.

There is a pause while Matthew remains uncertain how to answer his inane proposal for tackling his problem. Instead he vehemently strangles the life out of the napkin in his lap, then says with serious intonation: "Let's order, shall we?"

As the three of them order the traditional prime rib dinner. Matthew takes advantage of Tom's artistic perspective and runs an idea past him about designing and producing his own line of jeans. Tom loves the concept and offers to help design an ad campaign when Matthew is ready to market the pants.

Matthew, feeling a real connection to Tom, is blown away by his offer. This blossoming bond makes Matthew feel even more foolish for not trusting this affable guy with a cat named Tim. As a peace offering, he gifts Tom the shirt, pants, and shoes he admired during their first insane meeting on La Cienega Boulevard.

CHAPTER 43

If there was a pant you could wear out and know it would tame the opposition, wouldn't you buy it? Real blue denim, yellow piping, pearl snaps, bleached and softened. This was Matthew Street's design and his philosophy, and he needed a pattern maker.

Evelyn Bouvier was a veteran recommended by an instructor at the Fashion Institute of Design. She had worked in the Paris fashion industry before moving to the United States and striking out on her own. She was very French. Everything about her was very French. Her studio had the distinct aroma of lavender and rosemary. This was considered very French. She was now sixty-seven years old but looked forty-seven. In a word, she looked amazing. Matthew retained a few French words and phrases from his high school days. His accent was questionable but he went for it anyway. "*Vous* êtes *très belle*," he says. Translation: *You look amazing*. She by all means was flattered.

"Are you trying to hit on me, Monsieur Street?" she says in her pronounced French accent.

"Yes," he says, keeping up with this cute repartee.

"Oh, so I can only guess you are hoping your enormous flattery will maybe get you a far cheaper price for the pattern."

"Maybe. Yes. No. Not my intention. But if that'll help lower the cost, then yes. But if not, I still meant what I said about you being a most attractive woman. You have retained the glow and youthful look of a magazine model, Mademoiselle Bouvier. Good for you."

"Aw, Monsieur Matthew. I do so adore your honesty," she says with a charming smile. "You flatter me and make me blush like a schoolgirl in French braids and knee-high stockings. Will one hundred dollars work for you? If not, keep complimenting me and see how low I will go."

"You are truly a woman of sumptuous style. I don't usually talk that way, but being in your presence is intoxicating, Mademoiselle."

"Okay, eighty-five—and that's my last offer, young man."

"I would not be a true gentlemen if I didn't pay your original fee of two-hundred," he says.

She gives him an air kiss on each cheek.

"I've loved you American boys ever since the French Revolution," she quips.

§

Matthew was so certain this was a great business venture that he borrowed against he shares in the corporation. He was supremely confident, yet at the same time nervous because he didn't want to crash and burn in a blaze of obscurity. He didn't need James Alexander telling him he was a disappointment, just like his son. A month later Matthew and Scott Howard, who first helped him with the faded denim experiment, went into production at Scott's plant located deep in Van Nuys. Scott knew the apparel business better than anyone. Matthew watched rigidly as the sewing was done in an assembly line fashion, with each seamstress assigned to a specific function on rows of industrial sewing machines. It was an amazing symphony of needle, thread, and the humming machines performing together.

Matthew made sure the first pair off the line was in his size. They fit perfectly. This was cause for a celebration. With the absence of champagne, one of the workers passed around a bottle of tequila he had stashed in his locker. A rousing *felicidades* was heard throughout the plant.

§

Weeks later, their shelves were overflowing with the new jeans. This included the Marina store and the newest location in Hollywood. They weren't exactly walking out the door on every person but sales were pretty favorable. For now all they had was word of mouth advertising and a small ad in *The Los Angeles Free Press* (popularly known as *The Freep*). They needed a big push. A clever campaign.

Logan had a plan and wanted to talk. They decide to meet at the Marina store since he was already close by. It seems he and Emily were on the outs, so he's spending all his time alone on his boat. He decided to take a backseat as manager because his drinking became excessive when he and Emily started to quarrel more routinely, and he became more belligerent. Booze was hard for him to give up. It was his strength. His power. His control.

8:00 p.m. Matthew got there an hour before closing. The store was buzzing. The locals seemed to be thrilled by the Valley-inspired fashion trends they'd introduced to Marina Del Rey. The Pantages Theatre-type marquee was illuminated like a spotlight advertising a world movie premiere movie. Sheila was filling in as manager. Tonight, however, Matthew found her in the office, staring blankly out an open window into the thick, salty air. She was having a glass of wine, a diversion she normally never took, but tonight was an exception. She looked a little troubled. Almost pale.

"You okay?" Matthew asks.

There was a long pause before she turns to him and says, "I heard from Jon this morning."

Keep in mind, it's been over a year since they'd had any news of Jon Lewis. Most of them thought the Mafia finally had caught up with him and he was at the bottom of the ocean with a bag of cement chained to his dick. Not the case. In keeping with his love for prolific nineteenth-century novelists, he was living in London under the name of Charlie Dickens. Seems Tony Clarke, the English T-shirt vendor, helped him make his great escape through Canada. Through his own illegal connections, he supplied Jon not only with a phony passport but also an airline ticket in a matter of twenty-four hours.

Sheila did not hold back her emotions. She was overjoyed to find out he was still alive. The wine served as both a celebratory vehicle and a calming agent. She took a healthy chug before revealing some blistering news. He had contacted her using a pay phone in Palm Springs. This obviously jolted Matthew's senses.

"What? He's in the country?" he barked.

"Supposedly his mother died and he crossed over through Canada to attend the funeral. Could all be a diversion to fool the Feds," she says. "It was stupid and dangerous to say the least, but I'm anxious to see him."

It's all that Matthew can do to keep from picking up the phone, contacting Bud Collins and the Feds, and drawing them a road map showing his exact location. Sheila knows the hatred and contempt that Matthew has for Jon. Nevertheless, she asks for a personal favor—a favor, unbeknownst to her, that would cost her dearly. She plans to see him this weekend and asks if Matthew would give her time off, plus keep all this intrigue under wraps. There is a natural pause, giving Matthew time to clench his fist and massage his now throbbing temples.

Waiting for an answer, Sheila tilts her head at him. He senses she can detect his general wariness. Despite the fact he's corrupt, she can't help but still have these deep feelings for Jon. Her compassion outweighs the severity of his crimes.

Matthew crosses to the open window and sucks a deep draft of the salty air into his lungs. He then turns back to her, giving into her request.

"Sure, time off. Take the whole month. But when you get back, you should look for another job."

Sheila is stunned. "Really? You're serious? I'm fired for having feelings?"

"Here's how it is, Sheila," Matthew says, as calmly as he can manage. "I can't be linked with anyone who is so close to Jon Lewis. In my eyes he's crawling vermin, clearly responsible for me being watched and spied on like *I'm* the bad guy. Like *I'm* the drug pusher. Like *I'm* the one who embezzled twenty thousand dollars from the store."

"I'm truly sorry this happened," Sheila says, "but I'm not sorry I love Jon."

Matthew offers a warning: "Yeah, well, don't think you're out of the woods. They probably bugged your phone and have a set of binoculars on you day and night. Our conversation is over. Leave the keys before you let yourself out."

Sheila heads for the door, bewildered. Doesn't utter another word. Not even a sigh. She made a choice, and it was obvious whose side she had chosen. The side of the enemy, who hopefully will get what's coming to him someday.

§

Logan eventually shows up. Late, but sober, so that's a plus. On this night, he was unusually friendly. This was the Logan Alexander Matthew once liked very much. Clearheaded and alert. He first told him how he had just fired Sheila not more than twenty minutes ago.

"Pilfering?"

"Infatuated with the devil," Matthew corrects himself. "Don't ask. Long story. So what's all the excitement about?"

Logan gets right to it: He wants to franchise the Jon's Drawer brand.

A feeling of doubt punches Matthew in the stomach like the first drop of a roller coaster. Franchising sounds good when you're a huge corporation or a professional sports team, but to him, this titanic financial venture had all the earmarks of potential disaster.

Logan wanted to sell the jeans Matthew designed under their own label. He was rational and sensible and also brutally honest.

"Personally, I don't love the pants," he says. "The design's too fashion-forward for my taste. But merchandising them in the right markets could make us a lot of money."

"Logan, I don't—"

"Think about it. Sleep on it. Get back to me. It's not a decision that needs to be made right away. I have to get back to the boat—I have a Pan Am stewardess waiting for me."

Why he couldn't have said all this over the phone was a mystery. Maybe to prove he could talk without falling over.

Matthew immediately jumped on the phone and ran this notion past Chris and Tom Sparks on a conference call. They thought it wasn't an awful idea. Smart business move, they said. So Matthew went for it. Another arm of their already formed corporation was put into place. Logan had his father's attorney's draw up the papers.

They both agreed they needed a stellar campaign promotion ad to sell the public on the Jon's Drawer brand. Something stylized. Matthew sold Logan on the idea of using Tom Sparks in Hawaii. He called Tom in advance and ran by the whole campaign idea by him. Tom was excited to be involved. He insisted on offering his services as a favor.

"No way," Matthew said. "Charge us like any other client."

He had a good reason: It's hard to be critical or make creative suggestions when you're getting something for free.

§

Friday. Shortly after eight in the morning, Logan and Matthew hop a plane at LAX and head for Honolulu to meet with Tom Sparks. They flew business class because Logan needed leg space, comfort, and special attention. He also took the aisle seat, claiming that he suffers from claustrophobia.

They were both quiet for the most part until they reached cruising altitude, then Logan opened up about his personal life, primarily his marriage, which wasn't going so well. Seems he and Emily were separating indefinitely after four years.

"I predicted four and a half," Matthew says.

"Really? My dad gave it five. Either way, it's a lousy crying shame. Not every marriage makes it. There are so many reasons why they fail. The love runs out, the passion slowly dissipates, and communication stops."

"And then there's the womanizing husband who drinks too fucking much," Matthew offers.

"Yeah, that too."

Logan would see his kids every other weekend. Was he okay with that?

"It is what it is. I'm not the only guy whose marriage had failed. Thousands of us are out there. We should start a boys club, and meet once a week at a local bar to drown our sorrows, and exchange ideas on how we plan to scrape up alimony and child support payments and not go broke doing it."

"Who knows, maybe if you give it time—take a break from each other, go see a marriage counselor—things will work out."

"Can I be brutally honest?" says Logan.

"Please do."

"I'm not so sure I want it work out. It's been a rough road. She would be the first to say that I'm not the easiest person to live with. I have issues. On a good day, I drink myself into oblivion. Cheat on a regular basis. And when confronted, deny that I cheat. These are not traits that can be rectified by talking to a marriage counselor. So, my future as a husband looks bleak. The important thing though is making sure my kid is not traumatized by the separation."

Matthew wasn't sure what to do with that confession so he just shrugged.

Neither of them said another word for five hours and fifty minutes—until the sound of the landing gear lowered from the undercarriage. And even then Matthew only muttered, "We're here."

CHAPTER 44

Oahu. Tom picked them up at their hotel. He and his wife, Gina, had invited them to stay at their place, but Logan was not comfortable about inconveniencing himself. He had to be in full control of his own personal needs and because of that, Matthew was forced to stay at a hotel with him and forgo the luxury of a home-cooked meal and settle for idle conversation with room service. He's not complaining just stating facts. No, he's definitely complaining.

Tom's Jeep Wrangler hugged the Kamehameha Highway like it had driven over it a thousand times. A chorus line of palm trees vamped against the Hawaiian sky as Tom threaded his way through traffic and onto a two-lane open road.

"Could we stop and buy a six-pack?" Logan says.

"We'll be there in less than an hour and Gina has prepared us a brunch."

Logan makes a blanket statement—he only drinks Beck's German beer. Anything else is unacceptable. They stop at the first liquor store and wait while Logan jumps out and grabs his brew. This would be the first of many apologies Matthew would make to Tom.

"Is he always this, you know, wound so tight?" Tom asks Matthew.

"Tight? This is him on a laid-back day."

Just as Logan comes out of store, already drinking a beer, three unmarked cars screech into the parking lot and surround them like covered wagons on the prairie. Half a dozen men in blue nylon jackets with FBI stenciled on the back exit the cars in what appears to be a tactical maneuver. It literally becomes a shouting match as they instruct the guys to raise their arms in the air, and assume the position against the liquor store wall. Position? What position? It's not like they're familiar with their vernacular.

Matthew attempts to get answers but is abruptly told to keep quiet and follow instructions. They go into a standard pat down, checking for weapons and any sort of contraband.

Logan is irate. "We've done nothing! We're old enough to buy beer. And we're rich enough to buy and sell you guys twice over. This is fucking harassment!"

An agent spouts off: "There's always one guy who thinks he can ignore the rules."

"We're U. S. citizens. We have rights!" Logan insists.

"Oh, please, spare us the histrionics and just shut the fuck up, till we're done here."

Neither Logan nor Tom was in the dark about what this was all about. They knew. Tom looked a little scared.

"Okay, which one of you gentlemen is Matthew Street?"

"You would think by now," Matthew says with chilling equanimity, "you guys would know who I am—my height, weight and what I had for breakfast."

One of the agents sidles up close behind Matthew. "Okay, smart guy, where is he?" he demands.

"Where is who, the Lindbergh baby?" Matthew says.

"Your friend Lewis—and cut the wisecracks."

Matthew becomes frustrated and angry. He's had enough of their interrogations, their insinuations, and their being on his heels for the past two years. He loses it and spills his guts.

"You want Jon Lewis. I'm gonna give him up, so maybe you'll leave me alone. Last I heard he was in Palm Springs to bury his mother, Agnes. Probably lowering the casket as we speak."

"He's lying," Logan interjects. "Actually, Jon's in Pamplona, running with the bulls. I swear it!"

His smart-ass remark is not taken lightly. The guys are cuffed and detained at the scene for another half hour until a Special Agent shows up. He's not formally introduced, but he's a fireplug of a man, intense and all business. This Special Agent pulls Matthew aside and, speaking in a stage whisper, very straightforward telling him that catching up with Jon Lewis is imperative. A number-one priority. His testimony is an important component in taking down Vincent Longo.

"It appears that while Jon was making a drug run early one foggy morning on the Vincent Thomas Bridge in San Pedro," the Special Agent confides to Matthew, "he witnessed a woman being tossed into the briny deep by two unidentified men and failed to report it to the authorities."

"And how does that concern me?" Matthew argues. "And who reported Jon being a witness? Another witness? Certainly not the dead woman or the guys who tossed her off the bridge. A fish that was swimming by, perhaps? Or are you guys just guessing that Jon saw this?"

"Look, Street, the important thing here is that we need his testimony. The unfortunate lady who took a header was an assistant district attorney who had evidence that could put Longo away for tax evasion. Almost a carbon copy of the Al Capone conviction in 1931. And being that Jon Lewis was the only witness, Longo is willing to go to great lengths to shut him up and take him down. Even if it means screwing with your life until he does. Trust me, this dude will not rest until he finds Lewis and cuts off his balls."

The San Pedro bridge incident was the turning point for Matthew. Jon had gotten in deeper than any of them had imagined. Drug running, embezzlement, and now witness to a Mafia hit of a Los Angeles district attorney. At this juncture Matthew had an obligation to help track down Jon and bring this case to an end before someone else died—like himself.

Matthew assured the Feds the Palm Springs particulars were factual. After they were finally released, Matthew sat down, leaned against the wall, and felt a surge of guilt flow through him because he had given Jon up. But he figured by the time they send local agents to pick him up he may have already split the country. But you never know. They could break into his mother's dingy house and discover Sheila and him having crude sex on that rickety old kitchen table with the cat looking on from the windowsill. Whatever the result, Matthew was, in the words of the bad guys, a rat fink/stoolie. But there's a consequence to pay if they don't catch Jon—Matthew would still be on their persons of interest list. So he wasn't by any means in the clear. He was fucked. And the beat goes on.

§

Twenty minutes later, they were being served a platter of deli food, compliments of Gina and Tom. They of course explained why they were late and the whole unnerving ordeal with the FBI. This made both Gina and Tom anxious, thinking that now they're on the FBI's radar, and will be watched and have to sleep with one eye open until Jon Lewis is either apprehended or killed. Matthew apologizes, but he couldn't promise them being kept under surveillance was not going to happen. Truth was, it was probably a sure bet that they would be under the FBI's microscope until Jon was brought in. Not a great way to live for any of them.

As they sat on the veranda, Gina, noticeably on edge, changes the subject to something less sanguinary.

"So, Logan, what big plans are you hatching?" she asks.

Logan is caught off guard that the question is directed to him and not to Matthew. "Me? Hatching? You mean like formulating?"

"I guess I mean, what's your future look like?"

"In the grand scheme of things, divorce, child support, alimony." Whoa, that put the conversation under a dark cloud.

"Sorry to hear that," Gina says.

"It happens. Can't force happiness. And as far as the store, well, we're here doing it. Formulating a plan to make a highly sought-after brand name for ourselves in the world of clothing, specifically pants."

He gets up from the table, walks over to the edge of the veranda that overlooks the ocean. He watches the force of the waves crashing against the rocky shoreline. The sound is powerful. He's bothered by it.

"How do you people live with the noise? I know you guys see this place as a tropical paradise but for my money, living on an island with the chance of being caught in a tsunami, and hot lava running through my kitchen, would keep me up nights."

"Well," Tom says, "we don't think of it as noise as much as soothing music to our ears."

"It beats the sound of sirens, car horns, and an occasional gunshot strafing through the night air, in our neck of the woods," Matthew says with a slight laugh.

"I guess the sound of an occasional siren and a gunshot every now and then is music to my ears," Logan says with his own muffled laugh. He seemed in good spirits. But sometimes with him that's just a cover-up before all hell breaks loose and he launches into a tirade.

After lunch, it's down to business, checking out the ads Tom drew up. This became an instant issue. Logan was noticeably baffled. Says he wasn't aware that Tom had already been working on it. He presumed they were there to bounce ideas around. He obviously misunderstood Matthew when he said he gave Tom an early go-ahead, so that they at least had something tangible to see.

"Thing is, I expected to be involved from the start," Logan remarks. "Not come in midway when all the creative work is already done. This is as much my idea as it is anyone else's."

"No one is disputing that, Logan. This is a total team effort from beginning to end," Matthew says.

Tom jumps in. "In my opinion, the jeans thing you guys came up with is a great innovative idea. And I think I hit it on the nose. It says who you are and what you're selling. Style plus an ongoing commitment. It's clever, yet at the same time it displays a public image."

"Sure. Public image. Style. Got it. Let's take a look, why don't we?" Logan says with a snap of his fingers.

They gathered in Tom's home studio. It was an impressive area. Some of his best marketing artwork, framed in natural wood, hung on the teal gray walls. Also in evidence were advertising awards. Matthew was definitely in awe and confident they chose the right man for the job.

Tom tries to settle any nerves and offers them a joint. Logan passes, underscoring he didn't want anything to interfere with his appreciation of the artwork.

Tom then breaks out the Jon's Drawer ad. It fucking blows Matthew away. Two figures sketched in ink, a male and female in a sexy pose, with the words Wear Outs spelled out in a slanted rope font at the top of the page. Clever? No. Ingenious? Yes. They turn their attention to Logan for his reaction and comments. They assume he'll love it too.

He pauses before giving them his critique. "Look, I can appreciate your expertise, Tom. You're a helleva fine artist. Me, as a kid, I couldn't even stay in the lines in my coloring book."

A finger of doubt pokes Matthew. He felt like a bomb was about to explode. Call it a fearful premonition. Logan holds the rendering in his hand and studies it for a few beats. Then he looks up with trepidation in his eyes, his lower lip quivering.

"I'm gonna be honest. After all, I'm paying for this ad, and I think I have the right to be straightforward."

Now Matthew's lip started to quiver. Hold on, here comes the tirade.

"Yeah, you have a perfect right to be blunt," Tom says.

"It leaves me flat. Empty. Hollow. Disconcerted. I'm skeptical about using words like *bland* and *trivial*—but it's how I feel."

Matthew could feel his jaw drop and hit the floor. Tom, who never had his work branded as trivial, is in a complete state of shock and doesn't try to cover it.

Logan isn't done. Without missing a beat, he turns to Matthew and says this was a fucking wasted trip. "Thanks for the deli," he mutters right before he sails the rendering across the room like a

MATERIAL THINGS

Wear Outs

If there was a pant that you could wear out* and know...really know it would tame the opposition...wouldn't you buy it?

*Wear Outs: real blue denim, yellow piping, pearl snaps, bleached and softened $25.00.

Exclusively at Jon's Drawer

Jon's Drawer

Villa Marina Center 4371 Glencoe Avenue
Marina Del Rey 823-9114
436 N. La Cienega Boulevard Los Angeles 657-4680
13538½ Ventura Boulevard Sherman Oaks 783-9507

cheap Frisbee. He then storms out like a wuss. This was more than just a tirade; it was a fucking temper tantrum.

Matthew thought about chasing after him. But why bother? You can't fight stupidity. Without any means of transportation, Logan hitched a ride to the airport, then headed directly back to the mainland without checking out of the hotel. Left his clothes, left his maturity. Matthew felt sick inside.

Gina had witnessed the whole ordeal. Her evaluation? Logan Alexander needed someone to really love him and accept his flaws. Gina was a registered child psychologist who had seen this behavior many times in young children who lacked affection from their parents and tend to rebel when confronted by the enemy—the enemy being another adult who seems to be in charge of their feelings and their decision-making. Also, she's pretty sure his pending divorce, and the abandonment that comes with it, was the spark that made him fly into a rage.

§

Matthew left for the mainland on the weekend, hoping to reverse the tension and quell the animosity. He thanked Tom and Gina for their hospitality and apologized (for the thousandth time) for Logan's shitty behavior. And his equally shitty lack of appreciation of good artwork.

"Well, I'm off to try to bring this latest melodrama to a sensible and calm conclusion," he said after bidding them goodbye.

He's not Catholic or a religious guy, but he crossed himself as he said this.

CHAPTER 45

Logan Alexander and Matthew Street had known each other forever, longer than they'd known anyone else. In light of recent events they'd gone from being close friends to two guys with not much to say to one another. Matthew played the only hand he had left: swallowing his pride and reasoning with his estranged friend.

It's sunrise, and Matthew decided to get an early start, hoping to catch Logan on his boat in the Marina. Still playing the angry card, he refused to acknowledge that Matthew was standing on the deck of his Italian yacht trying to make amends, with coffee and fresh bagels. He banged on the cabin door several times. Maybe too loud. Maybe too hard. He saw movement through a porthole, so he knew Logan was there, avoiding him. From inside he heard a woman's voice: "He doesn't want to speak to you and asks that you get off his boat."

For the next few minutes Matthew tries to use common sense and sound judgment, suggesting they throw out what Tom did and start from scratch with an artist of his choice. Van Gogh if he wants. Humor didn't help the situation. Made it worse. Again the same female voice comes from inside, this time carrying an obvious threat: "He's calling the port authorities and having you arrested for trespassing and unlawful entry." That remark was a little harsh, even for Logan. Matthew guesses the girlfriend came up with that warning.

Defeated, Matthew tosses the bagels in the water for the seagulls to feast on, then leaves the artwork on the deck, hoping Logan would keep an open mind and see the value of the ad. None of this made sense, as franchising the Jon's Drawer name was his idea to begin with. Gina was right: Logan is rebelling against the people who always controlled him—the adult community he had to obey throughout his childhood. And unfortunately he now sees Matthew as the grown-up.

Matthew drove slowly, trying to gather his thoughts. Logan Alexander had lost it.

He couldn't have predicted what came next if he was given ten thousand guesses.

Matthew arrives at the Marina store at approximately 7:15 a.m. Give or take a few minutes. Doesn't matter because he's in store for a rude awakening that will throw his day into more turmoil. In front, blocking the door stands a burly sheriff, with his arms folded across his barrel chest like he's guarding the entrance to the Palace of Versailles. Matthew assumes he's there to beef up the security in the mall. He gives the guy a friendly nod, then tries to walk around this hefty hunk of flesh. The man shifts, impeding his path.

"Excuse me," Matthew says. "I can appreciate your commitment to keep this place safe from the bad guys, but I'm one of the good guys who just needs to get inside my shop."

"You must be Matthew Street," the sheriff replies assertively.

"I am. Nice meeting you."

Matthew makes another attempt to enter the store and is once again stopped when the sheriff plants his Frisbee-sized mitt against his chest.

"I'm afraid you've been legally prohibited from entering the premises, sir," he says.

Prohibited? What the hell is this fuck talking about?

"Wait. Stop. My name is on the lease. Doesn't that count for anything? Doesn't that give me the right to enter my own fucking store?"

The hulking sheriff, finally exhibiting a whiff of compassion, explains the horror of it all—that Logan Alexander ordered an injunction against him, violating a corporate agreement. He mentions James Alexander and his attorney but says he can't—or won't—divulge any other details. He was still in the dark and he wasn't about to argue with this cartoon cop who was actually allowed to carry a gun. He needed more of an understandable, lucid reason that would stop him from shaking and sweating and convulsing and clenching his teeth, his hands balled into fists and his mind racing in all directions.

He rushes to a pay phone and calls James Alexander's attorney. It was now 7:40 a.m. He didn't care if he woke him or if he was in the middle of fucking his trophy wife. It didn't ring fast enough.

"Jacob, it's Matthew Street. What the fuck is going on with my store? They won't let me in. Sheriff said it was because of some legal crap you and James Alexander drummed up. Pull your small dick out of your wife and give me answers." There's a pause. "No, I won't calm down! There is nothing so far that gives me reason to be even-tempered!" He's screaming to the point of almost rupturing his larynx.

The lawyer explains that when they drew up the original corporate papers, one of the stipulations was that any of the shares could be borrowed against or revoked at any time. Matthew used the money for his shares to fund the production of the jeans with Scott Howard. At the time, Logan wanted no part of this. He didn't believe in the pants. Thought they were unattractive and that there was no market for them. So when things recently went south in Hawaii, Logan became more of a tyrant and a bully and called back the stocks to force Matthew's hand, using the one weapon he knew would ruin him—financial recourse. Matthew's only choice was to pay back the loan or he'd lose total interest in the corporation and the store. Logan knew he had no way of paying it back, so he ordered a restraining order to keep Matthew out. He was screwed. All this because Tom Sparks went ahead and designed an ad without Logan's authorization. This was profoundly unscrupulous.

Matthew jumps in his car and speeds away, leaving the store and what appears to be his livelihood behind. There was nothing preventing him from taking out a loan with Longo, and reacquiring his corporate shares. But the more he thought about it, the more it didn't make sense. Why would he want to continue a partnership with a guy who hated him enough to ruin his life over a pair of denim pants?

This was not the end of Logan Alexander's streak of destructiveness and Matthew's angst. A more senseless act of aggression ensued. A week goes by and in the early misty morning the finance company hauls away Matthew's green Mercedes. Never got a warning. Like a thief in the night, creeping in the underbrush, the repo man towed his lonely, isolated car to wherever they take possession of delinquent loans on people who are considered bad risks. He's guessing the same chop shop across the Mexican border, where Logan's gull-wing Mercedes would've met its dismantlement if the theft had gone according to plan.

So now, Matthew is walking, hitchhiking, or taking public transportation. Alternative measures are escalator, elevator, or skateboard. Not exactly the upward mobility he thought he'd be experiencing at this point in his life.

§

The local Marina tabloid got wind of what went down about Matthew being prohibited from setting foot on what was once his domain, Jon's Drawer. Having heard about the legal ramifications, they took his side, feeling that Logan Alexander and his lawyers had overstepped their authority and were jeopardizing the reputation of the Jon's Drawer franchise, as well as sales—especially the innovative new jean that Matthew designed bearing the distinctive Jon's Drawer label.

Surprisingly, the news article brought on demonstrators, at both the Sherman Oaks and Marina Del Rey stores. A news report aired on the local TV station. The countless supporters overwhelmed Matthew to the point of tears.

The employees were forced to close the doors for fear there would be a backlash from angry consumers, who were loyal fans of Matthew Street. Someone had sent a message and tossed a brick through the Marina window. Leave it to the beach crowd to flex their muscle.

Logan Alexander was not available for comment. A bummer that it came down to this kind of language, but *chicken shit bastard* was the chant of the angry crowd gathered in front of the store on that foggy morning in the beach city. The consensus of opinion was that Logan was too drunk to realize he had been ostracized and ridiculed for his behavior and his bullying tactics.

When a beer bottle was hurled through the window like a mortar shell, and nearly took off Elaine's head, it was the last straw. She quit on the spot and decided to meet up with Michele in Puerto Vallarta. In the hands of Logan Alexander, she figured Jon's Drawer was on its last legs. About to slip into a prolonged coma.

In her parting note to Matthew, she wrote: "Really a shame—your dream has become a living nightmare."

CHAPTER 46

1974 creeps in. Matthew had some money stashed away, but with no other income and no car, he was forced to move into a much smaller, inexpensive place. Ruling out the YMCA or joining the Army, he found a duplex for rent next door to his seamstress, Dede. Awkwardly enough, it was located directly behind the Sherman Oaks store. But this did not discourage him. He was desperate for a roof over his head and crashing on another couch was totally out of the question.

Chris came over to help him move the small stuff—his toothbrush and what little self-respect he had left.

While they both packed up the memories and the damn fitted sheets that were rolled into a ball because they were impossible to refold correctly, Chris comes across a photo album of Matthew's wedding day. He holds it up for a judgment call.

"Your wedding album. Keep it or toss it?"

"I guess keep it," Matthew says.

"Yeah. Smart decision. You never know when you'll one day break it out and reminisce with friends around a cozy fire, about a marriage that didn't work, and a wife who didn't trust you."

"Okay. Good point. Start a cozy fire with it."

As Chris continues to rummage through the box of memorabilia, he comes across a picture of Matthew on the beach in Malibu standing next to a girl and her Doberman. Who took this picture? Doesn't matter. What matters is, he recognizes the girl as the Las Vegas hooker. It's not a hard puzzle to solve—this has to be Olive, the Doberman she was referring too. Dilemma—does Chris say something or let it slide? Why open up this can of worms? What will it accomplish? Nothing except hurt and anger, and destroy the reputation of a girl who Matthew once admired. A girl who was trying to survive a controversial vocation and lifestyle to make a better life for her and her daughter. Chris rips up the photo so there's no solid evidence of her memory to cause any grief down the line. This will remain his secret that he's pretty sure is not a secret at all, but rather a bizarre triangle they're all aware of, but for their own personal reasons, they refuse to acknowledge.

§

11:30 p.m. Matthew's first night at the duplex was less than comfortable. He tossed and turned and he wasn't even in bed yet. Tanya was also restless, so they took a leisurely walk around the block. The fresh air did them good. It was a quiet night, until he heard the sound of another dog howling in the distance. Or maybe it was the feral cry of a coyote in heat. From habit, he stopped in front of the store. No sign of a sheriff standing guard. He was safe from being extricated. As he gazed through the window, it felt like he was looking into his soul. Then an unforeseen circumstance presented itself—he still had the keys to the store. Logan, that genius, didn't even have the presence of mind to change the locks after his unscrupulous takeover.

Matthew took advantage of his mistake and went inside, with Tanya in tow. After deactivating the alarm, he stood there for a brief moment and took a deep breath. It was one of those "I'm back home again" moments—sweet, simple, without fanfare. He then settled into the barber chair that still sat in the center of the store like a three-dimensional sculpture. This was his throne. He was reminded of the old guy that sold it to him. Wondered if he was still above ground. Those kind of cantankerous dudes live forever. Tanya took up her once familiar station by the window, while Matthew pondered what went wrong. The answer came to him without a struggle—he trusted the wrong fucking people. Jon, Logan, and Logan's father. When he wasn't looking, they exploited him. Took advantage of his moral principles and ran him out of town. Chris had warned him. He listened but never thought it would actually come to fruition. Man, did they fake him out.

Matthew thought about leaving a ransom note, just to screw with their heads. *Pay thirty-two thousand dollars by midnight tomorrow, if you ever want to see your inventory alive again.* Clever, but an utterly ridiculous threat, so he smartly scrubbed that idea.

A young couple breaks the mood when they stop to window shop with their noses pressed up against the glass. The girl, very cute, pointed at the jean display, nodded in appreciation. Matthew accepted the silent compliment. They suddenly saw him, and he's guessing had no idea if he was real or a mannequin. He waved. Tanya barked like a good dog. They waved back. Tanya barked again. Then for some reason, they gave him this impassioned thumb's up, followed by the peace sign. Almost as if they knew who he was and were acknowledging his accomplishment as the guiding light and driving force of Jon's Drawer. At least that's what Matthew wanted to believe. They continued on their walk. Matthew has a hunch the cute chick would be back tomorrow to make a purchase.

A surge of bravery swept over him. He wrote a snide note with a black felt tip marker on the full-length mirror that read: *You guys have managed to bring mediocrity to the forefront of the apparel business. Yours truly, Mark Twain.*

It felt devious and unethical. He loved the rush, knowing that those who recognized the Jon Lewis pseudonym would freak out, thinking he's back. Logan would give a dismissive shrug, professing no knowledge of the whole incident.

After switching the alarm back to its "on" position, Matthew and Tanya leave, locking the door behind them. No sign of breaking and entering. Just as they're about to split, three squad cars pull up to the curb. A slew of officers jump out with guns drawn and surround Matthew. Matthew is instructed to lay face down on the sidewalk, spread-eagled. He may have spoken too soon about any sign of a sheriff.

Tanya growls, trying to protect Matthew. He quiets her down for fear they might use the stun gun on her. What Matthew hadn't realized is that Logan installed a backup silent alarm system. Matthew plays it naive.

"What's the deal, man? I was just out walking the dog, getting some fresh air."

The fuzz check the front door. It's locked. They scan the interior with their high beam flashlights. All is still. No sign of an intruder. No sign of disruption.

One of the officers explains how the silent alarm went off. Matthew volunteers his own theory.

"Clever. Silent alarm. Sometimes a rat can set off the motion sensors. This neighborhood is crawling with rodents. I think the guy who owns this store is actually a rodent." His rude comment only got him a deadly stare. "Sorry, just a little late-night humor to break the mood of being hassled for no good reason, other than you guys think I broke into this store. Slow night I guess, huh?"

The cops artfully surmise it's a false alarm. Matthew never mentions he was once connected with the store for the obvious reason—they'd see it as retribution. After checking his ID, they eventually let him go without as much as an apology.

Twelve hours later, they discover the note on the mirror. The cops returned and put out an APB on a Mark Twain. It never occurred to them he was a legendary, long-dead author. Putting this wild goose chase into motion finally gave Matthew something to smile about.

§

Almost a full month has passed.

Matthew has this friend, Buzz, who loaned him his old charcoal gray Ford Falcon station wagon, so he could look for work. It was painful to apply for a job at places where he was overqualified. Nothing came close to being a possibility. He received not a single callback. He was lost in a world that seemed to have turned its back on him.

Around this time an *LA Times* fashion critic writes a scathing article lamenting the fading cool factor of Jon's Drawer: *After Matthew Street's untimely departure, Jon's Drawer became less organic and charming and more rigid and artificial. Originally, the storefront was given over to a young, earthy crowd. Now it's like these guys are trying to compete with the department stores. It's like Peter, Paul and Mary giving Mary the axe. What were they thinking? Or should I say, not thinking.*

Although Matthew was flattered by the article, it served as a stark reminder that what he had accomplished was slowly and painfully crumbling before his eyes. Elaine had it right. The store was tragically dying. On its last breath.

§

Chris and Claudia Mancuso, the cute Italian chick with the overbite, were about to call it quits. Chris would never deny there was a long list of things he admired about her, but they really had nothing in common. Her interests were limited to clothes, rock 'n' roll, and sex. Worthy pursuits, but Chris required more of a progressive personality, someone with an interest in the visual arts, the theater—an intellectual type who could discuss Nietzsche and Kierkegaard. She did not fit the mold, but he knew she and Matthew would click on so many other levels.

Tuesday night, 7:00 p.m. It was the three of them having dinner at Antonio's Pizzeria in Sherman Oaks. It was publicized in the mid fifties that a Mob shooting once took place here involving notorious West Coast mobster Mickey Cohen, a former apprentice to Bugsy Siegel who became the self-styled "King of the Sunset Strip." Rumor had it that one of Cohen's flunkies did the shooting, but it was never disclosed who took the lead. The LAPD Gangster Squad tried to make the case but failed. Twenty years later it was still a cold case.

They're in a booth, backed up against a far wall, eating Claudia's favorite dish, classic spaghetti and meatballs. Matthew was sitting on one side of the crescent-shaped booth, Chris and Claudia on the other. They discussed everything from Chris recently signing with his first literary agent, to an update on Jon Lewis. The word on the street was that Jon had narrowly escaped being caught at his mother's funeral, and was able to safely leave the country unscathed.

"Where do you think he landed?" Claudia asks.

This simple inquiry made Matthew suspicious. The idea of her being connected with Longo scissored through him again.

"Not sure what became of Jon," he says.

"Rumor has it he fled to a small town just outside of Paris," Claudia offers. "Married a French girl and is now selling vintage American cars, under the pseudonym of Ford Weber."

Chris is flummoxed. "How did you know that? I'd love to know where you heard that."

Claudia shrugs. "You know, I hear stuff. Who knows how true it is. People lie to make stories more interesting."

She hears stuff? Where does she hear stuff? The local supermarket checkout line? At the hairdresser's? The mailman who delivers the white lilies? This was disturbing. Matthew knew he couldn't continue on the way he was going—suspecting every man, woman, and child of being a member of the Mob and wanting the inside track on Jon Lewis.

Suddenly he realized how tense he was, realized he hadn't been taking regular breaths, realized he'd been actually holding his breath. He had to break this recurring cycle, so he took Claudia home with Chris's blessing. He needed to learn how to trust people again. And being with her was a good place to start.

An hour later, they're in her bed having glorious unbridled sex. She was on top. Matthew discovers she likes to be in control. Her breathing was sensual. Her moans erotic. She didn't miss a beat, as she pumped to satisfy Matthew's every urge to get him off. She then, out of nowhere, puts on the brakes and stops her wild body language to have a discussion about trust.

"You thought I was a member of the Mob, didn't you?"

There was a pause to let Matthew take a needed breath. His penis shriveled to the size of an acorn.

"What? No. Yes. Maybe," he says, suddenly feeling caught.

"You stereotyped me because I'm Italian. All Italians fit the profile of being Mafioso in your mind. Right?"

Where was this sudden accusation coming from? Why was she accusing him of being discriminatory? Who told her, Chris? Although factual, he couldn't confess to this allegation. It would certainly mean the end of this new friendship. The end of this amazing sexual madness. Not to mention, it didn't help his problem trusting people again.

"You're wrong. I may have mentioned the Italian notion to Chris as a stupid joke, but never really meant you, per se."

"Not every Italian is a crime boss or running a numbers racket."

"I know that. That's very prejudiced to think so."

"My father, for example, plays jazz piano."

"And I'm sure he's great at it."

"Do we understand each other, Matthew Street? Because if you want to continue to fuck me, you have to scratch the idea that I'm in any way connected to Vince Longo or any other wise guy."

"Yes. Understood."

He poses a question to himself: why is she bringing this up? There has to be a well-founded reason. Maybe she actually is connected and is trying to throw him off his game. This did not help his effort to put his trust in everyone who crosses his path wearing a dark blue sharkskin suit.

"Do you also understand, Matthew Street, that I'm messing with your head and trying to be witty and sarcastic?"

With that comes an enormous sigh of relief. "I do now—and you're good at it too," he says.

§

The following morning, Matthew and Claudia are at his usual haunt, Tiny Naylor's. While Claudia is in the restroom, Matthew sits at a table drinking coffee and reflects on last night's incredible fuckfest.

As the waitress slides over and tops off Matthew's cup, a friend of his, Taylor Renfro, walks in, looking even more tan than usual. It's public knowledge that his ruddy complexion comes from a lotion—Man Tan. Some days he's a glowing shade of orange. Taylor is in the music business. Songwriter. Had one big hit with a California group. That was his only claim to fame. A one-hit wonder, as it were.

Taylor and Matthew exchange the standard hellos and what's happening in their respective worlds rhetoric. Rumor had it that Renfro recently offered somebody's girlfriend five hundred dollars for oral sex. The doctors had to wire his mouth shut from the broken jaw the boyfriend gave him. That was as oral as Renfro got. Renfro was a sexual junkie, so any kind of rude behavior like that was not unjustified.

Renfro stands over Matthew like a cloudy day and plops down a local newspaper. Staring back is an ad for Jon's Drawer, featuring the pants Matthew had dubbed the Wear Outs. The irony is, this was the same artwork Logan had rejected in Hawaii. The same ad he threw in Matthew's face. He remained cool-headed, shrugged and shook his head in disbelief. Just another childish, underhanded move on Logan's part, demonstrating his need to be in control. In his peripheral vision, Matthew sees Claudia on her way back from the restroom. As he gets up to meet her, he knocks over his coffee onto the newspaper ad. Probably an act of casual aggression. Claudia stops directly in front of Renfro. Stares him down. They are face to face. Matthew had no idea what this was about. It made him nervous. It obviously made Renfro nervous too. He backs off, not knowing how to respond to the fact their noses are almost touching, and being blissfully unaware he's about to get verbally assaulted in front of the Tiny Naylor's crowd.

"Remember me?" she says in a fairly loud, stern voice.

"Yes. I do," Renfro replies. "You once dated Chris Styles. Can't remember your name."

"You offered my friend Karen money for a blow job. Remember that name, you pig?"

"Whoa. Back off, honey. You must be mistaken."

"No way. She cried for a week. You made her feel cheap and worthless. Like some whore."

Taylor's eyes squint like he was waiting for something unpleasant to happen. And it did. With serious force, Claudia slaps Renfro's face. The sound reverberates throughout the restaurant, bouncing off the walls as far back as the kitchen. Heads turn, some even choking on their Spanish omelets.

"She owed you that, you sadistic little prick," Claudia says.

"Do that again and I sue you for assault," he warns her. He turns to all who are watching this bombardment go down. "I have all of you as witness to this vicious attack by this crazed broad."

Claudia's jaw drops. "Broad?" she repeats indignantly. She responds with another *smack*, only harder and louder. This time he reels backward. She then says something to him in Italian, when translated meant "midget piece of shit."

Before it gets any crazier, Matthew steps between them and suggests Renfro leave before he has to eat his breakfast through a straw.

As Claudia took Matthew by the arm and led him outside, they were met by a round of applause and some unfavorable murmurs from the crowd. Needless to say, this was the last Matthew Street ever saw of Taylor Renfro.

"That was ugly," Claudia says. "But worth it to defend my friend Karen."

With this incident, Matthew had gained a new respect for Claudia Mancuso. Good relations are built on trust, and she had just proven to him she was courageous and loyal.

§

Work. Matthew needed a job. He was going stir-crazy and his bank account was getting dangerously low. He had no idea where to turn next. He actually looked in the classified ads. Lots of openings for truck drivers, short order cooks, and nurses. Nothing in there about anyone looking for an experienced clothing store manager who recently got fucked in the ass by his partner.

He was planning to take a trip downtown to the clothing mart. Maybe rep a line. He got as far as Alvarado Street before he turned back, already knowing the end result—*go away kid, you're bad news*. Most of these apparel guys knew about his connection with Jon Lewis and were probably afraid they'd somehow be caught in Mafia crossfire.

He was lost. He had no place to turn. No sudden inspiration. No eureka moment, which was unusual for him. What's left? Death? Suicide? Jump off the Golden Gate Bridge like Selig Levy? (He still had no recollection of who he was.) He half seriously planned his demise: leaping off the California Apparel Building on Mart Wednesday. He'd be making a profound statement about how the clothing industry can steal your self-respect just by being honest.

Honesty was your worst adversary, not your competitors. You had to lie and cheat and make frivolous promises to be successful. All he needed was the guts to jump. In this absurd delusion, he didn't even have that going for him. So he abandoned that foolish idea and went back to making himself sick worrying.

Things really looked bleak and he was seriously considering selling his blood for cash. A few days had passed when he found an unexpected delivery waiting for him in his mailbox. No, it wasn't white lilies, thank you very much— although, he was extremely cautious removing the plain brown envelope, in case it was a letter bomb. To his delight and surprise the parcel was postmarked Hawaii and contained Tom Sparks' return address. He opened it frantically, discovering a business class airline ticket. A note was attached inviting him to spend an open-ended amount of time with him and his wife Gina, and that he might have a design gig that was right up Matthew's alley. Matthew was blown away and jumped at the opportunity.

§

Claudia and him weren't exactly in a mutually exclusive relationship, so leaving wasn't a big deal for either of them. It didn't draw any tears. They said their goodbyes over the phone. It was mild and unemotional.

"It's probably for the best," she says bluntly. "I need to move on with my life anyway, and not get stuck in a rut seeing people who I'm not compatible with. Nothing personal."

"Right. Understood. Compatible. I get the message. Moving on."

"I gotta jump," she says. "I was in the middle of entertaining a friend when you called." Entertaining was code for blow job.

Matthew expunged Claudia Mancuso from his mind and his Rolodex. He would never admit it to anyone, but he never really convinced himself she wasn't linked to Longo. Even if she were, so what? Her being an assassin and actually taking out Jon Lewis was a ridiculous notion. Or was it?

§

After a five-hour flight Matthew touched down in Hawaii. Tom kept his promise and got him a job redesigning the lobby of one of the big island hotels where he had scored a big advertising gig. Some place like the Maui Kai, Mauna Kea, Mauna Lani. Who knows? They all sounded the same, and they were all amazing accommodations promising the ultimate Hawaiian getaway charging an arm, a leg, and a thigh. Before undertaking the lobby project Matthew altered Tom's office space in the same Old West flavor as Jon's Drawer. That alone improved his skills and showed that he could be a creative force. When he completed the job on the hotel lobby, they were so thrilled with his work and design choices, he got a personal thank-you visit from the hotel's public relations officer. Her name was Sydney. Hawaiian. Beautiful. Green eyes. Dark complexion. No more than twenty-four years old.

Matthew is lying on the beach catching some rays in front of Tom's house when she approaches. And this is where it gets freaky to the point of being, well—just freaky. She's wearing a pair of his jeans—the Wear Outs, the ones with the yellow piping. He asks where she got them and if she knew they were his pants. Mail order from Los Angeles, she says. And yes, she knows who he is through Tom.

She sits down next to him in the sand and hands him a can of Big Swell IPA beer. "Ke aloha," she says, which was some sort of non-traditional Hawaiian toast. He is so hoping this isn't just another Anne Fraser fantasy because he likes her. She asks if he wants to take a walk.

"Sure, a walk. Who wouldn't like to walk on the beach in Hawaii with an attractive girl?" he says.

"You're sweet," she says.

"I like to think so."

The beach is almost desolate. Void of activity, only random birds and gulls searching for scraps of food left behind by previous beachgoers.

"Can I trust that you're not a narc posing as a PR person?" he remarks casually.

"Uh-oh. Why do I sense you're going to make a joint appear out of thin air?"

"Very intuitive of you."

As promised, he pulls a joint from his pants pocket and shares it with Sydney. The ocean is relatively quiet, no sailboats or surfers in sight. Another half mile and they finally run into life—a couple of old Hawaiian fishermen on the edge of the shore, loafing and drinking beer. Sydney gives them an aloha and says something else in Hawaiian, because they said something to her in Hawaiian. This goes on for a few back-and-forth exchanges before she interprets.

The fishermen ask if they're a couple. Sydney tells them no. The fishermen say they should be. She then explains how they just met and are sharing some weed together, and maybe after they get thoroughly stoned they'll be a couple.

It's a long explanation but Matthew likes how it ends. He smiles inside because he doesn't want to appear overanxious.

§

That night Matthew and Sydney go out to dinner with Tom and Gina. It started out as a remarkably pleasant evening, just spending time with new friends. It was a treat for Matthew to get away from the noise and hugger-mugger of LA and everything that made his life there so uneven.

On a high note, Sydney's company gave her the go-ahead to offer Matthew another design job— if he wanted it. But before he could answer a guy who looked out of place interrupted him. Wearing a dark suit. Looking stern and unfriendly. Nobody wears a suit and tie on the island, unless they're a chauffeur or a funeral director. And even then an aloha shirt and sandals was fitting attire. He speaks in a deep, gravelly voice, and tells Matthew that Mr. Longo needs to talk in private and apologizes for the interruption. But it's urgent. The idea that Vince Longo was in Hawaii looking over his shoulder was the ultimate slap in the face. These guys obviously counted on Matthew to bring Jon Lewis's head to them on a plate. There was nothing he could do or say to convince them that as a fount of information, he was all dried up.

Sydney looked worried. Matthew assured her this was a routine matter that shouldn't take more than a few minutes. He excuses himself, and then is led outside to a Lincoln town car with tinted windows. He stands and waits as the back passenger window begins to roll down slowly. Sitting in the backseat, smoking a cigar, is a man he's never seen before. If he tried to crack a smile his whole face would probably shatter. He speaks with authority.

"Street, I'm Vince's father, Paul Longo. You heard of me?"

"Of course. I watch the news. I read the papers. Saw your face on *Time* magazine's July cover naming you, what was it?—oh, yeah, disappointment of the year."

"I heard you were a smart mouth."

"Harassment does that to some people. Look, sir, this is not a good time for me. I'm having dinner with friends. Intimidate me after dessert."

Matthew starts to leave but is stopped by the limo driver's beefy hand pressed against his chest. "Is that considered assault? Do I have a court case here?"

"Look, kid, relax. I'm just here to talk about Jon Lewis and how critical it is that we get a hold of him."

"By the ankles to secure a block of cement?"

"Old school, kid. Look, the Palm Springs story about him at his mother's funeral was not nice. You had us all chasing after our tails. No more games. We have to be a team, understand? I can't end this if you don't share information. The truth. Not on wild goose chases that send me to hot desert communities. I don't do well in heat."

The window rolls up and the town car drives off. Matthew now understood why he got the surprise visit. When a guy like Jon witnesses a gangland hit, they step up their game and run on nervous energy. They bring in the big boys to make idle threats.

Later, at Sydney's place, she and Matthew drank to loosen up, then talked about their respective pasts. About everything from Matthew's recent nerve-racking encounter with the Mob and the Longo family, to him being ousted from his clothing company by a pathetic creature named Logan Alexander. He finds out she attended the University of Hawaii and got a degree in business. Her mother was native Hawaiian, her father an Irish American who left when she was three years old. On a low note, she was abused by an alcoholic stepfather who, while driving drunk, died in a car crash when his truck skidded out of control and wrapped around a palm tree. It was very cathartic for both of them to open up. Sex with her, by the way, was insanely crazy great and helped distance himself from his ongoing stress.

§

They got an early start and headed for the Hawaii Kai model home project on the eastern tip of the island. The hotel was owned by the majority stockholders. They waited in the courtyard, landscaped in the traditional Hawaiian flavor—waterfall, birds of paradise, lipstick palms, a Macaw parrot squawking mindlessly on its perch—for the developers to arrive. Three men in their mid-thirties approached in traditional aloha shirts, tan pants, and loafers without socks. Matthew knew these rather staid dudes would never go in for bell-bottoms and English tees. They exchanged a friendly but business-like aloha with Sydney. The developers were looking for someone to design the interior of one of their model homes, from the furniture down to the kitchen faucets. Sydney introduced Matthew as the perfect designer for the job. She couldn't have been more gracious, giving him high marks for his recent job on the hotel lobby of the Mona Lani.

That was all the résumé these guys needed. He had the gig. They shook hands, then had him sign a standard contract. This was to be Matthew's defining moment. He could not fuck this up.

The developers showed Sydney and Matthew the model home. He stared at the blank walls. They seemed to look back at him, stark naked, in need of color, shape, and design, desperately crying "help!" He displayed nothing but confidence, even though perspiration was forming on his upper lip.

A month later, job complete. The Hawaiian developers in the fancy silk aloha shirts appraised Matthew's work—overstuffed sofas, leather nailhead club chairs, bamboo wood flooring, gooseneck kitchen faucet, farmhouse sink, linen drapes. The list goes on. He brought in the full complement of furnishings, fabrics, and decorative accessories, all shipped over from the mainland. They were ecstatically pleased by the results. Covered him in leis up to his chin. Even offered another model home.

But it was time for Matthew Street to get the hell out of Dodge. He'd been gone for nearly a year, and even though Hawaii had acted as a powerful balm to his psychic wounds, and his new friends had helped him overcome his problems, going home seemed like the right thing to do. For one thing, he wanted to walk his dog again; funny how one misses the simple pleasures in life the most. Plus he was still paying rent on the duplex. And finally, he needed to face his own personal challenges and whatever demons he had left behind.

Shortly after eight the next morning, Sydney sees Matthew off at Honolulu International Airport. It's another picture-perfect day in paradise, tarnished only by the tears in Sydney's eyes and the look of pure sadness on her sweet face. As they walk through the terminal, hand and hand, she again tries to talk him out of going, promising him countless design jobs and more of the wonderful moments they shared during his stay on Oahu. She thought they made a terrific team and that they could fulfill greatness together. He didn't disagree. If not for her, he would've been just a no-nothing decorator seeking small jobs from do-it-yourselfers at home improvement centers.

She detours and slides inside the airport gift shop. After a quick scan, she buys him a black puka shell necklace as a reminder of their time together.

"You don't have to do this. I don't need a necklace to remember you," he says.

"Yes you do," she says. "Put it in your sock drawer. Every time you put on your shoes, you'll smile."

Sydney was something he hadn't counted on. It was very tough for him to leave her behind.

CHAPTER 47

Chris picks up Matthew at LAX. They're on the 405 Freeway headed back to the Valley. It was good to see Chris. He looked healthy. He'd stopped smoking and was able to lay off those damn Pepsis—which was harder to kick than the cigarettes.

Having a keen eye, Chris instantly notices the black puka shell necklace around Matthew's neck. He knows he wouldn't buy that for himself. He nods subtly towards the necklace.

"A gift from a sexy wahine surfer, I'm guessing," he says.

"Not even close," Matthew says, then gives him a detailed account of meeting Sydney, who captured his heart. He adds how both she and Tom gave him a platform to prove himself as a serious interior designer.

"Finally finding and cultivating a creative outlet that was missing from my life is a big deal," Matthew says, hoping he doesn't sound vainglorious.

"I'm glad for you," Chris says with sincerity. "It's hard to believe you've been away for nearly a year."

"Yeah? Fill me in."

A lot has happened. Chris gives Matthew a summary of events, starting with Claudia getting married to some guy named Juan José Ortega, and how Logan got drunk and ran his father's luxurious Italian boat aground on the rocks off the coast of San Diego. Punishment came in the form of forcing him to finally join AA. He suffered through two and half meetings before he went MIA. Needless to say, he'd never get the keys to the boat or any of the fancy cars for a long time. He was, however, allowed to use the damaged boat as his place of residence, since he got evicted from the Marina Del Rey Yacht Club apartments for harassing women in the laundry room.

Matthew asks, "Were you invited to Claudia's wedding?"

"I passed. It was a destination wedding, being held in Mexicali, in an abandoned bullfighting arena."

"What?"

"I know," Chris says, shaking his head. "Makes no sense."

Maybe there was some deep meaning behind it. Matthew wasn't knocking it, but such a barbaric venue just didn't seem like something Claudia would be attracted to. Then again, she was the same woman who had no qualms about smacking Taylor Renfro around in a public place. Later they would discover that this Juan José Ortega was an amateur matador, whose task is to actually kill the bull in front of a bloodthirsty crowd. Where do you meet a guy like this? Or better yet, who introduces you to a dilettante matador? And why in God's name would you marry a person who kills animals for a living?

§

Chris drops Matthew off at his duplex at around eight o'clock. As he enters the darkened room, he smells the distinct odor of cigarette smoke and pungent men's cologne. He can barely see but detects the silhouette of a person sitting in a chair in the corner of the room.

"Safe flight, I hope," a familiar voice says.

A click is heard as a lamp is switched on, spotlighting Vince Longo sucking on a cigarette.

Matthew nearly jumps out of his pants. "Jesus, you scared the piss out of me! What the fuck are you doing here? How'd you get in, anyway? Never mind—get the fuck out before I call a cop."

"Settle down, this won't take long," Longo says as he blows a smoke ring that hovers above his head like a cheap halo. "By the way, I heard you met my father. Said he found you gritty and thoroughly unlikable."

"Coming from a man who hurts people for a living, I'll take that as a compliment. Now say what you gotta say, then go. I'm exhausted and want to go to bed."

"I came to give you a message." He pauses a beat before continuing. "He's dead. It's over. He's taking a dirt nap." Matthew didn't have to ask who. It was evident he was referring to Jon Lewis. He suddenly felt weak and nauseous and had to sit down. Yes, it was upsetting, but he was glad this merry-go-round of a soap opera had ended. He didn't want to know how Jon died but Longo obviously felt the need to elaborate There's a strong note of pride in his voice as he provides the graphic details.

"He met with an unfortunate accident while vacationing in Zurich. Seems the brakes went out on his Saab rental car as he was driving down a treacherous road. He lost control. The car hurtled off the mountain like an Olympic ski jumper."

MATERIAL THINGS

Matthew puts two and two together and surmises someone cut the brake fluid line. It doesn't take a genius to figure out this callous act was Longo's handiwork.

"He was alone," Longo goes on. "No one else was hurt, except for the Saab—it was totaled." Longo then rises from the chair and walks across the room towards the door. "Oh, and one other thing. That senseless pursuit in Russian—we weren't fooled. No one flees to Russia to live a secure life."

"So I guess we can close the file on this source of annoyance in our lives, huh, Vince?" Matthew says.

"You'll never hear from me again, Street. I'm retiring from the family business. Plan to buy me a small farm in upstate New York, get myself a dog and some chickens, and watch the sun rise and set in peace. Far away from the sounds of the city and gunshots ripping apart someone's skull. It's been a tough racket but I'd rather do that than sell fucking pants." He then leans down to Matthew's level and speaks directly in his face. "Oh, I left an envelope of Polaroids of the car wreck on the coffee table. Just in case you need to corroborate the story with the Feds. Also, as added proof of the deceased's identity, I left his gold wedding band—still attached to his finger." Longo heads outside, leaving in his wake the stink of his cheap cologne and the bitter dregs of his sanctimonious attitude.

Matthew can't help himself from checking out the pictures and the finger. A big mistake. It's gruesome and repulsive. He gags, almost throwing up in the sack. He then puts the finger in the freezer until he can decide what to do with it. He's thinking he'll mail it to agent Bud Collins with the Polaroids and a note saying: *Fuck you—here's literally the middle finger for you to sit on.*

With Jon Lewis now out of the way, the Mob was in the clear about the Vincent Thomas Bridge homicide. From that day forward, Longo was no longer a nuisance or a threat to Matthew Street or his friends and was never heard of again. A few years later the *National Enquirer* reported that he was found dead in his barn with a pitchfork pierced through his neck and a bouquet of fresh lilies nicely arranged in his mailbox. Rumor had it he was killed by an angry neighbor who made it look like the Cosa Nostra took him out. It didn't matter. He was history, and Matthew would no longer find him or anyone else sitting in his living room with a dead man's finger stashed in a paper bag.

§

The genesis of Tapis Design was meant to be. Here's how it started. Matthew was sitting in a pew inside the Little Brown Church on Coldwater Canyon and Riverside Drive. A diminutive sanctuary in Studio City surrounded by multistory apartment buildings, the church had hosted more than 23,000 weddings. But it's probably best known as the site of the union between Ronald Reagan and Nancy Davis on March 4, 1952.

He was waiting for another wedding ceremony to begin. His sister Patti was getting married for the third time. He was there without a date because, well, he felt like he had used up his allotment for available crazy chicks with monumental issues and the emotional baggage they're hauling around. With no prospects waiting in the wings, he was officially single and actually feeling good about it. No romantic ties to bog him down and scramble his senses. He was in mid-conversation with Patti's friend, Betsy—the same sweet girl Logan tried so hard to get in the sack on the night they named Jon's Drawer.

"So, I hear you've had a rough time of it lately," Betsy says.

"Rough time of what?

"Of it," she says.

"Oh, yeah, it. It has definitely been rough."

"Any plans to fix it?"

"At the moment, none. Got any ideas?"

She goes on to suggest that he seriously consider working for Les, Patti's soon-to-be husband, Les Tucker, who was a highly successful interior decorator.

"Rumor has it you have this natural talent for changing shitty architectural structure into non-shitty architectural splendor," she remarks to Matthew. Betsy was not only attractive but had a colorful command of the English language.

As luck would have it, Matthew did end up working with Les Tucker. He was his mentor. His design guru. He learned his craft, at an entry-level position, picking up and delivering lamps, brass doorknobs, and tile samples in his newly leased Fiat hatchback. He felt like he was doing something worthwhile. Discovering what really gratified him—using a medley of ideas to make change. To make a difference. Just like he did with pants, only in this case, we're talking a bathroom vanity or window treatments, or parallel linen couches for an open floor plan.

§

Thirteen years later, having accumulated an abundance of experience under his belt, yet another unforeseen tragedy rattled Matthew's friends and family. They found Les slumped over on the toilet seat, dead from a massive heart attack. Unlike his sister's marriage to Jon, Les's death caused them lots of pain and distress. They had a service at the same Little Brown Church where they first got married. Cremation was chosen over burial, so there was no funeral cortege following a hearse through the streets of North Hollywood. The church was packed and Matthew preferred to stand in the back, away from the sobbing and the whimpering. Betsy, who first suggested he team up with Les, slides up next to him. She slips her arm through his, then tilts her head at him. He was sure she could sense his general fear.

"You're going to be fine, Matthew Street. It's your time to venture out and be your own person."

"I know. That's what scares the piss out of me. Relying on myself."

"You've been doing that since your hairstyling days. This should be a snap," she says.

All eyes are on the podium while a woman in her late sixties is just finishing up her eulogy about the deceased, but has trouble getting the last few words out because she is overcome with grief and sobbing uncontrollably. The audience waits patiently while she gathers her thoughts and emotions, and is finally able to speak once again.

"As I look out amongst you kind folks, and see the blank stares, it has come to my attention that I am at the wrong funeral." An uncomfortable murmur runs through the assembly. "Nevertheless, this does not lessen the grief we all share for the dead. Any dead. I appreciate you people witnessing a perfect stranger shed her tears and talk about a man who plunged to his death while on balloon safari in Kenya. Can someone please point me in the direction of The Laurelgrove Avenue Church?" She walks off to the disbelief of the stunned crowd.

Matthew decides he should say a few words that might help his own grief. He crosses to the podium and takes a long, deep breath, while nervously finger-combing his hair.

"How is it possible that someone ends up at the wrong funeral? I wish I were at the wrong funeral, but I'm not. I'm exactly where I'm supposed to be, eulogizing and sending off a man who left us far too soon. A man who was loved and respected on and off the field of interior design. A man whose death caught me off guard. A death that really pisses me off, fostering an extreme feeling of total resentment. Not exactly your typical heartwarming eulogy packed with accolades, but this is how I'm wired, folks. I'll go home, fold myself in the fetal position, and do my weeping in private, thank you very much."

As Matthew exits the podium to a sea of disapproving stares, he sees a beaming Betsy flash him a thumb's up.

§

Tapis Design, a name hatched by his friend Chris Styles, was born a week later. So there he was, brought back to life into yet another milieu, that he would label his third and final stop in a mixed bag of diverse careers. Plus, he reminds himself, if it wasn't for his sister Patti, who hooked up with both Jon and Les, who knows where he'd be today? Still cutting hair and suffering from a bleeding ulcer. She was the catalyst for his successes. She inadvertently sacrificed two very tough relationships for him, and you've got to love a sister for that.

In the years ahead, Tapis Design would flourish while Jon's Drawer was hanging on literally and figuratively by a thread. Not unexpected. The Marina and the Hollywood stores went belly up for lack of personal supervision and inventory selection. They were forced to sell its inventory to a jobber at twenty-five cents on the dollar. Logan Alexander would eventually make even more horrible business decisions and run the parent store in Sherman Oaks into the ground. He hired delinquent sales help who would give clothes away to their friends and pocket cash from the register. Once again proving beyond a shadow of doubt, to everyone who knew him, that Logan Alexander was a complete failure at whatever or whomever he came in contact with. Matthew firmly believes it's the result of him growing up with that proverbial silver spoon in his mouth. Logan's spoon finally turned green and tarnished. He resented his father because he was left nothing but the memories of once being financially solvent and having it all. He became a hermit in his own environment. Lost weight. Lost his willingness to stay sober and probably resented his present wife, Joyce, for saving him from being homeless.

CHAPTER 48

It's 1999. In his impeachment trial, President Bill Clinton is acquitted by the United States Senate of charges of perjury and obstruction of justice. Former heavyweight boxing champ Mike Tyson is sentenced to a year's imprisonment for the assault on two motorists following a minor traffic accident. The first Coachella Valley Music and Arts Festival is held in California.

Meanwhile, Matthew Street's social life is at an all-time low. It's his feeling he should've stayed with Sydney in Hawaii, when he had the chance. Maybe it's not too late. Maybe she's still available. Maybe he's desperate and grabbing at emotional straws. Lots of maybes. He blew it and he knows it. He's feeling the crushing loneliness, and has accepted the fact he might never have another meaningful relationship.

When all hope is lost, and bachelorhood appears to be a permanent state of mind, good fortune taps Matthew Street on the shoulder and surprises him to the point of creating a tiny implosion in his heart. If you wait long enough, good things happen. This came in the form of an angel wearing blue jeans and a maroon crop top sweater—Melinda Miles. Their eyes met across a room filled with clients at a wrap party for a loft design job he did in the Old Bank District located in the Historic Core of downtown Los Angeles. Eyes that beautiful would have looked fake if they weren't so alive with intelligence. Their initial connection was making sour faces at the Moroccan stuffed acorn squash and couscous that was being served. He made his move, asking smilingly if she wanted to go grab a chili cheeseburger. She flatly turned him down. He was crushed until she revealed she was a vegetarian. They shared a laugh, then escaped the circle of diners to go lean against a far wall to discover themselves. Of course, he mentions his early days as a boutique shop owner prior to jumping into interior design.

"I knew that," she says.

"Really?" he says with a great degree of curiosity.

She tilts her head before speaking. "Jon's Drawer, 1972. I bought my first pair of bell-bottoms at the La Cienega store."

This was the kind of recognition a person likes. The kind that caused his heart to pump faster and made the arduous journey to this moment in time worth taking.

The din of loud conversation became too much to handle so they went outside to take in the view of the downtown skyline. The horns and sirens that bounced off the buildings and echoed through the streets serenaded them like an out of tune symphony.

Neither of them were smokers, so they had no reason to break up the conversation with that frivolous occupation. She opens up and tells him she's an aspiring actress. In Tinseltown and its environs, actress and waitress are usually paired together, but in her case she also worked as legal secretary downtown. You can never be sure what really attracts you to another person but in Melinda's case it was an easy call—she was smart, pretty, blonde, and had an infectious English accent. Born in Eltham, South East London, she moved to the States with her parents when she was ten years old and, to Matthew's delight, had retained a bit of that British inflection. Very proper. Used the word *lovely* a lot. She didn't try to be someone she wasn't. There was a fresh honesty about her. When she said she hated broccoli, Matthew believed her. Why would anyone mention something so mundane unless they meant it? Melinda was real. She was not dependant on drugs or hung up on material things. There was something about her that made him feel comfortable and safe. So three weeks later, they moved in together with their cats, in his converted warehouse loft located in a highly visible commercial area on Hunter Street.

Matthew wasn't sure exactly what day it was when he discovered he had a detached retina, but it changed his life. Especially his appearance. He had to wear these goggle-like dark glasses with leather side panels that protected his pupils from radiant light. He resembled a welder. But it would become his quirkiest trademark.

As they were driving back from the optometrist he suddenly pulls over to the curb without warning. Melinda freaks out.

"What's wrong? Want me to drive? Your eyes giving you fits?"

Then, in a calm voice, he asks her to marry him. Wait, edit that …

"You *have* to marry me," he says. "If you don't, you'll hurt my feelings, and this is not a good day to hurt my feelings."

Resting a gentle hand on his shoulder, she never says yes but instead answers: "We should hurry back and tell the kids"— meaning their cats. "They should be the first to know." They kiss to seal the deal and make it official.

This tender moment filled him with emotion. In truth, it also felt like he was betraying himself because he had promised never to go through this ritual again. The long-haul commitment had put him in a vulnerable position and twice kicked him in the face. But he managed to rid himself of being afraid just by looking into Melinda's eyes, that seemed to tell him "don't be afraid."

The sun was beginning to rise, skimming over rooftops and billboards, and landing in their bedroom through a single window by their bed. Melinda turns to Matthew. Her morning breath is sweet on his cheek.

"You sure you want to do this? Get married?" she asks in a semi-groggy state.

Nerves cause him to launch a sarcastic missile. "What else have I got to do today?"

They share a laugh.

§

Los Angeles County courthouse. They stood in front of a female judge. Overweight. Reeking of some sort of lavender scent. But she appeared capable and spoke without missing a syllable, as if she performed this rite a thousand times a day—rather like the marriage vows answer to Jiffy Lube.

Chris and Matthew's sister, Patti, showed up as witnesses. After the twenty-minute ceremony, Matthew took them all for dim sum at this great place in Chinatown. Nobody threw a wedding bouquet and a three-tiered chocolate/strawberry cake was not served.

§

MATERIAL THINGS

Five years have passed when Matthew decides to call it quits and shut down Tapis Design. He's made his mark and is tired of the daily grind, putting together design ideas for bored housewives with too much time on their hands. It was a gratifying career, but how many soffits can you install?

And Melinda's acting career wasn't exactly skyrocketing. Sure, she got a gig now and then on an episodic TV show, or a small bit part in a movie that usually came out and folded in the same week. Nothing that was going to get her noticed. Not everyone becomes a star. Disappointing, sure, but you move on. That's the movie biz.

So, they made a mutual decision to leave the cutting-edge lifestyle of California and head across the Atlantic. They packed up the house, the cats, and Matthew's late-model Mini Cooper, and made a long, tedious journey on a cargo vessel headed to Scotland—taking up residence at Lower Granton Road, Edinburgh, to be precise. Finally, after all these years, they had made it to an earthly paradise, retreating from the pressures of modern civilization.

§

Life in Scotland was all they expected it to be. Lovely and magical. They would receive guests on a regular basis. For the people they left behind in the States, visiting them in Scotland was both a treat and a holiday.

The following spring, when their houseguests had just left to fly home to Los Angeles, Melinda complains of a headache. Aspirin and an ice pack doesn't seem to be the remedy. It progressively gets worst. They go to Western General Hospital. It's old and rundown and needs a facelift, but the skillful staff of doctors and nurses is great. They diagnose her symptom as a migraine, give her something for it, and send her home.

Three days later, in the middle of the night, Melinda wakes up screaming in pain. Matthew rushes her back to the hospital. After tests and MRIs, they get horrible news: Melinda has a brain tumor. Now Matthew is screaming *bloody ass Jesus*, through the halls of the hospital, disrupting the patients. People want him admitted to the psychiatric ward. A couple interns apply a straightjacket grip around his arms and waist, trying to calm him down.

"You don't understand," he yells, fighting them off, "my wife has a fucking brain tumor!" He loses all sense of reason. "Someone has to fix that now!"

His pleas do not go unnoticed. The doctors assure him they will do everything possible to make sure Melinda receives every appropriate medical procedure available.

What does that even mean? Was it even treatable? Sure, for a moment in time. But not long enough to be wiped clean and continue her life with some normalcy. Not to be negative, but patients with this disease typically endure pain and suffering during treatment that usually has no long-term effect, then die.

Matthew's feeling—God or whoever was in charge wasn't finished messing with his head. It was like a higher power said *Not so fast, pal, we're not done screwing with your emotions. You haven't suffered enough.*

He lost Melinda in the summer of 2016. Truly the most tragic day in his life. He didn't have the heart to tell their kids, the cats. But they knew by her absence, and the drops of salty tears that moistened their food when he fed them.

§

He loved the dead of night in Edinburgh. It came without the usual city rant of construction, or the scream of sirens off in the distance taking a heart attack victim to the emergency room, or choppers flying overhead in search of an addict who had just broken into a pharmacy. Calm. Peaceful. As he walked, he tipped his gaze to the sky. At least a million stars blanketed the inky sky above him. One of them blinked several times. He would like to think it was a sign—Melinda winking, reassuring him that her memory of their love story, their life together, though cruelly short, would last for eternity.

More anger surfaces. She's gone, and he's alone with nothing but winking memories. Fuck winking memories. He wants to make new memories with her, not dwell on things of the past. Thinking about the past only gives rise to more heartache. He hasn't slept through the night in over two months. He looks like shit. He and the cats have lost weight and their appetites.

CHAPTER 49

Present day. 2016. Valencia, California. The sun has set, and we're back inside the dark garage, absent of any joy, where Logan Alexander self-destructed.

Matthew, Chris, and Kate sit exactly where we left them. The bottle of wine is consumed and from the looks on their faces, so is the ingrained history.

"You wanted insight, you got it," Matthew says to Kate, whose eyes are rubbed red from wiping away a few tears and whose heart was broken a thousand times over.

"Sure, this was a tough pill to swallow but it should help you understand your father and the generation a little better," Chris says. "Who he was, who he wasn't, and who he could've been."

Kate heaves a heavy sigh. "The more I found out about my father, the less he seems to be the person I wanted, the person I needed him to be, all those years."

"I can only speak for myself," Matthew remarks, "but opening up these doors a crack, and peering inside the past, has been a very cathartic release. I've come to accept my delicate sensibilities and understand the man I despised."

"It's ironic that the first time in my entire life I feel remotely affectionate towards him—is when he's dead," Kate says.

Matthew and Chris say their good-byes. There are hugs and thank-yous and promises of keeping in touch through social media. Of course, it remains to be seen whether that will actually take place. Matthew thinks not.

They didn't go back inside the house to comfort any of the bereaved. They snuck out a side gate like common thieves who had just stolen a chunk of their past and couldn't wait to head back to their own safe reality. But before heading directly to LAX and dropping off Matthew at the international terminal, Chris needed to make an unscheduled stop and swing by his house in Valley Village. In twenty minutes they pull up to a Spanish-style house built in 1929. Full of character and ambience, parts of the home were refurbished and upgraded by Matthew when he was still deeply engrossed in his design company. Inside they are met by Oliver, Chris's golden retriever. He greets Matthew like a long-lost friend, jumping on him excitedly. Chris's wife, Lolo, a photographer, is on a newborn photo shoot in Ventura. She will be disappointed that she missed seeing Matthew before he headed back to Scotland.

"For whatever reason I'm here, I hope it doesn't take long," Matthew carps, "because I'm anxious to get back to my cats who are probably starving to death by now."

"What? You left the cats alone?" Chris barks, concerned.

"Of course not. I'm just trying to speed things up here."

"It'll only take a minute, I promise. There's an old friend in my office who's anxious to see you."

Matthew follows Chris through the backyard past the pool that's strewn with leaves and needs cleaning. This, by the way, is Oliver's private swimming hole. He takes a running dive into the deep end just to show off his skills. A few more steps and they near the office, a converted garage Matthew designed. Matthew had no idea who or what to expect. In his mind he was anticipating finding Sydney or Linda or even Anne Fraser. The mystery excited him, as well as making him a little nervous.

"How 'bout a hint?" Matthew says.

"Nope, a hint would give it away," Chris replies.

They enter and stand in silence for several moments as Matthew beholds a relic sitting idle in a corner of the space. His eyes widen with utter shock and surprise. He turns and stares at Chris in gape-mouthed wonder, struck speechless.

"Jesus, where'd you find it?" he says, finally recovering his voice.

"Rose Bowl swap meet, by accident. I was looking for a wrought iron gate," Chris says.

Matthew crosses the room and sits in the same barber chair that once adorned Jon's Drawer. His chair. The old geezer's chair.

Matthew settles in. A mystical feeling comes over him. He takes a deep breath and is able to visualize VIP Men's Hairstyling, Jon's Drawer, Acme Shoe Emporium, Jon Winkle's Books, Periwinkle, and all the multifaceted people who drifted through the doorway unannounced, but were never turned away.

Chris says, "The chair is like a time machine. I experienced a shiver of déjà vu, as if I were returning to a spectacular place that now only existed in my mind."

"So it's now, what, haunted? Cursed? A thoroughfare to the past?"

"Yes. All those things."

"You have any idea who Diane Zukie is?" Matthew asks.

"No. Never heard of her. Why?"

"She was the first customer we ever sold a pair of bell-bottom jeans to. Seven dollars. I have to say, that was an inspirational moment. It marked the beginning of our entrepreneurship."

"And you bring this up now because . . .?"

Chris listens as Matthew waxes lyrical. "It was always about the people. Not the money. Not the recognition. Not the prestige. But the fact that a pair of pants had changed people's lives. It was a philosophy. A statement. A way to express yourself without flowery language or a sign on your back that says 'I'm different.'"

Chris nods in agreement. "Jon never got that message, did he?"

"Nope. Too selfish. Too self-absorbed. Too wrapped up in his own mischievous lifestyle." Matthew pauses. "He almost got away with it too."

"It? Away with what?"

"His life. Got away with his life. We were the lucky ones who managed to survive the moral repugnance. Then again, I question sometimes if, in fact, we are lucky. Our collective memory is haunted by way too many deaths."

There's a pause as they both reflect what they know is true. Every year, on a certain date, they would remember a fallen friend, loved one, or adversary.

Chris breaks the downbeat mood. "It's yours. I'll have it shipped to Scotland."

It was like Matthew was suddenly thrown back into the seventies, again dealing with that rusty, bilious, tobacco-spitting dude who looked like Gabby Hayes and smelled like the inside of an old cowboy boot. It made him feel young and naïve, thinking this barber chair would be a monument of his former self.

Matthew asks, "How much you want for it?"

"Let's say $83.50," Chris says, recalling the original price. There's a pause because Matthew knew Chris had paid three times that in today's antique market.

"No deal. I'll give you two hundred, and you have it shipped to my doorstep."

They both spit on the floor to make the moment genuine. A plethora of emotions washes over them that only two nearly lifelong friends could share. They glance at each other and for the first time see two middle-aged men staring back at each other.

"You know," Matthew says, "I just realized, you've grown older and grayer. Got a couple more lines under the eyes since the last time I saw you."

"Thank you for noticing. As have you, my friend, grown older. It comes with age."

They burst into self-deprecating laughter, agreeing that the best part of living is to see another sunrise.

§

They finally make it to the airport with time to spare. Chris pulls up to the white curb—a traveler's nightmare that only gives you thirty-four seconds to pick up grandma returning from her European vacation. It was going to take longer than thirty-four seconds for these guys to say bon voyage. They narrowed it down and promised each other: no excessive sentimentality. No weeping, no sobbing, nothing misty-eyed or maudlin. At the curb, Matthew gives Chris one of those stoic looks when you're about to break up with somebody, and they know it's coming.

"So, this is it, my friend," Matthew says. "Time to end this oppressively solemn visit. Thank God it's over. I couldn't take another day of atmospheric pollutants in the Valley."

Chris thinks this is a smog reference but isn't sure, so he just nods and let it lie there unrecognized.

"Be sure and stay in touch," Matthew adds.

"Absolutely," Chris promises.

"Only please, no more calls about someone taking a gun to their head. Nothing horrific. Only good, lighthearted, sugary shit."

"Gotcha. But don't sell yourself short. It took guts to come here and face your demons. Not many people would have the balls to do that."

"I still think it was a mistake. Not sure if we helped Logan's kid understand the complexities of her father, or just made things more convoluted and tortuous."

"Know what? It doesn't matter. She takes from us, whatever she takes from us. It's no longer in our hands. We are not the masters of her universe. We're only the messengers."

It's time to go. They come together in an unabashedly affectionate bro hug.

"I love ya, man," Chris says.

"Me too. That goes without saying."

Chris watches as Matthew slowly and almost methodically disappears into the throng. He doesn't go directly to the security checkpoint but straight to the nearest bar. He needs a drink. He slides in and sits next to a woman who is nursing a beer. Early forties. Attractive. Casually well dressed. He orders a Scotch on the rocks.

He's not a hard liquor kind of guy, but he feels Scotch is the beverage that's going to settle his nerves. And he is anxious. His bar stool mate turns to him knowingly, sensing his jitters that seem to permeate through his pours.

"Not a great flyer, I take it," she says.

"It's not the flying, per se," Matthew replies, "it's the long arduous hours in the air sitting next to God knows who. My luck, I'll get a real talker aching to tell me their life story. I have enough of my own life to assess. Sorry, I don't mean to imply I'm not enjoying our conversation up till now."

"I understand," she says. "I promise to keep my life to myself. It's not that interesting anyway. I did most of my growing up in Vegas. My opinion, a crappy ass, hot town, that caters to losers. No place for a kid to be raised, if you ask me. C'mon, my bedroom night light was the Frontier Hotel marquee that burned like a fucking lighthouse on Bass Harbor, Maine."

As she ran on and on about the trials and tribulations of living in Las Vegas, it gave Matthew a chance to exhale and also take a closer look at this woman. She's young, vibrant, and what's more, she looked awfully familiar. Her green eyes were a giveaway that she was bright and quick-witted. His next line was your standard cliché but he didn't know how else to couch it.

He seizes an opportunity to get a word in edgewise. "Do I know you? I get the feeling I know you."

"I don't know, do you?" She studies his face for a moment. "You don't look that familiar to me. Unless maybe you've eaten at Moonshadows Restaurant in Malibu. Ever since my good-for-nothing prick of a husband left me and my daughter, I was forced to waitress there on the weekends. Part-time. Full-time would drive me insane.

You can only take so much abuse from drunks who like to pinch your ass. Men and women. Sorry, too much information. The one thing you're trying to avoid."

"No, it's okay, I'm not in the air yet."

This exchange seemed very familiar to Matthew. One of those déjà vu moments. He was getting a nervous sensation that he was close to realizing something relevant. Her physical presence coursed through him in a warm rush.

"You tell me—coincidence or just a fluke? But I once knew a girl who was a waitress there, God, I'm thinking at least a hundred years ago."

"Wow. A hundred. My guess is, she's not there anymore," she says with a cute smirk.

He stares at her. She's noticeably uncomfortable. He apologizes for staring. She says she didn't realize he was staring. The welder-like tinted glasses masked his eyes.

"I have what's called photophobia," he explains. "Sensitive to light. A lit birthday candle blinds me. Not a very interesting topic of conversation."

He then switches gears, mentioning how she reminded him so much of this girl he once knew in 1973. She tells him she was three in '73. He takes a sip of his Scotch, changes the subject again, and asks if she's flying today.

"No," she says, "I'm just waiting to pick up my daughter Olive. She's coming in from Cambridge University for spring break."

It was at this point he choked on a piece of ice. Okay, so the name Olive hit him like a ton of fucking bricks. He tried as fast as his mind would compute to make sense of all this. This girl, actually a woman, worked at Moonshadows and has a daughter named Olive. This was too uncanny to be mere coincidence. He was pretty sure he was having a conversation with Linda Tarlow's daughter. Her name escapes him at the moment, but he doesn't ask. He's too busy wiping the perspiration from his hands onto his pant leg. It was obvious he was having trouble breathing. She sensed he was maybe in trouble. Asked if he was all right. He just nodded because speaking was impossible.

He ordered another Scotch and downed it as soon as it was put in front of him. He goes back to staring, but this time via a side-glance. It was uncanny how much she resembled Linda. Her green eyes, her smile, her thin lips. Everything about her. In his head, he remembers the day this little girl begged him to be her father and he flatly turned her down. This broke his heart then, and even now as he relives it for a second time. The safe thing for him to do was just excuse himself, go catch his flight, and erase this one in a billion happenstance from his memory. He saw no reason to introduce himself and expound on a very uncomfortable time when she was three and in search of a father.

He stands up. His legs are wobbly and he teeters a bit.

"You sure you're okay?" she asks. "You look a little peaked."

"No, I'm fine. Pale is my natural color. Well, nice talking to you, young lady."

"It's Kirby. Have a nice flight to wherever it is you're headed."

Like a shock wave, the name really jogged his memory. Kirby, that was the kid's name. This was another chance to reveal himself, but he chose not to, because it would open up a surplus of questions and answers he was in no mood to delve into.

"Scotland. I live in Scotland. I'm headed to Scotland."

"Never been. Sounds romantic."

"It can be when the weather is right, and if you're sitting in front of a cozy fire with the right person. That is, if you have a fireplace, which I don't."

Her laughter is warm and genuine. "Look, without this seeming, I don't know, perverse," she says, "you mind if I give you a hug before you fly? It's just a silly feeling I have. That you're this good guy that I've met in maybe a past life—or when I was a kid, or even in a daydream. I'm kind of a believer in reincarnation."

Matthew felt an ache in his eyes. Or was it in his heart?

"Sure, a hug. Why would I mind if an attractive lady gave me a hug? If the plane crashes this could be the last hug I ever get."

After the hug, which lasts longer than he anticipated, he walks away, not knowing if he made the right decision to conceal his identity. Truthfully, he didn't want to know if Linda Tarlow was alive or dead or married or divorced or the oldest working hooker in Vegas. It was a conscious effort to cover his tracks. He was already too ensconced into his past and didn't want to dig deeper. Plus, he thought it best that Kirby kept her life a secret from strangers she met at an airport bar. Weird, here he was trying to protect her from being emotionally wounded. Why? Who knows? A Scotch-induced moral panic, perhaps.

"Well, have a nice reunion with your daughter," he says flatly.

"You know, I never got your name," she says.

"Right. My name." He mumbles for a few beats, then decides to lie so as not to arouse suspicion or further the conversation into a series of wows and astonished looks and possibly a few tears, followed by her saying she can't wait to tell her mother how she ran into him.

"It's Phillip. Phillip Marlowe."

"Sounds more like the name of a classic paperback detective."

"Yeah. I get that a lot."

"I've been told my dad ran into that same problem many times."

He didn't ask what she meant. Didn't have to. As he recalled, the dad was a deadbeat musician, always on the road, who abandoned Linda and her daughter for a notorious rock 'n' roll lifestyle. Never knew the guy. Vaguely heard of his band—The Limp something or other. Maybe Dicks. Not exactly a stellar name. A ways back someone in the band OD'd while playing a club in Boston. Died right on stage during a set. Think it made the eleven o'clock news. Could've been her father, but he couldn't swear to it. He was surprised Kirby never mentioned it. Then again, he did specify at the beginning of this conversation how he wanted to avoid true to life personal anecdotes.

Matthew heads straight for the security checkpoint. Halfway there, he looks back one more time and catches a glimpse of Kirby waving. It was one of those Queen Elizabeth waves. He didn't respond because, well, he wasn't sure if it was meant for him, or that she'd spotted her daughter somewhere in the crowd.

Either way, for an instant he experienced a cold flash of recognition, a shiver of familiarity, as if he had returned to a place that no longer existed—walking barefoot on the Malibu shoreline during a full moon. The only thing missing was a highly animated Doberman charging towards him with the objective of burying its nose in his crotch. It's amazing how these small moments of silent wonderment clicked in his mind, which maybe wasn't a click after all, but the sound of time passing.

Once Matthew disappears from view beyond the security checkpoint, Kirby sees her daughter Olive, toting her pink-wheeled carry-on luggage towards her. The plan was to meet up at this particular bar. Olive is a beautiful blonde girl of nineteen. She's the mirror image of her mother and also strongly favors her grandmother, Linda Tarlow. Matthew turns his gaze back one more time. He can't help but be almost proud that that little girl he once knew had grown up to be a responsible woman and mother, and gotten passed the disappointments in her childhood.

Both Kirby and Olive begin to wave and yell frantically, trying to catch each other's attention over the hubbub of travelers bound for God knows where.

Kirby, in her excitement, forgets her wallet sitting on the bar next to her unfinished beer. The bartender, quick to react, grabs it, checks the ID for a name, then calls out: "Uh, excuse me, Ms. Street—your wallet!"

ACKNOWLEDGMENTS

It goes without saying that this book never would have seen the light of day without the invaluable personal facts and contributions given to me by my friend of many years Lary Borkin. He dug deep into his heart and soul and pulled out a wealth of knowledge and shared it unsparingly.

Also, I would be remiss if I didn't give a special nod to all the employees and sales people who worked tirelessly to keep Jon's Drawer afloat. And although this book is the work of my imagination, I was inspired by their personal true-life experiences. Thanks so much to Nancy, Carol, Laurie, Dede, Freddy, Tina, Bob, Bill, Carmen, Teri and George. They were all credible witnesses to the 70s sensibility and lived to tell the tale.

Thanks goes to the countless number of customers who crossed the threshold and shopped at Jon's Drawer, making the store a huge success. Their loyalty and devotion to the days fashion, kept the 70s trend alive and brought with them their own stories that gave me fuel to strengthen the events relived in this book.

Putting together a book is nothing you do alone, and I had the best support from cover and interior designer Ghislain Viau, editor's Pamela Cangioli and Kevin Cook whose brilliance in helping me pick and choose the right words is evident on every page. And a huge thanks goes to Lolo Spencer whose camera made my author photo an artistic piece in itself.

Lastly, to my wife Laurie, who I am grateful for so many reasons but mostly for being there when I needed her most, as not only my bride, but my friend whose honesty was an asset, as I took this journey into the past and bringing it into the present.

And lets not forget our Golden Retriever Oliver who was by my side through just about every keystroke. Good boy.

ABOUT THE AUTHOR

As a writer/producer Larry Spencer has spent over twenty years working on a multitude of successful television shows, recently segueing into feature films, which then transitioned into authoring his very first best selling novel, *The Tipping Point of Oliver Bass*. After a successful television career, he moved into feature films, where he scripted an original screenplay called "In Search of Ina Byers." Spencer makes his home in Valley Village, California with his wife, Laurie and their golden retriever Oliver.

Printed in Great Britain
by Amazon